AND Dangerous TO Know

Darcie Wilde is the author of:

And Dangerous to Know

A Purely Private Matter

A Useful Woman

AND *Dangerous* TO *Know*

DARCIE WILDE

KENSINGTON BOOKS
www.kensingtonbooks.com

KENSINGTON BOOKS are published by

Kensington Publishing Corp.
119 West 40th Street
New York, NY 10018

All Kensington titles, imprints and distributed lines are available at special quantity discounts for bulk purchases for sales promotion, premiums, fund-raising, educational or institutional use.

Special book excerpts or customized printings can also be created to fit specific needs. For details, write or phone the office of the Kensington Special Sales Manager: Kensington Publishing Corp., 119 West 40th Street, New York, NY, 10018. Attn. Special Sales Department. Phone: 1-800-221-2647.

Kensington and the K logo Reg. U.S. Pat. & TM Off.

Library of Congress Card Catalogue Number: 2019950862

ISBN-13: 978-1-4967-2086-3
ISBN-10: 1-4967-2086-5
First Kensington Hardcover Edition: January 2020

ISBN-13: 978-1-4967-2092-4 (e-book)
ISBN-10: 1-4967-2092-X (e-book)

10 9 8 7 6 5 4 3 2 1

Printed in the United States of America

CHAPTER 1

The Darker Shades Of Morning

*He talks to me about the woman, and of the thing
being forgotten—is it so?*

George Gordon, Lord Byron, private correspondence

Adam Harkness pushed his way into the Brown Bear public house. April's bright, damp dawn had just begun to seep between London's chimneys, but the room was already crowded with working men after a mug of beer or a bowl of stew. Harkness touched the brim of his old-fashioned tricorn hat to Seamus Callahan, the landlord. In answer, that worthy spared one hand from plying his beer jug to wave Harkness toward the cellar door.

The Brown Bear was just like any of the hundreds of public houses across the length and breadth of London, save for one thing. This house stood directly across from the famous Bow Street police station. Down the years, the Brown Bear had become a sort of annex to the business of the station and its magistrate's court. Prisoners were held here, questioned here, even searched for stolen property here. A man might think he'd been invited in for a friendly drink, only to find he was being called out for his crimes by a witness sitting in the back of the room.

And sometimes, while men ate and drank upstairs, a much grimmer table was laid out in the cellar.

"I'm sorry to have roused you so early, Mr. Harkness." Sir David Royce straightened up from his work.

"I'm sorry you should have to." Harkness crossed the chill cellar to stand beside a long table with its sad burden. He had served long enough as a principal officer at Bow Street that the smell of death no longer alarmed him. Neither did the sight of a corpse.

She was a pale woman, and no longer young. Not even death had erased the lines around her mouth and eyes. But neither was she very old. A quantity of dark hair—clean and well brushed—tumbled loose about her shoulders. Her skin was only minimally marked by sun and wind. Her hands looked strong, but the nails were clean and the fingers were not obviously splayed or callused. She'd lived a life indoors, then, perhaps as a lady's maid or a shopkeeper's assistant.

A ring of bruises stood out sharply around her mouth.

"What's happened here?" Harkness asked.

"This unfortunate woman was brought here in a hired wagon, around two o'clock or so. The carters were extremely reluctant to stay while I was sent for." Sir David Royce was a portly, balding man with steady hands, sharp eyes, and a methodical mind. He held the office of King's Coroner for Middlesex County. It fell to Sir David and his subordinates to inquire into all unexpected deaths reported in a county that included both London and Westminster.

Sir David was constantly busy.

"I owe our host upstairs a little something for holding the pair of them spellbound with his beer and conversation." Sir David rubbed his hands on a piece of toweling, which he slung over his shoulder. "I began my examination as soon as I was called, and I admit, I've been wrestling with what to do since."

"How so?" With most crimes, such as theft, it was left to the victim to make complaint and seek redress, and to pay any costs that might arise in that attempt. But murder was a violation of the King's Peace. The coroner's sworn duty was to help uphold and preserve that peace by identifying the person or persons who broke it in the first place.

"Harkness, I believe this woman has been poisoned. You see those bruises on her mouth? She's been made to swallow a considerable quantity of laudanum, very probably mixed with brandy. You can still smell it on her."

Adam inhaled. Under the noxious odors that accompanied a death, he could still detect the tang of alcohol, anise, and camphor that made up a common blend of laudanum.

Harkness straightened and wiped at his mouth. "Is she . . . intact?"

"She's not virgin, but I can't find signs of force used on her, except those I already pointed out. I'll be looking again when the light's better, but I do not think rape is at the root of what happened to her."

"Could she have met with an accident?"

"To accidentally drink enough laudanum to die, she'd have to have accidentally emptied a full bottle into a pint of brandy and then accidentally gotten the whole lot down without falling unconscious or becoming violently ill. And there's no sign that she stumbled and fell because of intoxication."

"Then what is the matter?" asked Harkness. "Convene the inquest. If you need my help, you have it, of course." As coroner, Sir David could command the assistance of the Bow Street officers whenever he needed. The magistrates wrote out the warrants as a matter of form, and the Crown paid the fees.

Sir David sighed. "The problem, Mr. Harkness, is that this good woman was originally found at the gates of Melbourne House."

The coroner paused expectantly for Harkness's reply. When Adam just shook his head, Sir David deflated visibly.

"What have I missed?" Harkness asked. "I know Melbourne

House is in Piccadilly. It's home to Peniston Lamb, Lord Melbourne. Lord Melbourne's a gamester, a horseman, and in Parliament. And I believe his wife, Lady Melbourne has a name for herself . . ."

"Lady Melbourne is notorious," said Sir David. "Not only is she a leading political hostess, she has had any number of lovers. Including, they say, His Royal Highness the Prince of Wales."

"Ah." Harkness felt an unwelcome light begin to dawn in his mind. "That could become . . . delicate."

"And then there's the matter of Lady Melbourne's son, or more accurately, her son's wife, the infamous Lady Caroline."

Harkness looked again at the dead woman. "This isn't . . ."

"No, no. Whomever we have here, she is not Lady Caroline Lamb. I've had that lady pointed out to me at the theater. She's a tiny person with very red hair."

"Then how does this infamous Lady Caroline come into the matter? I thought you were concerned about Lady Melbourne?"

Sir David laughed. "Heavens defend us, Harkness! I forget sometimes how closely you focus on your own little world."

Considering that Harkness's world involved criminal activity across the length and breadth of the United Kingdoms, he would have disagreed with the epithet "little." But he held his tongue about that.

"Lady Caroline," said Sir David with theatrical patience, "is a public scandal in silk skirts. She might be genuinely insane, poor woman. But regardless of that, she numbers among *her* lovers, a certain George Gordon, Lord Byron."

That brought Harkness up short. "Byron the poet?"

"Poet, radical, madman, unrepentant seducer of women, and God knows who or what else," replied the coroner grimly. "The rumors are . . . most unsavory."

"Sir David, please tell me you don't think Lord Byron . . ."

"Mercifully, no. Lord Byron is currently in Switzerland, or maybe it's Italy. Lady David was reading about it the other day."

Which was a relief. Harkness did not care to imagine the public uproar if the celebrated Lord Byron was accused of murder.

"But you do think this woman may have been killed by someone in Melbourne House?"

"It's possible," answered Sir David. "The carters insist they didn't know what they were hauling. They were just paid, and generously, to take a load wrapped in canvas to the Brown Bear. But they were very clear that the load was heaved into their cart while they were *inside* the courtyard gates."

"Who paid them? Who helped them?"

"They could not, or would not, say. And that's only part of the problem," added Sir David sourly. "Any connection to Lord Byron, however tenuous, is going to set the whiskers of every single newspaper man from here to Landsend twitching. And here we have a dead woman who was found practically at the feet of Byron's Mad Lady Caroline, *and* the possibility that someone *in* Melbourne house tried to get the body *away* from Melbourne house . . ."

"And it has the makings of a bloody mess," Harkness finished for him. "But it's strange, Sir David. If someone simply wanted her . . . gone, they could have her thrown into the river. Or dumped her into an alleyway." Even Piccadilly had its fair share of deserted mews and dank lanes. "Why didn't they?"

"I don't know," admitted Sir David. "Some rudiment of conscience, or overconfidence, or even remorse? A bit of all three?"

"But not enough of any to risk the house's residents being called to testify at an inquest." Harkness sighed. "When will you issue the warrant?"

"I won't."

I can't have heard that right. Harkness frowned, but Sir David nodded.

"I'm not going to say anything at all about this woman. I will finish my examination, write down my notes in my private journal, and see her interred."

"You won't convene an inquest?" Surprise reverberated uncomfortably through Harkness. He had never seen Sir David hesitate when it came to carrying out his duty, no matter who he might be bringing into his court. "Even though you're certain this is murder?"

"As long as this stays quiet, whoever is responsible will think their measures have succeeded and will do nothing more."

Like flee the country, like call upon their influential friends, like bribe any witnesses to remain silent. Harkness nodded in reluctant understanding.

"But while they are, hopefully, sitting secure, we'll be busy in other ways." Sir David glanced toward the cellar door. "I need a favor from you, Harkness."

"If I can." Harkness respected Sir David, and liked him as a friend, but he would not give his word until he was sure he could keep it.

"You recently spoke to me about a lady, one who was of great assistance with that business at Almack's last year . . ."

"Miss Rosalind Thorne." Despite the gravity of their conversation, Adam felt a small smile form. He'd been fortunate to know a number of remarkable women in his life, but Rosalind Thorne was someone extraordinary. That lady was fiercely intelligent, with nerves of steel and a sharp sense of humor, all combined with a queenly demeanor.

"I believe she lent a hand sorting out the mess with Fletcher Cavendish and Mrs. Seymore as well?" said Sir David.

"Miss Thorne's made something of a specialty of being useful to ladies who have problems . . . outside the workaday."

"How high do her connections run?"

"Into the first circles." In fact, Rosalind Thorne had been born and raised among the *haut ton*. Her family lost their place when her father lost his money, but her family name guaranteed that she remained welcome in many aristocratic homes.

"Harkness, I need you to find out if she will use her connections to penetrate the walls of Melbourne House. If this woman"—he gestured to the body on the table—"ran afoul of any person in the house, and if that person is trying to keep the matter a secret, we'll need to discover all we can before that person decides to cover their tracks any further."

Sir David could call anyone to testify at an inquest. As a Bow Street officer, Adam might brandish his staff and his warrant to enter a house and search it for evidence. But the law neglected to grant him, or the coroner, the power to compel any man to talk.

Especially if that man, or woman, was bosom friends with the Prince of Wales.

Miss Thorne, however, was no rude officer. She was a gently bred lady. Those same families that would unite against Bow Street would open their doors to Rosalind Thorne— their doors, their diaries, and their secret hearts.

"Very well," said Adam. "As soon as I can, I'll go see if Miss Thorne is at home."

"I hope that she is," Sir David replied, more to the woman beneath her makeshift shroud than to Harkness. "For all our sakes."

CHAPTER 2

Early Callers

Tell me always when you see anything wrong &
believe me that greatest act of friendship will be
most gratefully felt and acknowledged.

Mrs. George Leigh, née Augusta Byron, private
correspondence

As it happened, Miss Rosalind Thorne was at home, but
she was not alone.

"Rosalind, tell George he's a shortsighted booby." Alice
Littlefield glared at her brother.

"Yes, do." George looked down his long pointed nose at
his sister. "And then you can tell Alice she's an unreasonable
child."

Rosalind Thorne put down her bite of toast. "Coffee?" she
inquired.

Rosalind's morning had begun somewhat later than Mr.
Harkness's. Unlike him, she had been permitted time for a
breakfast of coffee, toast, and marmalade in the small but
neat parlor of her house in Little Russell Street. Her intention
upon rising had been to spend a peaceful hour with her stack
of correspondence. This modest plan, however, was entirely
disrupted by the unexpected arrival of Alice and George Lit-

tlefield, both spattered by fresh spring mud and both in high dudgeon.

Brother and sister looked at her now in surprise as she lifted the silver coffeepot. Both shook their heads.

"As you please." Rosalind set the pot down again. "Perhaps you would settle for telling me what's happened?"

Rosalind and Alice had been friends for ages. When they appeared together, they made a striking pair. Like her brother, Alice was slim, dark, and quick, although George was much taller. Rosalind, on the other hand, was tall, golden, and dramatically statuesque. But that was not where the contrast ended. Even as a girl, Rosalind had been steady and thoughtful, while Alice had always been quick and rambunctious.

Despite their apparent differences, the two became fast friends as children, and for much of their childhood, the promise of futures had been a sparkling one. Alice's debut was one of the most highly anticipated of her season. For her part, Rosalind had achieved that elusive but much-sought-after dream. She had fallen in love. Even better, her chosen beau, Devon Winterbourne, returned the sentiment in full measure. There were problems, of course. Rosalind's parents— especially her father—were utterly determined that Rosalind should marry into both wealth and title. Devon Winterbourne was a *scorpion*, a second son, and so did not stand to inherit. But he was the second son of the Duke of Casselmaine, which was a distinctly respectable level of peerage, even by her father's soaring standards. Rosalind, her confidence buoyed by love, had been certain that she could talk her parents 'round, especially if she had her sister, Charlotte's, help.

Then, across the course of a year, disaster struck for both families.

Rosalind's and Alice's fathers nursed similar ambitions for their daughters, but they also nursed similar vices in themselves. Both men gambled, and drank, and engaged in speculation, and the results for both had been the same. After years of living beyond their incomes, they'd finally lost their ability to pay their debts, or borrow from friends, or anyone else for that matter.

When ruin finally threatened, Rosalind's father responded by running away.

Mr. Littlefield's response left his children not only penniless but orphaned.

Therefore, George could be forgiven for sounding genuinely distressed when he exclaimed, "Alice is intent on destroying her livelihood!"

"Oh, piffle, George." Alice, having refused coffee, helped herself to a slice of toast from the rack and dropped down onto the stool in front of the fire.

"And how is Alice doing this?" Rosalind asked the room at large.

"Tell her, Alice. Tell her what you're going to do!" The naked anger in his voice genuinely surprised Rosalind. Despite his family's hardships, George remained an easygoing man, and the pair enjoyed a close relationship that Rosalind sometimes envied. She and her own sister had not fared nearly as well.

"If you would sit down and calm down, I would be glad to tell her everything." Alice pointed her half-eaten toast toward the sofa.

But George ignored this direction and rounded on Rosalind. In tones he normally reserved for discussing Parliamentary corruption and failed drainage systems, he announced, "She's going to turn *novelist*."

Rosalind paused to suppress all possible traces of a smile. Only then did she raise her brows and look to Alice for confirmation of this outrage. Alice lifted her chin, which was really all the answer Rosalind needed.

"I've spoken with Mr. Henry Colburn. In fact, it was George who introduced us . . ."

"I wish I'd made you stay home!"

". . . and Mr. Colburn said that should A.E. Littlefield be inclined to write a novel, he would be delighted to consider the manuscript for publication at the earliest possible date."

Shortly after their father's suicide, George and Alice had both turned to writing to make their livings. The majority of the Littlefield income now came from the twice-weekly paper the *London Chronicle*. George was a feature writer, while Alice provided society gossip under the sobriquet of A.E. Littlefield. This and some other odd jobs enabled them to live, but not well. There were times, especially when the season was over and London quiet, that it became difficult to make ends meet.

"What Colburn wants," George sneered, "is another book of overwrought tittle-tattle, like that *Glenarvon* thing Lady Caroline wrote, and he thinks Alice can give it to him."

"Which she can," replied Alice. "And she can do it using prose that is a much less violent shade of purple and is sprinkled with rather fewer mawkish Irish ballads."

"And when she's sued for libel, and the Major removes her from her regular column, then what?"

Rosalind did not remark on this immediately. Instead, she poured a fresh cup of coffee and held it out. George stared at it and then, resigning himself to the inevitable, seized the cup, sat himself on the end of the sofa, and drank. Alice crossed her ankles, rolled her eyes, and held out her hand. Rosalind poured a second cup.

Now that she had their attention, and a moment of silence, Rosalind said, "George, this isn't like you. What is really the matter?"

"It's one thing to air the *haut ton*'s dirty linen when they're tossing you the titbits themselves, or if you're *Lady* Caroline, daughter of a duchess and married to a peer of the realm. It's quite another thing when you're a penniless nobody."

"If it sells, we won't be penniless," replied Alice tartly. "And I intend to publish anonymously."

"It won't stay anonymous. It never does."

"Have either of you spoken to any of Mr. Colburn's other authors?"

Brother and sister stared at Rosalind, both with their cups halfway to their mouths, their expressions such precise mirrors of each other that Rosalind's self-control finally gave way and she let out a long laugh.

"You're journalists!" she cried. "Has either of you considered interviewing the other persons Mr. Colburn is publishing to find out what manner of man he is and how he conducts his business? You could also speak with a solicitor about the libel laws. I should think, George, you would know at least one law clerk, but if not, perhaps Alice can speak to Mrs. . . . ."

It was at this moment that the parlor door opened, and Rosalind's housekeeper, Mrs. Kendricks, entered the room. Mrs. Kendricks was a rail-thin, competent, and usually unflappable woman. But just then a distinct color flushed her cheek and worry creased her brow.

"I do apologize, Miss Thorne," Mrs. Kendricks said. "But you have another visitor. Lady Jersey is . . ."

Wherever or whatever Lady Jersey had been before, she was now in Rosalind's front room.

CHAPTER 3

Unseasonable Arrivals

*. . . from far, from near, fashion and folly poured
forth their victims.*

Lady Caroline Lamb, Glenarvon

"Idid not expect you to have callers so early, Miss Thorne.
It is hardly the social hour."

Rosalind, George, and Alice all struggled to their feet as
Lady Jersey strode into the parlor. If the room had seemed
somewhat crowded before, it instantly became cramped.
Sarah Villiers, Lady Jersey, was a stout, short woman. Her
force of personality, however, was such that she instantly
filled any allotted space.

Ladies of the *haut ton* were instructed from infancy to be
quiet, modest, and entirely unobtrusive. At some stage, Lady
Jersey had thrown all such lessons over her shoulder. Ignor-
ing the trio standing in awkward surprise, she stalked about
the room, peering at Rosalind's few pictures and ornaments
as if bent on making an immediate purchase.

But then, Lady Jersey could afford to disregard those proprieties the world demanded of other women. She presided
over that great hub of social London—Almack's Assembly
Rooms. Newspapers and wits scoffed at Almack's weekly

subscription dances with their strict dress code and meager refreshments. But the fortunes of whole families turned on the matches arranged at those highly exclusive assemblies. As the foremost among Almack's gatekeepers, Lady Jersey held unrivaled social power, and she had no scruples at all about wielding it exactly as she saw fit.

There was no reason for the woman who ruled London society to be prowling Rosalind's narrow parlor before ten o'clock in the morning. Fortunately, proper manners provided refuge from the sudden shock.

"Lady Jersey, how do you do?" said Rosalind. "May I introduce Mr. George Littlefield and his sister, Miss Alice Littlefield?"

"Yes." Lady Jersey looked the Littlefields up and down through her quizzing glass with the same glare she'd used on Rosalind's Dresden shepherdess. "Not, I trust, related to that horrid newspaper gossip, A.E. Littlefield? I am aware that Miss Thorne is forced on occasion to have intercourse with such . . ."

"Heavens, no," murmured Alice. "I'm sorry your ladyship should think it. Well, George, it is past time we were on our way."

"Yes, of course." George did not bat an eye as he made his bow. "Miss Thorne. Lady Jersey. Pray, don't trouble, Mrs. Kendricks. We will show ourselves out."

As the Littlefields took their admirably prompt leave, Alice paused just long enough to give Rosalind a glance that spoke volumes. Specifically: *If I do not receive a full report of this visit, the consequences will be severe.*

Mrs. Kendricks, excused from having to attend to the departing Littlefields, retired to the chimney corner.

Lady Jersey sighed. "I do wish you would remember to keep regular hours, Miss Thorne. There cannot be a moment's delay in this matter."

"I am ready to help however I can."

Rosalind had made Lady Jersey's acquaintance during the previous season. Unthinkably, a man had been murdered inside Almack's. Rosalind had discovered the murderer, although to Lady Jersey's way of thinking, this was of secondary importance. For her, the vital acheivement had been that Rosalind prevented the scandal from destroying the reputation of the ballroom or its committee.

"Your sense of duty has always been most admirable, Miss Thorne. I said so to Lady Melbourne when I recommended you to her. 'You may depend on Miss Thorne in all particulars,' I said. 'She is entirely calm and levelheaded, and she understands that such affairs must be managed with the utmost discretion . . . "

"I beg your pardon, ma'am— "

"Was there ever anyone more unreasonable than that wife of his! Taking the most private family business to a *lawyer*! Perhaps her own parents are of no standing, but to demonstrate so little consideration for her nearest relations . . ."

Lady Jersey's volubility was the stuff of social legend. Rosalind knew from personal experience that waiting for her to draw breath would be an exercise in extreme patience.

"I suppose one could excuse *that* woman, perhaps. All things considered . . . The house *she* was raised in . . . the duchess was a great lady, there is no denying. These is none like her today. I met her several times, you know. Still, the irregularities of the domestic arrangement . . . and the general permissiveness. It had to have some effect on Lady Caroline."

While Lady Jersey flung forth this verbal whirlpool, Rosalind signaled to Mrs. Kendricks. The housekeeper moved silently to her side.

"Still. One would think any person would have been *grateful* to be admitted to such a household as Lady Melbourne's."

Rosalind made a discreet scribbling gesture. In response,

Mrs. Kendricks handed across her housekeeping book and pencil.

"It should have been a brilliant match! An unparalleled match."

Rosalind opened the notebook to a fresh page and began writing.

"If she'd only been *discreet*! If she'd only understood how long and how hard Lady Melbourne labored to help her!" Lady Jersey glowered at the tidy writing desk with its stacks of correspondence. "You just have time to change into something decent. You have something, don't you? I suppose I might loan you one of . . ." She turned, and stopped. "Miss Thorne, what in heaven's name are you doing?"

"A few notes for my housekeeper. Thank you, Mrs. Kendricks." Mrs. Kendricks made her curtsey and took the note, the breakfast tray, and herself out of the room. "If you will please sit down, Lady Jersey? Mrs. Kendricks will bring you fresh coffee while I get ready."

The fact that everything was moving in the direction she hoped for seemed to catch Lady Jersey off guard. "Yes. Very good. Very prompt. I was certain we might rely on you."

"I do have one question."

"Well? What is it?"

"Where are we going?"

Lady Jersey leveled Rosalind with a quelling glower.

"Oh, Miss Thorne, do try to pay attention! I've been perfectly plain! We are going to Melbourne House. Lady Melbourne is in need of your *particular* assistance."

This was no small pronouncement. Lady Melbourne was one of London's preeminent social and political hostesses. True, she was no longer in her prime, but the Melbourne name, the family, the house, and the lady herself still represented the highest circles of London society, and that was despite a level of notoriety that would have destroyed a lesser woman.

Indeed, if there was one person who wielded more influence over social London than Lady Jersey, it was Lady Melbourne.

"Of course," replied Rosalind calmly. "I do apologize. And the matter is . . . ?"

Lady Jersey sighed sharply. "Really, Miss Thorne! I have never known you to be so woolly-headed! Did I not just explain? Some very valuable, highly confidential letters have been stolen from Lady Melbourne's personal papers. It is to be your duty to recover them." She leaned forward and hissed. "They're about *Lord Byron*, Miss Thorne! And there can be no question but that they have all been stolen by *that woman!*"

CHAPTER 4

The Troubles Of Lady Melbourne

Few men can be trusted with their neighbor's secrets, and scarcely any woman with her own.

Elizabeth Lamb, Viscountess Melbourne,
private correspondence

What Rosalind knew about the connection between Melbourne House and the notorious aristocratic poet George Gordon, Lord Byron was limited. When Lord Byron and his epic poem *Childe Harold's Pilgrimage* had become London's ruling sensations, Rosalind was mired in the depths of her family's dissolution. Despite this, the salacious details of the poet's *affaire de coeur* had so pervaded society that they reached even her.

The facts, as Rosalind knew them, were these:

Lady Melbourne's daughter-in-law was Lady Caroline Lamb. Lady Caroline (who held that title in her own right, quite separate from her husband) was married to the Honorable Mr. William Lamb.

While married to Mr. Lamb, Lady Caroline had conducted a romantic affair with Lord Byron.

That, in and of itself, was not the problem (at least, not as these things were reckoned among the fashionable). The problem lay in how Lady Caroline conducted that affair.

She stalked Lord Byron through the ballrooms. She (apparently with his cooperation) visited his home dressed as a page boy. She allowed herself to be seen emerging quite alone from his carriage at all hours.

It hardly seemed possible that matters should escalate, but they did. When Lord Byron ended the affair to marry a Miss Anne Isabella Milbanke, Lady Caroline refused to give him up. Worse, she became increasingly and publicly hysterical at his rejection of her. At one ball, they said, she broke a glass and slit her own wrist. At another, they said, she tried to throw herself out a window.

Some of these stories were certainly exaggerations. Rosalind, for instance, refused to believe that Lady Caroline had actually lit a bonfire and burned all her correspondence from the poet while dancing round the blaze.

It was indisputable, however that Lady Caroline had capped off her indiscretion by writing an account of her torrid romance in the novel *Glenarvon*. The novel had, among other things, savagely satirized Elizabeth Lamb, Lady Melbourne. The woman who now summoned Rosalind to her home in Piccadilly Square. Regarding some missing letters.

Regarding Lord Byron.

Rosalind was no stranger to aristocratic houses. But even among London's many brilliant residences, Melbourne House stood out as marbled and gilded grace on the grand scale. The fabulous Grecian portico, the domed entrance hall, and the pair of sweeping staircases were all designed to inspire awe, and this they achieved admirably.

A liveried footman conducted Rosalind and Lady Jersey to a pale green salon on the second floor. While fairly intimate as compared to the public rooms below, it was still larger than an entire floor of Rosalind's rented house. A mural depicting the classical graces decorated the ceiling. Antique marble and alabaster vases stood in well-spaced niches. A pair of footmen and another pair of uniformed maids also occupied their appointed places. A fifth woman, quite probably the lady's maid, stood beside the mantel.

Elizabeth Lamb, Viscountess Melbourne, sat facing the doorway in a gilded, tapestried chair. Crossing to their hostess was like approaching the queen to be presented, and Rosalind felt certain this was not an accident.

"I am so very glad you could come, Miss Thorne." Lady Melbourne's voice was deep and low. One would have to stand close to hear her clearly. Rosalind suspected this was not an accident, either. "And thank you so much for bringing her to me, Lady Jersey. Do please sit down. I trust, Lady Jersey, you have given Miss Thorne some explanation as to what's happened?"

"I have informed Miss Thorne of the whole of the circumstances, Lady Melbourne. Indeed, I was able to positively confirm to her . . ."

While Lady Jersey explained to Lady Melbourne the depth and detail of her explanations to Rosalind, Rosalind had time to study the woman who had sent for her. Age had streaked her hair with white but had left her a studied dignity and a clear, knowing eye. It was easy to see the beauty that was reported to have captivated so many famous men. She still dressed at the height of the fashion. But where Lady Jersey's dedication to the current mode made her look fussy, Lady Melbourne seemed perfectly at ease in her burgundy damask frock with a magnificent Indian shawl draped loosely around her shoulders. The only concession she could find to Lady Melbourne's married state was a wisp of a cap held in place by a silver comb.

Despite this exquisitely crafted nonchalance, Lady Melbourne's hands betrayed her true situation. She gripped the chair arms as if she feared to release them, this despite the fact that her knuckles were scarlet and horribly swollen. In fact, the skin had split in several places.

Rheumatism, thought Rosalind, for the signs were unmistakable. *She must be in pain. But she will not betray any sign of weakness to a stranger.*

Lady Jersey was still talking. ". . . and I do assure you, Lady Melbourne, it will take Miss Thorne no time at all to discover what *that woman* has done with your letters and see them restored . . ."

"Yes, yes, dear Sarah," breathed Lady Melbourne. "You've been admirably thorough in your account of Miss Thorne's many virtues. But while I do recognize it must be a trial to your patience, perhaps you'll allow me to put one or two questions to your protégé myself?"

It took a great deal to divert Lady Jersey when she was in full flow, but Lady Melbourne had managed it. Rosalind was impressed.

"Well, yes, of course! Miss Thorne is quite prepared to answer any question. Miss Thorne . . ."

"And you do know how much I thank you for bringing her and for explaining all the circumstances to me. Again." Lady Melbourne continued smoothly. "It seems a shame you must sit through the whole dreary business yet again. I have a thought, Sarah. Why don't you leave Miss Thorne with me? I will entirely undertake the task of seeing she is safely returned to her home when we are finished."

It was a dismissal. No one dismissed Lady Jersey. It was unthinkable. Even Lady Jersey herself did not seem to know what to do.

She settled for drawing herself up and fussing with the fringed ends of her shawl. "I should hope I am never too busy to be of use to my friends."

"So we should all hope." Lady Melbourne smiled. "Do you not agree, Miss Thorne?"

"Most certainly, ma'am," murmured Rosalind, keeping her gaze properly directed to her own hands.

"Well," said Lady Jersey. "Well. I know Miss Thorne will

quickly bring this whole business to a satisfactory close. You must promise you will write to me *immediately* if—"

"*Immediately*, Sarah. Thank you so very much."

"Oh, no, my dear Lady Mebourne, thank *you!*" Lady Jersey curtsied. Lady Melbourne nodded in reply, without letting her eyes stray from that lady's countenance for a moment.

Propriety left her with no options. Lady Jersey had to take her leave. One of the footmen closed the door silently behind her.

"Tea," Lady Melbourne said. The footman on the left-hand side of the door bowed and withdrew.

Although they were now alone except for the servants, Lady Melbourne did not immediately make any fresh remark. She simply studied Rosalind with a gaze that was cheerful and gentle but also somehow relentless. Rosalind was by no means awkward in society, but she suddenly felt certain her dress was creased, her face was dirty, and her hands in an unforgivable state. Courtesy, however, absolutely forbid that she be the one to break the silence.

At last, Lady Melbourne relented. "Miss Thorne, Lady Jersey tells me you are Sir Reginald's daughter," she said. "I had the pleasure of meeting him once. I remember him to possess those engaging manners that are so rarely found these days. How does he?"

"Not well, I am sorry to say. He is in the country with my sister, looking to recoup his health." This was an old lie, and Rosalind was grateful to find it still flowed smoothly.

The small smile Lady Melbourne returned left Rosalind uneasy. *What do you know?* she wondered. *What did you expect to hear?*

Footmen arrived with the trays of tea things and several kinds of cake. Under Lady Melbourne's direction, the table was brought forward and all the things laid out with her quiet maid's confident assistance. Rosalind was served a cup of tea with lemon and a slice of seed cake. Lady Melbourne did not take anything and she, quite literally, did not lift a finger.

Rosalind sipped her tea and ate a polite bite of the cake, which was excellent. Lady Melbourne nodded her satisfaction. "You may all go," she said to the servants. The servants obeyed, save for the dark-haired lady's maid. She remained in her place beside the chimney, saying nothing but watching everything. She was, Rosalind noted, unusually tall and broad for a woman. Probably Lady Melbourne needed someone strong to help her walk on days when her rheumatism was very bad.

"Well, now, Miss Thorne, you must tell me truthfully." Lady Melbourne leaned forward just a little. "Did our dear Lady Jersey actually manage to explain to you the difficulty in which I find myself?" The sparkle in her eyes took the edge from her words. Indeed, she seemed to be on the verge of laughter and eager for Rosalind to share the joke.

Rosalind set cup and plate aside. "She did give me a few salient points but no details. At least, not in order of actual occurrence."

Lady Melbourne let out one sharp laugh. "Exactly! I have never met someone who could say so much and so little at the same time. Still, I admire her energy. Lady Jersey has accomplished great things for herself and her family. However, I think we might do better than follow the example she's set and instead try to speak plainly. Do you agree?"

"I will do my best, Lady Melbourne."

Lady Melbourne cocked her head. "When Sarah raised the possibility of my confiding in you, I felt I was grasping at straws. However, I think we will get on together." She spoke these words as a confidence, and Rosalind felt herself being drawn into it, whether she would or no. This, then, was the charm for which the lady was famous. "I must admit to you several things I would not normally speak of to anyone. Especially not, I'm afraid, to our dear Lady Jersey."

As Lady Melbourne said this, her hands spasmed around

the chair arms. A fresh drop of blood appeared on one swollen knuckle. She lifted the wounded hand. The lady's maid hurried forward with a white handkerchief to wipe away the blood, and retire. Clearly this was something she had done before, and often.

Rosalind saw all this only from the corner of her eye. She sipped her tea, kept her gaze fixed on the fireplace, and resolutely pretended that nothing was happening.

"Well, now." Lady Melbourne words indicated that Rosalind could return her attention to her hostess. "I shall begin with the obvious. As you can see"—she indicated the maid with a tilt of her head—"I am not a well woman. I am infected with a rheumatism that refuses to be shifted."

"I am sorry to hear it, ma'am," murmured Rosalind.

"What I have not told anyone else is that I do not expect to live for much longer. There. Now you have a way to demonstrate that extraordinary discretion Lady Jersey has assured me—repeatedly and at length—you possess."

Rosalind made no reply. She needed no such blunt declaration to understand that Lady Melbourne was testing her. She also knew by that lady's manner, any recourse to platitudes on Rosalind's part would end this conversation at once.

"Now, Miss Thorne, to our business. A packet of correspondence has been taken from my desk. Those letters are private and deeply personal. I may soon be beyond the judgment of men, but my children will not. I will not allow those letters to remain in the hands of anyone who might try to harm my family." A slight tremor shook her chin and her voice.

What could possibly be in these letters?

If the stories Rosalind heard were true, Lady Melbourne had thrived for years on conduct that would have destroyed a less adroit woman. She had married into the high life, and it suited her entirely. The minute she produced a legitimate heir, she proceeded to take on a whole string of lovers, none of whom were ordinary men. Indeed, rumors circulated that her fourth son, George Lamb, had been the result of a liaison with His Royal Highness, the Prince of Wales. In return, His Royal Highness had made her husband a groom of the bed-chamber. Because Lady Melbourne was not content merely to seek adventure for its own sake, she used the connections forged by her numerous affairs to move her family up the social and political ladders.

Rosalind understood very well all the ways a woman had to make shift to get along in the world and was not inclined to judge the lady's conduct. But it was clear that Lady Melbourne was not a woman to be worried by a few ordinary letters.

"Perhaps, ma'am, you could tell me how you discovered the letters were missing?"

The tremor in Lady Melbourne's chin grew momentarily more pronounced, but when she spoke, her low voice remained clear and calm.

"It was only two days ago. We were at dinner. Nothing formal—a few friends of my son's, a few political people. Some horse people. The tea had just been set out in the parlor when a card arrived for me. Mr. Scrope Berdmore Davies urgently desired an interview. Are you acquainted with Mr. Davies?"

"No, ma'am." The name sounded familiar but did not recall any face to Rosalind's mind. "Did your guests know who had arrived?"

Lady Melbourne paused. "I believe I made some remark. It would have carried to the whole of the company."

"And did you agree to see him?"

"I did. He and I have . . . certain friends . . . in common, and I was afraid of some emergency."

"Certain friends?" murmured Rosalind. Lady Melbourne looked sharply at her, but a moment later began to laugh.

"Ah! And I had promised to speak plainly. I am justly set

down. Yes, certain friends. But the one I am speaking of now is, as you have no doubt already guessed, Lord Byron."

Rosalind nodded. "What happened then?"

"I interviewed Mr. Davies alone in the blue salon. He had just returned from the continent and was carrying a message from Byron. He was asking after a series of letters he knew I had in my possession. He was worried that those letters might add fresh fuel to some old scandals and asked me to hand them over to Mr. Davies so that they could be destroyed."

They're about Lord Byron, Miss Thorne! whispered Lady Jersey from memory. *Byron and* that woman!

"Why wouldn't Lord Byron trust you to destroy these letters yourself? Or request that you return them directly to him?" asked Rosalind. "Why insist you give them to Mr. Davies?"

"Have you ever lived under threat of blackmail, Miss Thorne?"

Rosalind paused just long enough to be certain of her voice before she lied. "Thankfully, no."

"It preys upon the mind to know that your name and position rest entirely in the hands of some reprobate. If one is a sensitive or melancholy individual, it can become difficult to think calmly, or to trust even the oldest and best of friends." For a moment, resentment burned brighter than the pain in Lady Melbourne's eyes. "Mr. Davies made his case to me forcefully and at length. He said Lord Byron had every reason to believe some person or persons meant to steal my letters and release the contents to the world. He insisted I produce them all so that he could see for himself that none were missing."

"Did Mr. Davies say whom Lord Byron thought might try to steal the letters?"

"No. As I questioned him, it became clear that Mr. Davies was . . . not entirely well."

He was drunk, Rosalind translated. *This Mr. Davies turned up drunk at an unreasonable hour asking you to hand over some compromising letters about Lord Byron.*

Rosalind's flow of thought stopped, and turned cold.

Did they also involve your daughter-in-law, Lady Caroline? Were these letters written during their affair?

Possibly written between Lady Caroline and Lord Byron?

Suddenly, Rosalind found herself wondering if these missing letters that so worried Lady Melbourne really belonged to her at all.

CHAPTER 5

The Complex Travels Of Correspondence

*You may know I suppose that Lady B[yro]n
secretly opened my letter trunk before she left
Town, and that she has also been . . . in
correspondence with that self-avowed libeller &
strumpet [erased] wife.*

George Gordon, Lord Byron, private correspondence

"**D**id you give Mr. Davies the letters?" asked Rosalind. Lady Melbourne did not seem to be able to choose whether to be more amused or annoyed at the question. "I did not. I told Mr. Davies that if he was not prepared to trust my word, he should come back in the morning when he was . . . better. In the meantime, I would write a note for him to forward to Lord Byron. In it, I would assure Byron that I would keep the letters locked safe away, or destroy them myself." She paused. "You will have heard that Byron has left the country?"

"I had heard something to that effect, yes."

In fact, the papers had breathlessly followed every inch of the poet's journey to the coast. Much was made of his juggernaut of a carriage, said to be modeled after Napoleon's personal conveyance. To satiate the reading public's demand for details, Alice had been driven to pure invention to describe its attributes. She was particularly proud of the cloth of gold hammock.

"Lord Byron may not ever return to us." Lady Melbourne's chin trembled again. "It is his wife's fault." She said this as a fact, as immutable as the laws of gravity. "Lady Byron has allowed herself to be persuaded to seek a complete legal separation, Miss Thorne, and to keep his infant daughter entirely from him. Did you know that?"

"I had heard," Rosalind admitted. That she felt a distinct sympathy with the lady's action was not an opinion it would be wise to voice at this time. "How did Mr. Davies respond to your refusal?"

"Mr. Davies made it clear he was not satisfied, but as I offered him no alternatives, he acquiesced and took his leave."

And where, Rosalind wondered, *did he go?*

"The next morning, I went to my writing room immediately upon rising," said Lady Melbourne at last. "I intended to fulfill my promise and write to Byron, but the fears Mr. Davies had expressed the night before had touched me. I opened my desk to make sure the letters were still in their place. They were not."

She was trembling again. Rosalind took up her teacup to drink, thus giving her hostess time to recover.

"There was no possibility of the packet being accidentally misplaced, if that is what you are wondering" said Lady Melbourne. "No one ever goes into that desk save myself, and I keep my old correspondence strictly in order."

"And of course, the servants have all been questioned?" said Rosalind, mostly for form's sake. In her experience of such matters, the servants were much blamed but seldom truly at fault. "From what you have told me thus far, it would seem any thief would have needed to be familiar with the house." *And familiar to its occupants.*

"A thorough search was instituted at once. Claridge took

charge of it." Lady Melbourne tipped her chin toward her maid. "She is as close to me as my right hand, and somewhat more dear to me, given the state of my hands. . . ." Lady Melbourne laughed, but only a little. Claridge lowered her gaze.

"Did Mr. Davies return as he promised?" Rosalind asked.

"He did. I did not, however, tell him what had happened. Mr. Davies is . . ." She paused again, choosing her words with care again. "He is devoted to Lord Byron. He might consider it his duty to write and say what had happened before we had a chance to recover the letters."

"Have you received any demands for money?"

"None! And that is the most alarming thing, Miss Thorne. A common blackmailer could be paid off. But what am I to make of silence? I fear Mr. Davies, and Lord Byron may have been correct. Someone intends to have the letters . . . my most private correspondence . . . published in the gutter press." She shuddered. "I do not wish to spend the last of my time on this earth fending off old scandals, Miss Thorne."

"Could your daughter-in-law have taken them?" Rosalind asked, leaving out the fact that Lady Jersey had been so adamant that Lady Caroline was the thief. After all, if Lady Melbourne knew who had taken the letters, what would she need Rosalind for?

But if the letters concerned Lady Caroline, or possibly even belonged to her . . .

"It is possible Caroline had something to do with this," admitted Lady Melbourne. "Between her fits of outrageous behavior, she can be quite clever. She is also horribly suspicious of those who have her welfare at heart." Lady Melbourne leaned forward again, but not so far that she had to release her death grip on the chair's arms. "She has more than once tried to injure me personally during a fit. But her rooms were searched as thoroughly as the rest of the house. If she did take the letters, they have already been spirited away."

Rosalind's next point was a delicate one, but she could not neglect it. "Is it possible that Mr. William Lamb, Lady Caroline's husband, had a hand in this matter?"

"You do not know my son, or you would not ask that. He is quite without guile." This thought seemed to oppress Lady Melbourne even more than the loss of her property. "Caroline barely had to raise a finger to ensnare him, and she continues to bewilder and fascinate him. He is very kind, my poor son. Whenever she fears she is in danger of losing him, she plays expertly upon his sympathy."

Rosalind listened to this assessment and wondered. There was definitely something out of the ordinary about William Lamb's relationship with his wife, Lady Caroline. Very few husbands—even the most kind and loving—would have permitted a woman who behaved so outrageously to remain under their roof, let alone agree to allow them to publicly publish the family gossip. And he must have agreed. As a married woman, the law forbid Lady Caroline from entering into any kind of contract without her husband's consent.

Years of practice allowed Rosalind to keep the depth of her perplexity from showing on her face. Usually, when a husband and a husband's family tolerated a difficult wife, it was because of complications over money or property. Could that be the case here?

"Miss Thorne, there is one final point I feel I must raise. Lady Jersey has assured me that you could conduct your inquiries entirely unobserved. Is this true, or is it another of her exaggerations?"

For a moment, Rosalind was tempted to allow herself to be insulted. She could rise to her feet and say that this matter was beyond her abilities and that she was very sorry. Lady Melbourne might be telling the truth, but Rosalind had the distinct feeling she was not telling all of it. There were layers of secrets here, and they might well turn out to be far beyond the ordinary, just like the lady in front of her.

And if I do leave, then what? What will Lady Jersey say, to me and the rest of the world, when she knows I turned my back on her friend?

Whether she liked it or not, Rosalind depended on the good opinion of society women. She had no independent income. She made her way entirely on the genteel charity of those women who still fit neatly into society's puzzle. Because she was "a gently bred girl of good family," there would be no question of actual payment if she returned Lady Melbourne's letters and named the thief. But there would be gifts, and other considerations. Most important, word of her useful abilities would be passed on to Lady Melbourne's friends when they might find themselves in need of similar assistance.

If she turned away, those recommendations would not come. So, despite her unease, Rosalind could not leave this matter, or this woman, before she had done her best.

"I must establish some reason for my presence," said Rosalind. "Would it be possible for me to take the character of your confidential secretary?"

Lady Melbourne considered this. "Yes. I can say that because of my current indisposition I require assistance with my correspondence. I assume you are capable of composing a neat letter and organizing a visiting book and so forth?"

"Yes, ma'am. I have assisted several ladies in this fashion."

"Hmm. Well, we shall try your capabilities. I have a large acquaintance and you will be very busy. Still, it will explain this interview and the fact that you are staying here for the time being."

Rosalind had no notion of actually taking up residence in Melbourne House, however temporarily. Something close to panic overtook her, and that for the simplest of motives.

She had nothing to wear.

Her wardrobe was barely adequate to ordinary levels of society, and Melbourne House was a cut above. Lord Melbourne was, after all, a member of the royal household, and Lady Melbourne . . . well, she was practically so if the rumors were correct.

"You will of course need to pack your things," Lady Melbourne went on, oblivious of how Rosalind's expression froze. She turned to her lady's maid. "Claridge, go speak with Bell. Miss Thorne is to have the use of the chaise as long as she is with us. Put Ormande in charge of it." Claridge curtsied and departed. "Now, tell me, Miss Thorne, how do we begin?"

Rosalind took a steadying breath.

"I will make a few discreet inquiries among my acquaintance in the press." *Alice will be beside herself.* "If letters from Lord Byron are being offered for publication, there will be rumors. However, it may be that whoever took them is waiting until the search has died down before approaching a buyer. Of course, if the thief stole the letters for personal reasons, they may already have been destroyed."

This thought did not seem to calm Lady Melbourne at all. If anything, it raised a brighter blush in her cheeks.

Why should that be the possibility that genuinely upsets you?

"I also may speak with a gentleman of my acquaintance, a Mr. Sanderson Faulks. He knows a great deal about the affairs of various gentlemen of the *ton* and may be able to shed some light on what is driving Mr. Davies's sudden interest in these particular letters."

"I should have thought that was obvious. It is Lord Byron's wish."

Rosalind nodded. "And indeed it may be, but there may also be other factors to consider. People seldom act for only one reason."

Lady Melbourne narrowed her eyes thoughtfully and then nodded. "Well, I leave the matter in your hands. I will expect you here at eleven o'clock tomorrow, ready to assume your duties."

"I must apologize, Lady Melbourne, but that will be difficult. I have an engagement Thursday night, and it is of long standing." It was Tuesday. Removing herself to Melbourne House would take the better part of a day, and augmenting her wardrobe longer than that.

Lady Melbourne waved this away. "You can go from this house as easily as any other." She paused. "I assume this is young Louisa Winterbourne's engagement party you're attending?"

"Yes, ma'am. Miss Winterbourne is a friend of my family, and I helped with the arrangements for the ball."

Lady Melbourne's look was far too knowing for Rosalind's comfort. She told herself she should not be surprised. Lady Melbourne obviously kept herself up-to-date regarding social matters, and of course she would have talked with Lady Jersey about Rosalind's background. She would know that not so long ago, Rosalind had been engaged, or almost engaged, to Louisa Winterbourne's cousin, Devon Winterbourne, who was now the Duke of Casselmaine.

"I shall send her a note with my congratulations," said Lady Melbourne. "She's attached herself to young Mr. Firth Rollins, I believe?"

"Yes, ma'am."

"Excellent choice. A very good family, and the connection should suit both sides admirably. I will be happy to receive her after the wedding. Ah, Claridge, is everything ready?" The door had opened and Claridge entered, followed by the liveried footman. Lady Melbourne did not wait for her maid to answer. "Bell, you will show Miss Thorne to the carriage. You will forgive me, won't you, Miss Thorne? I have afternoon callers and must get ready."

"Of course, ma'am." Rosalind stood and curtsied. "Should I learn anything from my initial inquiries, I will write to you at once."

"Thank you," replied Lady Melbourne. Once again she fixed Rosalind with that gentle, relentless gaze.

"I am not ashamed of what I have done in my life, Miss Thorne," Lady Melbourne said. "I have lived well and done well by my family. But the world's opinion is unforgiving when it comes to women. I would not have my children suffer because I am not there to defend them. Do you understand this?"

"Yes, ma'am. I do."

Seemingly satisfied, Lady Melbourne eased herself back in her chair, clearly exhausted by her efforts. "Claridge, I am ready to retire."

Rosalind pretended not to hear and followed the footman out. She did not look back, although she heard the sharp cry as Claridge helped raise her ladyship to her feet.

Lady Melbourne deserved privacy for her pain.

CHAPTER 6

Grave Omissions Of Fact

. . . About the Trunks—Could not I say something true to contradict such a vile Calumny!

Mrs. George Leigh, née Augusta Byron,
private correspondence

The neatly sprung chaise was a much more modern and nimble vehicle than Rosalind expected. Clearly, Lady Melbourne was not one who clung to past affectations once they ceased to serve.

When they reached Little Russell Street, the driver, Ormande, helped Rosalind out. Rosalind asked him to return at ten o'clock the following morning.

"But my instructions were quite clear, Miss Thorne," Ormande replied with a respectful touch of his hat brim. "Myself and the boy"—he jerked his thumb at the youth balanced on the chaise's back step—"are to remain at your disposal."

Rosalind found herself taken aback. It had been a long time since anyone except Mrs. Kendricks had remained at her disposal. "Very well. Please introduce yourself to my housekeeper. There is a livery stable three streets over, I believe." The horses could not be kept standing in their traces, and she had nowhere to house them on the premises.

"Ah. That'd be Chalmers's," Ormande said. "A good establishment. Thank you, miss. Is there anything else you'll need?"

"Not at this time, thank you, Ormande."

Satisfied, Ormande turned to shout at the boy holding the reins and climb back into the driver's seat.

Rosalind's morning at Melbourne House and the magnitude of her new task had left her feeling a little breathless. She was looking forward to the quiet hour or two. She needed to gather her composure. But as soon as Mrs. Kendricks met her at the door, Rosalind knew that this was not to be.

"Mr. Harkness is here, Miss Thorne. From Bow Street," she added, as if she hoped Rosalind had forgotten her previous acquaintance with the man. "He says the matter is urgent and that he could not just leave a message."

Rosalind was conscious of an unusual impatience. She was already uneasy. Stabling a pair of horses and putting up two extra people in her house for even just one day was going to be a strain on the space, and her pocketbook. Before she'd left Melbourne House, the footman, Bell, had handed her an envelope he said was from Lady Melbourne. Rosalind suspected its contents would help deal with her immediate expenses, but she wanted time to think, and to plan, and to speak with Alice and . . . well, and so many other things.

Rosalind set all this aside. Mr. Harkness was not a frivolous man. If he said the matter was urgent, then it surely was.

"Thank you, Mrs. Kendricks," she said. "We will need coffee, and probably something to eat. Then I will need you to begin packing for an extended stay."

"Very good, Miss. Where is it to be?"

Rosalind told her, and when Mrs. Kendricks blanched, Rosalind nodded her head in silent agreement. They were both thinking of Rosalind's meager wardrobe and how the recent additions, as new and neat as they might be, were not going to be sufficient to maintain the pose of a lady's companion and assistant in such a house for more than a few days.

If only the problems ended there. Rosalind straightened her shoulders and walked into her parlor.

As soon as she entered, Adam Harkness turned toward her.

Rosalind's various activities on behalf of the ladies of the *ton* had meant that she and Mr. Harkness met several times as colleagues of a sort, and even as friends. But although she might have preferred it, Rosalind's feelings for Mr. Harkness did not begin or end with polite collegiality. Rosalind had by now come to realize she was never going to become used to the first sight of Mr. Harkness's intense blue eyes, or to the clarity of his brow, or the quiet intelligence of his demeanor. That she knew him to be honorable, brave, kind, and with a fine sense of humor did nothing to make matters easier.

Neither did the fact that once, perhaps twice, he had almost kissed her, and once, perhaps twice, she had almost let herself be kissed.

"Miss Thorne." Mr. Harkness made his bow. He was in his workaday clothes—a plain, dark coat and the scarlet waistcoat that gave the Bow Street officers the nickname of "Robin Redbreasts." His tricorn hat lay on the table, and she had no doubt that his white staff of office was tucked inside his coat pocket. "I apologize for disturbing you."

"Not at all, Mr. Harkness. But you must forgive me if I'm a little distracted. I've had . . . a somewhat complicated morning."

"I'm afraid I'm not going to make it any simpler."

"Well, what a good thing I've already sent Mrs. Kendricks for coffee. Won't you sit down?"

Mr. Harkness took the cane-bottomed chair, and Rosalind took her usual place by the fire. He sat for a moment, his hands on his knees, gathering his thoughts.

"I have a favor to ask of you, Miss Thorne," said Mr. Harkness finally. "It is difficult, and it may be dangerous. I must also ask that no one hear any detail of this conversation."

"Then perhaps I should stop you before you go any further. I have just undertaken to assist a lady with a personal matter. I'm afraid I will be fully occupied for some time."

"There is no way you can put this lady off for a few days? My business is extremely urgent."

"I'm afraid the lady will not be put off. In her eyes, this matter is also extremely urgent."

"Does it involve murder?"

The word pulled Rosalind up short. "What has happened?"

"Miss Thorne, Sir David Royce, the king's coroner, sent for me early this morning so I might view the body of a woman who was poisoned and left at the gates of Melbourne House."

"*Where?*" Rosalind cried, mortified at the break in her voice.

"Melbourne House," repeated Mr. Harkness.

Thankfully, Rosalind was already sitting. Otherwise her knees would have surely buckled.

"And this happened last night? This woman died there last night?"

"She was found there. Where she died, I can't yet say. But yes, it was last night."

"Why wasn't this in the newspapers?" Rosalind asked, her dazed mind seizing on trivialities. The paper sellers should have been crying it from every street corner as she drove away from Melbourne House. The gates themselves should have been besieged.

"Sir David is doing everything in his power to keep the matter quiet," Mr. Harkness said. "He does not want the publicity. Given the nature of Melbourne House and its occupants, he's afraid there might be an attempt to shield the guilty party."

Lord Melbourne is a member of the royal household. One

son is a member of Parliament, another is in the diplomatic corps, another is probably the natural son of His Royal Highness the Prince Regent, and her daughter-in-law is . . . who she is.

Yes. There might be some attempt to shield these persons.

"Miss Thorne?" said Mr. Harkness, but Rosalind was not listening.

Anger swept through her—abrupt, cold, and unexpected. Trailing close behind came the sick helplessness she knew from the darkest moments of her life, when she discovered another set of lies, these told by her then-beloved father.

The difference was that this time, she was no helpless, ignorant little girl.

She told me her story of trust and pain and letters and wanting to spare her children. She told me about drunken Mr. Davies and evil Lord Byron and mad Lady Caroline, but she did not tell me someone is dead.

"Mr. Harkness, this woman who was found . . . who is she?"

Mr. Harkness's answer was delayed by Mrs. Kendricks, who entered with the fully loaded silver coffee tray and a disapproving frown. Mrs. Kendricks did not like Mr. Harkness. She still cherished the hope that Rosalind would yield to the gentle campaign of persuasion Lord Casselmaine had launched last season. In the meantime, Mrs. Kendricks considered Adam Harkness little more than an impediment to Rosalind achieving a secure, and even enviable, future.

Despite this, or perhaps because of it, Mrs. Kendricks was always scrupulous with her hospitality toward the officer. She made sure her coffee was fresh and that her food was suited to a man of active occupation. As a result, there were ham sandwiches on her tray, along with ginger biscuits and a cold salad of early peas.

"We do not know who she is," said Mr. Harkness while Mrs. Kendricks went about the business of moving the table and setting out the things. "At least, Sir David did not know this morning. She was a handsome woman and had the appearance of having been in health up until she died. She was well dressed, but not wealthy. If she was married, she did not have a ring on her hand. Her complexion was pale and quite fine, her hands smooth but not soft, and her face was only slightly pocked. I would have guessed her for an upper servant or governess, or perhaps a lady from a shop."

"What happened to her?"

"She was poisoned, Miss Thorne, by a large quantity of laudanum."

"Will there be anything else, miss?" asked Mrs. Kendricks, and Rosalind could not help but notice the uncharacteristic furrows on her brow.

"No, thank you, Mrs. Kendricks."

Mrs. Kendricks sailed out of the room, and Rosalind turned again to Mr. Harkness.

"Did the woman . . . did she have any papers with her? I'm wondering specifically about any letters?"

Mr. Harkness lifted a brow. "Not that I know of."

Rosalind poured coffee for Mr. Harkness and herself. She bit into a ham sandwich. She drank. Mr. Harkness helped himself from the plate and let Rosalind have her silence.

Was is possible Lady Melbourne didn't know what had happened? She was ill. She believed she was dying. Her family might be attempting to shield her from the shock.

The memory of Lady Melbourne's clear and piercing gaze rose in Rosalind's mind, along with the pervasive sense that something had been left out of their conversation.

No. Lady Melbourne did know. She had chosen not to tell.

Rosalind felt the red flush of anger creeping into her cheeks. This would not do. She gulped her coffee gracelessly. That would not do, either. Mr. Harkness saw how upset she was. He was waiting for her explanation. She had to tell him something. But what to tell? It was a serious matter to break

confidence with even an ordinary acquaintance. If someone—
Lady Jersey, for example—found out that Rosalind shared
the secrets of one of the most powerful women in London society . . . Rosalind's entire future would be at risk.

And the matter of the letters might have nothing to do
with the matter of this unfortunate woman.

*Yes, and pigs might sprout wings and fly on Thursday
when Lord Byron is crowned King of England.*

Rosalind made her decision.

"It would seem, Mr. Harkness, that our paths have con-
verged," she said. "The house I visited this morning was Melbourne House, and the lady I spoke with is Lady Melbourne.
Some private letters have been stolen from her desk. She is
afraid of either a blackmail attempt or publication and wants
me to try to recover the missing correspondence before either
possibility is realized."

Mr. Harkness had a habit of holding himself very still
when he was startled. Another man might have looked stiff,
but Mr. Harkness had the demeanor of a horse at the starting
line—a restrained, alert anticipation, waiting only the proper
signal to unleash a flurry of reaction.

"Tell me," he said.

Rosalind obeyed. She told Mr. Harkness the whole of the
story she had been given—of the dinner party and the arrival
of Mr. Davies, who carried a plea he said came from the distant, melancholy, and scandal-breeding Lord Byron. About
the letters going missing, the fruitless search of the house and
its occupants, and how she had been summoned.

"This is why you wanted to know if our unfortunate had
any papers with her," Mr. Harkness said once Rosalind had
finished. "You thought she might be the thief?"

"Or a go-between in the thief's pay. But why would anyone kill such a person before the letters were recovered? And if
the letters have already been recovered, why was I sent for?"

"If she was being paid, she might have been trying to go

around her employer. Thieves are notoriously untrustworthy," he added with studied blandness. "It also might be that the person who recovered the letters has not yet told Lady Melbourne." Mr. Harkness considered his own words. "But we are getting ahead of ourselves. We do not know that the two matters are linked."

Rosalind met his gaze, and Mr. Harkness responded by curling the corner of his mouth just a little. He did not believe the death of the unknown woman and the theft of Lady Melbourne's letters were separate any more than Rosalind did.

"I'll need to get this news to Sir David at once. Miss Thorne . . ." For one of the few times in their acquaintance, Rosalind saw Adam Harkness hesitate. "I have absolutely no right to ask you this. Less now than when I first walked in. But will you go along with Lady Melbourne's scheme? Having you in the house might be our only chance of discovering who this woman is and how she died."

Now it was Rosalind's turn to hesitate. For the second time that morning, she was keenly aware of the desire to simply walk away from whatever troubles had lodged themselves in Melbourne House.

Why am I so afraid?

Rosalind had been in danger before. She had confronted lies, theft, blackmail, and murder—all of the most genteel and hidden, and therefore dangerous, sort. Why did this feel different?

She had no answer. She only knew that it did.

There it was again—Mr. Harkness's vibrant, patient stillness. He needed her, but he would not press her, because he also trusted her to know what she could and could not do.

It was that trust she could not refuse.

"Very well, Mr. Harkness," said Rosalind. "I am engaged."

CHAPTER 7

The Vulgar Mention Of Money

From this view his adoption (if not invention) of my being a Picklock is easily explained—for such a suspicion of my means of information would entirely discredit my testimony.

Anne Isabella Milbanke, Lady Byron, private correspondence

After Adam Harkness took his leave, Rosalind sat alone in her parlor for an unusually long time.

I will do this, she told herself.

She would, she felt sure of that. But it was also true that she had never embarked on a task with such a sense of ambivalence. The only comfort she could find inside herself was rather cold.

I will do this because I have given my word.

With this fixed firmly in her mind, Rosalind rang the bell.

"Well, Mrs. Kendricks," she said when her housekeeper arrived. "It seems we may be about to enter another storm." She braced herself for some cool disapproval. In Mrs. Kendricks's estimation, making herself useful to ladies and other gentlewomen was acceptable because of Rosalind's reduced circumstances. Dealings with Bow Street in any capacity, however, was unsavory and unsafe. It certainly was not suited to a lady of Rosalind's birth and breeding.

Much to Rosalind's surprise, her housekeeper delivered no tart observations. In fact, she seemed unusually hesitant.

"This woman . . . the one they found at Melbourne House . . . what was her name?"

"Mr. Harkness could not tell me," said Rosalind. "But if you'd rather stay at Russell Street during this business—"

"No, miss," Mrs. Kendricks cut her off. "I'll go with you."

"I know you think what I do is . . . unwise."

"So I do," Mrs. Kendricks answered promptly. "But from what that Mr. Harkness said, this woman—whomever she might be—would be of my station, or near enough. We are all in God's hands," Mrs. Kendricks added with soft sincerity. "But it's not right that someone should die without even their name left to them, and it's not right that those persons who hold so many lives in their hands should not take proper care of the ones who are dependent."

Mrs. Kendricks did not beg Rosalind's pardon for speaking so freely, nor was Rosalind going to admonish her. The housekeeper had seen a great deal in her time. Rosalind was not about to deny her a say in this turn their lives had taken.

"Well, miss, we had best make a start on packing." Mrs. Kendricks smoothed her skirt, quite unnecessarily. "That driver, Ormande, has made himself quite at home in the kitchen. He can make himself useful bringing the trunks down."

"Yes. Oh, and let me see what I have here." Rosalind opened her reticule and pulled out the slim packet she had been handed as she left the house. "This may be of some use to us as we make our arrangements." She broke Lady Melbourne's seal, unfolded the paper, and froze.

Inside the paper was not a letter, or the few pound notes she expected. It was a draft from the Bank of England.

For five hundred pounds.

Rosalind stared at it, unable to think what to do or say.

"What is it, miss?" Mrs. Kendricks came round to peer over her shoulder and see what had so startled Rosalind. When she did, she clapped her hand over her mouth.

Rosalind folded the papers together. "You will please send Ormande to bring down the trunks," she croaked.

"Yes, miss," murmured Mrs. Kendricks, and she practically took to her heels.

As soon as she was gone, Rosalind refolded the draft into its outer paper and shoved the packet into her desk drawer. She stared at the drawer, as if she thought it might bite. Or burn.

I am being ridiculous, she thought, but she could not calm herself. It was not any kind of joyous surprise that disordered her nerves. It was confusion, and anger.

What was Lady Melbourne thinking?

The amount too large. Shockingly. Unthinkably. Rosalind could live on this much for an entire year, with a larger house, a carriage, a full staff, and new wardrobe in the bargain. If invested carefully, this was the foundation of a lifetime annuity.

This was no "gift," nor was it carelessness from a lady who did not understand the value of a pound coin.

This was a purchase price. Lady Melbourne was making a blatant attempt to buy Rosalind's loyalty. Or at the very least her silence.

But what *for?* Rosalind had already agreed to do what Lady Melbourne wanted. Why would she feel she needed to ensure such a level of gratitude, or dependence?

Could Lady Melbourne fear what Rosalind would think, or do, when she found out about the dead woman? Adam Harkness believed that someone in Melbourne House was already trying to cover up the facts of the murder.

Could that someone be Lady Melbourne herself?

CHAPTER 8

The Art Of Concealment

Your informant was as usual in error—Do not be-
lieve all the lies you may hear.

George Gordon, Lord Byron, private correspondence

What on earth have I done?
The question that followed Adam Harkness as he walked from Little Russell Street to Bow Street.

The problem was, of course, he knew the answer.

You've asked Miss Thorne to enter a house where a noto-
rious madwoman lives in order to unearth a murderer. Or
you would have asked it if Miss Thorne had not already been
invited there.

Which was a coincidence. To Adam Harkness, coincidences tended to be like broken twigs in a hedge—a telltale sign of something dangerous waiting to be found out.

Adam trusted Rosalind Thorne implicitly. He knew her to be both competent and steady. In fact, she had enough nerve for ten men.

If Miss Thorne's not afraid, then why should I be?

Except she was afraid. More than that, she was deeply angry. He had seen it in her eyes and heard it in the slight hesitation that preceded some of her answers.

*And should you be paying such close attention to her,
Harkness? Is that a good idea?*

The answer to that question at least was simple. No, he
should not be, and no, it was not a good idea. He was certain
of this because he could still remember the first time he had
truly watched Rosalind Thorne, and that had been almost a
year ago.

The circumstances were strained and their time was short.
She'd managed to contrive a moment when they could speak
privately, but it involved putting herself in what would be
considered an immensely improper situation—Miss Thorne,
an unmarried woman, went alone into a room with an unmarried man who was far beneath her class, and she shut the
door.

To Adam, it was something else altogether.

He remembered the play of candlelight across her skin, the
determined spark in her eyes as she spoke—offering solutions,
considering actions. He remembered the moment she turned
to him, caught him watching her.

How very still she became.

His back was to the window then. He had not come between her and the door. He was that careful at least. He
should have gone further. He should have backed away and
kept his silence. She should have gone straight to the door
and removed herself.

But he did not, and she did not.

You deserve better, he'd said to her. *You should not be
condemned to a life of polite artifice and deciding what fatu-
ous man sits next to what prattling woman at dinner.*

What am I to do? she'd asked. *I am shaped for one thing
and one thing only—to marry a gentleman and run his house.
If I had other choices, they were taken from me long ago.*

She spread her hands, he remembered that, because he remembered everything about that exact moment—the slant-
ing shadows across her face, the darkness in her eyes.

That is not true, he'd said. *I will not let that be true.*

She'd watched him come toward her. He'd moved slowly, carefully. He'd wanted to give her time to decide, to run, to throw something at him if she needed to. He remembered thinking that. He remembered thinking he should tell her that thought so she could laugh at him, but he had lost the power of speech.

I cannot, she'd whispered. *Even if I wanted to.*

No. Only if you wanted to.

He remembered the touch of her cheek beneath his fingertips. He remembered how he wanted to kiss her the same way he wanted his heart to continue to beat. But he had not. And she had not. Now, a year later, there still remained only that one touch between them. That touch, and an infinity of looks, and Adam's feeling of standing on a cliff's edge but finding himself unable to back away. He could not even resort to the spurned man's agonized shout that she led him on, because she did not do that. He stayed of his own free will, and he knew that because he stayed, sooner or later, he might forget himself.

What kept him sane was the perfect knowledge that if he ever did, that moment would be the last time he ever saw Rosalind Thorne.

Which made him a fool. He knew that. And yet, here he was. Again.

Harkness wrenched his thoughts away from Rosalind's face, her hands, and her demeanor to focus on the work ahead.

It was imperative that he untangle this mess as quickly as possible. There was too much about this business that left him uneasy. The coincidence was only one part of it. Another part was that it would have been so easy to conceal this entire matter from the officers of the king's justice, and yet it was brought directly to their attention.

Miss Thorne had surely considered that, or she would, once the facts had time to sink in. That spoke to arrogance, ignorance, or . . .

Or what?

*   *   *

Overhead, the bells began their staggered tolling, alerting all London to the fact that it was going on the hour of four. Nothing had changed inside the Brown Bear. The men at the bar and on the benches might have been the same ones who had filled the room when he left that morning, and they paid just as much notice to Harkness, which was to say none at all. Adam claimed the iron key to the cellar from a distracted Seamus Callahan and started down the stairs.

Of course, he should not be here. He should have first gone round to the Bow Street station itself. As a principal officer on his shift, it was Harkness's responsibility to check in as often as possible and be sure that nothing had happened requiring his attention. The problem was, Harkness was one of only eight principal officers at Bow Street. He, like any of the others, might be called up by the magistrates to assist with any matter of law, protection, or investigation anywhere across the length and breadth of England.

If Harkness returned to the station, it might be hours before he could leave again. He did not want to wait hours.

In the cellar, Harkness pulled out his tinderbox and lit the nearest lamp. It was a fine spring day outside, but down here Harkness's breath steamed from the cold. Blocks of ice wrapped in straw and canvas had been stacked against the wall. The smell of earth and damp hung everywhere.

The first table still held its morbid burden. The canvas sheet remained drawn over the body, hiding it from view. Harkness felt its presence, though, as clearly as he felt the cellar's cold against his skin.

The woman's clothing had been tossed into a basket in the corner. Sir David would have it removed to be cleaned and sold, or given to charity. What could not be salvaged would go to the ragpickers. Nothing would be wasted.

She was not dressed for being out after dark. There was neither coat nor gloves, and the nights were still chilly. But there was a bonnet of good straw, freshly lined in gray woolen flannel. Her stockings were thick wool.

Strange, he thought. *Why such this bonnet and these stockings but no coat?*

Her dark blue dress was a thoroughly practical garment. It had a round skirt, high collar, and crisp white cuffs. The cuffs and collar had been mended and turned, but the garment had plenty of wear left.

Harkness spread the dress on the table and ran his careful hands across its inner lining and the hems. This was a London woman, he was certain of it. If she had something valuable on her person, she would not be so careless as to carry it in a pocket that could be picked.

And if she'd had a reticule or valise of any kind, it had not come into the cellar with her body. If she'd worn a separate pocket underneath her skirt as many servant girls did, there was none in the basket.

Harkness ran careful hands over the skirts. He flipped up the hems and examined the stitching. He also examined the back and the bodice.

If this woman had been involved with the theft of Lady Melbourne's letters, there was no real reason to believe she had evidence of that theft with her. It was far more likely that whoever had killed her had taken what they wanted.

But there was still a chance. Everything Miss Thorne told him said there was far more to this situation, and this woman, than there first appeared. Harkness was determined he should leave no possibility, or hiding spot, unexamined.

Adam searched the flannel petticoat. He also searched the corset and the good, new linen chemise.

Nothing.

The boots were stout and graceless, and caked with mud, but they were new as well. Harkness pried up the inner soles. He should have started there. It was a favorite hiding spot for thieves and the wary.

Nothing again.

Harkness leaned both hands on the table and stared at the line of clothing, willing it to explain itself to him. Was it simply coincidence, or accident that this woman was found so close to a blatant theft? He could not believe it. Perhaps she had been robbed by her murderer. That would explain why she had no bag or pocket. *Or coat.* Perhaps she really had been careless or naive and left the letters where they could easily be found and removed.

He considered the clothing again. This time he felt the familiar studied stillness fall over him. A heartbeat later, he moved again, although not without a few choice curses at his own stupidity. He'd forgotten the hat.

Harkness snatched up the bonnet and held it close to the light. He found the seam where the flannel had been sewn into the straw frame, and then he found the knotted darn in the seam. He ran his palm across the surface of the flannel.

There. Right there. The unmistakable outline of a folded paper pressed against the cloth.

Harkness yanked out his pocket knife. He slit the lining with a single stroke and pulled the paper free.

It was a letter. Wherever it had come from, it had traveled a long way under hard conditions that left it battered, wrinkled, and water-stained.

The seal was not so much broken as crumbled. Adam opened it carefully, not wanting to tear the fragile paper. The writer—whomever it was—had a careless but emphatic hand. The author stabbed the paper and underlined every third word with great black slashes.

This writer also thought a great deal of their correspondent. Adam read:

> *But I have never ceased nor can cease to feel for a moment that perfect and boundless attachment which bound and binds me to you—which renders me utterly*

incapable of real *love for any other human being—. . .*
we may have been very wrong—but I repent of nothing
except that cursed marriage—and your refusing to con-
tinue to love me as you had loved me—

Adam let his gaze drop to the signature, but there was only
a single initial:

B.

B as in Byron? Harkness wondered. Possibly. Probably. He
turned the letter over to see the direction. It was written in
the same careless hand, with much splotching and daubing of
the ink. After a minute, though, Adam made out that the letter was addressed to a Mrs. A. Leigh. The address at the top
of the letter was for someplace called Six Mile Bottom.
Adam's brows lowered.
Miss Thorne said she'd been tasked with retrieving some
letters for Lady Melbourne at Melbourne House. He had no
idea if the Melbourne country estate was this Six Mile Bottom. He'd have to ask Sir David about that. But he did know
that Lady Melbourne's family name was Lamb, not Leigh.
He turned over the other names Miss Thorne had mentioned
to him—William Lamb, Lady Caroline Lamb, Mr. Scrope
Davies, the famous Lady Jersey . . .
Adam frowned at the letter, at the collection of clothing on
the table, and finally at the corpse beneath its makeshift
shroud.
"So, who the devil is Mrs. Leigh?"

CHAPTER 9

The Presence Of Past Sins

*. . . the rumours of which I was the Subject—if
they were true I was unfit for England, if false
England was unfit for me.*

George Gordon, Lord Byron, private correspondence

Alice and George Littlefield shared a three-room flat in a
genteelly shabby street. Brother and sister kept their own
house and "did" entirely for themselves. Rosalind had no
doubt that she would find Alice home and most likely still
working, even though it was already early evening. George
wrote exclusively for the *London Chronicle*, but Alice turned
her quill to anything that came her way. In any given month
she might pour forth an entire potpourri of essays, editing, or
translations in addition to her gossip columns.

Her assumption proved correct. A bare moment after Rosalind knocked, the door flew open to reveal Alice in an ink-
stained pinafore and cap.

"Rosalind! At last! I was afraid I was going to have to
barge into your parlor and harangue poor Mrs. Kendricks
for your whereabouts. Come in and sit." Alice seized her
friend's hand and dragged her over to the ancient sofa. "I
think there's still some tea left in the pot." She lifted the pot's
lid and squinted. "We're in luck."

She poured out the black brew, pushed the cup into Rosalind's hands, and then dragged a slightly lopsided chair away from the paper-covered dining table. "Now. What did Lady Jersey want?" Alice dropped onto the seat and leaned forward, elbows on knees, hands clasped. Rosalind could hear the ghost of their former deportment mistress howling in despair. "Has some new and dreadful crisis arisen to stalk the gracious halls of the storied Almack's assembly rooms? And when can A.E. Littlefield have the details?"

Despite everything, Rosalind laughed. "Believe it or not, Lady Jersey's visit had nothing to do with Almack's. At least, I don't see how it does."

"You amaze me! What else could get Lady Jersey out of bed before noon?"

Yes, what? Rosalind took a swallow of tea and then, despite her best intentions, made a face. Alice frowned, took the cup from Rosalind's fingers, drank some, and made a similar face. "Oh. I'm sorry for that, Rosalind. I'll put the kettle on again."

Alice filled the battered copper pot from the pitcher and hung it on the hob. While her friend bustled about the tiny flat, Rosalind tried to gather her thoughts. It was not as easy as it should have been.

"Where's George?" she asked as a way to delay having to answer.

"I have no idea," announced Alice tartly. "He never sees fit to talk with me these days unless he wants to complain." Despite her tone, it was easy to see Alice was worried.

Oh, Alice, so am I. About so many things.

Rosalind took a steadying breath and decided that the best approach was the direct one.

"Alice . . . have you heard any rumors about someone who might be selling letters written between Lord Byron and Lady Melbourne?"

Alice whirled around and stared as if Rosalind had just uttered a rude word. "What on earth . . . ? Rosalind, you must be joking."

"I'm not." A spasm of conscience ran through her. Rosalind reminded herself that she was not actually breaking confidence. She'd told Lady Melbourne at the beginning that she meant to let Alice know about the letters. "Lady Jersey came to take me to Melbourne House. Some of Lady Melbourne's private letters have gone missing and she fears blackmail, or publication. Or both."

Upon hearing this bare minimum of facts, Alice abandoned kettle and pot and instead crossed to the sofa and took Rosalind's hands.

"Rosalind," she said quite seriously, "if this business has *anything* to do with Lord Byron, I'm begging you, as your friend, turn the invitation down. Anyone who gets near that man is incinerated. Especially if they're women."

"It's too late, I'm afraid."

"I know Lady Melbourne is very influential, but she's brutal. I can't print half of what I've heard about her, and she discards people who disappoint her like clipped coins. If she's made you any promises . . ."

As Alice clearly had a dozen other arguments to make, Rosalind swiftly cut her off. "I'm not doing this for Lady Melbourne. I'm doing it for Mr. Harkness."

"Mr. Harkness? Your runner? When did he come into this?"

"After I got back from Melbourne House, and he's not mine and he's not a runner. He's a principal officer."

Alice narrowed her eyes. "I think, Miss Thorne, that you'd better begin at the beginning."

So Rosalind did. Alice rummaged in the pantry for her hidden stash of tea and discovered that George had already plundered it ("I will be murdering him later," she announced firmly). She responded to this outrage by raiding his room for the tin she knew he kept there, and then she managed to find a remaining lump of sugar and some milk that was still in excellent condition. As her friend darted about, Rosalind talked about her interview with Lady Melbourne and her subsequent interview with Adam Harkness, about the lady's fear that her secrets would be made public, and about how one of those secrets seemed to include the death of a woman whose name was not yet known.

Rosalind finished at about the same time that Alice handed her the fresh mug of sweet, milky tea. Alice sat back down holding her own mug and was unusually silent.

"I think I like it better when you're managing visiting books and passing me tidbits."

"I think I do, too."

Alice drank her tea. "Well, to answer your first question, no. I haven't heard any rumors about letters like that being offered for publication, and believe me I would have. The Major would give up a year's salary to get anything of that nature for the *Chronicle*." Alice stared at the wall past Rosalind's shoulder, turning the mug in her restless hands. "I met him once, you know."

"Lord Byron?" Alice nodded. "Alice! You never told me."

"It was not my finest moment. I'd just started with the *Chronicle* and was attending some party or the other. You know how it happens. A new hostess wants a favorable account of her crush in the papers, so A.E. Littlefield and a dozen other social writers get invitations. It was the little season, so there was not a great deal happening. The Major sent me in the hopes of getting some on-dit about who would be the new sensations.

"Well, there I was in the corner, trying to see as much as possible. I remember the quadrille was particularly complicated, and the punch particularly bad, and this voice beside me announces, 'Not dancing? What excellent taste you have, Miss Whomever-You-May-Be. I'd as soon impale myself on one of the butter knives as throw myself into that crush. I expect the evening shall end with an incident of grievous bodily harm.' "

"I remembered turning. I'm sure I meant to say something devastating. I mean, it was so rude, and so obvious, and then I saw him . . ." Memory made Alice blink.

"There are some people . . . they burn, and when they're nearby, even the most sensible of us turn into moths. He was like that. I don't even remember what I said, or what he said. He didn't stay long. A friend came and he left, and I swear upon my life, Rosalind, I thought I was going to faint.

"I think he knew who I was. I saw him eyeing me later, and his friend was whispering to him. He might have purposely made that remark, hoping I'd print it."

"Did you?"

"Oh yes. I couldn't fail to include a remark from Lord Byron in my column. And I certainly can't fault him for making sure he got his name in the papers. I mean, a poet has to keep himself in the public eye. But I watched him move about that room, and there was that light, that fire . . . he knew what he did to people, and when you know you have power over the moths, you use it."

"And then the moths fawn over you and flatter you and give you whatever you want so you'll shine for them. But when they burn up in the flame, the flame gets dirtied by the effort," said Rosalind.

"Round and round," agreed Alice. "Each side using and degrading the other. And when you're a young man in London, and you've discovered you can get away with . . . well . . . anything, you do that, too."

"How did the Byron light come to shine on Lady Melbourne's world?"

Alice considered this. "I *think* it was Lady Caroline Lamb who managed that. She'd fallen into an obsession with Byron, and he with her. You've heard about that by now, I expect? Well, it turned out Lady Caroline did not have the head or the heart, or maybe the liver—who knows when it comes to all these internal organs?—for an affair with a man such as Lord Byron, and Lady Melbourne decided she needed to intervene before her daughter-in-law was fatally compromised." Alice paused. "I think Lady Melbourne meant well, at least according to her own views. I think she really was trying to stop the scandal and get Lady Caroline away from Byron. When it became clear that Lady Caroline wouldn't listen to her, Lady Melbourne took another tack and set about charming Byron, and incidentally trying to get him married off so he'd settle down."

"Because when a man is inclined to dissipation and is feeling his own power in society, marriage is always an effective deterrent to further bad behavior," murmured Rosalind.

"Isn't it amazing how that conviction persists even among our cleverest women? Well. Lord Byron returned the favor of Lady Melbourne's attentions by charming her."

"For her social influence, or just because he could?"

"A bit of both, probably."

"And what happened?"

"Lady Melbourne proved to be as much of a moth as the rest of us," said Alice quietly. "She fell in love with him."

CHAPTER 10

The Affairs Of Unruly Hearts

*If ever I return to England—it will be to see
you—and recollect that in all time—& place—and
feelings—I have never ceased to be the same to
you in heart.*

George Gordon, Lord Byron, private correspondence

"Alice, you can't mean it." Rosalind remembered Lady Melbourne—regal, calm, and charming in spite of her pain. It was unimaginable that she could lose her experienced heart to the famously rude and unruly poet.

But Alice simply shrugged. "That's what I've heard, anyway, and my source is very well placed. Now, was the feeling real? Or did she feign it as part of her flattery of him? I don't know. But they did grow very close. They corresponded constantly. He called her his *corbeau blanc*, his white raven, and when he decided he did need to marry, he let her choose the candidate."

"*Why?*"

Alice sighed. "Among his less admirable qualities—and those are many—the man is a social climber. He wooed all the prominent hostesses, and I rather imagine he wanted a wife who would help keep society's doors open for him. Anyway, Lady Melbourne pushed forward one of her nieces, Anne Milbanke. Now, you must admit, Rosalind, that if Lady Melbourne really intended to put some distance between Lord Byron and Lady Caroline, she'd have selected a wife from further afield than her own family."

Rosalind was silent for a moment, searching for a flaw in Alice's reasoning. But she could find none. If Lady Melbourne truly had wanted Lord Byron to leave her family alone, why would she marry him *into* her family?

A knock sounded on the door.

"Who could that be?" Alice started to her feet. "George can't have forgotten his key again."

"I expect it's our supper," said Rosalind.

"Supper!" Alice worked the latch.

Ormande stood on the stairwell with his young outrider, Acre, and a thin, weedy looking boy wearing an apron. Between them, the youths carried a stout hamper. Warm, delicious scents wafted into the flat.

"Rosalind!" cried Alice. "You shouldn't have!"

"Yes, I should. I am milking you shamelessly for information and drinking all your tea. Supper is the least I owe you." In fact, once Ormande had dropped her off at Alice's, Rosalind had sent him directly to the corner cookshop to order them a dinner. "You can bring it all in here, Ormande, thank you."

They cleared Alice's papers from the table, spread a cloth, and let the cookshop boy bring out his treasures. There was roast lamb, bread and butter, and some very new potatoes. These were joined by ham pie and parsley sauce, young greens, treacle pudding, a jug of cider, and a flask of hot coffee.

"Well, George will be furious he missed it all!" Alice's eyes sparkled. "And since when did you acquire a manservant, Rosalind?" She nodded toward the door that Ormande closed behind himself.

"Since I became Lady Melbourne's assistant. She has loaned him, and one of her carriages, to me."

"I thought you looked abnormally warm and tidy when you walked in. Her ladyship is being very generous."

"Yes," agreed Rosalind, thinking of the bank draft in her desk. Alice noted the brevity of Rosalind's reply but thankfully did not pursue the issue. Instead, she pursued a plate full of roast, pie, potatoes, and greens, along with a glass of cider from the jug.

"I suppose we should set something aside for George, should he ever decide to come home." Alice glanced at the little carriage clock on the mantel. "Do you think I should be concerned?"

"Perhaps he doesn't want to risk an argument," suggested Rosalind.

"Coward," muttered Alice around a mouthful of potatoes.

Rosalind sliced her pie. "I take it there's been no resolution to the disagreement over your plan to turn novelist?"

"We've achieved a truce, of sorts. I've agreed not to mention it, and he's agreed not to take my head off."

"Alice . . . is this so important to you?"

Alice took a very long time chasing a bit of mutton around her plate with her fork.

"It's not that it's important to me personally, it's . . . well, it's insurance, if you like."

"I'm not sure I understand."

Alice sighed. "As things stand, the people who give me my gossip items talk to me because they know me. Mostly, they're girls we went to school with, and their friends. But those girls, well, they're marrying and settling, aren't they? Oh, they're still very much in the middle of the social scene, but there are new families, new girls, and new matrons taking over. They don't know me and are much less likely to talk to me. One day I might find myself left entirely out on the doorstep, and then what? I need something else before that happens. This could well be it."

"You might marry," suggested Rosalind. She had been to the *Chronicle*'s office with Alice and seen more than one man there cast a longing look in her direction.

"I might. But there's no guarantee that any man who would marry purely for the love of Alice Littlefield would be able to support a family without some extra income. Not all of us keep dukes in our pockets, you know." Alice stopped. "I'm sorry, Rosalind. That was unkind of me."

Rosalind indicated her complete unconcern by helping herself to another potato. "Perhaps that's what's worrying George."

"What? Dukes in pockets?"

"Money. I'm sorry to pry, but is it possible there's something you don't . . ."

But Alice waved her knife dismissively. "Of all the things George might do, lying to me about money troubles is not one of them. Besides, with the new season underway, things have been relatively good, despite the fact we are all supposed to still be in mourning for the princess." She glanced at the clock again. "In fact, as much as I hate to do it, Rosalind, I'm going to have to send you away soon. A.E. Littlefield is on duty tonight, and I've got three balls to attend and write up for Thursday's edition."

"I understand. But since Lady Melbourne's been so good as to let me have the use of her carriage, I can drop you off wherever you need to go."

"Well, of course, I won't say no to that. Be sure to thank Lady Melbourne for me, and my shoes, not to mention my hems." Alice sipped a little more cider. "You are being careful, aren't you, Rosalind? About Lady Melbourne?"

"I'm trying," said Rosalind. "She is clearly bent on doing all she can to get me on her side, which raises certain . . . suspicions."

"Especially when there's a dead woman in her yard. You've said very little about her, you know, Rosalind."

"That's because I know very little. Nothing at all, in fact. Mr. Harkness could only guess that she was some upper servant or a shopkeeper, or something of the kind."

"And she didn't have any letters on her?"

"He promised to look again, but so far, no, nothing was found. Not that this means a great deal. They could have been stolen again, or still be hidden somewhere." Rosalind cut into her pudding and watched the sweet treacle pool onto the plate. "Now, let me see if I understand what you've told me so far. Lord Byron had his affair with Lady Caroline. Lady Melbourne, alarmed at the growing scandal, entered into a friendship with Lord Byron. Her initial plan, as far as is known, was to try to break things up between the two." She ate a thoughtful bite of pudding. "Instead, Lady Melbourne and Lord Byron grew close."

"And began to correspond," added Alice. "Considering we are talking about missing letters, this is significant. At some point, Lady Melbourne began urging Lord Byron to marry her niece—one Anne Isabelle Milbanke, known as Annabelle by her friends and family." Alice poured herself some strong coffee from the flask and drank with frank and open relish. "A marriage which has been a public disaster, and ended with Lady Byron née Milbanke taking their baby, returning to her parents, and seeking a complete legal separation."

Rosalind nodded somewhat absently. That aspect of the deeply layered scandal had shocked society for months. It was all but unheard of for the private affairs of a prominent family to be laid before a lawyer. Many wondered why Lady Byron would even bother. A wife's petition for legal separation from her husband had next to no chance of succeeding. As a married woman, Lady Byron could not even engage the lawyer without her husband's express consent.

"So, in addition to the ongoing disaster with Lady Caroline and Lord Byron, Lady Melbourne has to watch the destruction of a marriage she engineered to keep Byron near her." Rosalind frowned at her plate. "And all of this might be in those letters."

"It might," agreed Alice.

"But it's not enough," Rosalind spread her hands. "She says she wants to protect her family, but I cannot see from what. Losing some letters is unseemly, but Lady Melbourne has navigated far worse. She cannot really be afraid that anyone in her circle would be so ill-bred as to cut her or her children, over such a minor matter. Even I've heard some of the stories. They say her fourth son, George, was fathered by the Prince of Wales! If I know that much, imagine what her real friends know, and yet she is still constantly celebrated."

Alice became very busy cutting her pudding into increasingly smaller pieces. "It might be . . . it might be that there's something in those letters she hasn't told them."

"But what?"

Alice grimaced and pushed her plate away. She looked into her coffee cup and then pushed that away, too. Instead, she poured a fresh measure of cider out of the jug. "It might be that she knew about one of Byron's less savory relationships."

Rosalind frowned. "There are rumors he prefers . . . the company of men. Sometimes, at least."

This was not something one spoke of openly, but Alice and Rosalind had moved in society for years now, and they both knew much more about the private lives of its inhabitants than a pair of unmarried young women were commonly supposed to.

"If it were only that particular preference, we still probably wouldn't be having this conversation." Alice downed a credible measure of the cider. "Do you know Mrs. George Leigh?" she asked suddenly.

Rosalind drank some coffee and considered. "I think . . . is there a lady-in-waiting to Queen Charlotte by that name?"

"Yes. That's her. Well. Mrs. George Leigh was born Augusta Byron. She's Lord Byron's half sister."

"Good heavens, Alice! Now a lady-in-waiting is caught up in this? This is worse than the Wars of the Roses! How is this Mrs. Leigh involved?"

Alice set her glass down, and for a moment Rosalind thought her friend was going to change the subject.

"Rosalind, are you certain you want to hear this?"

"No, but I think I need to."

Alice nodded. "I would never, ever even hint at this to anyone but you, and never unless . . . unless it was life and death."

"Which it is. Alice, what do you know?"

"Mrs. Leigh—Augusta Byron—is the real reason Lord Byron had to leave the country."

"What did she do?"

"It's what he did. Or they." Alice swallowed, and swallowed again. "He fathered her youngest child."

Rosalind set her cup down. "Alice, you don't mean it. You just said they're brother and sis . . ." She stopped, unable to finish.

"I do mean it," said Alice hoarsely. "And what's more, everything I've heard indicates that Lady Melbourne knew about . . . matters between them, and that she knew while she was persuading him to marry her niece."

Rosalind had come to believe she had heard every scandal that society could manufacture, but this was something well beyond the pale. Alice could not even meet Rosalind's gaze as she continued.

"I do not doubt Lady Melbourne's ability to weather any ordinary scandal. Her wealth and general influence can certainly cause society to look the other way in most matters.

But if there's ink on paper showing that she badgered her niece into marrying a man who carried on an affair with his own sister . . ." Alice stopped. When she spoke again, it was very softly, and very seriously.

"If that's what's in those letters, Rosalind, Lady Melbourne has every reason to be terrified of having them made public."

CHAPTER 11

What May Be Learned After Sunset

. . . and, if she closed her eyes, visions of murder
floated before her distracted mind.

Lady Caroline Lamb, Glenarvon

After that, there was little left to be said. Rosalind and
Alice packed away the remains of the meal into Alice's
tiny pantry and piled the dishes into the hamper for the
cook's boy to take away.

Then, with Rosalind acting as lady's maid, they dressed
Alice in her simple yellow satin gown that had been trimmed
with fresh ribbons for the season. They put her hair up into
tidy braids woven with strings of artificial pearls.

"And still no George," sighed Alice as Rosalind fastened
her grandmother's garnet necklace around her throat. Annoyance was beginning to give way to real concern. "Honestly, Rosalind, I don't know what to do about him."

"Should I ask Devon to talk with him? Or Sanderson
Faulks?"

"Perhaps." But from Alice's tone, it was clear she did not
hold out much hope that either man would be able to talk
sense into her recalcitrant and tardy brother.

The knock at the door proved to be only Acre telling them

that Ormande had the chaise ready. Outside, dusk was turning into genuine darkness. Lanterns shone in the carriages and doorways.

With some slight argument from Alice, it was agreed that Ormande would first take them to Little Russell Street and then continue on as Alice's driver for the rest of the evening.

"May I take it that you are not going to write a polite note declining Lady Melbourne's invitation?" said Alice as the driver touched up the horses.

"No," said Rosalind. "If this business were only about Lady Melbourne and her letters, I might, but there's this other matter. . . ."

"Yes. That," agreed Alice solemnly. But she did not stay serious for long. A spark lit in her dark eyes that had nothing to do with the lights outside the carriage. "You never did tell me, Rosalind, how is Mr. Harkness?"

"Much as he ever was." *I will not be led, Alice.*

Alice did not seem to notice Rosalind's cool tone or the equally chilly glance that went with it. "And you're still going to Louisa Winterbourne's engagement ball Thursday?"

"And you're coming with me," Rosalind reminded her. "A.E. Littlefield will most certainly want to describe the glittering affair for the Sunday edition, so Mrs. Wilverton Showell who so expertly shepherded her niece to this most successful engagement will be able to look back on the grand occasion with complete satisfaction. And given everything else that's going on right now, I don't expect to have time to write it up for you."

"I would never ask you to. Especially since I expect you'll be very busy during the ball. And of course you'll be seeing his grace, the Duke of Casselmaine, there. There may even be a dance or two."

Rosalind sighed. If she would not be led, it seemed Alice would not be deterred. "Devon seldom dances voluntarily, you know that." Except there had been one time, recently, when he'd not only danced, he'd danced with grace and enjoyment.

"No. *Devon* does not, at least not often. Nor do you, as I recall. Except with *Devon*," remarked Alice with bland and utterly false nonchalance. Rosalind opened her mouth, but Alice did not give her room to speak. "Rosalind Thorne, if you attempt to say that this confluence of your runner and your duke is anything but interesting and awkward, I shall be deeply disappointed."

"I will not attempt any such thing. In fact, I may go so far as to say it might be . . . fraught."

That took Alice entirely off guard. "Oh, Rosalind! Has Lord Casselmaine . . . has he said he wants . . ."

"Yes. He has." Her fingers were fidgeting with the drawstring of her reticule. Inexcusable. She stilled them. "Not formally, of course but we have . . . had a conversation."

She remembered Devon in the sunshine of the park. He'd been holding a horse's reins at the time, and the beast had been determined to get at her straw bonnet, which made the whole thing more than a little absurd. But what was not at all absurd was how he'd turned to her and told her he loved her. He had never stopped loving her.

Alice let out a very long, slow breath. "What are you going to do?"

"I don't know yet."

"Do you still love him?"

"Sometimes I do. Sometimes . . ." But she could not bring herself to finish.

Alice touched her hand. "Sometimes what, Rosalind?"

Rosalind didn't answer. She felt keenly aware of their surroundings, the comfortable carriage, the robes, the neat and well-matched horses. A competent driver sat on the box, ready to ease the workaday business of running and fetching. All these were things that both she and Alice has once taken for granted.

"Sometimes I wonder if I love who I used to be, and who I will be if we marry."

Alice, of course, understood. "That's hard. I'm sorry."

Rosalind shook her head. "It's not as if it's a new problem. A resolution will come."

Fortunately for Rosalind's composure and self-worth, she was not required to say anything else on this subject. The carriage had turned up Little Russell Street, and Ormande drew the horses to a halt.

"I'll call for you at nine on Thursday," Rosalind told Alice as the boy helped her out.

"I'll be ready. Rosalind . . . promise me you'll be especially careful at Melbourne House?"

"I will, Alice." Rosalind paused. "Alice . . . did you tell me that your publisher, or your potential publisher, Mr. Henry Colburn, also published Lady Caroline's novel *Glenarvon*?"

"Yes. Why do you ask?"

"A thought. Nothing more."

Alice lifted her chin. "That, Rosalind Thorne, is a blatant falsehood. However, as I am pressed for time, I will let it pass, for now."

They said their farewells, and Rosalind went inside her house. Mrs. Kendricks had left a lamp burning in the hall, but she was nowhere in evidence. Rosalind removed her coat and bonnet. From the sound of the footsteps and thumping overhead, her housekeeper was surely deep in the throes of packing for tomorrow.

Tomorrow. Rosalind hung her things on their pegs and took up the lamp to light her way to the parlor. Everything she had heard from Alice left her troubled, and strangely tired. This did not matter. She had given her word, and she must make ready to go to Melbourne House, carrying an unexpected layer of additional pretenses and blossoming suspicions.

Not to mention one or two utterly unfounded suppositions.

For instance . . . suppose Lady Caroline Lamb, with her well-documented desire to wreak revenge on her mother-in-law, had stolen a packet of desperately scandalous letters. Who better to entrust these valuable documents with than her publisher, Mr. Colburn, who had already demonstrated a willingness to profit from the family's scandals?

Lady Caroline might have smuggled the letters to her publisher with the understanding that he would bring them out for the public, suitably arranged and edited for best effect. If that was the plan, Mr. Colburn was not likely to talk about it with any resident of Melbourne House, even if they thought to ask him.

But he might just talk with Rosalind. Or A.E. Littlefield, or even George Littlefield.

Rosalind's thoughts stopped in their tracks, and she had the odd feeling of looking over own her shoulder. But it was not anything about the infamous, and so far invisible, Lady Caroline that gave her this sensation. Nor even about Lady Melbourne.

It was Alice herself, or rather her invitation from Mr. Colburn to submit a manuscript, that gave Rosalind her sudden pause. That, and George's strenuous but ambiguous objections.

Was it possible that honest, open, amiable George knew something unsavory about Mr. Colburn?

Rosalind set down the lamp with a sigh that felt terribly self-indulgent. A new, unopened letter waited on the mantelpiece. Rosalind picked it up, aware of a surge of unreasonable irritation that there was yet one more thing that needed her attention.

The letter was unfranked, which meant it had been delivered by hand. She read the direction, and her irritation vanished because she recognized the writing.

This was from Mr. Harkness.

Rosalind broke the plain seal at once and found that a second sheet of paper had been folded inside the first.

Mr. Harkness's note was brief and without salutation:

> *Our unfortunate had the enclosed concealed in her bonnet lining. We still have no name to put to her, but it looks as though Lady Melbourne's fears of blackmail are justified.*
> *A.H.*

Rosalind sat down at her writing desk.

Everything I've heard indicates that Lady Melbourne knew about . . . matters between them. . . . Alice's words echoed through Rosalind's mind.

She steeled her nerves and opened the second sheet. It was clearly a copy of whatever letter Mr. Harkness had found. The ink and paper were both quite new. Rosalind read the declarations of love and devotion directed to one Mrs. Leigh by some person with the initial *B*.

Mrs. Leigh, who was born Augusta Byron.

. . . if there's ink on paper showing that she badgered her niece into marrying a man who carried on an affair with his own sister. . . . Alice's words returned from memory. *If that's what's in those letters, Rosalind, Lady Melbourne has every reason to be terrified of having them made public.*

Rosalind folded the two sheets together and slid them into her drawer beside the other letter containing Lady Melbourne's unseemly bank draft. Was this what that five hundred pounds was for? To make sure Rosalind would continue with her work and keep her silence, even when she found out what Lady Melbourne had done?

Rosalind turned the key in the lock.

Remember this is no longer about Lady Melbourne. This is about helping Mr. Harkness find out who this poor woman is and what really happened to her. She slipped the desk key into her reticule.

And why she had this letter concealed so carefully about her person.

And whether Lady Melbourne was so desperate to recover those letters, she had murder done.

CHAPTER 12

The Business Of Bow Street

*I shall therefore not only take all proper & legal
steps—but the former correspondence shall be
published—& the whole business from the beginning investigated in all the courts . . .*

George Gordon, Lord Byron, private correspondence

For all its fame, there was nothing fancy, and very little
comfortable, about the Bow Street police station. The entrance hall was as busy as the street out front. All kinds and
conditions of people crowded around the clerks' desks, bom-
barding the men with their complaints, questions, hopes, or
fears. The chief clerk, Stafford, along with his deputies tried
to sort them out, deciding which should be sent on their way
and which should be referred to the magistrates.

The ward room was somewhat less crowded but scarcely
less noisy. Constables, runners, and patrolmen lounged on
the benches waiting for fresh assignments. They shouted
their greetings at Harkness as he passed, and he doffed his
hat in answer.

The patrol room waited on the far side of the ward room.
Indignant letter writers might describe it as a hive of dissolution and incompetence, but in truth, it more resembled a

cross between a bank office and the reading room of a circulating library.

"Hello, Harkness." Sampson Goutier, who was the only other man in the room, waved his hand in casual greeting as Adam entered. He sat at one of the scarred tables that had been set in the middle of the room. Goutier was a black man who'd been born in Paris to parents who had arrived in that city from Barbados and fled it when the revolution spilled into the streets. His given name was not actually Sampson. His shipmates on his first voyage had rechristened him owing to his size and strength. Goutier had decided the appellation suited him better than his mother's gift of Parcival. He'd come to Bow Street after working with the river police and Harkness was glad to have him. Goutier had a keen eye and a careful ear, and very little got past him.

"How goes the day here?" Harkness asked him.

Goutier brandished his pen. "I am fighting all the devils of the details for Stafford and his mighty recording angels."

"No one tells you how much time you're going to spend writing reports when they offer you promotion."

"Because if they did, we'd all stay patrolmen."

The newspapers might call anyone who worked at Bow Street a "runner," but there was a particular hierarchy among the men at the station. Where Harkness was a principal officer and might be called to lead inquiries anywhere in England, Goutier held the rank of patrol captain. The captains and their men were most concerned with guarding the streets of London. But they also might be sent out by the magistrates to scour a neighborhood and question witnesses in the event of a theft; or they might form a special squad to break up a brawl or a mob. Goutier had assisted the post office with thefts from the mails and had more than once been requested by the Bank of England to work on a case of forgery.

Harkness chuckled and started helping himself to a number of newspapers from the racks that were arranged against the walls between the cabinets and the bookshelves. The station subscribed to most of the London papers, as well as some from across England and Scotland, and even one or two from Paris, but most of the space was taken up by Bow Street's own publication, the *Hue & Cry*.

Hue & Cry was published for the expanding network of policing stations that attempted to emulate Bow Street's model. It carried descriptions of crimes, criminals, and missing items. The idea was that if the stations could share such details, it would become that much harder for those who broke the peace to successfully flee from one district to another or to slip their stolen goods into unsuspecting hands.

According to the law, housebreaking was a matter for officers of the peace. Retrieving any missing property, or persons, however, was held to be a private matter to be resolved by private means. Shopkeepers sometimes banded together in cooperative societies to hire a thief-taker or investigating officer. For most persons, though, experienced assistance cost more than they could afford. Instead, they advertised. Until a witness came, or was pushed, forward, Harkness's best starting point to discover the identity of the unknown woman lay among these public pleas for information and promises of rewards.

Harkness deposited the papers and himself across the table from Goutier.

"I hope you're not planning on actually getting through that lot," Goutier said. "Old man Townsend's been looking for you since noon."

Harkness sighed. "I suppose I should have known. Is he in there now?" He nodded toward the side door that led to Townsend's private office.

"Pacing like a caged panther," Goutier assured him amiably. "What have you been getting up to now, Harkness?"

"I'll tell you later." Harkness got to his feet. "If I survive."

"Good luck." Goutier bent back to his report, and Harkness crossed the ward room to the station's lone private office, and knocked. "Adam Harkness reporting, sir!"

"Ah, finally!"

Taking this exclamation as permission, Harkness let himself in.

Like Harkness, John Townsend held the rank of principal officer. This, in theory, made them equals. In practice, however, John Townsend was the head of the Bow Street station and oversaw all the men who worked there. He was a man who'd grown in consequence, and girth, across his years at the station, and he liked to have his worth on full display for the world to admire. The rest of the station might be a bare-bones place, but Townsend's office was filled with his luxurious collection of carpets, candlesticks, clocks, snuff boxes, and enough objet d'art to furnish a half-dozen pawnshops. Much of it had been gifted to him by grateful patrons, a large number of whom were members of the aristocracy, and the royal family.

Harkness would be the first to admit that Bow Street's reputation, and its finances, prospered because of Townsend's connections. At the same time, those who patronized Mr. Townsend felt it was part of his job to assiduously guard those "rights and freedoms" that belonged "naturally" to Englishmen of particular classes and qualities.

Townsend had always agreed, and obeyed.

This was the real reason Sir David was so reluctant to make it known where the dead woman had been found. Townsend would not be at all happy with a real inquiry that might affect the members of Lord and Lady Melbourne's household. It was also why Harkness had agreed to keep his silence.

"Well, Mr. Harkness, you seem to have been out and about a great deal today. " Townsend stood behind his gleaming desk of good English oak. Normally, he dressed to match his rich surroundings, favoring plenty of colorful silk, linen, and superfine wool. Just now, though, he wore black from head to toe, a gesture of mourning for the late Princess Charlotte. Townsend was a friend of the Prince of Wales and was frequently called to Carlton House and Kensington Palace to oversee the security of the inhabitants, so this might have been considered politic. The whole nation, after all, was still supposed to be in some form of mourning, even though the death of the princess and her son had been five months ago. But there was more to it. Townsend cherished his association with the royal family, sometimes to the point where he seemed to consider himself a member of that august clan.

"I was on business for Sir David Royce." Harkness took the chair Townsend waved him toward. "I apologize for not leaving word with Stafford, but as I was called out before dawn . . ."

"Yes, yes. Sir David explained that. I've a letter from him here." Townsend lifted the single sheet of paper that graced his blotter. "In it, he requests your assistance for what he says is likely to prove a lengthy matter. The details of the situation are proving—and these are his words—'stubbornly difficult to untangle.' He calls you Bow Street's best man and says he needs you to track down several witnesses for him before the inquest can be convened." Townsend lowered the paper. "I am assuming your work today has been with these stubbornly difficult details. Have you made any progress?"

Harkness thought of the travel-stained letter nestled in his coat pocket and the copy of it that he'd written at a back table in the Brown Bear and sent to Miss Thorne. If he told Townsend he had found a letter concealed in a dead woman's clothing, Townsend would—properly—demand to see it. He would—also quite properly—demand a full explanation to go with it.

Harkness looked his ostentatiously patient superior in the eye.

"No, sir. Unfortunately, I've found nothing yet."

Townsend waited, letting the silence stretch out and inviting Harkness to fill it. But there was nothing more that Harkness could safely say.

Townsend paced to the window. "Sir David's requesting you more frequently these days, Mr. Harkness. I'm hearing your name in other circles as well." Townsend spoke to the windowpanes, and the street beyond. "All favorable mentions, I hasten to add! In fact, I would say you're acquiring a most impressive reputation. And it's well deserved, sir. Yes. For the most part, very well deserved indeed."

For the most part. Interesting exception, sir.

Harkness waited. Townsend did not give compliments randomly. He wanted something.

Or he's planning something.

"It's past time you gave some serious thought to your position, Harkness," Townsend went on finally. "You have every possibility of a brilliant career. But day-to-day work, however brilliantly done, and my praise, however widely spread, can take you only so far. It's past time, Mr. Harkness, that you started to become personally known in the *right* circles."

Harkness had intended to keep up a neutral façade, but something must have showed on his face, because Townsend laughed. "I know, I know! You're not one to put yourself forward. You know your place, and you want your deeds to speak for you. These are admirable qualities, Mr. Harkness. But!" Townsend raised one finger. "You also need to know your worth, and not just to your family, but to your fellow officers."

"Sir . . . you're asking me to . . ."

"I'm asking you to go out where you can be seen," said Townsend patiently. "That's all. Attend a few routs. Eat a few dinners in elevated company. I'll select the invitations." He paused, as if something had just occurred to him. "In fact, you can begin on Thursday night. I've an invitation to the engagement ball for Louisa Winterbourne. She's cousin to his grace, the Duke of Casselmaine."

The mention of Lord Casselmaine caused Harkness's vitals to contract sharply, and he could only hope that Townsend would take Harkness's sudden choked look as part of his general reluctance regarding formal events.

"I will not be able to attend," Townsend continued. "Their Royal Highnesses the Dukes of York and Kent have indicated they will be attending the performance at the Theatre Royal in Drury Lane. It will be the first time any of the family has been out in public since the tragedy." He touched the lapel of his black coat. "As such, their presence will occasion more than the usual interest from the public. I have been commanded to personally take charge of the security details at the theater. Therefore, you will go to the ball in my stead." Townsend looked down his long nose at Harkness. "I will not accept any complaint or protest, Mr. Harkness. His grace, the duke, is becoming a force in the House of Lords, and he is very close with those who control the Civil List. Bow Street must be represented."

"Perhaps Mr. Lavender . . ." But even as he spoke the words, Harkness already knew it would get him nowhere.

"It will be you, Mr. Harkness," said Townsend flatly. "We're dependent on Parliament. You know that. And as usual, the house is arguing expenditures. If we don't keep the lords, and their wives, contented and duly impressed, Bow Street stands to lose its money. And if all they get is this nonsense in the papers about how we're nothing more than a gang of rude thief-takers, they'll find it easier to deny us, d'ye see? I have the honor of the Prince Regent's patronage, but he has many calls on him, and now, in his grief, we cannot ask any more of him." Townsend's solemn expression broke into a sudden grin. "Come, come, Mr. Harkness! Don't look so stricken! I'm doing you a favor, man. Surely, you're not going to turn such an opportunity down?"

Surely not. But he couldn't help seeing how Townsend exuded the particular sort of satisfaction that never failed to make Harkness uneasy. Townsend might be overly interested in his own position, but he was no fool. He'd been a principal officer and a crack investigator in his time. He earned his formidable reputation by ferreting out spies and radicals, and he remained a superb politician.

"I have a letter here from a consortium of shopkeepers in Mayfair. They say that there have been a series of break-ins and robberies. They want a man out there to look into it, lead a patrol or whatever else may be necessary. They fear that in their situation, in a new neighborhood, they are vulnerable, and these crimes may soon rise to more than just breaking and thievery. I want you to go out and see what may be done, take the descriptions, work out the schedule for a patrol—assuming they are willing and able to pay the fees, of course. They assure me they are, but we should confirm it." He smiled. "I'm afraid as we advance in the world, Mr. Harkness, we find there's a deal more money and a deal more paper than we might have hoped for."

"But, Mr. Townsend, I've this business for Sir David, and I want to be able to clear it up as soon as possible."

"Yes, yes, and that needs to be done, of course." Townsend beamed. "Therefore, I want your opinion. Who's best to put on this matter for Sir David?" He gestured toward his desk and the coroner's letter. "After all, we want him to have confidence in the entire officer corps."

So. That was it. Townsend had flattered Harkness. He'd honored him. Looked to bring him into the administration of the station and have a hand in the management of the new districts. Now, Townsend was setting him aside.

There was something more to it, though. A knowing gleam shone in Townsend's keen eyes, and Harkness had the distinct and lowering sensation that he'd let himself get backed into a very tight corner.

"Mr. Townsend . . ." Harkness hesitated as his mind raced

for an argument, any argument, that might persuade the man. "You've always held that a thorough investigation requires continuity." Which was true, and also one of the points on which Harkness agreed with his superior. "Certainly Sir David needs a better acquaintance with all our officers, especially the newer men. However, since I've already begun to look into this matter, it might be best for the continuity of the inquiry, if I was the one to continue."

"And if you had any progress to report, I'd agree at once." Townsend smiled at him. "But unless you've got something more to add to the very little bit you and Sir David have told me so far . . . ?"

There it is. Townsend suspected that both Sir David and Harkness were keeping secrets. This was not a situation he was prepared to tolerate. Therefore, Townsend offered Harkness a choice: Harkness could break confidence with Sir David, or he could be removed from the Melbourne House inquiry.

Not that Townsend knew Melbourne House was involved. Because Townsend was, of course, right about who was keeping secrets.

Which does not make this business any better.

Harkness watched Townsend, standing proud and confident in his expensive mourning. There must be some way around this, but Harkness could not see it from here. All he could see was the Prince Regent's friend, on one hand, and the nameless woman who'd made some powerful enemy, on the other.

And if there had been a third hand, that one would have cradled Miss Thorne. Because anything Harkness told Townsend would involve her. Townsend, though, did not like Miss Thorne. Harkness thought about all the ways Townsend's maneuvers could add to the trouble Miss Thorne faced inside Melbourne House, and he found his decision was already made.

"No, sir," Harkness said to the man in front of him. "There's nothing yet."

Townsend sighed. "Well then. Who should take over?" Harkness hesitated, and Townsend clapped his meaty hands together. "Come, come, sir! These are exactly the sorts of decisions you're going to have to get used to making as you advance in your career. Perhaps Mr. Lavender?"

Lavender was a young man, keen and intelligent. What little Harkness knew of him, though, said he was cut a little too closely from Townsend's cloth. But what if he named someone and Townsend took that as an excuse to *not* use that very man?

Harkness scrubbed the back of his neck and forcibly put down all his second guesses. He would not try to play Townsend's game. It was one he would lose.

"I'd say Mr. Goutier. He's only a patrol captain, I know, but he understands his work as well or better than any man in Bow Street." Harkness paused, then added, "And I've heard him say he's eager to learn from you directly, sir."

This was flimsy, naked flattery, and the words felt brittle as they left him. But Townsend took them in without hesitation, and his chest swelled.

"Yes, yes, he's a very likely prospect and fair to continue his own rise. I've thought so since I persuaded him over to us from the river police. Very good, Mr. Harkness. Now, you will attend to your other duties, and I will make sure you have the invitation to the Casselmaine ball. And Mr. Harkness," added Townsend heavily. "I fully expect you to make a good showing on Bow Street's behalf."

Because he did not trust his voice, Harkness simply bowed and let himself be dismissed.

Goutier was still in the ward room when Harkness returned, adding a full stop to his report.

Harkness reclaimed his seat and stared at his piles of unread newspapers.

"What did old Townsend want?"

Townsend wants to make sure I know I'm being reined in and that my future is dependent on his good opinion. Therefore, he gives with the left hand and takes with the right, and that includes taking away my ability to help Sir David or Miss Thorne. Not that he knows that's what he did. Yet.

"Harkness?" said Goutier. "You're a long way away. What's happened?"

Harkness pulled himself back to the present. "Mr. Goutier," he said quietly. "I expect you're about to get called into Townsend's office. Will you take a mug of beer with me afterward? I'll be across at the Brown Bear. There's going to be a few things we need to discuss."

CHAPTER 13

Enter, A Lady

*. . . you seem to have been apprehensive—or men-
aced (like every one else), by that infamous
Bedlamite—If she stirs against you, neither her
folly nor her falsehood should or shall protect her.*

George Gordon, Lord Byron, private correspondence

The concentrated effort between Rosalind and Mrs. Kendricks carried on late and recommenced early. Mrs. Kendricks handled much of the physical labor of packing. She
sorted and folded, judged, mended, and made lists of what
should to be purchased. But there were bills to be paid and
redirected, accounts to be suspended or reopened, and as
with all things, a lengthy list of personal letters to be written.
These were matters that required Rosalind's personal attention.

In addition to the letters telling friends and tradespeople
where to direct their correspondence for the foreseeable future, a letter must be sent to Sanderson Faulks, saying she
must speak with him as soon as possible. Another had to be
sent to her sister, with whom Rosalind had recently reentered
communication.

What on earth will Charlotte think when she hears the

whole of this? Rosalind wondered. Her sister might just laugh at it all. In fact, she probably would.

Rosalind wished she had that luxury.

Finally, a letter must be written to Mr. Harkness, thanking him for the information he'd forwarded and suggesting that if he had anything further to communicate, he could make use of Alice and George Littlefield at the *London Chronicle* as intermediaries.

Because, she wrote, *I think a certain level of discretion will be required of us both.*

Which returned Rosalind to the question of George, and whether he might hold some secret about the publisher, Mr. Colburn, and whether it could explain his distaste for Alice's idea of writing a novel, and whether that secret might somehow be found to relate to the missing letters. At another time she might have dismissed this possibility as too much of a coincidence, but now she found she was not sure at all. The fashionable world was small, and the places where the fashionable world met the literary world were smaller yet.

All Rosalind could do was hope that her return to Melbourne House would show her how to begin to straighten this tangle.

In the end, Rosalind and Mrs. Kendricks's combined efforts met with success. Ormande drove the chaise through the gates and into the courtyard of Melbourne House, just as the city's bells began tolling eleven.

Theirs was not the only carriage in the yard. A simple two-wheeler pulled by a broad-shouldered chestnut was being driven away. A lean man in a dark coat with a tall beaver hat on his head and a valise in his hand strode up the steps. The sight of the black bag sent a jolt through Rosalind.

A doctor? Could Lady Melbourne have had an attack of some sort?

Unfortunately, by the time Rosalind and Mrs. Kendricks

had been helped from the chaise, the doctor had already disappeared inside the house. But Rosalind's worry intensified as the footman led her into the domed foyer, where the lady's maid, Claridge, was waiting alone. It wasn't often Rosalind met a woman who was taller than she, but Claridge looked down on her.

Literally and metaphorically, Rosalind thought.

"Lady Melbourne's compliments, Miss Thorne," Claridge said. "She has asked me to show you to your rooms. If you'll follow me?"

This indicated to Rosalind that if something had happened, it was probably not too serious. Probably.

"How does Lady Melbourne this morning?" Rosalind asked as Claridge led them up the right-hand stair.

"Very well, thank you," replied Claridge placidly.

"I am glad to hear it. I thought I saw the doctor arrive, and was a bit concerned."

"Dr. Bellingham is here to see Lady Caroline and Master Augustus," Claridge informed her. "Both of them suffered from an infectious fever a fortnight ago, and he is come, I believe, to check on their progress."

"Oh, I see." Rosalind paused. "Is Lady Caroline often ill?"

"Nervous people like to have a doctor about them," said Claridge. "It gives them something to do with themselves, and is better than some things they might choose."

Rosalind felt Mrs. Kendricks's silent disapproval at this little speech burning cold against her back. It was entirely out of bounds for any servant to say so much about their household. The transgression was worse for an upper servant, such as a lady's maid, who regularly shared their employer's confidences. But Rosalind filed away the moment for later consideration.

It was important to know that Claridge was willing to talk, if only about Lady Caroline.

Claridge conducted them to the third floor, and the front of the house. There they were shown a pleasantly furnished

suite—sitting room, boudoir, and dressing room, all decorated in pale blue and cream. Ormande and a pair of footmen arrived shortly afterward with Rosalind's boxes. Mrs.
Kendricks immediately began giving directions and produced
the keys to unlock the trunks.

"Is everything to your satisfaction, miss?" asked Claridge.

"Yes, thank you," replied Rosalind. "Everything looks
beautiful."

"Her ladyship has asked me to say she will meet you in her
private sitting room. I can show you the way just as soon as
you are ready."

"I am ready now." Rosalind would have said this whether
she was truly ready or not. One did not ever keep one's hostess waiting.

Trusting Mrs. Kendricks to unpack and get her things settled, Rosalind followed Claridge down to the second floor.
They met no one on the way. Either most of the inhabitants
were from home at this time of day, or Melbourne House
was one of those residences where people could go for days
without seeing each other except at meals.

Or a bit of both.

Claridge opened the door to a graceful room that overlooked the walled and highly formal garden spreading out
behind the house.

"Beautiful!" exclaimed Rosalind.

"It is her ladyship's own design," Claridge told her with
distinct pride. "She wanted to bring some sense of the gardens at Brocket Hall to the city house."

"She is a remarkable woman."

"Yes, miss." Claridge's reply was soft but strangely flat.
"But she's known so much trouble. It is a great pity."

At these words, Rosalind turned, but this time Claridge
seemed aware that she had overstepped her boundaries and
schooled her features into the properly impersonal expression.

"If you will excuse me, miss, I will let her ladyship know you are arrived." Claridge made her curtsey and departed.

Left alone, Rosalind knew what she should do. She should select a chair, sit, and wait. Acceptable activity was limited to browsing through the art folio on the round table beside the sofa.

That was not what she did, because this was clearly Lady Melbourne's writing room. An elegant marble-topped desk stood under the arched window where the light was the best. Pens, crystal ink wells, a leaf-bladed letter opener, and all the other necessary tools waited in perfect order for their mistress. A fresh blotter had been laid down. A curving glass-doored cabinet held several shelves of account and correspondence books.

Rosalind glanced over her shoulder, feeling a bit like the guilty schoolgirl she used to be. Satisfied that no one was approaching, she tried all the desk drawers and found them locked. She made a note to ask Lady Melbourne where the key was kept and who knew its location. The gilt and enamel box on the mantelpiece was a tempting possibility.

She glanced at the door again. It was still closed.

The box proved to hold an entire ring full of keys of all shapes and sizes. There were far too many to sort through quickly. But there was another possibility for a would-be thief.

Rosalind returned to the desk and reached for the letter opener. She paused again, and listened again, and still there was no sound from the corridor.

Rosalind's formal education had been erratic. There were times when she had a bewildering number of masters and tutors, and other times she was left alone with just such books as might fall under her hand. But for one eventful year, Rosalind had been sent to an exclusive "dame school" for young ladies. This was where she met Alice. It was also where she had learned a number of useful skills, such as clamoring through windows while wearing skirts; listening at doors; and, of course, breaking into the headmistress's desk.

Rosalind slid the letter opener into the crack between the drawer and the desk, held her breath, and batted at the latch.

The latch clicked, and the drawer came smoothly open. Lady Melbourne's desk had been selected for beauty, not utility or security. Rosalind returned the letter opener to its place. She also bent down more closely to look at the front of the drawer. The delicate brass was clean and perfectly polished, and so was the wood. Rosalind could not make out any scratches or chips to indicate the drawers had been forced. But it certainly could have been. She had just proven that very much to her own satisfaction.

"Well, well," said a woman's voice.

Startled, Rosalind straightened and, to her shame, blushed. Caught entirely red-handed, she watched a slender, pale woman glide through the door she had not heard open.

"Nibble, nibble, little mouse," said the woman languidly. "My mother-in-law will be extremely put out to find you nibbling at her house."

Before Rosalind could make any reply, the woman put her hands on her hips, as if talking to a naughty child.

"Well? Nothing to say for yourself, Miss Mouse? Exactly what is it you are doing here? This room is an Olympus and is entirely out of bounds to us mere mortals."

"You came in," Rosalind pointed out.

The woman drew herself up to her full height.

"Ah, but you see, I am the infamous, insane, and thoroughly irritating Lady Caroline Lamb. Now, who the devil are you?"

CHAPTER 14

The Mad Wife In The Sitting Room

I'm mad
that's bad
I'm sad
that's bad
I'm bad
That's mad

Caroline Ponsonby (later Lady Caroline Lamb),
private correspondence

There was, Rosalind knew, exactly one correct response to such an introduction as Lady Caroline offered.

She curtsied.

"Very pleased to make your acquaintance, Lady Caroline. I am Miss Rosalind Thorne."

"Thorne? A pointed reply!"

"My. There's a quip I have not heard for some time."

Two spots of red appeared on Lady Caroline's white cheeks. But then, to Rosalind's surprise, she broke out into a laugh and collapsed onto the pretty green and white sofa.

"A hit! A hit! I am quite set down." She pressed both hands dramatically against her heart.

Lady Caroline was a tiny person, and thin to the point of emaciation. Most unusually, her red hair had been cut down to short ringlets. The combination lent her a boyish appearance, despite her neat blue dress and the broad blue ribbon that bound her hair back from her forehead. The impression of youth, however, was spoiled by the dark circles under her eyes, which stood out sharply against her pale, freckled skin.

Her collapse did not last long. In the next heartbeat, she back sat upright. "But I ask again, what are you doing here, you bold and clever Miss Thorne?"

"I am to assist Lady Melbourne with her letters and appointments. She asked me to wait on her here."

This produced another peal of laughter, "Letters? Merciful Heavens, yes! She needs help with her letters. She needs to run into the streets and cry, 'Help! Help! The letters! The letters!'" Lady Caroline waved one arm lazily overhead.

Rosalind took a moment to make sure her tone would remain only mildly curious.

"Has something happened?"

Lady Caroline let her head fall back and blew a sigh up to the ceiling. "So many things have happened. One would hardly know where to begin."

What do I do? How do I go about this? Rosalind blessed all her practice at concealment. She could not afford to look disconcerted. Rather, she moved to sit beside Lady Caroline on the sofa. "Is there a beginning?" she asked, as if this were some perfectly normal conversation about weather or the roads.

Lady Caroline frowned and leaned close. Her wide blue eyes moved back and forth, restlessly searching for something in Rosalind's face. Despite the brightness of the room, her pupils were unusually wide. There was a smell on her breath too—a harsh, tainted mixture of rose water, aniseed, and alcohol. It was an odor with which Rosalind was, regretfully, very familiar.

In the past hour or so, the lady had taken, or been given, a quantity of laudanum.

"Are you a nice person, I wonder, Miss Thorne?" Lady

Caroline asked. "Nice people should not come here. Her lady-ship baits all her traps with shining lies. You come close to watch them sparkle and then *snap!*" She closed her fist in front of Rosalind's startled eyes. "You're caught!"

"And who has Lady Melbourne caught in her traps?" Rosalind knew she should hold her peace. Men might speak of there being truth in wine, but in laudanum there was little beyond confusion and sleep. But if Lady Caroline was willing to speak, Rosalind was unwilling to miss the opportunity to hear, no matter what the circumstances.

"Oh, she's caught all of us," Lady Caroline drawled. "I, for instance, am supposed to be resting quietly in my own cage, but the underkeeper's sleeping in, you know, and while the cat's away, we poor mice shall play, and nibble." She giggled and clapped her hand over her mouth. She seemed to lack the strength to maintain the gesture, though, and her hand slid down and landed in her lap. Her eyes closed, and Rosalind feared she was about to drift into sleep.

"I read your novel, Lady Caroline," Rosalind tried.

This, it would seem, was the right tactic. The lady let her eyes flutter open. "Did you? And how did you find it? No, don't tell me. Turgid and indecent, rambling and vindictive." Once again, she delivered this declaration to the ceiling.

"In point of fact, I thought your description of setting was quite effective, and your characters chilling."

Lady Caroline pushed herself upright once more. "I think you might mean that."

"I do mean it," replied Rosalind. "And I believe that you are someone who observes things very keenly."

"You should know, Miss Thorne, that as a specimen of flattery, that one is blunt and lacking in finesse." But even as she said this, Lady Caroline smiled. She also leaned very close. Rosalind smelled her laudanum-tainted breath again. Her stomach curdled, but whether that was from the odor or the memories of her mother's sick room, Rosalind could not tell.

"What is it you want that makes you be so nice to me, Miss Thorne?" asked Lady Caroline. "You should know I have no power, or money, or anything else that is of use to anyone."

"But you do have knowledge of this house," replied Rosalind. "And its traps."

"Would you even believe what I could tell you, I wonder?" Lady Caroline murmured, but her eyes soon drifted back to the ceiling. "No one believes what I say."

"You could try me, then we'll both know."

This idea seemed to appeal to Lady Caroline, and her lazy smile slipped back into place. "Well, now. What would you say to the fact that my mother-in-law has enormous difficulty in retaining staff? They vanish from the house at an alarming rate."

Rosalind felt her hands go quite cold. "Who has vanished, Lady Caroline?"

But if Lady Caroline heard the question, she didn't seem to consider it important. "She lies, Miss Thorne," said Lady Caroline, but she stopped again. A faint sheen of perspiration appeared on her forehead. She rubbed at it. "My mother-in-law lies," she repeated. "I promise, she has lied to you."

Rosalind met that clouded gaze and decided to hazard a simple truth. "I know."

Lady Caroline drew back, wary and much more closely focused than she had been just a moment ago.

"Who has vanished, Lady Caroline?" asked Rosalind again.

Lady Caroline, however, had no chance to answer.

CHAPTER 15

The Doctor

Who can care for such a wretch as C——, or believe such a seventy times convicted liar?

George Gordon, Lord Byron, private correspondence

"Ah! Lady Caroline, I thought I heard your voice."

Rosalind clamped her mouth shut against a groan of disappointment as a man in a plain black coat strode into the room.

"Forgive me for intruding. I was just on my way down to see how Master Augustus is doing."

Lady Caroline stared at the man, her laudanum-mired thoughts struggling to adjust to this new arrival.

"Oh, Dr. Bellingham," she said at last. "How good of you to come." She held out her hand without getting to her feet. The doctor took her fingers and made his bow.

"This is Miss Thorne," Lady Caroline added. "Miss Thorne, Dr. Phillip Bellingham."

Dr. Bellingham made another bow. He was a neat man in every sense of the word. His sharp chin was freshly shaven, and he kept his gray hair closely cropped as if he kept to the old-fashioned habit of wearing a wig, but there was no sign of powder anywhere about him. Rather, Dr. Bellingham dressed quite plainly. His only ornamentation was a single watch chain stretched across his black waistcoat. Rosalind mused that he might easily have been taken for a clerk or curate until one noticed that every aspect of his dress was of the finest possible quality.

"Augustus is doing much better today, Dr. Bellingham," Lady Caroline was saying. "He was able to eat all his breakfast and sit with his tutor for his morning lessons."

"I am very glad to hear it," replied Dr. Bellingham. "But it still might be advisable to have a look, as long as I am here."

Rosalind frowned inwardly. Dr. Bellingham, she remembered, had arrived at the house just ahead of her and Mrs. Kendricks. At that time, Claridge had said he was here to see Lady Caroline and Master Augustus. But if he had not done that yet, she couldn't help but wonder where he had been all this time.

"Will you come with me?" the doctor asked Lady Caroline. "He'll be more patient with my poking and prodding if his mother is present."

But Lady Caroline was not fully attending to this. Her gaze had drifted to the empty hallway beyond the doctor. At first, Rosalind thought this must be the laudanum tightening its hold, but then Lady Caroline said, "You've not brought Mrs. Oslander with you today, Dr. Bellingham." She spoke each word with great care. "I trust she is well."

"Perfectly, thank you," replied the doctor. "But since everyone here is so much improved, I did not see any need for a nurse today."

"Ah. Of course that is what it is." Lady Caroline turned her vague eyes toward Rosalind and smiled. "That and only that. Naturally. Well, Mrs. Oslander is so very good at her work, we cannot be selfish and keep her to ourselves, can we? Now, you must excuse me, Miss Thorne." She patted Rosalind's hand. "I have my family duties to attend to."

The doctor chuckled then, and waved one hand toward

the doorway. "Except, ma'am, it seems family duty has come to you."

Rosalind turned in time to see a boy teeter across the threshold. "Mother?"

"Augustus, my dear!" cried Lady Caroline. "You are supposed to be with your tutor."

"I don't want him." The boy dashed up to Lady Caroline and buried his face against her shoulder. "Make him go away. He has a red nose."

The boy's legs were thin and unsteady, but he was not a small person. In fact, he might have been as much as a full stone heavier than his mother. His belly protruded and his eyes receded under a broad brow. An orange smear ran down his round cheek, and he was rubbing his face against Lady Caroline so it now smudged her dress.

But what was truly remarkable was the effect the disheveled boy's arrival had on Lady Caroline. She grit her teeth and levered herself to her feet, as if attempting to drag herself from the laudanum's seductive fog by sheer force of will.

"He cannot help his nose, sweetheart." Lady Caroline kissed the boy's brow and ruffled his limp curls. "You must try to pay attention to him, you know, so you will grow into a clever gentleman."

"I don't want him!" The boy's round face flushed scarlet, and his hands both tightened into fists. "I don't want him!"

"There, there, it's all right, Augustus," said Lady Caroline. "Here. Come and make your bow to Dr. Bellingham." Lady Caroline turned her son toward the doctor. Dr. Bellingham bowed gravely, and the boy made an unsteady attempt to return the gesture. His mother patted his shoulder approvingly. "And this is Miss Rosalind Thorne. Miss Thorne, my son, Master Augustus Lamb."

"A pleasure to meet you, Master Augustus." Rosalind executed her most polite curtsey. Augustus bowed, but he also scowled.

"Who *is* she?" he demanded of his mother.

"Why, Miss Thorne is a friend of your grandmama's." Lady Caroline paused. "And I think she could be a friend of mine."

Augustus pulled away from his mother and walked up to Rosalind, coming far too close. He smelled of sweat, sour milk, and peppermints, and he stared at her without blinking.

"She doesn't like me," he announced. "Her friends never like me."

Rosalind opened her mouth to deny this, but Lady Caroline caught her eye and shook her head. Rosalind obeyed the signal and kept silent.

"Augustus," said Lady Caroline brightly. "Let's you and I and Dr. Bellingham go speak with your tutor. Maybe mama can talk him into a different nose."

The furrows in the boy's brow deepened. "You can't. People can't change noses."

"Well, if we don't try, we'll never know. Don't you agree, Miss Thorne?"

"I do indeed, ma'am."

The boy considered this carefully, pushing his lip out with the effort.

"Perhaps I could take some measurements," suggested Dr. Bellingham. "It might be useful, medically speaking."

"You can measure noses?"

"Most certainly," answered the doctor. "I've a special instrument just for noses. Shall I show you?"

"Well, I want to see," declared Lady Caroline.

"And what on earth are you even doing here?"

At this, everyone in the room stiffened. Lady Melbourne had arrived at last.

CHAPTER 16

The Private Business Of Families

What could I do? A foolish girl, in spite of all I could say or do, would come after me, or rather went before . . .

George Gordon, Lord Byron, private correspondence

"**W**ell?" The chill of Lady Melbourne's disapproval ran across Rosalind's arms. Lady Melbourne entered the room slowly, leaning on Claridge for support. As she drew near, Augustus shrank back, grabbing up a bunch of his mother's skirt in one fat fist. Dr. Bellingham bowed, but Rosalind could feel the tension radiating from him as well.

Lady Melbourne retained her capacity to charm, but it seemed she did not trouble herself to use it on members of her household.

Claridge lowered her ladyship into her chair beside the window.

Lady Caroline recovered first. "Why, good-day, Mama! And how are you feeling?"

"I asked, Caroline, what you are doing in my private study?"

Lady Caroline smiled brightly. "Why, I'm meeting your

new inmate—or perhaps I mean intimate—Miss Thorney Rose, and of course I'm looking after my son like a dutiful mother should do." She laid both hands on Augustus's shoulders. "Dr. Bellingham, we should go. Good luck, Miss Thorne! Augustus, I know what! Let's race!"

Lady Caroline hiked up her skirts and ran from the room. Her son shrieked with laughter and thundered after her. Dr. Bellingham hesitated, uncertain of what to do in the face of such abandonment of customary manners. In the end, he settled for making a fresh bow and moved to follow the pair down the corridor, albeit at a more sedate pace.

Rosalind was conscious of staring at the departing group with a kind of hopelessness. It was impossible to miss Lady Caroline's naked hints that this nurse, Mrs. Oslander, had gone missing. It was equally impossible not to think of the description Mr. Harkness had been given of the dead woman. He said she possessed pale skin and clean hands and was neatly dressed but of the working classes. Mr. Harkness had guessed an upper servant such as a lady's maid, but the description might apply equally well to a nurse.

She must find a way to speak with Dr. Bellingham before he left Melbourne House.

"I hope Caroline did not upset you, Miss Thorne," said Lady Melbourne.

Rosalind forced her attention back to the woman beside her. Lady Melbourne had dressed to receive her visitors in a simple day dress of dark green muslin trimmed with antique lace. Her still luxurious hair had likewise been simply styled. But her face was strained, and the color beneath her dusting of powder was far too flushed for good health. Rosalind noted that her swollen hands were covered in net gloves, which only partially hid the bandages that encased them. The fingers of one hand scrabbled at the chair arms, and she winced. She smelled of lavender, but also vinegar and bitter medicine, and Rosalind thought it must be Lady Melbourne's hands that had kept Dr. Bellingham so busy since his arrival.

"I know you are a woman of steady nerves," Lady Melbourne went on. "But my daughter-in-law can be a shock at first."

"She seems to be possessed of very high spirits."

"How diplomatic of you." Lady Melbourne laughed. "Yes, she is indeed possessed of high spirits, when she is not sunk in one of her melancholies. She also talks a great deal of nonsense. I'm sure she had some remarkable things to say about me."

It was an invitation to gossip, if Rosalind so chose. Rosalind did not choose, but it did provide her a useful opening.

"For some reason she mentioned that you've had some difficulty retaining staff of late."

Lady Melbourne did not so much as blink. "What can she have meant by that? It is difficult to tell when she's in one of her moods."

"I'm sure you realize that if any servant has been dismissed, they might be the one who took the letters," Rosalind tried.

"But I assure you, none have. I am still able to run my own household, Miss Thorne." Lady Melbourne laughed to erase any hint of admonishment. "Caroline, among other things, is a lover of drama and mischief. She could easily have been trying to worry you, like a child teasing a governess. I hope you will not find it necessary to have too much to do with her."

Why not? Surely you know that it is at least possible she's the one you're looking for?

The reality of Rosalind's position relative to Lady Melbourne settled heavily into her thoughts. She was no longer here to act for this woman as assistant and agent. Her task was, and must be, entirely different.

Rosalind chose her next words carefully. "It might be helpful if I could gain Lady Caroline's confidence. It is still possible she might have had something to do with the disappearance of your letters."

"But William tells me he has seen nothing, and he swears nothing was found when her room was searched. While Caroline is capable of anything, my son would never deceive me."

Lady Melbourne spoke this last as decided fact, but her gloved and bandaged hands spasmed. Rosalind glanced to the corner where Claridge stood sentry.

Claridge was looking out the window at the garden.

"Lady Melbourne," said Rosalind slowly. "Are you certain you have told me everything regarding the letters' disappearance? I cannot help if I am not in possession of all the facts."

"If I knew more, Miss Thorne, you would not be here. I would have been able to attend to this matter myself." What energy and humor Lady Melbourne had been able to muster drained from her as she spoke. "In my days of health, no one would have dared to commit such an outrage against me. As things are, however, I am sensible of my dependence on you. You may be sure you know as much as I know."

Perhaps it is only the lady's fears I am hearing underneath her words. She is used to being the absolute mistress of her world. To find herself helpless while her plans fall apart would be an enormous burden for any person.

And yet . . . and yet . . .

Rosalind gave herself a mental shake. Such speculation would do her no good. She did not know enough.

Yet.

"Lady Caroline might have had nothing to do with the letters' disappearance," Rosalind said. "But I imagine she is about the house a great deal?" Lady Melbourne inclined her head in agreement. "She may have useful information, and time is of the essence."

"Well, I suppose you must do as you see fit. I warn you, however, Miss Thorne, Caroline is a skilled liar. She wields a kind of animal magnetism that can affect women just as easily as men."

"I shall be on my guard." Rosalind assured her.

You do not want me to believe what Lady Caroline says. You wish for me to understand she is a liar. And you gifted me with five hundred pounds to purchase my loyalty.

And you very much do not want me to believe your son could keep secrets from you.

Rosalind longed to speak, plainly and clearly. She wanted to ask if the dead woman in the yard could be the Mrs. Oslander whom Lady Caroline had brought so prominently to the conversation. She wanted to see Lady Melbourne's reaction, and hear what story she would tell.

She needed to find Dr. Bellingham.

She had no way to know how long his examination of Augustus Lamb might take, even with some pantomime about the tutor's offensively red nose. If she missed this chance, she would have to make shift to organize another casual meeting, and that would take time, which she did not have.

"Now, let us have done with Caroline and all her perturbations." Lady Melbourne's announcement cut through Rosalind's thoughts. "I'm sorry to have asked you so early, but I am expecting a large number of callers this afternoon, and Mr. Scrope Davies is to be among the throng. I thought you would wish to meet him."

"Excellent," said Rosalind. "I will just . . ." She glanced about her. "Oh, I am so sorry, I've left my work and notebook back in my rooms. I'll go fetch them." She stood.

Lady Melbourne frowned. "Claridge can do that."

"But I know exactly where they will be, and Claridge should remain here, in case anything is needed."

Lady Melbourne cocked her head. She did not know whether to believe Rosalind, and she did not like this fact.

"If I am your assistant, rather than simply your guest, it will look strange if my hands are not busy," Rosalind pointed out.

"Yes, of course," said Lady Melbourne reluctantly. "Tell me, Miss Thorne, do you find it uncomfortable to live a life with so much dissembling in it?"

Rosalind met her gaze. "Do you?"

There was a pause. Out of the corner of her eye, Rosalind noted Claridge was staring at her, shocked out of her professional detachment by this blunt question. But Lady Melbourne only smiled. "Go fetch your things."

CHAPTER 17

Afternoon Calls

To Scrope I leave the details.

George Gordon, Lord Byron, private correspondence

Rosalind's first instinct was to go find Dr. Bellingham directly. However, the house was huge, and there was no way to be certain where the nursery was, or to know whether the doctor had gone there or to Lady Caroline's private rooms. She did not want to draw attention to herself by asking for directions.

Instead, Rosalind hurried up the stairs to her own rooms. Thankfully, Mrs. Kendricks was in the boudoir, laying Rosalind's small collection of brushes and creams out on the dressing table.

"Miss Thorne, is anything wrong?"

"Not yet," answered Rosalind. Her notebook, pencil, and workbasket waited on the table at the bedside, as she knew they would be. Mrs. Kendricks had been arranging rooms for her in other people's houses for years. "But there is a Dr. Bellingham in the house. I need you to ask him to please wait when he is finished with Lady Caroline and her son."

"Is her ladyship ill?"

"No. But I'm going to be developing a slight headache

while Lady Melbourne is receiving callers. I'm subject to them, as you well know."

Their eyes met in understanding. "Yes, miss. If you will allow me one hour . . . ?"

"That will do admirably, Mrs. Kendricks."

Rosalind slung her workbasket on her arm, tucked the book inside, and hurried back to Lady Melbourne.

Lady Melbourne had not exaggerated her number of callers.

Her visitors arrived in groups of twos and threes, even as many as four at a time. The formal structure of social calls was observed in every particular. Arrivals would sit and be served with tea or coffee and cakes by the footmen and maids, with Claridge of course supervising over all. The news and the gossip flowed freely, with Lady Melbourne managing the conversation as skillfully as Claridge managed the tea things. This lasted approximately a quarter hour, at which point, Bell would enter with a silver tray, bearing the visiting card of the next group seeking admission. Lady Melbourne would give her permission, and they would be conducted to the sitting room. Each party who came in greeted the previous. Small remarks about the weather or the health of mutual acquaintances were exchanged. Then, this ritual observed, the first party would declare it time to take their leave with all appearance of spontaneity. The hostess might invite them to stay longer, if she chose, but it was not an option Lady Melbourne exercised. She kept her stream of visitors moving as quickly and as neatly as a captain supervising the changing of the guards.

That same etiquette that ruled the comings and goings of the callers declared that Rosalind must remain in perfect, although subordinate, attendance on all persons who came through the sitting room door. She must make notes that would be later entered into Lady Melbourne's visiting and correspondence books, fetch items from the desk—and, incidentally, endure Claridge's cold gaze whenever Lady Melbourne asked something of her rather than directing Claridge to perform the task. She must help pass cups and keep the conversation flowing whenever it seemed to flag. This last, though, was infrequent. Lady Melbourne's energy was truly astounding, at least as long as there was someone in the room to see.

All the while, Rosalind struggled to keep her impatience in check. A physician such as Dr. Bellingham would be a busy man. He would wait only so long on a person of such little account as Rosalind. In a more casual household, Rosalind might have been able to make some excuse to remove herself, but the formal rules Lady Melbourne lived by declared that Rosalind could not ask to leave until there was a pause in the flow of guests, and that pause did not come.

The one hour Mrs. Kendricks had allotted passed. And then a quarter hour after that.

Rosalind smiled in greeting to Mrs. Candlewood, with whom she shared a mutual acquaintance, and asked after her son, who had gone into the navy. This unleashed a long complaint about how the peace had spoiled any chance of his advancement.

Another quarter hour slipped away.

Dr. Bellingham has surely left by now. I will have to think what to do next. I cannot let myself worry. There will be something.

Mrs. Candlewood and her two daughters said their goodbyes, and for the first time since the calls began, the room was empty except for Rosalind and Lady Melbourne.

Lady Melbourne glanced at her clock. "And still no Mr. Davies," she remarked, and Rosalind was conscious of a small jolt of shame. She had been so worried about whether she would be able to speak with Dr. Bellingham that she had all but forgotten they were waiting on Mr. Davies, whom she also very much needed to meet and speak with.

If this continues, I will have to start my own visiting book.
"I hope he does not mean to disappoint us." Lady Melbourne sighed. "But you look a little pale, Miss Thorne. I trust you are not one of those pathetic objects who succumbs to a headache after a few calls?"

Rosalind opened her mouth to declare that of course she was not, but she was too late. Bell arrived with his tray yet again. All the muscles in the back of Rosalind's neck tensed as Lady Melbourne picked up the card he presented.

"And here is Lady Jersey. Probably she wants to see how you and I are getting on. I suppose we should not disappoint. You may tell her I am at home, Bell."

Bell took his leave. Rosalind entertained a brief vision of herself charging past him and fleeing down the corridor.

Lady Caroline would do it.

For an odd moment, Rosalind found herself wondering if there was something to be said for Lady Caroline's approach to life.

She was left with no time for internal debate on this philosophical point, however.

"My dear, dear Lady Melbourne!" Lady Jersey sailed into the room, her heavily embroidered India shawl billowing behind her. "How *are* you! Is everything quite as you hoped?" Lady Jersey drew her chair up without asking permission or waiting for reply. "Is not our Miss Thorne a treasure? I am sure she has made great strides already!"

"Good day, Lady Jersey," replied Lady Melbourne. "I trust you are in health?"

This bland greeting with its implicit reminder of expected manners caused Lady Jersey to draw back and blink. "Oh. You are very right, of course. But I have been so worried, I have not been able to sit still a moment. Yes, I am in excellent health, thank you. And you, you look marvelously well."

"Thank you. And what is your opinion of Miss Thorne's looks?"

"Now, Lady Melbourne, you mean to put me in my place, and you are quite right. I have arrived in a state. I know that I have, but the matter is so grave . . ." Lady Jersey paused long enough to accept a cup of tea from Claridge. "I simply cannot, I *will* not, be casual about it. Admonish me if you please, but it is *your* best interests I have in mind."

The door opened again, and Rosalind all but jumped. *You are losing your nerve, Rosalind Thorne. It will not do.*

This time, though, it was not Bell with his tray. Instead, a maid Rosalind did not recognize presented a note to Claridge, who carried it to Lady Melbourne, who inspected the name on the paper.

"For you, Miss Thorne," she said, and nodded for Claridge to take the note to Rosalind.

Rosalind recognized Mrs. Kendricks's writing at once and unfolded the paper. She read, and she sent up a silent prayer of gratitude for her housekeeper's good sense.

What she said aloud was, "Oh dear. Lady Melbourne, Lady Jersey, I am sorry. I must beg to be excused."

"What is the matter?" asked Lady Jersey. "Is it to do with . . . ?"

"Sarah," sighed Lady Melbourne wearily.

"Oh no. It is not business. My maid has had a fall," said Rosalind quickly. "I should go see to her." She made herself pause. "Do you suppose Dr. Bellingham might still be about the house?"

Lady Melbourne cocked her head. Lady Jersey's eyes narrowed at the same moment. Rosalind suppressed the urge to squirm like a schoolgirl.

"Surely, it cannot be that urgent, Miss Thorne," said Lady Jersey. "Your maid is most capable, and I cannot believe a moment's carelessness would cause you to go rushing off when you are needed here."

Rosalind considered letting the matter go. Lady Melbourne was still uncertain of how much lead to truly give her, and

Lady Jersey was very much on watch. If she sparked fresh concern in either woman, her position in the house—and her ability to carry out her real task—would be in jeopardy.

But it was that task that drove her now.

"No, I think I must go," she said. "Mrs. Kendricks has been with my family for ages." Rosalind met Lady Melbourne's gaze, implicitly asking permission, and she flicked a finger toward Lady Jersey.

Lady Melbourne did not miss the gesture. Rosalind hoped that she translated it as meaning that Rosalind had something that must be done and that she could not speak freely about that thing in front of the voluable and excitable Lady Jersey.

Which was the truth, after all.

Lady Melbourne lifted her chin. "Well, Miss Thorne," she said. "I suppose you must go see to your servant. Bell will find you the doctor, if he is still here." She leaned toward Lady Jersey and smiled indulgently. "Young women these days, they are so *nervous* when it comes to their households. Why I remember one time, when my dear friend the Duchess of Devonshire . . ."

Rosalind did not stay to hear what had happened with regard to the duchess and her household. She simply made her retreat as decorously as she could and hoped she was not already too late.

CHAPTER 18

Unpleasant But Necessary Revelations

...All that is said of C(aroline) L(amb)...is another effect of fear in order to invalidate any future disclosure which he may suspect or know it is my power to make.

Anne Isabella Milbanke, Lady Byron, private
correspondence

When Rosalind returned to her sitting room, Dr. Bellingham was already there. Mrs. Kendricks, quite unharmed, stood beside the hearth, her hands properly folded. Rosalind did not know what her housekeeper had told the doctor, but she apparently did not feel any need to pretend to him that she had actually suffered a fall.

"Miss Thorne." Dr. Bellingham bowed as Rosalind entered. "How may I be of service? Does her ladyship require anything?"

"Lady Melbourne is quite well, Dr. Bellingham, and I trust you will forgive me for delaying you in your rounds."

Dr. Bellingham waved this away. "Whenever possible, I leave Melbourne House until last. With so many patients under one roof, matters may arise unexpectedly." He smiled stiffly. "Lady Caroline tells me you will be with us for some time."

"I may be. I am assisting Lady Melbourne until she is better."

The doctor nodded in tacit acknowledgment that the possibility of any return to health for Lady Melbourne was a polite fiction. "So I have heard—at least, it is among the things I have heard." He regarded Rosalind with fresh curiosity. "I don't know if you realize it, Miss Thorne, but you've made quite an impression on Lady Caroline. Unfortunately, it is not entirely a favorable one."

Rosalind raised her brows. "How extraordinary. We met only a few moments before you arrived."

"Well, she spent a great deal of energy urging me to speak with you. She is certain you are suffering from a variety of nervous complaints but could not seem to decide whether you were more in danger of lapsing into a fit, which would shock Lady Melbourne into a stroke, or were carrying some dread disease. So, you see, even had your maid not come to find me, I still would have found it necessary to wait on you." He smiled, again stiffly. He was a man used to professional courtesy, but it seemed it did not always come easily to him.

"And now that you have seen me, what is your impression?"

His eyes narrowed, just a little. "I cannot say. With your permission, I'll take your pulse."

Rosalind obligingly turned up her hand, and Dr. Bellingham closed cool and competent fingers about her wrist. He looked at his watch, and his lips moved as he silently counted. Rosalind tried to bear the procedure with calm and humor, but her eyes kept straying toward the porcelain clock on the mantel. She needed to conduct this conversation with Dr. Bellingham and return to Lady Melbourne as soon as possible. If Scrope Davies arrived, her window for meeting him was a short one. At the speed and frequency with which Lady Melbourne's callers refreshed themselves, she could not count on his visit being longer than the minimally acceptable a quarter of an hour, even if Lady Melbourne should wish to detain him.

Perhaps Mr. Davies will not come today. The time for polite calls was rapidly giving over to the time when all persons were expected to retire and rest before changing into evening clothes. No. He must come. Lady Melbourne promised him a message for Lord Byron.

Dr. Bellingham released Rosalind's wrist and tucked his watch away. "A bit fast, but otherwise sound. Your color and eyes indicate you are quite in health. Therefore, I must state that I cannot agree with Lady Caroline's diagnosis."

"That is a relief, sir."

"I would not worry about it too much. Lady Caroline is extremely changeable. One day the whole world is her friend. The next, all are conspiring against her, and somewhere in the middle she suddenly discovers herself to be a horrible wretch and must beg forgiveness from everyone. As a medical man, my best advice is to not try to manage the tide of her emotion. It cannot be done, at least not by good will alone."

"She truly is mad then?" Rosalind asked. At the same time, she reflected that if Lady Caroline was mad, it was a very organized madness. First, she had made it clear that Rosalind should speak with the doctor, and then she had done her best to make sure the doctor would linger on his rounds and speak to Rosalind.

"Would it frighten you if I said yes?" Dr. Bellingham asked, but he waved away Rosalind's answer before she could speak. "But, no. I can see already you are made of sterner stuff. I will tell you, Miss Thorne—and again, this is my professional opinion—that Lady Caroline is not what we could consider truly mad. She does not hallucinate, for example, nor is she subject to fits, but neither is she a normal woman. Her humors are far stronger than average. This makes them more prone to abrupt shifts, which can lead to periods either of extreme melancholy or euphoria, beyond the capacity of the female's naturally weaker constitution to tolerate."

Rosalind did not venture any comment on this assessment of the female constitution. She did note that here again was someone urging her to discount whatever Lady Caroline said. And yet here they were together, exactly as Lady Caroline wanted.

"Does she frequently take laudanum?" asked Rosalind.

"It is most efficacious in regulating elevated and changeable spirits, although I could wish she'd take somewhat less of it." The doctor sighed. "What Lady Caroline needs is complete rest and quiet. I have tried to impress this upon her husband. Perhaps this latest outburst will help convince him that it is time to remove her from London, to the family estate in Ireland, for example."

Rosalind needed to frame her next question carefully. The clock on the mantel ticked loudly. She felt sure that Mr. Davies must be going up to Lady Melbourne right this instant.

"Dr. Bellingham, you say Lady Caroline does not hallucinate. Does she . . . imagine things? Things she might become convinced are true?"

The doctor frowned. "I'm not sure what you mean."

Rosalind folded her hands to keep them still. The clock ticked on. "She seems to believe that someone among the household staff has gone missing. It is a strange thing, and a little disturbing. But now that I know she is subject to fancies, I suppose I will just disregard that as well."

"Very wise. If it will reassure you, however, I can say I know of no one among the staff who left the house suddenly, or at all, at least not recently, and I am almost as familiar with the state of things belowstairs in this house as above it."

"No one at all?" pressed Rosalind. "Not even this Mrs. Oslander?"

For the first time since their conversation had begun, Rosalind saw a flicker of hesitation in the doctor's keen eyes.

"If you're speaking of Judith Oslander, she is not a family servant. She's my nurse. One of my nurses, I should say, as Mrs. Oslander will often head a staff of assistants. Now, I will admit she is frequently at this house. When Lady Melbourne has one of her more serious episodes, she prefers Mrs. Oslander to oversee her care. She was also in charge of the nursing staff when Lady Caroline and Master Augustus suffered through their recent fever. She . . . is an excellent woman," he added with sudden vehemence. "A superior woman. I cannot understand why Lady Caroline would mention her in the context of a household servant." He paused and then asked sharply, "What exactly did she say?"

Rosalind hesitated. The doctor's change of mood caught her by surprise. She found herself wondering if his relationship with Mrs. Oslander was perhaps more complex than simply that of a physician and a trusted nurse.

But she did not have time to pursue such a delicate inquiry. She needed to get back to the sitting room and Lady Melbourne. Mr. Davies might have already come and gone. The door was thick and would mask the sound of footsteps up the marble stairs, even feet in a man's boots. She did not have any more time to hint, or probe.

"Miss Thorne," said Dr. Bellingham firmly. "I must insist you tell me what Lady Caroline has said about Mrs. Oslander."

The doctor set his jaw. He would not let her go without explanation.

I'm sorry, sir. I would be more gentle if I could.

"Dr. Bellingham, I recommend that you go to the Bow Street police office . . ."

"Bow Street! What in the name of God has Bow Street to do . . ." Dr. Bellingham pulled back hastily. "Forgive me, Miss Thorne. That was inexcusably rude. But what can Bow Street have to do with Mrs. Oslander?" He stopped. "Or you?"

"I apologize that I cannot be more forthcoming, but I urge

you to speak with Mr. Adam Harkness at Bow Street. He is a principal officer there, and he may have news of Mrs. Oslander."

The doctor retreated two steps. The color drained from his sharp face. He passed a hand over his brow and stared for a moment at his fingertips, as if he expected to diagnose something from the perspiration left there.

"How is it . . . no, no. I see you have already told me all that you are certain of and would rather say no more than that. That's admirable. Yes. Discretion is important."

"I'm sorry, Dr. Bellingham," said Rosalind.

He looked up at her, and for a moment she saw the startled and naked grief on his face. But he shoved it away with ferocious speed.

"Yes. Well. I had best go now, I think. I must . . . well, thank you, Miss Thorne." He turned away.

Rosalind felt a keen sympathy for the man. He now knew something very serious had happened to this woman he had worked with and at the very least respected.

One question filled her now: How had Lady Caroline come to know so much? Rosalind had told Dr. Bellingham that something was amiss with Mrs. Oslander. But who had told Lady Caroline?

CHAPTER 19

Parlor Games

*Tho she may in some instances exhibit the appear-
ance of sincerity, you must not forget that she can
deceive, & has been in the habit of deceiving.*

Anne Isabella Milbanke, private correspondence

Rosalind wished she could dive into the depths of the
house and find Lady Caroline, but that was, of course,
impossible. She must instead climb the stairs and return to
her place at Lady Melbourne's side.

"Ah, there you are, Miss Thorne!" cried Lady Melbourne
when Claridge readmitted her to the sitting room. "I was beginning to fear you had deserted me for more congenial company. How does your maid?"

A gentleman sat on the sofa reserved for callers. Unlike all
the other visitors, he had been given neither tea nor coffee.
Instead, he held a glass of wine in one thin hand. Rosalind
felt a thrill of hope. Her luck might have held after all. This
person could well be Mr. Scrope Berdmore Davies.

"I do apologize, Lady Melbourne," Rosalind said, addressing her hostess without acknowledging the gentleman.
She could not do so properly until Lady Melbourne introduced him. "It was just a scare—a slip on an unfamiliar stair,

and she is no longer young. A warm vinegar compress will put matters to rights." She would apologize later to Mrs. Kendricks for implying that she could be befuddled by anything so minor as an unfamiliar back stair.

"I am glad to hear it," Lady Melbourne replied, but the look in her eyes said *I will have the truth from you later.* "And I am glad you have returned, otherwise I would have had to send Claridge in search of you. Here we have the gentleman I have been promising so faithfully to introduce you to. Miss Rosalind Thorne, may I present Mr. Scrope Berdmore Davies."

"Your servant, Miss Thorne." Mr. Davies set aside his wineglass so that he could stand and bow, a movement he executed with grace, and rather more flourish than was necessary.

Whatever else he might prove to be, Mr. Davies was a throughgoing dandy. His dark green coat was exquisitely cut, and his crisp white cravat was a perfect waterfall of loops and folds. His buff breeches were spotless, and his gold-buckled shoes gleamed as if he polished them with champagne, as the "Beau" Brummel was once rumored to do with his Hessian boots.

While Mr. Davies's clothes were meant to convey perfect, studied confidence, his bloodshot eyes told a different story. They were restless, and tired. Dark circles marred his pale cheeks even though it was late in the afternoon.

Mr. Davies, however, was not too tired to keep from openly assessing Rosalind with the quick skill of an experienced man of the *ton.* After all, one's first priority upon meeting a new person was to assign them a place on the social ladder, otherwise how did one know how to treat them?

Mr. Davies's mobile expression, and the way he had already turned his attention back to Lady Melbourne, and his wineglass, suggested she had been judged, found wanting, and dismissed in the time it took her to make her curtsey.

"Mr. Davies," said Rosalind, "I think perhaps you and I have an acquaintance in common. Do you know Mr. Sanderson Faulks?" This was a guess, but given that Sanderson was also a confirmed and long-standing member of the dandy set, she felt confident in making it.

"You know Faulks, Miss . . . Thorne?" Mr. Davies arched his brows in genuine surprise.

"Mr. Faulks is an old friend of my family's." Rosalind resumed her chair, which allowed Mr. Davies to take his. "We have known each other from childhood." In fact, her father at one time hoped they would marry, but neither one of them ever mentioned that fact.

With this, Rosalind was treated to the sight of Mr. Davies mentally reassigning her to a better social standing. Mr. Davies was clearly a snob as well as a dandy. This also did not come as a surprise.

Rosalind felt, rather than saw, Lady Melbourne's quiet amusement.

"Well, well," said Mr. Davies. "How does Faulks? I haven't seen him in . . . well, an absurdly long time. Do tell him I said hello. Yes." He smiled, but somewhat vaguely. "Very good to meet you. Yes. Very good. But, my dear Lady Melbourne, I am entirely and inexcusably remiss. I have not yet inquired after you. How does your ladyship today?"

Lady Melbourne laughed. "Much as she did yesterday. Now, Mr. Davies, there is no need to stand on any sort of ceremony. You can go straight on with what you were saying before."

"Ahem." Mr. Davies very ostentatiously dropped his gaze. "I had meant for this to be a confidential conversation, ma'am . . ."

Rosalind got immediately to her feet. "You'll forgive me, Lady Melbourne, but I believe I should go see . . ."

"You should sit down directly, Miss Thorne. There is no need for you to go anywhere." Lady Melbourne smiled, her manner benevolent but firm. "Mr. Davies, Miss Thorne is my particular friend. Anything you would say to me, you may to her."

Mr. Davies looked as if he would protest this, but Lady Melbourne laughed again. "Now, now, you are not turning shy, are you? It is not as if she is a stranger. After all, you already acknowledge a dear friend in common."

They had acknowledged no such thing. Mr. Davies's gaze strayed to Rosalind again. He did not understand her, or her presence, and he did not like it. Nor did he miss the fact that underneath her easy charm, Lady Melbourne was quite deliberately baiting him.

Mr. Davies responded to all of this by taking a long swallow of wine.

"Very well, Lady Melbourne, since you insist. As you know, our friend abroad is very anxious about that correspondence we spoke of previously. I had hoped you might have some good news for me."

"Yes, of course," replied Lady Melbourne amiably. "Miss Thorne, there is a letter on my writing desk. If you'll oblige me and hand it to Mr. Davies?" Rosalind did as requested, and Lady Melbourne continued. "There, Mr. Davies, is my reassurance for Byron, just as I promised you. Please be so good as to send it to him straightaway. These continental mails are such a muddle, it could well be Christmas before he receives it."

Davies watched Lady Melbourne, and Rosalind watched Mr. Davies. He was clearly nonplussed at his hostess's candor, and her calm. What had he been expecting? His gaze slipped again to Rosalind, looking for some sign. Or excuse. Or reason.

"Lady Melbourne," he said slowly. "We have been friends for some time now . . ."

"Since Byron introduced us," Lady Melbourne added, seemingly for Rosalind's benefit, but there was a stern undercurrent there Rosalind knew was not for her but for Mr. Davies.

"What I am about to say . . ." He laid the letter down on the coffee table beside his empty wineglass. "I am sorry, but this must be said. I would not for the world impeach your integrity especially in front of a . . . well . . . another. But, you do still have all the letters, do you not?"

The delicate humor vanished from Lady Melbourne's manner. She drew herself up as fully as she was able.

"Mr. Davies, that is an abominable presumption!"

Mr. Davies held out both his hands. "You urged me to speak freely, Lady Melbourne, and that is my question. Have you an answer?" He leaned forward, not eager but expectant. In fact, he was bracing himself. But, for what? Did he want the letters to be here?

Or did he know they were not?

"Mr. Davies . . ." began Lady Melbourne sternly.

"Lady Melbourne, if you will allow me," Rosalind interrupted. "I believe this matter can be cleared up quite quickly."

Her hostess's eyes narrowed, and for a heartbeat Rosalind thought she would be told to keep silent. Charmingly and politely, of course, but unmistakably.

But her ladyship just quirked her brows. "By all means, Miss Thorne," she said, and now it was Mr. Davies' turn to look worried.

Rosalind crossed to the writing desk. "May I have the key, Claridge?"

Upon receiving Lady Melbourne's nod, Claridge opened the enamel box on the mantel and took a small brass key off the ring. Rosalind opened the desk's right-hand drawer. Inside lay several folios and several neat bundles of letters. More or less at random, Rosalind selected a bundle secured with green tape and held it up.

"Here are the letters, Mr. Davies. Intact, as you see. Do you wish to verify their contents?" She held the letters out for him to take.

Mr. Davies stared at the letters, and at her, his distaste perfectly plain. She'd offered him an insult that could not be missed, and there was nothing he could do.

Lady Melbourne raised her chin. "Well, Mr. Davies?"

"Well, I must say, Miss Thorne, you place me in a most awkward position." Mr. Davies spoke slowly, and there was a keen edge to the words. "Indeed, if you were a man, I might take offense. If I take those letters, I am openly suggesting that I think my good friend Lady Melbourne is lying. Not only that, but I will have inspected a lady's private correspondence. And if—as you assure me—those are the letters Lord Byron is inquiring about, then my flagrant discourtesy is all for nothing and I must slink away." He gestured dismissively toward the door. "And it may be that news of my conduct will not stay in this room, and so my own reputation becomes quite tarnished."

He met her gaze, and she saw his meaning quite plain. *But you know that*, he said silently to her. *And now I have your real measure.*

Mr. Davies rubbed his fingertips together. "On the other hand, if this is a ruse, and those are not the letters, *I* expose *you*, Miss Thorne, and I must write to Byron and tell him all is as he feared. Lady Melbourne has failed in her charge. His letters are gone."

CHAPTER 20

What The World Well Knows

*. . . the temper of the whole letter is decidedly
that of a conscience enraged by anticipating
judgment . . .*

Anne Isabella Milbanke, Lady Byron,
private correspondence

"Well, Mr. Davies, do you mean to keep us all in this agony of suspense?" quipped Lady Melbourne. "You pride yourself on being a betting man. On which side do you lay your stake? Are these the letters, or are they not?"

Davies met Rosalind's gaze directly. She saw him question, saw him dare, and one strained heartbeat later, saw him decide.

Mr. Davies inclined his head. "I must apologize, Lady Melbourne. Truly. I beg you will not be offended. It was only Lord Byron's concerns I meant to address. You know how the smallest of ideas can become so firmly fixed in his mind."

The words flowed easily, but they were too glib. No genuine feeling bolstered them. Rosalind returned the letters to their drawer, locked the desk again, and returned the key to Claridge to return to the box on the mantel. All the while, she felt Mr. Davies watching her.

He was not the only one. Lady Melbourne was allowing the silence to stretch out, waiting to see where it would lead.

Rosalind made a decision, and turned, displaying an artlessness she did not feel in the least.

"Ma'am, am I remembering correctly that Mr. Davies was the one who first came to you with this story of missing letters?"

"Indeed, he was." Lady Melbourne cocked her head toward Mr. Davies. "He disturbed what had up until then been a very pleasant evening."

Mr. Davies's lips thinned. "And I told you at the time, Lady Melbourne, Lord Byron . . ."

"Yes, yes, our poor, dear Byron and his oppressive fancies." Lady Melbourne sighed with affected weariness. "But if it was Byron who sent you, who is it that put the idea into his head? Come now, we are quite alone and you can tell me the whole story. As the letters are quite safe, there is no harm done at all, is there?" She spoke lightly, easily, as if she believed every word and was slightly fatigued by the trivial nature of it all. "Surely, it makes no difference if one old lady knows you tried to pull the wool over her weakened eyes. Goodness, I have been accused of far worse, and by men of far greater standing than you!" She paused to make sure this verbal blow had hit home. "What concerns me is that your actions make it plain that the rumor that these letters have gone missing is being spread about. As a friend, you can see that you really *must* tell me who is responsible for it so I can contradict them absolutely. Then you can send Lord Byron word of that as well. Think how relieved he will be!"

A dozen calculations played out behind Mr. Davies's bloodshot eyes. Nothing about this meeting was going according to his plan. Lady Melbourne caught Mr. Davies's gaze and held it. Rosalind watched, and thought she might have to reassess her opinion of Mr. Davies's steadiness. It would take a great deal of nerve to endure such a look as Lady Melbourne leveled at him now. Rosalind was not sure she could have done it.

A firm knock on the door made Rosalind start, much to her shame.

With no pause for permission, the door opened and a man in a plain black coat leaned into the room.

"Hello, Mother! I hope I'm not interrupting. Hullo, Davies! I heard you were in the queue for today."

"Well, do come in, William," said Lady Melbourne smoothly.

William. Rosalind felt her eyes widen as the man crossed the room to kiss Lady Melbourne's upturned cheek. This then was the Honorable Mr. William Lamb, Lord and Lady Melbourne's second son. He was also Lady Caroline's patient and long-suffering husband.

It was difficult to imagine someone more different from that quixotic and elfin lady. William Lamb was tall and square-shouldered. His dark waving hair had been slicked back from a high, clear brow. He had a long face, and his brown eyes bulged slightly in their sockets. But apart from his height, he gave the impression of being entirely ordinary. He exhibited none of the impatient energy shown by his wife or his mother. Quite the reverse, in fact. To all appearances, this was a placid man, ready to take things just as he found them.

"Just passing by. I'm on my way out again and wanted to know if you had any commissions for me in the city."

"Nothing today, William. Oh, William, this is Miss Thorne. She will be staying with us for a time. Miss Thorne, my son, William Lamb."

Rosalind made her curtsey, even as she saw a thoughtful expression steal across Mr. Davies's face. Inside, she shrank back, but she could not let that show.

On the surface, nothing at all had happened. Social reflex had taken hold. Introductions must be made. That was the hostess's first duty.

But Lady Melbourne had told Davies that Rosalind was her particular friend. She'd intimated their acquaintance was of long standing.

If that were true, Rosalind would not need an introduction to Lady Melbourne's dutiful son.

Mr. Davies now knew Rosalind was entirely new to the household. Yet another deception had been revealed.

"Well, I'm off then, and I'll not be home until late," Mr. Lamb was saying. "There's some tiresome speeches tonight, and Heaven knows what they're plotting over in Commons, because the prime minister certainly doesn't." Lamb laughed, and Mr. Davies joined in.

Mr. Davies also got to his feet. "I think I'll walk out with you, Lamb. I've no wish to overstay my welcome." He spoke the words with a smile, but he also spoke them directly to Rosalind.

Lady Melbourne did not miss this little detail. "You are always welcome here, Mr. Davies. Do not forget my note." She nodded toward the letter that still lay on the coffee table. "I'd like that sent to Byron as soon as possible so he can be fully informed regarding that little matter he's somehow become so very concerned about. And do tell him I am eager to read the latest installment of his adventures on the Continent."

"Of course, of course." Mr. Davies's assurance was as glib and as false as his earlier apology. He tucked the letter into his coat pocket. "Your servant, ma'am." He bowed to Lady Melbourne. He turned, just a little, and bowed to Rosalind. She thought she saw a gleam in his eye, a hint of danger and possibly of admiration.

Rosalind found she did not care for either.

As soon as the door closed behind the men, Lady Melbourne allowed herself the luxury of a deep sigh.

"That was neatly managed," she began, but she took another look at Rosalind's expression and her brows lifted. "But you are very grave, Miss Thorne. Are you not pleased with the results of your little gamble?"

"Indeed I am not, ma'am."

"What do you mean?"

Rosalind became aware that she was still staring at the closed door. She chided herself silently and turned toward Lady Melbourne. "Mr. Scrope did not believe me," she said. "He knows that the letters are missing."

"How can he!" cried Lady Melbourne.

"I don't know. But he was certain of it before he even arrived. I suspected as much, but the way he reacted to the letter I tried to give him has confirmed it."

Lady Melbourne stared at her, quite openly surprised. Then she nodded. "Well. I am most impressed, Miss Thorne." Then her voice dropped. "Do you think he stole them himself?" Lady Melbourne asked.

"He might have. You say that he came on a night when there was a supper party?"

"Yes. But he did not stay long."

But the doors would be unlocked, and when there is a dinner party in a house such as this, the guests and the staff are all crowded into a very few rooms. Most of the house would be quiet, and dark.

She might have thought that Mrs. Oslander had been on duty that night and had surprised Mr. Davies in the act of searching for the letters. But that would not explain why Mrs. Oslander would have concealed one of the letters so deliberately about her person.

Therefore, the real question became, Was there a connection between Mr. Davies, and Mrs. Oslander?

"Lady Melbourne, have you told anyone that the letters are missing?"

Lady Melbourne did not miss the stumble. "No one," she said. "Not even William."

"But you did tell Lady Jersey."

Lady Melbourne smiled and looked relieved. Rosalind wondered at this. "You want to know why I would tell anything to a woman called Sarah Silence, known universally for an inability to keep her mouth closed for two minutes together? Well, Miss Thorne, it is because in this one matter, Lady Jersey also has a great deal to lose, and she knows it."

Rosalind felt her brows lift in surprise, and Lady Melbourne sighed. "Yes, the webs that Byron's scandals have spun have caught a great many of us, and Lady Jersey is among them. I knew if I told her, she would take it very seriously and do everything that was in her power to help, and that on this one matter at least, she could be trusted to say nothing." Lady Melbourne's tone was not only confident, it was perfectly and genuinely calm. "So, wherever Davies got his intelligence, it was not from her."

"Could it have been from Lady Caroline?"

"What?" demanded Lady Melbourne. "Caroline knows nothing about this!"

"But she does. Lady Caroline told me about the letters when she first found me here. She was making a joke of it, but it was entirely evident she knew they were gone." *She needs help with her letters. She needs to run into the streets and cry, 'Help! Help! The letters! The letters!'* "Could Mr. Davies be in communication with her?"

Mr. Davies and Lady Caroline shared a connection to Lord Byron. If there was one thing that Rosalind understood, it was how tightly the web of acquaintance and friendship bound members of the *ton* together. Mr. Davies could have approached Lady Caroline. He could have invoked the name of her former lover, perhaps even telling her that Byron still harbored tender feelings for her. He might have persuaded her to take the letters and use Mrs. Oslander as a go-between to smuggle them out of the house.

Or, it could be the reverse. Lady Caroline could have approached Mr. Davies.

"You mean were they in partnership?" said Lady Melbourne, echoing Rosalind's thoughts. "To what end?" But she did not wait for Rosalind's answer. "Well, for Caroline the answer is easy. To bring about my public humiliation and ruin. Davies, of course, will fulfill any commission from Byron, and Byron no longer trusts me." She spoke these words stoically, but her swollen and wounded hands spasmed around the chair arms, showing the true power of the emotions coursing through her. "Yes. Those are motivations that could spawn a partnership." Lady Melbourne shook her head again. "But if it is true, why try to make me confess that they are gone? Do you think Davies intends blackmail?"

"Do you think him capable of it?"

Lady Melbourne was silent for a long time. "I would not have believed it before this, but now . . . I do not know. Caroline, of course, is capable of anything."

In her mind, Rosalind took this declaration of ruthlessness and laid it next to the woman she had seen with her son. Augustus Lamb was clearly not well, and perhaps had never been. Even when her mind was clouded by laudanum, Lady Caroline took charge of the boy with a mother's understanding. Rosalind knew full well that motherhood did not confer sainthood. At the same time, many families would have sent a child such as Augustus away and never mentioned his name again. Lady Caroline kept her son by her. She engaged doctors and tutors for him and tried to see to his care and comfort.

But it was not just Lady Caroline who cared for her son. It was Lady Caroline and the very ordinary Mr. William Lamb. He was the child's father. He had full and final say over where any child he acknowledged lived and how that child was cared for. Like his troubled wife, his troubled son remained here in this house.

That was not the behavior Rosalind would have expected of a simple, placid, unassuming man.

Rosalind laced her fingers together to keep them still. She had been in this house for less than a day, and yet she had already seen so much, she felt quite dizzy. Despite all the rest of it, she did not forget the dead woman who still waited to have her name restored to her.

If that woman did prove to be the nurse, Mrs. Oslander, she was a person Lady Caroline would have easily spoken with.

Lady Caroline—who could charm, disarm, and manipulate—might have persuaded Mrs. Oslander to steal the letters. On her own behalf, or on Lord Byron's.

Or Mr. Davies's.

"What are you thinking now, Miss Thorne?" asked Lady Melbourne.

Rosalind straightened her shoulders. "I am thinking I would like to be excused for tomorrow, ma'am. I am thinking it is imperative that we learn more about Mr. Davies's present situation." She paused. "Unless there is something more you can tell me?"

Lady Melbourne cocked her head toward Rosalind. Her hands spasmed, and the shadow of their pain dimmed the lady's bright eyes.

"No, there is nothing."

This is what you say, ma'am. Rosalind nodded in acknowledgment. *But can I believe it?*

CHAPTER 21

Unwanted Introductions

*But there also seems another disposition in parts
of the letter—to alarm and annoy you . . .*

George Gordon, Lord Byron, private correspondence

Sampson Goutier watched Dr. Phillip Bellingham walk into
the Brown Bear. The physician clutched his valise as if he
feared it might make a sudden escape, which it might, with
help. He looked around uncertainly and began to make his
way over to the barman. Goutier stood and beckoned. Dr.
Bellingham started, stared, and then threaded his way around
the tables and benches to join him.

"Are you Mr. Harkness?" the doctor asked. It was early in
the evening, and the crowd in the public room was at a low
ebb, meaning it was possible to speak in normal tones.

"No, sir. I am Patrol Captain Sampson Goutier." Goutier
bowed. The doctor made no answering courtesy. "Mr. Harkness is called away on other business. I am here to act for
him. He sends his regrets that he cannot speak with you himself."

In point of fact, Harkness's feeling went far beyond regret.
The horror that overcame the man's normally stoic face as he
contemplated an evening in the regulation white silk breeches

of English formal wear was magnificent. Sampson would have to make sure to replicate it for Sal when he got home tonight. She'd laugh herself breathless, which was a magnificent sight in its own way.

Now, Dr. Bellingham, he just looked dubious. Goutier was used to this. In the aftermath of Napoleon's wars, trade was booming for England, and the British navies were ringing the globe. This meant London was filled to its busy commercial brim with every cut and kind of humanity. Despite this, some Londoners still found a large black man with an accent that mixed French, Caribbean, and Cockney an uncomfortable presence. Most of them, however, settled down fairly quickly once it was clear their surprise would not alter the fact of him.

Goutier gestured to the corner table, inviting Bellingham to sit. Dr. Bellingham made up his mind to accept what he could not change and took his place, tucking his valise away underneath the table.

"Mr. Goutier." Bellingham folded his hands on the table and looked at Goutier with a kind of forlorn hope. "I was told that you might have news about Mrs. Judith Oslander. She is a nurse I have . . . some acquaintance with, and she has been missing for . . . for several days now."

"I may, sir." Goutier reached into his coat pocket for his wallet and pulled out two pieces of paper. He laid the first on the table. It was a pencil sketch of the nameless woman. Having learned all he could from the corpse, Sir David, the coroner, had ordered she be taken away for burial. Just before that, Goutier had been given time to take her likeness.

Dr. Bellingham picked up the sketch. Goutier was a decent artist, and as a medical man the doctor surely recognized that the image he had drawn was not that of a sleeping woman.

For a moment, Bellingham's face was an utter, pale blank. Then he blinked. Then, slowly, by strange fits and starts, his brow furrowed and his mouth softened and sagged.

"Yes," Bellingham croaked. "Yes. That is Judith Oslander. God," he breathed. "God Almighty save us. How did she come to be *here*? How is it even *possible*?"

"The corpse was brought late at night, by a hired cart. The driver could not, or would not, say who paid him."

The doctor stared at him. "How is it even possible?" He repeated, then held up his hands. "I'm sorry. This is ludicrous. The whole thing . . . who would have even believed that would be . . . ?" He stopped. "No. I will pull myself together," he said, and it was an order.

Goutier got to his feet, shouldered his way to the bar, and then returned with two large brandies. He set one in front of Dr. Bellingham, who swallowed the dose in one go.

"Thank you," Bellingham said to the bottom of the glass. "Exactly what I would have prescribed."

Goutier tucked the sketch back into his wallet. "Can you talk now, sir?"

A flicker of panic crossed the doctor's face, but he smoothed it away. "Yes, yes. Forgive me. I had hoped . . . I had very much hoped . . ." He stopped and looked at the glass again, like he very much hoped he had not finished all the brandy in that first gulp. "I want to, I wish to . . . a proper burial, sir. A Christian service, and a headstone for her. I can do that much." He fumbled in his pocket and finally pulled out a gold sovereign. "That's enough, surely?"

"Surely." Goutier took the coin quickly to remove it from view. Yes, the place was filled with Bow Street men, but there was no need to let the doctor become a target of those who were not. "It will be seen to."

"Thank you, Mr. Goutier." Bellingham drew in a great breath. Goutier waited with easy patience while the doctor pulled himself back from the gulf of his shock. He wanted Dr. Bellingham to be comfortable. The man would talk much more freely if he was relaxed and knew he had a sympathetic listener.

"I imagine there are questions to be answered," said Bellingham at last. "I am entirely at your disposal."

"Thank you, Doctor. Can you tell me how you came to know that Mrs. Oslander was missing?"

"I needed her services for a patient. I went . . . I sent round to the agency she works through, but they said they could not reach her. I was concerned by this. I went to her rooms. Her landlady told me she had not been home for several days. She was angry but would not give me any other information."

"When was this?"

Dr. Bellingham looked into the bottom of his glass again. "Five days, perhaps six now."

This was interesting. Mrs. Oslander's body had been found only two days ago. But if what Bellingham said was correct, she had been missing for much longer.

"I will need her address, and that of the agency that employed her."

Bellingham pulled out a small notebook, wrote both down, tore out the leaf, and pushed it across the table.

"Thank you, sir," said Goutier. "What else can you tell me about Mrs. Oslander?"

Bellingham considered. "She was an excellent nurse. Completely capable. Absolutely unflappable. Precise and dedicated in all her business, and clean," he added. "I insist on cleanliness in all my nurses."

"Was she married? Did she have any family?"

He tipped the empty glass toward him. "She told me she had been widowed young." Possibly he did not believe this. Many an unmarried woman smoothed her way by bestowing the title of "Mrs." on herself and inventing a dead husband.

"Was Mrs. Oslander an honest woman?"

The doctor's eyes narrowed. "Under other circumstances I would consider that an insult, sir."

"As you should," agreed Goutier easily. "Under other circumstances."

The doctor reddened. "My apologies. We must sometimes ask unpleasant questions in my profession as well. Yes. She was scrupulously honest."

His eyes shone brightly in the lamplight, and Goutier suspected the man was on the verge of tears.

Did you love her, Dr. Bellingham?

It was possible. They had worked closely together and had known each other for a long time. Both in their middle years and yet neither had a spouse of their own. At least, Goutier assumed the doctor unmarried. If he had a wife, she was so far absent from his consideration or conversation.

And if he did have a wife, he would not be the first or only man to also love elsewhere.

"I must ask, Dr. Bellingham, because this was found among her things." Goutier laid the second paper on the table. This was the travel-stained letter Harkness had found and entrusted to him. "It was carefully hidden, so that it was missed at first."

Dr. Bellingham's hand shook as he carried the paper to his face to squint at the blurred direction before unfolding the paper.

The doctor took his time reading the letter, and Goutier began to suspect the man was deliberately delaying the moment when he would have to speak again. Goutier felt for him. If Mrs. Oslander was proved to be a thief, that would reflect badly on Dr. Bellingham in a professional capacity. But if Bellingham had loved her, it would be another blow to his already grieving heart.

Even so, Goutier felt the muscles in his back begin to tense. He did not like it when people had to think so carefully about what to say to him.

That's because they're usually trying to get round you somehow, said his wife, Sal, from the back of his mind, although she probably would have added a few more choice words. Sal kept a second-hand clothes shop, and saw her fair share of dodgy customers. In fact, Goutier had met her because she'd summoned his patrol to deal with a fellow who'd tried to pawn off an entire chest of clothes on her. The fellow claimed it had belonged to an uncle who'd recently passed on. If it hadn't been full of petticoats, the story might have worked.

Goutier had arrived to find Sal standing guard with a broom and cleaver in front of the storeroom in which she'd locked the fellow. As soon as they'd opened the door she began lecturing him—using many a salt-tinged Biblical quotation—about the immorality of attempting to dupe a poor, honest shopkeeper into becoming a receiver of stolen goods.

Goutier had fallen in love on the spot.

When the doctor lowered the letter, his cheeks were flushed with much more than just the recent dose of brandy. "Why would Judith . . . Mrs. Oslander have . . . this . . . with her?" His voice was as stiff as his expression. It was as if he was trying to find the correct question to ask.

Goutier looked the other man directly in his bewildered eyes. "Some personal letters have been taken from Melbourne House. This may be one of them."

"No!" he croaked. Then, suddenly, he shouted, "You're a liar! I would have *known* if she was planning . . . if she meant to . . . !"

Around them, heads turned. Glasses were set down.

Goutier held up one hand. "Dr. Bellingham, I say only that this letter was found with Mrs. Oslander's things, that it was purposefully concealed, and that it was clearly not addressed or directed to her." Goutier rose, a gesture that would incidentally remind Bellingham that he was a good three inches taller and a full stone heavier. "Your glass is empty, sir. Let me get you another."

By the time Goutier returned with the second brandy,

Bellingham had composed himself, at least somewhat. His eyes still gleamed too brightly, and beads of perspiration glimmered on his forehead.

Goutier put the glass in front of him. Bellingham stared toward it, seeing what passed through his thoughts more clearly than what stood on the table in front of him. At last, the doctor raised the brandy to his lips, but he paused before he drank and then set it down untouched. Instead, he pulled out a handkerchief and wiped down his bright red face.

Goutier sat back, content to let the man take all the time he needed to come to his decision.

By the time Bellingham tucked his handkerchief away again, it was clear he'd made up his mind.

"I should not tell you any of this. It is incumbent upon me to keep strict confidence about what happens in my patients' homes."

"The circumstances are difficult." Goutier took a swallow of his brandy, and Bellingham automatically reached for his own glass. Again, though, he did not drink. He just stared at it.

"At the time, I did not think anything of it," he said. "Or, at least, I did not think much of it, but I was at Melbourne House, two weeks ago? No, three now. At least three. I would have to check my book I . . ." He wiped at his sweating face again. With such a constitution, it was as well the man lived in chilly England. "I was there to examine Lady Caroline. She suffered from an infectious fever. I . . . I was earlier than expected. An appointment had been cancelled, I believe. . . ."

"Your book will surely provide that information, if it is needed," said Goutier.

"Yes, of course. I'm sorry. This is inexcusable of me. A physician should be able to keep his composure, whatever the circumstances." Bellingham pressed both hands onto the table in an effort to steady himself, and this time he managed to meet Goutier's gaze. "I came upon Lady Caroline and Judi . . . Mrs. Oslander. Lady Caroline was gripping Mrs. Oslander's wrists. It was entirely against my instructions that Lady Caroline should be on her feet at all, and at first, I just thought Mrs. Oslander was trying to persuade her back to bed. But then I saw . . ." His eyes narrowed as he strove to make certain he relayed his details accurately. "I saw Lady Caroline press a package into Mrs. Oslander's hands. She wanted it to be taken somewhere and refused to go back to bed until Mrs. Oslander agreed."

"And did Mrs. Oslander agree?"

"She did. It was to humor Lady Caroline, or so I thought at the time. Lady Caroline did return to her bed," he added. "Her fever was very high. She was at a truly critical stage."

"Then, Lady Caroline may have been in a delirium?"

"Just so. Yes." Dr. Bellingham nodded. "I told Judith afterward that she should put the package in Lady Caroline's study, or give it to Lady Melbourne or Mr. Lamb to deal with. Although, I hardly thought she needed such directions . . ."

"Experienced as she was?" filled in Goutier.

"Yes. Yes. So. As that was what I instructed, I assumed that was what she did. Mrs. Oslander was always ready to abide by my judgment. She'd never gone against me in even the smallest matters before."

To Goutier, that was the least believable thing the man had said yet, but now was not the time to interrupt.

"I never would have *believed*, even when I saw with my own eyes, I did not believe . . ." Again, Goutier noted the way the doctor's expression crumbled in painful fits and starts. "She had a fold of pound notes tucked in her sleeve. I saw them peeking out as she reached for—something, I can't seem to recall what it was. Odd.—But I did see them, and I failed to grasp the significance at the time."

"And now you do?"

"I think so." Bellingham's voice grew steadier now. "I think that Lady Caroline did not just beg Mrs. Oslander to take that package. I think she paid to have it done."

"Do you think Mrs. Oslander did as Lady Caroline asked?"

"She must have. At least, she must have taken the packet away, that packet must have contained these missing letters."

"Where did Lady Caroline want Mrs. Oslander to take the letters?"

Again, Dr. Bellingham hesitated. Again, Goutier watched him pick and choose from among his possible answers. In his mind's eye, Goutier pictured Sal behind him, arms folded, mouth pursed, as if she were watching one of the neighbor boys whom she'd caught with his hand in the money box, swearing up and down he was actually putting the sixpence back.

Now Dr. Bellingham did drink his brandy, all in a single gulp. When he put the glass down, he had made his decision.

"They were to go to that man who helped Lady Caroline write that disgraceful, gossiping book. I advised Mr. Lamb against agreeing to its completion. Such agitation and exertion is harmful to an already overburdened constitution. And I was proved correct in this. I . . ."

"What man is this, sir?" interrupted Goutier.

Bellingham looked at him as if the answer was obvious. "To the publisher, of course. Mr. Henry Colburn."

CHAPTER 22

A Chance To See And Be Seen

*Am I a timid girl, who turns from your suit bash-
ful and alarmed?*

Lady Caroline Lamb, Glenarvon

Whenever Rosalind needed information from the strictly
male preserve that was depths of Clubland, she turned
to Sanderson Faulks.

"Miss Thorne, how delightful it is to see you." Mr. Faulks
bowed over Rosalind's hand. "At last, there is something to
render this so-called exhibition worthwhile."

Rosalind took her place beside him and studied the paintings that had been lined up in the center of the wall. "May I
take it you are displeased with the selection?"

"Displeased?" Sanderson snorted. "I'm appalled. I am going to sponsor a mass evacuation of our so-called painters.
They are all to go to Paris, where they can see some actual art."

As a meeting place, a gallery exhibition such as this offered
several advantages. First and foremost, of course, it was an
unexceptionable location for Rosalind to be seen with Mr.
Faulks. The fact of their family's friendship allowed some of
the rules to be relaxed, but as neither of them was married,
the majority of the social proprieties remained in full force.

The exhibition would also provide them opportunity to talk without having to worry about who might hear. Lady Melbourne had assured Rosalind she was welcome to receive her own visitors while she resided at Melbourne House. Given her doubts about Lady Melbourne, however, Rosalind did not want to risk the details of this particular conversation reaching her hostess prematurely.

The program Rosalind had seen in the gallery's entrance-way announced that "Compton's Gallery is pleased to present its annual exhibition of rising artists from across the United Kingdom." It further promised, "Only the very finest and most select works will be presented to our esteemed patrons."

There must have been a great many artists rising across the United Kingdoms this season, because the walls were filled from the ceiling to the wainscoting with an extraordinary jumble of paintings of all sizes and subjects, hung so close together that there was scarcely an inch of wall showing between them.

Mr. Faulks contemplated the closest specimen of these select works as if he wanted to rip it from the wall and toss it onto a fire. He was a tall, slender, pale man. Today, he dressed in moss green and rich cream with gold embroidered waistcoat. His green-gloved hands rested lightly on his gold-headed cane. As the third son of an aristocratic family, Mr. Faulks had been expected to go into the law, the military, or the church. Instead, he had dived into the world of art and antiquities. There, he acted as a professional patron and a kind of agent for sales and as a consultant for those who wished to create and expand their private collections.

"While I am the last man to praise Napoleon in any particular, at least he sponsored French painters of merit rather than giving space to any mountebank with a brush who was not actually color-blind, although there's some of these who . . .

You have an amused light in your eye, Miss Thorne. Am I rambling?"

"A little."

"How utterly inexcusable of me! Do accept my most sincere apology. How shall I make amends? A pot of tea perhaps? That balm universal for all social ills?"

"That would be lovely, Mr. Faulks, thank you."

"May I offer my arm, then? Excellent. Let us leave these mediocrities to their devices."

Mr. Faulks steered Rosalind deftly through the crowd. Whatever his assessment of the offerings, the exhibition had been well advertised, and a wide selection of fashionable and not-so-fashionable London had turned out for it. Patrons might occasionally pause to contemplate one canvas or the other, but mostly they seemed interested in each other and the chance to exchange greetings and gossip.

This made for slow progress. Rosalind and Mr. Faulks were both frequently stopped by acquaintances wanting to have a few words or share a bit of news. Therefore, Rosalind did not think anything of it when, after at last reaching the gallery's entrance hall, yet another gentleman bowed to Sanderson. This man was a fellow dandy, and if not genuinely wealthy, he managed the appearance of wealth. His coat, cut full about the skirts, was the same shade of blue as the sapphire nestled in the folds of his cravat. He wore a pearl gray beaver hat and matching kidskin gloves. A lace handkerchief trailed artfully from his sleeve. The pomaded hair beneath his hat was iron gray, and his face was well lined, particularly around his keen, pale eyes.

"Why, hello, Fullerton." Sanderson greeted the man in his usual bored drawl, but Rosalind felt his arm tense beneath her hand. "How unexpected to find you among these works of supposed art."

Fullerton? The name caused Rosalind to draw up short.

She warned herself not to jump to conclusions. Fullerton was a reasonably common name.

If Sanderson noticed her discomfort, he gave no sign. "Miss Thorne, allow me to introduce you to Mr. Russell Fullerton. Fullerton, Miss Rosalind Thorne."

"Rosalind Thorne," Russell Fullerton repeated as he bowed over Rosalind's hand. He drew the syllables out slowly as if reluctant to let them go. "What a lovely and unusual name. A man would remember it for a long time, and the woman it is attached to." His pale eyes glittered.

Rosalind felt her spine stiffen.

"I believe I've heard your name as well, sir." She met his gaze. He was inclined to stare. She would let him, and he would see she was not intimidated. "I think you must be that Mr. Fullerton who has such a reputation as a collector of overlooked artifacts. Is that what brings you here today?"

Rosalind was very aware that Mr. Faulks watched for clues as to how to proceed. As her escort, he could remove her from this conversation if she so much as pressed his arm—which might be prudent, but Rosalind did not choose to show weakness.

"As it happens," said Fullerton, "there are one or two persons I hoped to speak with about items that might interest them. I trust that will not trouble you any, Miss Thorne?" Mr. Fullerton bestowed a smile on her that was thin, unpleasant, and deathly cold.

"That entirely depends to whom those items previously belonged."

Sanderson evidently decided that this was quite enough. "Well, Fullerton, gazing upon all these bland expressions of English sentiment has left me profoundly weary. Miss Thorne promised me tea, and I will not be denied. Good day and good luck to you. Miss Thorne, shall we proceed?"

"Of course, Mr. Faulks," she answered.

Fullerton bowed to them both. "I'm certain we will meet again soon. Miss Thorne."

Mr. Faulks walked them out the gallery's open doors and down the stairs. Despite the growing distance, Rosalind still felt Fullerton's gaze on the back of her neck.

"My dear Miss Thorne," said Mr. Faulks as they turned up the broad walkway toward the high street. "You know how I despise gossip, but I must know what was at the back of that extraordinary exchange you just held with Fullerton."

The weather was beautiful, the sort of spring day that drove poets to their inkpots in an attempt to find new rhymes for sunlight and blooming flowers. The fashionable neighborhood was busy, inside and out, with doors standing open and ladders set up against windows so servants could scrub and polish and sweep.

Rosalind watched this busy, ordered world for a moment before she answered.

"Last season, I was helping a young woman who had fallen victim to a private money lender."

"Ah." Mr. Faulks swung his walking stick. "Let me guess. She had played too deep at cards but did not want to confess her debt to her husband. So when a sympathetic gentleman said he would willingly lend her the trifling sum she required, she seized upon this kindness."

"Yes."

"And of course gave him some small but easily identifiable object to hold in guarantee of her intent to pay him back." He sighed. "I am going to make it my mission in life to start a school for young wives just coming up in society. In it, I will teach them all possible games of cards, and how to win and lose sensibly at them."

"I would willingly subscribe to the effort."

They walked on in silence for a little. "Do not trifle with Fullerton, Miss Thorne," Mr. Faulks said at last. "He is one of those who takes a genuine delight in exploiting the vulnerable, particularly women. He might choose to overlook your interference in his blackmail schemes, but he will not forgive your refusal to cower before him."

Rosalind remembered that cold, narrow smile and had to suppress a sudden shudder. "You may believe me, Mr. Faulks," she said crisply. "My sincerest wish in this world is to stay far away from Mr. Fullerton and all his works."

CHAPTER 23

A Cup Of Tea And A Quiet Chat

*S[crope] is on his return to England and may
probably arrive before this. . . . I hope Scrope will
carry them all safely, as he promised.*

George Gordon, Lord Byron, private correspondence

Rosalind had heard that in Paris, unmarried women regularly dined in public without censure or even comment. Indeed, there was reported to be a burgeoning fashion for eating-places where ladies could not only enjoy a meal but could do so without any prior arrangement and—most shockingly—in full sight of any gentlemen who might also happen to be in the establishment.

Rosalind thought this sounded positively paradisiacal. English mores required that ladies restrict their dining to private homes or, occasionally, the private rooms of established hotels. Even this could be viewed with suspicion, however, and a request for such a dining room required written agreement from the hotel, well in advance. Therefore, it was generally simpler for ladies to dine in their rooms, where they could not cause offense or rouse suspicion.

One of the few exceptions to this state of affairs was the tea shop. These establishments operated only during the most unobjectionable times of day and offered exclusively light, sweet food that was universally considered both suitable and beneficial to a woman's delicate constitution.

Sanderson settled Rosalind at an unoccupied table and went to give an order for tea, fruit tarts, watercress and egg sandwiches, and sugar cake. Then he settled across from her and removed his hat and gloves, which he laid aside along with his walking stick.

"Now, Miss Thorne, I received your communication and read it with great interest. You must tell me how it is you come to be a resident at Melbourne House, of all places."

"Lady Jersey sent me to Lady Melbourne. Her ladyship is in need of my particular assistance."

"Is she, b'ghad? Don't tell me Byron's snuck back into the country or some such?"

Rosalind lifted one eyebrow.

"You are joking, Miss Thorne. Surely, you must be!"

"I am," she admitted. "A little, at least. But I don't get to see you surprised very often."

"You are a heartless tease." Mr. Faulks pressed his hand to his breast. "I am quite done in."

"Byron's name does enter into the business, though." Rosalind leaned a little closer and softly told Mr. Faulks about Lady Melbourne's missing letters. Still more softly, she told him about the woman found in the courtyard, whom she believed to be Mrs. Oslander. Then she told him about the letter that had been eventually found among her things.

Sanderson's eloquent eyes widened.

"Scrope Davies is involved with this business, you say?"

"He is, and I need to determine how deeply. I was hoping you could tell me something of him. I have met him only once, and that was when he came to the house determined to try to get Lady Melbourne to admit that the letters were indeed missing."

The tea and food arrived then, and they paused their conversation while the cups and dishes were laid out.

"Will you pour for us?" Sanderson asked. "I myself shall help you to this tart. It appears excellent."

Rosalind dutifully poured out two cups of tea and in return let herself be served a slice of tart rich with strawberries, rhubarb, and marzipan.

Mr. Faulks sipped his tea and nodded in satisfaction as if testing a new vintage of wine.

"I do know Davies, as it happens," he said. "We've a few clubs in common, and we've had . . . business doings in the past." From the way he spoke, Rosalind suspected that Mr. Faulks did not mean he'd supervised any art purchases for Mr. Davies. Among his other activities, Mr. Faulks privately lent money to those who needed it for short periods.

Mr. Faulks took a sandwich and a slice of tart. "If you want my assessment of the man personally, I would say Scrope Berdmore Davies is one of our young men who gives himself over to excess. His personal resources are of a limited kind, but like so many others, he feels honor bound to maintain himself in the expected style, so he has turned to the usual resources."

Rosalind busied herself with tart and tea until she was certain her voice would remain steady. That combination of honor and expectation was what had ruined her father, and with him her family. She tried not to look back, but sometimes old feelings rose unexpectedly and required a moment before they could be banished.

"Does Mr. Davies gamble or borrow?" she asked at last.

"He gambles." Faulks finished his delicate sandwich, took another and then another. "He prefers the horses to cards and dice, although he is not entirely averse to those. Unfortunately, he is one of those for whom excitement overwhelms good sense. So, while he is skilled, he can easily lose himself in the moment and play too deeply, just like any housewife at her first card party."

In her mind's eye, Rosalind once again saw Mr. Davies's expression as she held out the letters. So many calculations passed behind his features, driven by so many emotions. But among them she had seen a suppressed excitement. There was dare, a risk in front of him. On some level, he was calculating the state of play, and the odds, and enjoying himself doing it.

If—as you assure me—those are the letters Lord Byron is inquiring about, then my flagrant discourtesy is all for nothing . . . if this is a ruse, and those are not the letters, I expose you, Miss Thorne . . .

But Davies had not chosen to expose himself, even for the possible reward of exposing her. In that moment, he had weighed the risk and protected himself and the game he was playing. But he had also clearly enjoyed that small but unexpected thrill.

"He gambles, he loses, and then, naturally, he borrows?"

"Just so. To be fair, he does generally try to repay what he owes, and when he is in funds, he is generous to his friends."

Rosalind took a sandwich. There were only two left. She gave Mr. Faulks a hard look, and he had the grace to appear apologetic.

"Would Mr. Davies be considered a soft touch?" she asked.

"Cant expressions, Miss Thorne? I'm shocked. But no, he is not in general, but he is quite loyal, and he does have the desire to be of use when he can."

"He certainly seems to be loyal to Lord Byron," she remarked as she refilled Sanderson's cup. "He is going to great length and inconvenience to secure those letters for his lordship."

Mr. Faulks cut himself a fresh slice of tart. "I wonder . . . with this talk of money and obligation, I am reminded of something. It is known—perhaps not generally, but it *is* known—that Lord Byron is in debt to Davies. When Davies left for the Continent to visit Byron this last time, it was supposed that he went to try to pry some of those funds loose."

"And now who is guilty of cant expression?" Rosalind smiled over her cup's rim, but only briefly, for an unpleasant idea struck her. "Lord Byron must owe Mr. Davies a considerable sum for him to go to such trouble to try to recover it."

"I believe that it is considerable, yes. Of course, the story that he could get Byron to pay may have been a blind Davies put up to delay his own creditors. Some of us were rather surprised when he did return."

There was a long history of men exiling themselves to escape their debts. The "Beau" Brummell had removed himself to Calais for that reason. Rosalind's father and sister, Charlotte, had lived in Paris for a number of years before Charlotte was able to move them back to England.

"Could Lord Byron have used the prospect of payment to try to convince Mr. Davies to retrieve these letters from Lady Melbourne?"

"It is possible. Byron habitually makes the most abominable use of his nearest and dearest."

Rosalind watched the steam curl across the surface of her tea. "I am beginning to take a severe dislike to Lord Byron."

"You would not be the first, Miss Thorne."

"Do you know him?"

Sanderson shrugged. "I've met him. You will recall, I myself recently traveled to the Continent. Not, I hasten to add, for reasons of debt, but on a buying trip for certain clients of mine. It was during that dreadful cold summer we had. Along the way, I'd gotten an invitation to visit Byron and his friend Shelley where they were staying near Lake Geneva. I went, more out of curiosity than anything."

"And because you thought you'd get some good gossip out of it."

Mr. Faulks saluted her with his last bit of sandwich. "You know I love a story to dine out on, but I will now be both frank and discreet. Much of what I saw I would not repeat in company. It was altogether a strange, uncomfortable cohort." He finished the sandwich thoughtfully and wiped his fingers on his napkin. "I expect you might have gotten on with one young lady I met, Mary Wollstonecraft. Odd girl, very much of a literary bent in her own right. She was working on a novel when I was there. I've wondered if it's this thing everybody's giving Shelley credit for . . ." Faulks cut himself off with another shake of his head. "The rest of their particular society would not have suited you, though, most especially Byron. Not only is he prone to wild and disordered behaviors, he is perfectly aware of his personal attractions, and he is happy to use them for his own benefit." Mr. Faulk's mouth twitched. "I can see how someone like Davies might have become dazzled, and ensnared, by such a man."

Rosalind frowned. "So, Lord Byron owes money to Mr. Davies. His lordship wants a set of letters that Lady Melbourne has. He sends Mr. Davies to get the letters. To motivate Mr. Davies, Lord Byron either calls on the strength of friendship or promises to pay the money he owes." Rosalind dragged her fork through a smear of custard. "Mr. Davies returns to England. Sometime afterward, Mr. Davies goes to Lady Melbourne, in the middle of a supper party, with a story of how Byron is afraid the letters have gone missing."

"Which turns out to be true," Mr. Faulks reminded her.

"So, how did Lord Byron hear of it? The letters would have had to have been stolen months ago for word to get to him all the way out in Switzerland."

"Italy now."

"Yes. Now, Mr. Davies says this notion of the letters being missing is an idea Lord Byron had gotten stuck in his imagination. I could not quite believe that."

"Having met his mad lordship, I can." Sanderson paused and quirked his brows. "But I think I see some idea forming in you, Miss Thorne."

"Yes. You tell me that Byron owes Mr. Davies, and Mr. Davies needs the money badly."

"Quite badly, or so say all the little birds."

"Then what if Mr. Davies wants those letters, not to give to Lord Byron—"

"But to extort Lord Byron," Mr. Faulks finished for her. "Yes. Now that line is straight and clear, and that might drive a man to extraordinary acts."

Rosalind nodded. "Consider this. There is something I want. I have perfectly good reasons to need it. The item is held by another person. That person knows that I want the item, but will not part with it. Now, if the item simply goes missing one day, suspicion will at once fall on me."

"Artifice is therefore needed," put in Mr. Faulks.

"Yes. So I compose a story. I approach the item's owner, and I am extremely worried. I ask, Is the thing secure? Are they certain? I am told it is perfectly secure. But in a day, or two, or three, the owner goes to look at the item, and it is not there."

"And you, or *I* in this charming narrative, have a story. I heard rumors. I warned the owner. I asked the owner to take better care, and so forth." Mr. Faulks waved his hand. "I can invent whatever ghost circumstances dictate, perhaps even point suspicion toward some mutual enemy . . ." He paused and met Rosalind's gaze. "Especially one as conveniently located and universally distrusted such as Lady Caroline Lamb."

"Exactly," said Rosalind. "But if that was the plan, it is failing. Lady Melbourne refuses to believe that Lady Caroline had anything to do with the matter."

"Now there, you surprise me, Miss Thorne. I would have thought that given the chance, Lady Melbourne would be standing up in open court and denouncing Lady Caroline before the bar of justice."

"It seems Lady Melbourne's son, William Lamb, says Lady Caroline had nothing to do with the matter. Lady Melbourne assures me her son is entirely without guile and would never think to deceive her."

Mr. Faulks blinked. "This would be William Lamb, the rising politician who has spent his entire life watching his mother's astounding social machinations? This is the man whom she declares without guile and incapable of deceit?"

"Yes."

"Maternal love is truly an amazing thing." Mr. Faulks considered the situation. He also took a bite of tart and a sip of tea.

Rosalind smiled, and agreed. "But to return, for the moment, to Mr. Davies. He is familiar with the house. Despite everything, he has remained on visiting terms with Lady Melbourne, as we can see from the fact that he expects to be admitted no matter what time he arrives at her door. He is also friends with Mr. Lamb. He might plausibly have seen and even spoken to the nurse, Mrs. Oslander, during one of his visits."

"And offered her money, or other inducement, to take the letters."

Rosalind nodded absently. "Although Mr. Davies need not have bought off Mrs. Oslander directly. He might have approached someone inside the house and poured out his supposed troubles to that person in order to persuade them to act for him. Lady Melbourne, after all, is not the only person in that family susceptible to the name of Byron and the possibilities"—*or threats*—"he represents."

"Do you mean Lady Caroline?"

"Possibly Lady Caroline, but I was thinking of someone else."

"Who?"

Someone steadier, who has already dared to protect what they hold dear at great personal cost. "Mr. William Lamb."

CHAPTER 24

The View From Clubland

*My husband received letters telling him he would
be the public ridicule and jest if he supported
me—I was proved mad.*

Lady Caroline Lamb, private correspondence

St. James Street was a broad and ancient thoroughfare that
cut across the heart of London. Any number of remarkable parades and events had crossed its cobbles. Its most enduring point of interest in the modern day, however, was the
major artery through the precinct known as Clubland.

Most gentlemen of the *haut ton* belonged to as many clubs
as they could afford, and each had its particular specialty.
Clubs like Watier's were prized for their chef and cellar. Others, like Boodle's and White's, held out opportunities for
high-stakes gambling as their primary attraction. Politics, of
course, was well represented. Clubs for Tories jostled against
clubs for Whigs, and both looked down on the shabby rooms
haunted by radicals and reformers.

But no matter what their bent or speciality, the ultimate
purpose of all these institutions remained the same. They
provided a place where men could meet and come to know

one another. The social web so artfully spun by the ladies of the *ton* in their parlors was replicated by their husbands and sons in the confines of the clubs.

For a gentleman with a position to protect and maintain, therefore, time at a club was not just a respite, it was a social necessity. So it could not be considered at all strange to find that at roughly the same time that Rosalind Thorne was being escorted back to Melbourne House by Mr. Sanderson Faulks, the Honorable Mr. William Lamb was sitting in the member's room at White's with his newspapers and his drink. Nor was it entirely surprising that the thin gentleman in the sapphire blue coat should approach him there, and inquire, "Am I addressing the Honorable Mr. William Lamb?"

Lamb bent down one corner of his paper. "Do I know you, sir?"

"You do not, sir, but we have a mutual friend, Mr. Scrope Davies. My name is Fullerton." The man bowed, deeply and fussily.

Lamb inspected the fellow for a moment before folding his paper and gesturing toward an empty chair. He had work to do this afternoon, and he needed to get home before it grew too late. Things were brewing. Caro had been thoroughly agitated of late. He would need to take steps, and soon, or risk things falling out of control yet again. Now was not a good time for that.

As if there ever was a good time.

But the forms must be observed, and there was no knowing who this fellow was. His name had a ring of familiarity. Nothing distinct, but still Lamb felt reluctant to dismiss him out of hand.

"What is it I can do for you, Mr. Fullerton?" he asked amiably.

Fullerton folded his hands across his walking stick. The gloves were the same delicate shade of pearl gray as his spotless breeches and the hat he laid on the table.

"I believe your mother's taken on a new private assistant," said Fullerton. "A gentlewoman in reduced circumstances, as they are called. A Miss Rosalind Thorne."

Lamb frowned. "Sir, if you knew my family, and particularly my mother, you would know that no good comes of watching over her affairs. I grant her the respect and duty owed by a son and allow her to govern her house as she sees fit."

"Just so. But many would say it's a son's job to help protect his family, especially from unscrupulous characters."

"Your meaning, sir?"

"That having Miss Thorne in a household is not conducive to domestic harmony. She is perfectly capable of manipulating the credulous and the vulnerable to her own ends, and her own ends include feathering her own nest."

The two men stared at each other, each attempting to size up the force and affect of their words.

"You seem very well informed on the matter," remarked Lamb.

Fullerton inclined his head modestly. "I make it my business to be well informed on many things. You should also know that Miss Thorne wears enough faces for an entire crowd. Why, just the other day she was seen talking quite publicly with a runner from Bow Street."

For the first time since the man started speaking, Lamb felt the cold touch of fear. He began searching through the copious list of names lodged in his prodigious memory.

Do I know this man? Surely I've heard something of him somewhere. What was it?

Lamb chuckled to cover his alarm. "Mr. Fullerton, if you're here to frighten me with rumor and innuendo, you will have to do better than that. And you must be far more specific. For instance, does this garrulous runner happen to have a name?"

"Adam Harkness," replied Fullerton promptly, and Lamb's brows lifted. "He and Miss Thorne are thick as thieves, if I may use the expression. He comes and goes from her house freely. *Quite* freely," he added, and waited for Lamb's reaction. When there was none, he touched the side of his nose, just in case Lamb had missed his meaning. "I'd be very careful about keeping such a woman in my home if I were you, sir."

It is not my house! Lamb wanted to shout. *It is my father's house, damn you! And if he gave a damn about anything but his horses, he'd have curbed his wife years ago and I wouldn't have to endure the insults of scoundrels like you!*

But something in Fullerton's sly and urgent tone tripped a memory, and Lamb finally realized whom he faced. He picked up his glass of port and took a smallish swallow.

"Well, Mr. Fullerton," he said as he set the glass down. "You have delivered your warning. In return, I give you a piece of advice." Lamb caught the man's pale gaze and held it. "The nature and composition of my family's household is our private business, and I'll thank you not to expound upon either in public. Should you continue to do so, you may find that I am forced to take an interest in your business. Your business, Mr. Russell Fullerton, will not stand the scrutiny."

"Well then, sir, I can only ask your pardon. I meant no offense." Fullerton stood and executed another fussy bow. Lamb inclined his head and kept his mouth shut.

On the very long list of things Lamb chose not to speak about in that moment was the fact that this was the second time in as many days someone had warned him about Miss Rosalind Thorne. Scrope Davies had brought her up yesterday when they were leaving mother's sitting room.

How did your mother come to know that Thorne woman? Davies had asked.

Oh, much the usual way, I expect. I think Lady Jersey introduced them.

Mmm. Well, I'd keep an eye on her if I were you, Lamb. She's too sharp for anybody's good. Especially your wife's, I should think.

And now Miss Thorne's name was in the mouth of Ambrose Fullerton, who was a money lender and a blackmailer and had a number of influential men in his pocket. Lamb watched Fullerton as he crossed the club room, heading toward the foyer. He took careful note of who Fullerton stopped to speak with. Had anyone thought to watch Mr. Lamb, they might have noticed how very relaxed he appeared and how little his eyes blinked as his gaze followed the other man to the doorway. They might easily have concluded that Lamb had just passed a very pleasant moment in the other man's company.

But no one watched William Lamb. No one thought he could be worth the effort. This was yet another fact of which Lamb was very well aware.

CHAPTER 25

Preparations For An Evening Out

*. . . it would be much better at once to explain
your mysteries—than to go on with this absurd
obscure hinting mode of writing.*

George Gordon, Lord Byron, private correspondence

"How are you getting on belowstairs, Mrs. Kendricks?"
Rosalind sat at the broad dressing table in her Melbourne House rooms. She was already dressed in her new dark-gold ball gown—an extravagance she had planned and scrimped for as soon as she received Louisa Winterbourne's breathless letter announcing her choice of a groom.

"I'm getting on well enough, miss." Mrs. Kendricks clenched her teeth around a cluster of pins. "It is not a very settled house." She deftly bundled Rosalind's curls into a high crown and speared a pin into the heart of the mass.

"What do you mean?"

Mrs. Kendricks didn't answer until she had forced three more pins into their places. Rosalind's hair was quite thick and full, and securing it often seemed to require every pin in London.

"The whole staff believes her ladyship is dying. That means everyone was on edge even before this fuss about letters. No one knows what will happen when she passes. Normally, one of the daughters, or one of the son's wives, would step in and take over the running of the household. But no one's got confidence in any of that lot, and that is exactly how I heard them referred to."

"Not a good sign," murmured Rosalind.

"No, miss," agreed Mrs. Kendricks blandly. "But my impression is the house was breaking even before then. Everyone here has taken up sides one way or another. There's those that are absolutely loyal to her ladyship. There's those who are in sympathy to Lady Caroline, and believe her to be a poor mad creature. One or two younger girls, think she's *awfully* tragic and has broken her heart over her hopeless love, or some such nonsense. I'd say there's a footman or two finds her *awfully* romantic as well and fancy themselves the hero type to take her away from all this. Others think she's simply wicked and should be sent away in disgrace, and they pity Mr. William, and wish the viscount, Lord Peniston Lamb, would remember this is *his* household and step up and take charge of his family as he should . . ."

"Good heavens, Mrs. Kendricks! You heard all that in so short a time?"

"I have never been in such a house for gossip, miss, and I tell you, there is no surer sign of a place that's ready to topple." To Mrs. Kendricks, flowing talk was like flowing water: It eroded the ground and left the family nowhere to stand.

Rosalind mulled this over in silence for a moment. Then, thinking back on her conversation with Mr. Faulks, she asked, "Is anyone talking about the corpse?"

"Almost no one, but they all know something happened. The kitchen girls were whispering to one another about not wanting to go out alone on their half day. And I was helping one of the upstairs girls with her mending, and she says she heard about a body in the yard from one of the undergrooms.

She says she didn't believe it and that she thought he was just trying to put a scare into her. But he swore it was true, and now she's talking about going back home to her mother in Lancashire."

"What else did the undergroom say?"

Mrs. Kendricks shook her head. "That was all she could tell me."

"That's very strange. I should think that there'd be much more talk about such a thing."

"Not if it was cleared up quick," Mrs. Kendricks said. "And if it was only one person, *and* that person found it in their best interest to keep their mouth shut."

That was rather a lot of ands, thought Rosalind.

The soft knock of a servant sounded on the door. Mrs. Kendricks laid down her pins and went to answer.

"A letter for you, miss." Mrs. Kendricks handed Rosalind the sealed paper.

"Thank you. May I read it now?"

"If you hold your head absolutely still."

The direction was written in Alice's hand, but that proved to be only a sheet of paper folded and sealed over another letter.

Rosalind frowned and broke the fresh seal. Mrs. Kendricks set about adjusting and pomading her coiffure. Rosalind, careful to keep her head entirely motionless, broke the second seal.

The letter inside was written in a very clear, very small hand, as if the person considered ink and paper entirely too precious to waste.

She read:

> *Dear Miss Thorne:*
> *I trust you will excuse my writing without introduction. My name is Sampson Goutier. I am a Patrol Captain at the Bow Street Station and was given your name and current residence by Mr. Adam Harkness.*

As you are under direction from Sir David Royce to help inquire into the matter of the woman found in the courtyard, I judged it desirable to let you know the results of my own inquiries as soon as possible.

Yesterday evening, I spoke with Dr. Phillip Bellingham, and he informed me that the woman of our inquiry is indeed Mrs. Judith Oslander. He further informed me that three weeks ago, by his estimation, he had seen Mrs. Oslander with her patient, Lady Caroline Lamb. He described a scene wherein Lady Caroline insisted that Mrs. Oslander must take the package to a Mr. Harry Colburn and paid her to make the delivery.

He further told me that Mrs. Oslander had vanished almost a se'en night before she was found at Melbourne House.

Miss Thorne, I must tell you that in my opinion, this was not the complete story. Dr. Bellingham was distraught when he spoke. This might have been because he was far closer to Mrs. Oslander than he has been willing to admit. But there may be another reason that we have not yet discovered.

I wish you very well, and as I am sure our mutual friend would do, I urge you to caution in this matter.

Your Obedient Servant,
Sampson Parcival Goutier

Rosalind read the letter again, and yet again.

"I need to stand up, Mrs. Kendricks."

"One moment please, miss." Two more pins were slipped into their places. "Now, miss."

Rosalind got to her feet and carried the letter to the hearth. She read it a third time, crumpled it up, and tossed it onto the fire.

Why was this man Mr. Goutier writing her? Had something happened to Mr. Harkness? Rosalind frowned as the paper blackened and turned to ash. She was aware of her chest tightening. Mr. Harkness was a man in a profession that met with daily violence. Could he be hurt? No one would think to tell her if that were so.

Stop it, Rosalind. You have no reason to think that. He may have been called out of the city on some urgent business and could not write before leaving. Had any emergency occurred, Mr. Goutier would have mentioned it.

After three repetitions, Rosalind managed to draw in a full breath and to convince herself she believed this.

Behind her, Mrs. Kendricks said, "If you're quite finished, miss? We still need to do your gloves."

"Yes. Of course." Satisfied that the paper was fully consumed, and that she was in no danger of trembling, Rosalind dutifully returned to her dressing chair.

"Hands please, miss."

Rosalind held out both hands and let Mrs. Kendricks slip her white satin gloves onto her arms and do up the many buttons. The long pause gave her mind time to settle and to turn over the actual contents of Mr. Goutier's letter.

. . . Mrs. Oslander had vanished almost a se'en night before she was found at Melbourne House.

Could this be true? Where was she? What happened to her? Considering the manner of her death, there were a thousand possibilities, ranging from the banal to the dark possibility that she had been held in duress.

Unfortunately, the best source of information would be Mrs. Oslander's own home, and Dr. Bellingham's assertion that Mrs. Oslander had been missing for at least a week, longer now, raised a new and very real danger.

It was probable that Mrs. Oslander kept rented rooms in a house, as most women of her class did if they had no family. After a full week, the landlord of that house might have decided that Mrs. Oslander had vanished, possibly to avoid payment of her rent or some other debt. That landlord might have seized Mrs. Oslander's things and locked them away against her return, and would not hand them over until the rent was paid.

Or they might have simply decided not to wait and sold them off. They might now be part of the great river of London's secondhand goods, and any hint as to what might have happened to the remaining letters would be gone with them.

"That's done, miss." Mrs. Kendricks words startled Rosalind out of her reverie. Or almost out of it. Because her thoughts had very much stuck on the idea of this scene Dr. Bellingham described between Lady Caroline and Mrs. Oslander.

She wondered if it was true. Or if Dr. Bellingham, who might love Judith Oslander, was trying to protect her somehow by blaming Lady Caroline for the missing letters.

Dr. Bellingham had, after all, urged Rosalind not to believe anything Lady Caroline told her.

"Mrs. Kendricks, what is Claridge's opinion of Lady Caroline?" Rosalind asked.

Mrs. Kendricks opened Rosalind's jewel case and brought out the pearl necklace with the topaz clasp that was one of the few pieces remaining from the family's more prosperous days.

"I think Claridge blames Lady Caroline for Lady Melbourne's collapse and general ill health." Mrs. Kendricks fastened the necklace around Rosalind's throat and then added the matching pearl and topaz drops to her ears. "She definitely believes that Lady Caroline's 'antics' result more from being spoilt and wicked than they do from madness, or a broken heart, or any such."

"Could Mrs. Claridge be persuaded to talk with you about Lady Caroline?"

"Fairly easily, I should think." Mrs. Kendricks started closing up the jars on the table and laid the brushes back into tidy lines. "She wants to observe propriety, but she's under a strain. It's beginning to show."

"I need to find out if anyone has been visiting Lady Caroline, quietly, perhaps even secretly. Or if she's been passing letters to any person that she might not want seen by her husband, or Lady Melbourne."

"Well, I can try," said Mrs. Kendricks. "But to be frank, miss, if anything like that was going on, I'd have expected her to say something already."

Rosalind paused again, turning over all she had heard and learned, and all that she had not. "You might also ask her about Mr. Davies, and that first night he came asking after the letters. Perhaps she saw something, or remembers something her ladyship did not . . . care to mention in casual conversation."

"That may be more than I can promise, miss."

"I know. Do what you can."

"As always, miss."

"Yes, Mrs. Kendricks. As always."

This was not much of a move forward, but it was what she could do this evening. Now, she must try to set this problem aside, for a few hours at least.

Rosalind stood and let Mrs. Kendricks have a full look at her handiwork. The new dress was a relatively simple garment. Public perception had relegated Rosalind to the role of permanent spinster and assistant to gentlewomen. Therefore, she was expected to shun excesses in lace, beading, or ruffles. Rosalind did not mind, because that made it possible to concentrate on simple, well-drawn lines and good fabric for her dress and still remain acceptably fashionable. The slim gown was deep bronze brocade with wide gold velvet trim and a modest lace train dyed to match. More ribbons and Mrs. Kendrick's skill created a simple crown for her hair in the "Grecian" style that was currently popular. It also, thankfully, suited Rosalind better than costly dyed plumes, or the massive "Turkish" turbans that had begun to invade the ballrooms.

"You look lovely, miss. His grace is sure to remember all you have meant to each other."

"Thank you, Mrs. Kendricks," replied Rosalind, but neither one of them missed the fact that she turned away from this particular compliment a little too quickly.

Devon had already made it clear he remembered, and felt, a great deal. And Rosalind still had no idea how to answer him. The reasons for her doubts were slowly mounting, and included the fact that the mere possibility of Mr. Harkness being hurt made her want to run straightaway to Bow Street and demand to know where he might be.

Of course she did no such thing. Of course she simply took her fan and her reticule as Mrs. Kendricks handed them to her and stepped calmly out to keep her promises.

CHAPTER 26

While Otherwise Engaged

*She shall marry for the purpose for which
matrimony was ordained among people of birth—
that is, for the aggrandisement of her family,
the extending of their political influence—for
becoming, in short, the depository of their mutual
interest.*

Susan Edmonstone Ferrier, Marriage

The first words Devon Winterbourne ever spoke to Rosalind were hardly the stuff of grand romance. But then, at the time, neither was he.

That initial meeting occurred at Portland House, the night of Augusta Farrowdale's debut. Rosalind's own come out was still fresh in her mind, and she was eager to see how Augusta's dress and the house's decorations compared to her own. Rosalind's sister had been out for two years but was still not married or even seriously proposed to and was, from Rosalind's point of view, becoming filled with self-pity.

Charlotte had already breezed away to a cluster of her own friends. Rosalind remembered feeling relieved, even though standing alone by the wall was the last place she wanted to be. She didn't see anyone she knew immediately, and etiquette forbid she talk with anyone to whom she had not been introduced. But even that was better than having to listen to Charlotte's acid commentary on every single man she laid her eyes on.

Later, Rosalind would understand this was their father's influence. From her position as younger daughter, Rosalind knew that she and Charlotte were expected to marry well. "My daughters are shining stars!" their father repeatedly declared. "Their lights shall never be hidden away on fusty country estates." What she did not know then was how Father had made it clear to Charlotte, and their mother, that an exquisite match was not an aspiration for her. It was an absolute requirement.

Rosalind had felt herself fading backward, trying to be inconspicuous. It was an awkward time. Mother was despairing over her height, and her figure, which had begun to round out to the point where she hardly knew herself, and as a result, Mother had begun to scold her for eating too much.

That was when a masculine voice said, "I know I'm impertinent and forward and all the rest of it, but please, miss, will you rescue me?"

Rosalind turned and saw a thin young man her own age or slightly older. His face was pocked, and he was trying to grow side-whiskers to hide the marks, but the project was not going well. He wore his black hair in the new longer style, and that wasn't going well, either. But his gray eyes were earnest, and there was a glimmer of humor in them that made Rosalind set aside the tart reply she had initially planned.

"What is it I'm rescuing you from?"

"A friend of my brother's. He wants me for a game of cards, but he cheats, so if I play, I'm going to have to either lose or call him out, and neither one will go well. If we're talking, though, he can't interrupt to drag me off to the card room. That's him there."

He nodded toward a young man in a silk coat that was a

truly astounding shade of buttercup yellow. She also noted that the young man who spoke to her was dressed in a much more becoming—and far less fussy—coat of rich burgundy over a waistcoat of patterned black silk.

"Why me?" Rosalind asked.

"Because you look steady and will not giggle at me," he answered. Her pride and her spirits sank together. "And you're so lovely that no one will think that cards could possibly be more important than speaking with you."

He smiled then, and his whole face transformed. Those gray eyes lit with intelligence and all the humor they'd only hinted at before. Rosalind felt her heart take wing.

And that was all before she'd even found out his name.

Eight long years had passed since that night. Now Rosalind stood in the entrance hall of another great house. Once again, light blazed through the doors of the ballroom, thrown open to reveal the brilliance of the gathering. The merry strains of a country dance filled the air above the burr and rumble of voices.

This time, though, Rosalind was with Alice Littlefield rather than Charlotte, and instead of avoiding his brother's disreputable friends, Devon stood beside his radiant cousin Louisa and her aunt, Mrs. Showell, to play the host and help greet all the guests.

Louisa saw Rosalind first.

"At last!" Louisa ran forward to grasp both Rosalind's hands. "I'm so glad you're here! Hello, Alice! Isn't everything marvelous? It all came out perfectly, and it's all thanks to our dear Miss Thorne!"

Rosalind had spent much of the little season—that space of time just before Parliament opened and the real season roared into life—closeted with Louisa and Mrs. Showell helping select the flowers, the decorators, and musicians, not to mention the extra staff, and generally making sure the whole affair would be *à la mode et à la minute.*

"I'm sure you're giving me far too much credit, Louisa," Rosalind murmured.

"I'm sure she's not." Mrs. Showell had excused herself from Lord and Lady Burgess and come over to greet Rosalind and Alice. Devon Winterbourne, Lord Casselmaine, trailed behind her.

He looks well. The fashion in black coats suits him.

Devon was no longer thin; rather, he had grown muscular and carried himself with a confident air. He'd abandoned all thought of side-whiskers, and Rosalind tried not to let her gaze linger on the straight lines of his jaw.

The Duke of Casselmaine had only arrived in town with the opening of Parliament, so she hadn't had much time to see or speak with him yet this season. He was glad to see her, though, and he thought she looked well. She could read this much in his quiet eyes and soft smile. Rosalind tried to steel herself against the particular warmth that came from a combination of genuine welcome and satisfied vanity.

She failed.

Alice's sharp kick against her ankle informed Rosalind she was staring. She jerked her attention back to Mrs. Showell, who, thankfully, did not seem to have noticed her lapse.

But Devon did notice, and his smile had broadened.

". . . we'll be quite depending on you for help with the wedding plans, Rosalind," Mrs. Showell was saying. "I know all the warehouses, if I may say, but finding a dressmaker who can design something appropriate to the moment will be a challenge."

The kingdom was still recovering from the sudden death of the Regent's only legitimate heir, Princess Charlotte. Therefore, all celebrations held this year were expected to be relatively modest and subdued. Originally, it had been anticipated that Louisa would be married in the grandest style from Grosvenor Square at the last possible moment of the season.

That was now set aside. Instead, she would be married in summer from the Casselmaine estate.

"I'm sure Madame deChevalier will answer perfectly," said Rosalind. "She designed Lady Barrett's clothes, and her wedding was perfection."

"Mrs. Showell thinks I should have six attendants," said Louisa. Behind her, Devon rolled his eyes. "But I can't possibly . . . oh!"

This time, Alice kicked Louisa's ankle. The means of communication was proving startlingly effective, because Louisa broke off in midsentence to cover her mouth with one white-gloved hand.

"Oh, I almost forgot! Alice, you haven't met Firth yet, and you must! Immediately!" Louisa seized Alice's hand and dragged her away.

Rosalind looked up at Devon. All trace of a smile had vanished, and his expression was studiously sober.

"I think Louisa is enjoying an evening with the reins slackened just a little," she remarked.

"Perhaps a little too much." Mrs. Showell sighed fondly. "I'll take her aside and remind her that she's still required to observe one or two of the proprieties. But in the meantime, you'll excuse me I'm sure? So much to do." A successful ball was like any other successful campaign, in that the leader must remain constantly vigilant. Mrs. Showell would have no rest tonight.

And she'll declare herself exhausted to everyone of her acquaintance, and enjoy every minute of it. Mrs. Showell had been Louisa's chaperone for her season, and this evening was her triumph as much as Louisa's.

Rosalind smiled after Mrs. Showell as she sailed through the crowd. She was not, of course, delaying the moment when she had to look at Devon again. She was certainly not concerned that the sight of him had affected her more strongly than it should.

It was just over a year since Rosalind had found herself once again tossed up against Devon Winterbourne. Each of them had just begun to find their feet after years of hard change and hard loss. Rosalind's work had steadied her financial condition. Devon had at last reached a point where the responsibilities he had inherited upon his brother's death had begun to bear him up rather than weigh him down.

But the scars of abrupt change marked both their spirits, as did the years of silence between them. It was a great deal to navigate around, even leaving out the gulf of their relative positions in the world and the extra complication of Adam Harkness crowding into Rosalind's heart.

She thought again about the letter from Sampson Goutier. She needed to send back some word via Alice—no, it had better be George, who was known at Bow Street. She had to arrange a meeting and learn what she could from Mr. Goutier, and make sure Mr. Harkness was all right.

"We seem to have been abandoned by our nearest and dearest." Devon's remark cut across her thoughts, and Rosalind blushed at her own inattention.

Enough of this.

Rosalind faced Devon fully. She also spared a moment to be angry at her complexion, which was refusing to cool as she met his familiar gaze.

"They are behaving ruthlessly, heartlessly, and thoughtlessly," she agreed.

"You seemed fascinated by the ballroom just now. Are you interested in seeing how your decorations came out?" He paused. "Or would you care to dance?"

The musicians were striking up another country tune. Beyond the threshold, guests milled about, claiming partners and forming up into three long lines.

"Your waltz has become perfectly serviceable," said Rosalind with an air of affected criticism. "But has your jig step improved any?"

"Not a bit, I'm afraid." Devon smiled. The familiar expression lit his eyes and eased some nameless tension under Rosalind's ribs.

"Then you'll have to forgive me," she said, answering his smile with one of her own. "I'm afraid I've only the one pair of good slippers."

"Then may I suggest a turn on the terrace? It is a very fine night."

"That would be lovely. Thank you."

Devon held out his arm. Rosalind laid her hand on his sleeve and let herself be led away into the lights.

CHAPTER 27

The Gentle Perils Of Reunions

"You should have a softer pillow than my heart."
"I wonder which will break first—yours or mine?"

George Gordon, Lord Byron, and Anne Isabella Milbanke,
Lady Byron, in conversation

While the gathering could not be labeled a genuine crush, the ballroom was quite crowded. Rosalind and Devon made their way slowly through the great room. Devon, in his twin roles of host and Lord Casselmaine, was obliged to stop and speak with any guest who wanted to speak with him. Rosalind smiled and made her curtsies, took her share of the conversations, and coolly returned the curious and challenging looks she received.

This was the world to which she had been raised. She knew its ways perfectly and could follow its rules without thinking. She could also acknowledge that she missed this beauty and ease, and the instinctual understanding of how and who she should be.

She knew full well this beauty was gloss, and a very thin gloss at that. And yet, and yet . . . when she was in her role of helpmeet to others, she sometimes felt like a parlor maid in front of a dress shop, longing for the beauties inside that would transform her into something more than she was. That she had carved out a role for herself, that she had faced danger and made her part into something beyond the ordinary, was a matter of pride. But there were still days when that pride was still not enough.

Which was petty, and she knew it. It was foolish as well, and yet the feelings would not leave her.

The tide of guests ebbed for a bit, and Devon and Rosalind were able to finally make their way out onto the terrace. After the combined heat of bodies and scores of candles, the cool night air was entirely welcome. Rosalind and Devon were not the only couple seeking relief, and enough quiet so that they did not have to shout to be heard. Several others strolled back and forth along the carved stone railing or ventured into the garden below.

"Now, do we still make small talk?" Devon inquired drily. "Or have we proceeded beyond that stage?"

Rosalind felt her pulse beating softly at the base of her throat and found she was suddenly very aware of how comfortable it was to have Devon's arm under her hand. "I think I'd prefer small talk for now."

"Would you care to pour out for us?"

Rosalind laughed. "Let us see what is left in the pot. Ah. I know. Louisa seems very happy."

"She is."

"And I take it you approve of the groom?"

"Aunt Showell approves, and I wouldn't dare to try to stand against her. But, for what it's worth, I do like the fellow. He's young, but he's got sense and some ambition, and he genuinely adores Louisa. His parents are proving civil and reasonable, and the settlements are all going well." Louisa's family did not spring from a prosperous branch of the Winterbournes, and Devon was shouldering the cost of her dowry.

"I'm glad of it." Rosalind paused, and searched for the next unexceptional remark. She was aware that Devon was smiling at her and felt a fresh blush rise, which annoyed her.

They reached the end of the terrace, and turned together. As they did, movement caught Rosalind's eye. A gentleman had emerged from the ballroom and was making his way straight to them.

A moment later, she recognized him.

Oh, but of course. He was on the guest list. Along with five hundred other people, so it was not surprising the name should have slipped her mind. It was not only Louisa's friends and their families who were invited tonight, but persons of social and political consequence to the Casselmaine title and the Winterbourne family.

Still, she thought, *Considering the circumstances, I should have remembered William Lamb might be here tonight.* She felt Devon's arm shift under her hand. *Well, perhaps not. Under the circumstance.*

Mr. Lamb reached them, and bowed.

"Lamb." Devon and Lamb shook hands. "I'm glad you could come. How are you?"

"Very well, thank you, m'lord. Just wanted to offer felicitations to you and your cousin. All according to plan, eh?"

"My aunt's plan, certainly. Still, everyone seems pleased."

"And you'll be glad to be done with the expense."

Everyone laughed. Mr. Lamb's attention turned to Miss Thorne, and he bowed. "How do you do, Miss Thorne? Mother said you were going to be here tonight. I'm sorry I couldn't be on hand to escort you myself."

Another man might have made the remark sound suspicious, or even insinuating, but Mr. Lamb said it openly and casually, confident that everybody in the conversation was well informed of all the facts.

Devon's brows lifted. "Do you know Miss Thorne?"

"She's stopping at the house. Guest of mother's," said Lamb. "Likewise, I didn't realize you knew Lord Casselmaine, Miss Thorne?"

"I've been helping Mrs. Showell with her planning for Miss Winterbourne's engagement," responded Rosalind. If Mr. Lamb noted her hand on Devon's arm, and took into account the fact that they had lingered in the semiprivacy of the terrace for what must be considered a long time for the host at such an event, he was too much of a gentleman to remark on it.

And yet, he did note it all, and closely. Rosalind felt certain of that, and her certainty left her disquieted.

"Well, Miss Thorne, you do manage to keep yourself busy. No, no." Lamb held up his hand. "Sorry. Phrased that badly. Personally, I think many of us could use more occupation than we have. Boredom leads to so much mischief."

"That explains the bills that've been coming to the floor of late," said Devon. "Drafted during the depths of winter when everybody's bored off their heads."

"Ha! Exactly. Speaking of bills, sir . . ."

"Hold up a minute, Lamb, I expect this will be a long conversation. Can I find you later?"

Mr. Lamb's open, amiable gaze settled again on Rosalind, but only for a moment, and of course not in any way that could be considered insulting or even overly curious. "Yes, yes indeed, if you would. Or I can call 'round tomorrow if that would suit you better?"

"I'll find you."

"Thank you, sir. Your servant, Miss Thorne." William Lamb made his parting bow and ambled away, disappearing entirely amid the knots of gentlemen all in black and white.

"You're stopping at Melbourne House?" Devon asked Rosalind as they continued on.

"You hadn't heard? I asked Louisa to tell you in the letter I wrote her when I accepted Lady Melbourne's invitation."

Devon greeted this bit of news with a stoic expression. "I think perhaps it slipped everybody's mind. They've been very busy. I take it this is one of your particular visits?"

"Yes, it is."

They had reached the terrace stairs. By unspoken agreement, this time they descended to the lawn, but that was as far as they could properly go. The length of their friendly stroll was limited by the brightest torchlight and the shifting tide of guests.

"How are you finding the famous Melbournes?" Devon looked out across the gardens. All the torches were lit, and guests strolled up and down the gravel paths between the terrace and the Italian marble fountain that had been turned on full in honor of the festivities.

She searched for some answer she could make in a conversation that was, after all, only partially private. "Confusing," she admitted at last, remembering the bank draft that was still locked in her desk drawer at Little Russell Street. "Unsettling. Lady Melbourne is very . . . considerate, but . . ."

"Yes. But," agreed Devon seriously.

They had reached the edge of the lawn. Rosalind turned to look back at the house. The ballroom windows shone white and gold in the darkness. The rest of the house stretched out beyond the range of her vision, as solid and dark as a thundercloud.

"What are you thinking?" Devon asked.

"I am thinking about parties and houses," Rosalind said quietly. "I am thinking about how on a night like this, a house can be filled with people but almost entirely empty."

"I'm not sure I understand."

"Five hundred and three people," said Rosalind. "That's how many people were on Louisa's guest list, and most of them have come. And yet they're all crowded into perhaps four rooms. The rest of the house is quite empty, because all the servants are here, or in the kitchens. Anything could happen in those empty rooms, and no one would know."

"Should I ask why it is you're thinking about this particular thing now?"

Rosalind tipped her head back to look at the stars. She found quite suddenly she did not want to talk about the Melbournes and their troubles anymore.

"We've been here before," she remarked. "Just like this."

"Now we have reached a point in common." Devon smiled. "I was thinking something similar."

"That summer ball your mother gave."

"Her last attempt to get Hugh married. I tried to tell her it wouldn't work." He paused. "I might have tried harder, if I hadn't known you'd be invited."

They'd snuck away then. Laughing. Teasing. Daring each other to go out just a little bit farther, looking back over their shoulders as they darted forward just a few steps more, waiting to see if they were being watched yet.

Trying to see how far they could get into the shadows.

Not far at all, as it turned out. Rosalind's mother caught them. Mother could wield courtesy like a steel blade. She was perfectly polite to the second son of Casselmaine and yet somehow managed to slice him to ribbons before she took hold of Rosalind's elbow with two fingers and led her back inside.

She'd had the bruise for a week.

Mother was gone now, her heart and mind broken by her husband's abandonment. Father also was gone, although he still drew breath. He was kept close in a country retreat where the house and attendants were paid for by Charlotte's efforts. This time the only thing that stopped Rosalind from stepping into the twilight with Devon was Rosalind herself.

"It is good to see you again, Rosalind," Devon said. "We haven't been able to spend much time together since last season."

"You chose to stay in the country until the last minute."
This is not what I want to say. Why can't I say what I want?
"Yes. I could plead estate business, but it wouldn't be true.
I wanted time to think." Devon folded his hands together be-
hind his back, and he too looked up at the sky.

"Rosalind?" he whispered, as if he needed to speak to
Heaven in order for her to hear him.

"I know what you're going to ask." She spoke to the sky.
She picked out the Great Bear, Orion, and Polaris. "And no,
your attentions are not unwelcome."

"But are they welcome?" He attempted to soften the words
with a smile. "Being active in Parliament, you see, is teaching
me the fine points of debate."

Rosalind felt her pulse pounding hard enough that she
feared the onset of the dreaded headache. She told herself not
to be ridiculous. She was not a fainting debutante anymore.
She could interrogate her own heart and her own life without
hysterics.

She could acknowledge that some corner of her heart had
always been reserved for the man beside her. She could, and
she would, look squarely at the attractions of Mr. Harkness,
which were not limited to his bright eyes but included his understanding and acceptance of her living. And more. He fully
trusted her and her abilities.

That trust was different from any emotion, any desire, that
had ever been expressed to her by any other man. Devon
tried to extend something similar, but he struggled.

*Do I hold that against him? That he needs time to learn
and understand?*

If that was true, it did not speak well of her.

But there was nothing simple about Devon either, nor the
attraction of him. The enticement, and the difficulty, of Devon
Winterbourne came from the same source. Devon, Lord
Casselmaine, represented absolute security, as well as long-

standing affection and that particular kind of independence that came with elevated position. If she married him, she would no longer have to consider how women such as Lady Jersey, or even Lady Melbourne, viewed her. In the space of a single morning, Miss Rosalind Thorne could become Lady Winterbourne, Duchess of Casselmaine. With that change, the world would turn upside down.

I will not marry him for the title. I will not do that to either of us. To any of us, she corrected herself. *Because I am not the only one whose life is changed if I say yes to Devon. There is still Charlotte.*

Charlotte, her sister, whom she had found again only a few months ago.

"I have an invitation for you," said Devon suddenly.

Rosalind closed her eyes. "I'm sorry, Devon, I don't think I can make it through a dance right now."

"It's not a dance."

"I'm not doing very well today, am I?" Rosalind smiled wanly.

"Believe it or not, I'm highly encouraged. This invitation is to come out early to Casselmaine." Casselmaine was the ducal estate. Rosalind had never been there. "Aunt Showell was planning on asking you as soon as you two had finished what needs to be done here in London, but I wanted you to know the invitation is mine as well as hers."

So he could court her, again. Quietly, away from prying eyes and from the worry and scramble that was Rosalind's life. He was offering her a month or more of security and peace, a space of time when she could make up her own mind.

Of course she didn't need him for that. All she needed to do was to take the draft that Lady Melbourne had given her to the bank. Then she would have her own peace, without the inherent complexity that came with accepting an invitation from Devon.

That she was conflating Devon's invitation with an attempt to buy her loyalty, even in the privacy of her own thoughts, made the ground shift beneath Rosalind's feet.

What am I becoming?

"Let me finish with my visit to Lady Melbourne first," she said. "Then I'll answer you."

I'll find some way to end this.

He took her hand and raised it to his lips. She watched him, and she did not see the Lord Casselmaine. She saw Devon—her friend, her first love, the good man who struggled with whom he had been forced to become, even as she did.

"Thank you," Devon said, and Rosalind felt a fresh piece of her heart crumble away.

"Rosalind!" A familiar and urgent voice broke through all their tension, and the illusion of privacy fell away like broken glass.

Alice, thought Rosalind. *Oh, thank heavens.*

"There you are!" Alice glided up to her, maybe a little too quickly. She also threaded her arm tightly through Rosalind's. "Excuse me, your grace," Alice said to Devon. "I must steal her away."

Devon made a sound somewhere between a laugh and sigh. "Hello again, Alice. How are you enjoying yourself?"

"Very much, thank you. Everything is magnificent. I apologize for George. He was unavoidably detained, but I promise you Mrs. Showell will be delighted with her write-up in Sunday's edition. Come along, Rosalind." Alice yanked hard on Rosalind's arm.

With Devon chuckling behind them, Rosalind let herself be dragged away through the ballroom.

"Alice! What on earth is the matter?" she exclaimed as soon as they were out of earshot.

"I had to get you away from Devon."

"Why!"

"There." Alice pointed through a gap in the crowd. Rosalind followed with her gaze, and her mouth rounded into an O.

Because standing just inside the ballroom doors, looking painfully uncomfortable in black coat and white breeches, stood Adam Harkness.

CHAPTER 28

The Attractions Of The Ballroom

*I can't make out . . . what your melancholy—&
mysterious apprehensions tend to—or refer to—
whether to Caroline Lamb's novels—Mrs.
Clermont's evidence—Lady Byron's magnanim-
ity—or any other piece of imposture.*

George Gordon, Lord Byron, private correspondence

Rosalind's first feeling was one of relief. Mr. Harkness was whole and well, if a bit discomforted by his surroundings. Her relief, however, did not last.

Why is he here? His name most definitely had not been on the guest list. That, she would have remembered. *Something's happened.*

Rosalind gathered her hems a fraction of an inch higher. A moment ago, Alice had been tugging her along; now Alice was struggling to keep up.

"Do you need me with you?" said Alice. "Or should I go distract Devon?"

"Thank you, Alice." Mr. Harkness was not in his working clothes and red vest, but in formal attire—a black coat, blue waistcoat, and white breeches with white stockings and buckled shoes. None of them fit particularly well, and he held himself as one conscious of this fact. *If there was some genuine threat, he would not have dressed for the ballroom.* "I think I can manage Mr. Harkness."

"I'm sure you can. As you can manage Devon. Alone. But tog—"

"But they are not together. *Thank you,* Alice."

Alice shrugged, clearly a little irritated at Rosalind's tone. "Well. Should you change your mind, you may find me with the refreshments. And Lady Thomas. She said she had something *most* particular to pass on to A.E. Littlefield."

Alice separated their arms and took herself off to her professional tête-à-tête. Rosalind was sure she did not imagine her friend's nose as lifting ever so slightly in the air.

I will have to apologize.

That apology, however, would need to come later. Rosalind took a steadying breath and crossed the last several yards to the doorway.

"Mr. Harkness!" she cried with a good imitation of a hostess's easy delight at the arrival of a friend. "Good evening! I'm afraid I wasn't told you'd been invited."

He bowed, a smooth, spare motion that made him look much more himself. "I wasn't. Bow Street in the person of Mr. John Townsend was. He could not attend, as he was called to duty with the royal dukes tonight. I'm under orders to present myself on the station's behalf, and to make every possible apology for our second-rate showing."

Rosalind smiled. "Well then, we'd better get that out of the way at once. I see our hostess. Shall I take you to her?"

"I'd be most grateful."

Mrs. Showell was perfectly gracious in her reception of Mr. Harkness, as Rosalind had known she would be. She was also perfectly charmed by his frankness, and his blue eyes. Mr. Harkness had that effect on ladies.

"Now, I'm afraid I must leave you with our very good and

capable Miss Thorne. Wilford is trying to get my attention. We may be running short on the wine again. Dear me, I'm afraid Casselmaine's cellar will be a long time recovering from us! Please do enjoy yourself." Mrs. Showell hurried away, looking genuinely flustered. Rosalind felt a twinge of guilt. She really should be helping more rather than indulging herself with Devon and confusing ideas about her possible future.

First, though, there was Mr. Harkness and all the business he represented. Rosalind sighed inwardly and remembered her early thoughts about beauty and intricacy and gloss.

"Shall we take a turn about the room, Mr. Harkness? I've some things to ask you."

Mr. Harkness surveyed the room with every appearance of casualness, but Rosalind knew he was drinking in its details. "I'm sorry, Miss Thorne. That might not be the best idea. You see, my superior, Mr. Townsend, has . . . expressed some reservations about my being the one to conduct the inquiries about the matter of Judith Oslander. He's taken me out of the inquiry until I learn to behave properly."

"Oh," breathed Rosalind. "I see. Which would be the reason my recent letter came from the patrol captain, Mr. Goutier, rather than from you."

He nodded once but kept his gaze on the ballroom itself. Rosalind understood this tactic, and emulated it, gesturing to this person and that as he spoke. To anyone who watched them, it would appear that they were speaking about the other guests as they passed, a perfectly casual and natural conversation and a way of familiarizing him with his surroundings.

Given the general level of noise, someone would have to get quite close to know what they were actually talking about.

"Station politics, Miss Thorne, are just as messy as any other kind. I will tell you that Mr. Townsend doesn't yet know that you are at Melbourne House, or that Melbourne House is tied up with Mrs. Judith Oslander's death. However, he does know something is being kept from him, and he doesn't like it. He has not yet made up his mind what to do, but we may not have much more time before he learns what is truly going on. If we do not have enough answers to justify our actions before then . . ." Mr. Harkness did not finish the sentence. But Rosalind did not need to hear. Mr. Townsend had power and he had influence. If he was driven to anger, he would use them both, and not just against Mr. Harkness. John Townsend had taken a cordial dislike to Rosalind the last time they met. On one level, Rosalind understood why he should object to her. She was, after all, an untrained person, and female to boot, and had nothing to do with law or civil service. Despite this, Rosalind found she could not muster much sympathy for him.

But neither she nor Mr. Harkness had anything to gain by further rousing Mr. Townsend's suspicions.

Rosalind nodded. "I will do everything I can."

"I know that you will. In the meantime, let me assure you, you can trust Sampson Goutier absolutely."

"Thank you, Mr. Harkness. And you, or he, might want to speak with Sanderson Faulks as soon as you are able. He has some information about Mr. Scrope Berdmore Davies." *He's in debt, and he may have stolen the letters, or had them stolen to force Lord Byron into repayment.*

She wanted to tell him right now. For a moment, she considered taking the risk. They were not particularly observed. With their backs to the wall as they were, it was unlikely they could be casually overheard. But no. There were names that could turn heads. There were friends and acquaintances who would want to know who this gentleman was, and find out if there was anything new to talk over, especially since Rosalind had just left the company of Lord Casselmaine.

Where is Devon? Rosalind scanned the ballroom but did not find him. Perhaps he had gone to find Mr. Lamb.

"Has Mr. Goutier been to Mrs. Oslander's rooms yet?"

"He intended to go tonight, but his patrol was called out on a housebreaking. He tells me he will go in the morning."

"I hope we are not too late."

"Are you concerned someone has gotten there before us?"

"It is possible. But what concerns me most is that Mr. Goutier's letter said that Mrs. Oslander may have been missing for some time. If her landlord decided that Mrs. Oslander left to avoid the rent, they might have seized her things."

"Seized or sold," murmured Mr. Harkness.

"Yes."

They stood in silence for a moment, considering this and looking over the glittering celebration. Rosalind saw Louisa standing beside her fiancé, a broad, cheerful youth who held her hand as if he thought it might break and had spent the evening alternating between looking stunned at his good fortune and looking as if he'd just been crowned emperor.

"It might be useful if you could come with us," said Mr. Harkness. "To Mrs. Oslander's. You've a knack for understanding a woman's life and unearthing her particular secrets. I think the search might go more quickly if you were with us."

And time is short. Neither one of them had to say it out loud.

"As it happens," murmured Rosalind, "Lady Melbourne is not at home tomorrow, so I should be able to make an excuse to get away, at least for a while." The excuse would not, of course, be for Lady Melbourne, who knew her business, but for anyone else who might be watching. Like Claridge. Or Lady Caroline.

Or Mr. Lamb.

"Excellent," said Mr. Harkness. "There's a house in Kentish Town, No. 12 Wolverton Mews, hard by the lock on the new canal. Do you think you could find it?"

Rosalind lifted one brow. "I think so."

"We will meet you there at one, if all goes well."

She smiled and he smiled, and she opened her fan and plied it. He understood. "Now, Miss Thorne, as glad as I am to spend a minute in friendly company, perhaps I'd better take my leave. I strongly suspect Mr. Townsend will be quizzing his acquaintance on how I behaved tonight, and whom I spoke with, and for how long."

"Well, then, allow me to suggest that you begin your campaign of charming the *haut ton* by going to say hello to Alice Littlefield? She's in the refreshment room just now. If you go quickly, you might still catch her with Lady Thomas Epping. Lady Thomas knows everyone and invites them all to her dinners. If you can make her acquaintance, you will probably be presented to half of the *ton* before the evening's out."

"I think I would rather spend the evening hiding behind a hedge waiting for highwaymen."

"Say that to Lady Thomas, and your success is assured. She'll find it terribly daring and amusing. Good luck, Mr. Harkness."

He took her hand and bowed over it. Surely she only imagined the soft warmth of his breath against her fingers. She could not really feel it through her satin gloves. She did catch his eye as he straightened, and it was much harder than it should have been to turn away.

As she did, Rosalind once again caught sight of the Honorable Mr. William Lamb. He stood in the center of the grand staircase, his hands folded behind his back, looking right down through the doors into the ballroom and at Rosalind.

How long have you been there watching? Why are you there at all?

But even as this thought flickered through her, Mr. Lamb turned away to greet another gentleman who descended the stairs. Rosalind took up her hems and retreated more deeply into the bustle of the ballroom. She also tried to reproach herself for unreasonably allowing such a cold sensation to creep slowly up her spine.

Somehow, though, she couldn't quite manage it.

CHAPTER 29

The Possibility Of Advancement

*When men begin to speak of duty, they have
ceased to love . . .*

Lady Caroline Lamb, Glenarvon

Sampson Goutier tossed his hat onto the bench in the patrol room, leaned forward so his elbows were planted on his knees, and scrubbed his head with both hands.

God Almighty, he ached. His knuckles were bruised. So were his ribs. He straightened up and winced.

Please let it be just a bruise, he prayed to whichever saint might be on duty to look after patrol captains in the cold hours just before dawn.

He should have been home hours ago. But Captain Haslipp's girl had come round to say her dad was sick with a fever, which meant there was no one to lead his patrol tonight. So Goutier had sent the girl to tell Sal not to wait supper and took charge himself.

Goutier leaned back against the wall carefully. The horses were wiped down, fed, and stabled. The men were sent home to their own beds. He just had to write a note or two in Stafford's book, about where they'd been and what they'd seen, sign his initials to it, and he'd be on his way, too.

But it seemed that whatever saint God had assigned to the night watch was asleep, or getting himself a cup of tea, because there was the sound of a door opening back in the ward room.

"Mr. Goutier!" cried Mr. Townsend with the joviality of a man who was used to keeping society hours. He was in white satin breeches and a black coat. The rumpled strip of linen that had been his cravat hung loose about his neck. "What's kept you here, sir?"

By the time Goutier turned, he had a pleased smile fixed on his face. "Mr. Townsend! I did not expect you, sir. It was a dispute between neighbors. Turned into a brawl. Seems some of the sons of the houses were determined to settle a score or two. Windows got broken, some heads as well. Took the boys a while to calm it all down and sort it out. I'll have the report to you . . ."

Townsend waved off the end of his sentence. "It will get done in good time, I've no doubt. But you look all in. Will you take a drink with me?"

Goutier pictured Sal turning over in their bed, peeling an eye open, and finding him still gone. "I'd be glad of one, sir. Thank you."

The lamp was already lit in Mr. Townsend's private office, and the coals in the hearth glowed red beneath their bed of ashes. While Goutier settled himself gingerly into a chair, Townsend opened one of his cabinets and brought out a crystal decanter and two delicate glasses.

"Now, this is something to savor, sir. This bottle was given to me by His Royal Highness the Prince of Wales at Christmas." Townsend poured out two generous measures and handed Goutier one glass. "Your health, sir."

"And yours, sir."

Both men raised their glasses and drank. Townsend dropped himself into his own chair behind his desk and crossed his legs.

I'm sorry, Sal. I'll be home as quick as I can. Goutier took another small drink and did his best to shove his exhaustion and his spreading aches into the back of his mind. "How did things go tonight at the theater, sir?"

Townsend smiled. "Well, Mr. Goutier, I think I may say we put on an excellent showing. The theater was filled, and the crowd displayed their affection for the royal dukes most liberally. Insisted they bow, not once, but many times. Mr. Keane made a most humble and eloquent address from the stage. Indeed, I saw a tear in the Duke of Kent's eye. And we caught ourselves two pickpockets," he added, hoisting his glass and drinking once more. "His Royal Highness the Duke of York shook my hand. 'Townsend,' he said. 'I don't know what any of us would do without your watchful eye.' Yes." He smiled at the memory. "That's what he said. Worth being proud of, wouldn't you agree, Mr. Goutier?"

"Indeed, sir." *What do you want from me, old man? Why are we here?*

"Now, tell me how this business for Sir David is going."

Ah. "We've found out the dead woman's name. She was Judith Oslander. She was a nurse, on the books of an agency run by a Mrs. MacKennan."

"Very good. Very good. What else?"

Goutier considered. "She appears to have been robbed, I'm afraid. She had no coat or gloves or bag or pocket with her."

Townsend pursed his lips. "A shame. And no family?"

"None that we've been able to trace so far."

"Does Sir David think that she was killed in the robbery? Perhaps on her way home from her posting?"

Goutier swirled the brandy and considered again.

"That could indeed be what happened," said Goutier. "Save for the fact that she died by poison, not by a blow to the head or any such, which is what I'd expect from a footpad or hooligan."

Townsend considered this. "Poison, you say?"

"Laudanum, Sir David tells us." Goutier raised his glass again. "Mixed with brandy."

"Poor soul," murmured Mr. Townsend. "Lured to a carriage house or tavern, perhaps, put off her guard with drink."

"I shouldn't be at all surprised to find out that's just what it is. There's one or two more questions to ask—at the agency, with her landlady. Then I'm sure we'll be done and be able to report to Sir David."

"Well done, Goutier." Mr. Townsend nodded and polished off his brandy. "I want you to know I've my eye on you, sir. I approve of a man who does his duty in a workman-like fashion. No drama, no distraction. All the men speak well of you, and the officers. Mr. Harkness, for instance, personally recommended you to take on Sir David's inquiry."

Goutier took another drink but made no answer. He needed to step carefully. It was easy to see Mr. Townsend wanted something, and it was even easier to see that the thing wasn't going to be any good when it came.

"What do you think of Mr. Harkness?" Townsend asked.

"I think he's a fine officer," said Goutier. "He does his duty. He has the respect of his men. He's got a good eye and a good mind and is as honest a man as I've ever met."

"But is he a smart man?"

"Sir?"

Townsend smiled. "A smart man has priorities, Goutier. He understands the way of the world. He knows there's more to duty than laying hands on individual lawbreakers." Townsend stretched his legs out in front of himself and rolled the brandy glass back and forth in his long hands. "We're charged with keeping the peace, Goutier, with making sure that order is maintained. That's a different charge and a far greater charge than solving this riddle or that." Those long hands stilled the glass, and Townsend cocked his head toward Goutier. "Do you see what I'm getting at, Mr. Goutier?"

"I do, sir."

"After all, we've seen what happens when order breaks down. You've seen it." Townsend pointed at him. "You were in Paris as a boy, were you not?"

"I was born after the worst of it," he said. "And my parents crossed the channel before Napoleon took over."

"But can you imagine what it would be if those forces of bloody revolution, those forces that killed a *king*, came to ravage our home here?"

Now's probably not the time to mention that you English have killed a king or two in your time. "It doesn't bear thinking about, sir."

It was as noncommittal an answer as Goutier could imagine, but Townsend took it for enthusiastic agreement. "No, sir! It decidedly does not! So, as officers it is our duty to keep our eyes on those larger ideals—quiet order and the king's peace. As His Majesty's subjects and servants, *that* is where our duty lies. Mr. Goutier, I worry that sometimes Mr. Harkness, for all he is a good and loyal officer, is liable to forget that."

Goutier took another slow swallow of brandy. "Surely you don't suspect Mr. Harkness of being a radical, sir?"

"Oh, no, no, no! Of course not! Although . . ." Townsend paused and stared out the window, where the dawn was slowly turning the sky silver above the rooftops. Already lines of workmen trooped up the street, some with bundles or pickaxes on their shoulders, some pushing their barrows. "If there were any such signs in him, it'd be you who'd be in a position to see it first."

Goutier looked into his empty brandy glass.

"Let me refill that for you, Goutier." Townsend poured out another measure. "It's on all of us to preserve Bow Street's reputation. There's only so much I can do on my own. I need to be sure of my men, particularly my principal officers." He touched the side of his nose. "A position, I may say, sir, that is not out of reach for an intelligent man, a man who understands what we truly have to lose and what we truly have to defend. Now." He tossed back his own brandy. "I expect you'd much rather be in bed than listening to me ramble. A very good night to you, Mr. Goutier, and I don't want to see you back here before noon. That's a direct order, sir!"

Which left Goutier no option but to gulp down the drink and get to his feet as steadily as he could. "Thank you, Mr. Townsend."

"Send my greetings, and my apologies to Mrs. Goutier."

"I'll do that, sir. She's a good woman. She knew what she was getting when she married a Bow Street man."

"Marriage is good for a man. Keeps him focused on what's really important in life." Townsend beamed. "And I think I may count on you to keep me up-to-date about any further developments? Anything that might be useful? You've made an excellent impression on me, Goutier. A most excellent impression."

Goutier bowed and let Mr. Townsend clap him on his shoulder. Then he took himself out into the very welcome cold of London's dawn

Well, Sal. Wonder what you're going to have to say to all this? He swung his arms over his head unthinkingly, and winced and grabbed at his injured ribs. Not even the brandy could muffle the pain there.

"Damn," he gasped. "Damn housebreakers all, and damn Mr. Townsend with them."

His plan had been to spend the day making inquiries at the agency that employed Mrs. Oslander and then searching her rooms and questioning her landlady, assuming she had a landlady. That is, after he'd been home to show Sal he was still among the living with a (mostly) whole skin and slept long enough that she stopped shoving him back into the bed.

But what with all Mr. Townsend had said, it was looking like he'd better go hunt up Mr. Harkness so they could have themselves their own little talk, someplace other than the station.

After all, sir, Goutier thought toward the window where Mr. Townsend was surely watching, *we wouldn't want to disturb the proper order of things.*

CHAPTER 30

An Early Morning Meeting

Such a monster as that has no sex, and should live no longer.

George Gordon, Lord Byron, private correspondence

"Three of the clock and all's well! Three of the clock and all's well!"

The watchman's call startled Rosalind out of her doze. Overhead, Ormande clucked to the horses, and the carriage slowed its rhythmic sway, turning as it went. Rosalind peered around the curtain edge and saw the entrance of Melbourne House come into view.

She nudged Mrs. Kendricks, whose gentle snore broke into a snort as she started awake.

"Yes, miss," she murmured, and blinked. Rosalind smiled in sympathy.

Rosalind did not know the footman who was on duty to open the door and take charge of Rosalind's things. Mrs. Kendricks took up the extra lamp from the table and led the way up the stairs. Rosalind could feel the marble step's cold straight through the thin soles of her slippers, and her tired feet cramped up against it. The only thing that kept her climbing was awareness that her bed waited at the top.

But as they passed the first floor, Rosalind caught a glimmer of light out of the corner of her eye. She was too tired to keep her head from turning, and she saw the bright glow of lamplight shining under one of the doors.

"Who is awake at this hour?" she murmured.

Mrs. Kendricks blinked. "I believe that is Lady Caroline's writing room."

Lady Caroline? Rosalind raised her hand to rub her eyes, but at the last second remembered her gloves, and her light dusting of cosmetics, and lowered it again. She was exhausted. Her scalp itched from the gentle scrape of the pins holding her hair in place. It would be dawn soon. She wanted to retreat to her bed and stay there until noon, at least. But could she afford to miss a chance—any chance—to speak privately with Lady Caroline?

Rosalind sighed and handed Mrs. Kendricks her fan and reticule. "Go to bed, Mrs. Kendricks. It appears I need to stay up a bit longer."

Rosalind smoothed her skirts and turned down the gallery. She did not look back to see whether Mrs. Kendricks obeyed, or what her opinion of this change of program might be. She just positioned herself in front of the door and raised her hand to knock.

The moment her knuckles touched the wood, the door drifted open.

After the dark of the gallery, the writing room appeared as brightly lit as the Casselmaine ballroom. Four lamps blazed on four tables, and a fire leapt high and fierce in the hearth. A fresh sheen of perspiration formed on Rosalind's brow and palms.

Lady Caroline's writing room was a graceful chamber, with a beautifully painted ceiling and arched windows hung with velvet draperies. Another door hung open to reveal a small connecting room that held a comfortable-looking daybed and settle.

Both chambers were in a single state of absolute disaster.

Paper had been strewn across every surface and even drifted across the floor into the connecting room and the daybed. Books had been taken from their shelves to be stacked on top of the paper, or replaced backward and upside down and every which way.

Lady Caroline sat at the chipped and ink-stained desk, bent close over her paper. A loose, plain wrapper had been flung hastily over her nightdress. She scribbled furiously with a silver pen, scattering so much ink across the page, Rosalind wondered how she would be able to read anything afterward.

"So, you have returned to us, Miss Thorne," Lady Caroline said without looking up or pausing in her frantic writing. "I'm afraid I have no time to exchange witty banter and gossip about your evening. As you can see, the muse has taken hold of me."

"I'm sorry to disturb you and your inspiration, but I was very much hoping we might speak privately."

Lady Caroline reared back, stared at her page, dipped her pen in the inkwell, crossed out an entire line, and began a fresh one underneath. "About what?"

"Lady Melbourne's inability to retain household staff."

At last, Lady Caroline turned to look at her. There was nothing left in her manner of the sorrow or the opium-assisted vagueness Rosalind had seen before. Instead, her eyes narrowed in an expression of keen interest and suspicion.

A drop of ink fell from the tip of her pen to the paper. Lady Caroline ignored it. "I'm sure my mother-in-law did not authorize you to make any such inquiry."

"Nonetheless."

Another drop of ink fell. Lady Caroline looked to the pen, as if she could not understand how she came to be holding such an object. She laid it down in its tray and studied it there. "And how may I know that you will not run off tattling to her?"

"By the fact that you know she does not want me to ask, and yet here I am."

Lady Caroline leaned back, regarding Rosalind carefully. Dots of ink stood out amid the freckles on her cheeks. She did not invite Rosalind to sit, or extend any other courtesy. She just fell into a contemplative stillness.

All at once, Lady Caroline burst into motion. She darted across the room, shoved the door shut, seized Rosalind's hand, and drew her to the sofa, pushing her down with a hand on her shoulder so that she must sit or be toppled. Paper crinkled underneath Rosalind's skirt. Lady Caroline looked at Rosalind there and, seemingly satisfied with the tableau she presented, made to sit herself down. Something else struck her, though, and she darted back to the writing desk. She swept the papers she had been working at so diligently into a heap and deposited that heap into a drawer, which she locked with a key attached to a chain on her wrist.

Only once Lady Caroline had tugged on the drawer to be sure it was securely fastened did she come and plop herself down on the sofa, knee to knee with Rosalind.

"Tell me quickly, Miss Thorne. The door may not stay locked. Even at such an hour, I am not permitted my privacy. What do you know?"

"I know a woman named Judith Oslander was a nurse here, and that she is no longer."

"Yes, yes, and?" Lady Caroline leaned closer, alight with eagerness. "And!"

"I know that she was murdered."

Lady Caroline closed her enormous eyes, let out a long slow breath, and collapsed backward on the sofa. "Thank the merciful Heavens!"

CHAPTER 31

Lady Caroline's Story

What 'tis she may tell or what she may know or
pretend to know—is to me indifferent.

George Gordon, Lord Byron, private correspondence

That response was something of a surprise, even coming from Lady Caroline. Before Rosalind could trust herself to calmly ask what was meant, Lady Caroline's eyes popped open and she pushed herself upright.

"I was desperate to tell someone, but I did not know who. I was afraid, you see, of what they might do or say about me. I was . . . I am ashamed of that, but I have no heart left to me. It has all been drained away, you see? They have left a hollow doll where poor Caro used to be."

"Hollow dolls do not write books," said Rosalind.

Lady Caroline's cheeks turned a bright and sudden pink. "You are kind, Miss Thorne. Oh, I do wish we could be friends! But never you mind that. We must speak of Mrs. Oslander now, not me. She was our nurse, and my nurse, for a time. I had a fever. I was allowed to stay in here, because it is my room alone and there would be less risk of contagion. My son, Augustus—you have seen—he is not strong." She seized Rosalind's hand. Her fingers felt weak and delicate. "Mrs. Oslander was a *spy*, Miss Thorne."

Rosalind did not bother to question whether this might be true. "Who did she spy for?"

Lady Caroline stared. "My mother-in-law, the Lady Melbourne Almighty, who else? I woke from my nap early one day and I found her rooting about through my desk!" She flung one hand out toward that much abused piece of furniture. "In my most private papers! I sprang from my bed at once and pushed her away. We struggled. Of course she was the stronger. I am very weak, and I was ill. . . . She pushed me back into my bed and she leaned over me. I remember the smell of her, and the way her nose twitched . . . her great pale mouth . . ." Lady Caroline shuddered.

"She told me I must behave. She did not want to have to tell the others I could not behave. They would believe her, you see." Lady Caroline peered suspiciously at Rosalind's face again. "Like you do."

Rosalind struggled to master her expression. It was vital that she remain calm and impartial, or Lady Caroline might decide to stop talking. "I do not know what I believe yet."

"Perhaps. Perhaps not. Sometimes I do not know what I believe yet." Lady Caroline got to her feet. Another person might have begun to pace, but Lady Caroline *flitted*. She moved lightly, randomly from the sofa to the desk, to the windows, to the bookshelves. She touched things briefly and peered in every direction.

Like a canary in a cage when it knows the cat is watching.

Lady Caroline's nervousness was contagious. Rosalind wanted to plead with her to, please, just be still a moment. Then Rosalind caught a fresh glimpse of the haunted look in her eyes. It occurred to her that Lady Caroline wanted to be still, but she could not.

Because she knows the cat is watching, thought Rosalind again. *Or at least fears she is and she cannot bring her fears under control.*

"Lady Melbourne liked Mrs. Oslander, you see," Lady

Caroline went on. "She was steady and competent. Also very good at hiding and obeying and watching. Exactly the kind of spy my mother-in-law adores."

Round and round went Lady Caroline. From the desk, to the door, to a book, to the desk again and the window, to the book, and the hearth, and back again.

"I know, Miss Thorne, that I do not behave as a lady should. There are those who believe that since I cannot obey the rules, I do not understand them, you see? That is not true. I know them all by heart, and yet I still cannot take them *to* heart. I do wish my heart were not as it is. I wish it was like other people's. I wish I was a good woman. I know that my husband loves me more than I love him, and I do try. But with such a heart as mine, what can I do? William will not take us away and I . . . must try to endure.

"But some nights, even if I have had all my medicines, I cannot sleep. I cannot stand to be indoors. I was raised in the country, you see. When I was a girl, I would run and climb and ride all day. But here I am not allowed, not when anyone can see, and there are all the walls, you see? But some nights, I go down to the garden or the courtyard. There I can at least see the sky. Some nights it takes hours to manage even this small escape. I . . ." Lady Caroline stopped in midstride and swallowed, making a massive effort to still her frenetic motion. "That night I did manage it. I went out, just to see the sky and have a little air to breathe when there was no one to scold. That was when I saw her."

"Mrs. Oslander?"

Lady Caroline nodded. "She came staggering across the yard, her hair streaming loose down her back. At first I thought she was laughing. Then I thought she might be the worse for drink, but that was not in her nature. Serious, level-headed people capable of spying for others do not lose themselves to drink."

"Did she see you?" Rosalind asked.

"I did not want to be seen, out in the dark, quite alone, so I hung back, you see? I thought she would simply leave, and I would flee and all would be right again. But she fell, right in front of the gate." Lady Caroline was warming to her narrative now. Her eyes went distant with memory and creation. She was finding the right words to fit to her story, as if she planned it for the page.

"At first, I froze in my terror. I did not know what to do. I willed her to rise, but she did not. I knew I should get someone to help, but who was there who would not betray me? Still, I could not leave her there. I am not entirely without human feeling, no matter what others might say. So, at last, I went forward, and I turned her over and . . ." She shuddered. "Her eyes fell open, and her jaw. Her hands uncurled. She was dead, Miss Thorne, and stared at me with the awful, accusing eyes of the dead.

"I suppose I retreated then. I do not know. I remember bumping up against the wall of the house. I could go no farther. My mind could not force any further obedience from my limbs.

"I do not know how long I stayed there, paralyzed. Then I saw a man bolt across the yard."

"Who was he?"

"I could not see. He was muffled against the damp. He sprinted to Mrs. Oslander and crouched beside her. While he was thus occupied, I fled back to the house and my room." Lady Caroline gripped the sofa arm, shaking from the effort it took to hold herself still. She licked her lips.

Rosalind looked about for some water or other drink and spied a teapot and cup. A quick look showed something left inside it. She poured out the dark and bitter liquid and gave it to Lady Caroline, who gulped it down gratefully. Rosalind watched, wishing there were a second cup. She tried to think calmly. Underneath all those sensational details, Lady Caroline had said something important, but Rosalind could not lay a finger on what it was.

And then, quite suddenly, she could.

"You said Mrs. Oslander's hair was streaming down her back."

Lady Caroline blinked. "Yes. I remember. It was most majestic in the darkness."

"Where was her bonnet? Her coat?"

"She clutched her bonnet in her hand, but she wore no coat. She wore no coat," repeated Lady Caroline. "She must have been so cold. Her hands, like ice, even before. Even before . . ."

"What happened then?" Rosalind asked quickly.

Lady Caroline shook her head and clutched her cup so tightly that Rosalind was afraid the delicate china might shatter in her hands.

"When the morning came, I expected the house to be in an uproar. It was not. No one said a word. Not one. Not even my husband."

"And you said nothing about what you'd seen?"

Lady Caroline's knuckles were turning white. "What could I say? When everyone is keeping secrets some subject, who will listen to Caro? Especially when she has been drifting about the courtyard at night as she should not and now claims to see a woman fall dead at her feet? A woman who has now vanished as surely as the morning mist? And if they do hear, if they do believe, what will they believe of poor, mad Caro?"

Rosalind looked down at her hands, laced tightly together in her lap. She could well understand how Lady Caroline might come to feel this way and could not blame her for it.

"Can you tell me anything about the man? Whether he was tall or short? Stout or thin?"

Lady Caroline shook her head. "I saw a coat with legs. I am sorry."

Rosalind felt her brow furrow. She was so tired. Her thoughts could only wade forward slowly. "Where did he come from?"

"What do you mean?"

"Which direction? Did he come from the house or from the street?"

"Oh. I see. I see." Lady Caroline narrowed her eyes again. One hand waved in the air and her lips moved. After a moment, Rosalind realized she was sketching out the scene in her mind.

"The house!" she cried triumphantly. "The house, and . . ." She swallowed, and what little color she possessed drained from her cheeks. "And perhaps even the door I left open. He could have been anyone. Any servant, any guest, anyone at all . . ."

Rosalind leaned forward and lifted the cup from Lady Caroline's cold fingers. She squeezed her hand gently. "Thank you for your confidence, Lady Caroline."

Lady Caroline looked down at their hands and drew in a long breath. "You will not tell them what I have done? You will be my friend despite all?"

"I hope to be your friend." Silently, Rosalind also hoped this was the truth.

"I knew you would. Oh, I am glad!" Lady Caroline wrapped her in an abrupt embrace. "I will prove true, you will see! You must trust me, and I will be your helpmeet in all your labors!"

"Thank you, Lady Caroline." Rosalind extricated herself as gently as she was able. "But for now I must return to my rooms before anyone begins to wonder about my absence."

"Yes, of course!" Lady Caroline cried. "We must not rouse their suspicions. They must not know we are united to our single purpose now!"

Rosalind hesitated. "Lady Caroline, there is something I have to ask, but I'm afraid you'll be angry with me."

"How could I! We are friends now, united . . ."

"Have you recently sent anything to Mr. Henry Colburn?"

"Where did you hear that?" Rosalind moved to answer, but Lady Caroline did not wait. "They tell lies about me,

Miss Thorne. All of them. Lady Melbourne, the strangers in the newspapers, B . . . Byron. They will say anything about me." She pressed both palms against her temples. "You need to go before they start telling lies about you, too. And I must finish my writing." Her eyes gleamed. "And when *that* is done, I will have something to send to Mr. Colburn." She smiled archly. "Perhaps I will ask you to take it."

"Then I had better get my rest." Rosalind hoped that Lady Caroline did not hear the strain in her voice.

"Yes, yes. Good-night, Miss Thorne. Good night!" Lady Caroline unlocked the door. "Be quick, before someone sees the light!" she hissed.

Rosalind ducked through the door as quickly as she was able. She stood in the gallery and waited for her eyes to adjust to the darkness. After the heat of Lady Caroline's room, the chill made her shiver.

She did not want to think about what she had just heard. Indeed she should not. She was far too tired to make good sense of it. But her thoughts would not still. There were too many possibilities.

The first and foremost was that Lady Caroline might indeed have stolen Lady Melbourne's letters. She would have had ample opportunities to do so. She might have bundled them off to her publisher, a man who understood there was a great deal of money to be made from sensation and scandal.

Such a man might not inquire too closely as to whether Lady Caroline had permission to publish those letters she sent him. He might tell himself it could be assumed, given that she had already been given permission to publish a novel that drew so heavily from very personal sources.

Lady Caroline was not mad, not given to visions, but she was capable of concocting a story to get persons to do what she wanted, even if that person did not entirely believe her.

She was prone to fits of anger that brought down the desire for revenge.

William will not take us away . . . so I must endure . . .

What if Lady Caroline had reached the end of her endurance?

Hectored, confined, conspired against—and not just in her own mind—she might have concluded she had nothing left to lose by letting loose another scandal in Byron's name, if she could ruin Lady Melbourne.

It was plausible. It was even possible. But how did it lead to Judith Oslander's death?

The answer was a simple one. Judith Oslander snuck a look at what she had been given and understood the significance. She decided that she could make some money for herself from the sale of those letters, beyond whatever fee Lady Caroline had offered her. So she had taken one letter as proof, and then . . . what?

Who had she told? What had she done? She had come back. She had planned to meet with someone. Who would that be?

And how does Mr. Davies come to know for certain the letters are gone? Could Lady Caroline have told him what she planned? Or could someone else have done that?

Lady Caroline said Judith Oslander was a spy.

What if she was a spy for Mr. Davies?

CHAPTER 32

A Conspiracy Over Coffee

*... but anything which is to divide us would drive
me quite out of my senses.*

George Gordon, Lord Byron, private correspondence

"**W**ell now, Mr. Goutier!" Harkness heard his mother
exclaim as she opened the door. "Come in and sit
down!"

Goutier took off his hat and ducked his head under the
low beams of the kitchen ceiling. Harkness pushed his empty
pottage bowl away and waved the man to a seat at the broad,
well-scrubbed table.

The Harkness family home was an old one. Half-timbered
with flagstone floors and gabled roofs, a bit of a stoop out
front and a bit of garden behind, it had probably stood in
this street since Good Queen Bess passed this way. During all
that time it had been kept as clean and snug as generations of
Harkness wives and daughters could make it. It was also generally filled to the brim and past it with the next lot of Harknesses.

Just now the tide was at low ebb. Harkness's married sister
and her three children were out in the garden, feeding the geese
and hens. Laughter and scolds, not to mention clucks and

honks, drifted in through the open window. Jenny's husband was away with his ship, and Adam's two younger brothers were out on their apprenticeships—one with a carpenter and the other with a cooper and wheelwright. They'd be back tonight, as they still lived at home, thus saving the Harknesses having to pay for their bed and board with their masters.

When people asked how Harkness managed to keep so calm at his post, he told them it was because when you lived in an old house in the middle of London with as many as ten other people, it took a lot of noise to make you flinch.

"I'll have a bowl of pottage up for you directly." Mrs. Harkness pointed her spoon at the table, an implicit order for Goutier to sit. A widow now, Mother Harkness was a round, bustling woman who wielded her ladle and her tongue with cheerful dispatch. "Have some of that bread as well, and the butter's new."

"Thank you, ma'am." Goutier took the chair Adam nudged out for him. "But I've had my breakfast. Sal wouldn't let me out the door until I'd been fed."

Mother laughed in appreciation. "Your wife's a good woman, and I've always said so. But you'll take a mug of coffee. You've eyes like burned holes in your head."

The description was accurate. Wherever Goutier had been, bed had not been on the list. There were fresh scabs on his knuckles as well, and a bruise turned the brown skin of his right cheek a dark blue. He winced when he sat, too.

"You've been busy," Harkness remarked.

"Wish I could say it was on the right business." Goutier scrubbed his damp head with his hand and winced again. "Or that certain people are not taking an interest."

Mother Harkness set a thick crockery mug in front of Goutier. Even though he clearly needed the stimulating brew, Goutier still sipped gingerly. Harkness smiled. Goutier had some experience with Mother's coffee. It was always hot as the devil, thick enough to stand a spoon in, and strong enough that an incautious man might well not sleep again for a week.

"What's happened?"

Goutier took another sip of coffee, let out a growling sigh, and began to tell Harkness about his chat over Mr. Townsend's brandy in the small hours of the morning.

Harkness spread the new butter on his bread and listened.

Damn.

He should have known. He did know. Townsend had made it plain he intended to bring Harkness to heel. If he couldn't do it one way, he'd do it another. Carefully, of course. No brute force for John Townsend. That wasn't his way.

Mr. Harkness glanced over his shoulder to the hearth, where his mother was stirring a kettle with her stout wooden spoon. Harkness pressed his hand hard against his mouth and mumbled all his curses into his palm. Goutier grinned.

"If you were a good Catholic man, you'd need confession for that."

"Say me one of those Hail Marys, then."

"I might. It couldn't hurt you."

Harkness looked again to make sure his mother hadn't overheard. She was an easygoing woman, but on that particular subject, she would most surely not agree.

"What will you do?" Goutier asked him.

Harkness didn't answer. A shriek of laughter and the sound of outraged chickens tumbled in from the yard.

"Georgie!" scolded his sister. "Stop that right now! She won't lay for a month!"

Harkness dunked the last of his bread in the coffee and chewed. "I'll do what I'm told," he said at last. "I'll report to the station. There's a group of shopkeepers in Mayfair having trouble with a gang of thieves, and they want Bow Street to sort it out. I'm to go listen to their complaints. In the meantime, you're going to get us two horses from the stables and come to meet me."

Goutier blew some steam off his mug and sipped. "You don't trust me on my own now, Mr. Harkness?"

"I trust you absolutely. I don't trust whatever we may find out today. Like as not, it'll take two men to get it sorted, whatever it may be. This thing has only been on our doorstep for two days and it's already turned into a pig's breakfast. No, I lie. A pig wouldn't touch what this has become." He stopped and controlled himself. "This would be a personal favor, Goutier. You're putting yourself at risk here."

Goutier demonstrated his essential fearlessness with another swallow of Mother's coffee. "This morning, the old man made it clear he thought I'd spy on a fellow officer because I wanted his position," he said. "I find I don't care for that estimation of my character. So yes, I'm willing to do this little favor for you."

"Thank you," said Harkness seriously. "I'll meet you at Mayfair." He pulled the merchant's letter from his pocket. "The address is in there. We'll go from there to Kentish Town at one. Miss Thorne will be meeting us as well."

"Miss Thorne?" said Goutier. "I thought you were keeping her inside Melbourne House listening at keyholes?"

You're lucky she's not here to answer that, Goutier. "We might not get a second chance at this, and I want as many eyes on the business as we can get."

"I'll see it all done. Now, a favor from you, sir."

"Anything."

Goutier set down his mug and lowered his voice. "Get us out of here before your mother pours another cup of her coffee for me."

CHAPTER 33

The Effect Of Rather Too Much Conversation

A Great House makes a bad Figure without Suitable Living.

Peniston Lamb, Viscount Melbourne, as reported
in private conversation

"Good morning, Miss Thorne." Dr. Bellingham walked into Rosalind's boudoir and bowed. "I am sorry to find you are not well."

"I'm sure it's nothing, really." Rosalind was sitting up in bed, her wrapper around her shoulders, her plain cap on her head, and the remains of a breakfast on the tray on her lap. "But my throat is sore, and I did not want to risk it turning into a cold."

Much against the wishes of her weary heart—and her thoroughly exhausted head—Rosalind asked to be woken by nine o'clock. Mrs. Kendricks had been prompt and provided with a fresh cup of tea. Rosalind drank it all down, scarcely pausing for breath.

As soon as she had finished, she asked Mrs. Kendricks to send for Dr. Bellingham and gave over the story of the sore throat so that Mrs. Kendricks could repeat it for whomever might ask.

For his part, Dr. Bellingham had arrived so quickly, Rosalind wondered if he had been waiting for a summons.

He set his valise down on the bedside chair, and Rosalind mustered a sheepish smile. "I'm already feeling much better. Perhaps I ought not have troubled you."

"Well, do we not always say it is better to be safe than sorry? If I may take your pulse? Excellent."

The procedure gave Rosalind a moment to study the doctor. His hand on her wrist was perfectly steady, but his eyes spoke of a sleepless night. Further, Dr. Bellingham had not shaved yet. Salt-and-pepper stubble stood out on his chin, and his collar was crumpled, as if he had not changed it since yesterday. His boots and the hems of his stovepipe trousers were mud-spattered.

Rosalind had a sudden vision of Dr. Bellingham walking the streets late into the night, lost in his own unquiet thoughts. Then she remembered Mr. Goutier's letter, and his assertion that Dr. Bellingham's relationship with Mrs. Oslander might well have been far more than professional.

Looking at him now, Rosalind found herself inclined to agree.

"Now, if you will please open your mouth as wide as possible . . . thank you."

The doctor sniffed at her breath and then tilted her head gently back, peering closely at her tongue and down her throat.

"Well, Miss Thorne." Dr. Bellingham released her. "It is my opinion that you are suffering from nothing more than a slight irritation, probably caused by shouting to be heard in a crowded ballroom." His smile was brief. "I will give you a prescription for a sweet syrup. Your maid can probably make it up right here in the house, or you can take it 'round to Mr. Jones, the apothecary in Tracer Street. I do advise you to rest your voice as much as possible today, but otherwise there is no reason why you should not be up and about your regular business." He removed a fresh handkerchief from his pocket and wiped his hands. "I would ask, suggest, perhaps . . ." but he didn't finish. He only glanced uncertainly at Mrs. Kendricks.

Rosalind understood the issue. "Just a moment, please, Doctor," she said. "Mrs. Kendricks, will you take the breakfast tray? And I think a fresh pot of tea is needed."

Rosalind held Mrs. Kendricks's gaze longer than was strictly necessary, and her housekeeper returned a small nod. She then took the tray, and herself, out of the room.

The tea would be rather a long time coming. While Rosalind felt quite comfortable saying anything in front of Mrs. Kendricks, Dr. Bellingham clearly did not, and Rosalind very much wanted to hear whatever weighed on his mind.

The door closed. Rosalind folded her hands on the coverlet and waited.

"Miss Thorne." Dr. Bellingham bowed his chin to his breast, clearly reluctant to speak, even though it was just the two of them. "I met your runner, or rather the man he appointed, a Mr. Goutier?" Rosalind nodded in encouragement. "He told me that Judith—Mrs. Oslander—is dead."

"I am sorry for your loss, Dr. Bellingham." He waved her words away. "You had known her for some time, I believe?"

"Yes. Yes, I had."

The doctor looked Rosalind over again as searching for some sign or symptom he'd missed during his brief examination. "How did you know about any of this? Who exactly are you, Miss Thorne?"

"I am here to assist Lady Melbourne who is, as you know, going through a difficult time," she answered calmly. "I was recommended to her attention by a mutual acquaintance."

"I see." But he clearly did not like what he saw. His face had a strange trick of moving in tiny jerks, as if he was trying to make sure he got his expression right. In this case, that expression was a deep frown. "Miss Thorne, I think you should leave this house."

Rosalind drew back, startled. "Why is that, Dr. Bellingham?"

Dr. Bellingham dug his fingers into his waistcoat pocket as if searching for his words along with his watch. "Miss Thorne, it is possible that Mrs. Oslander's death was . . . brought about deliberately and it might be . . . well, it would be better that a respectable lady such as yourself, one without protection, not be associated with such danger, or scandal."

He clearly expected to alarm her and for her to find the possibility of scandal more alarming than mere danger. Rosalind, however, did not so much as flinch, and confusion clouded the doctor's face.

"Will you be discontinuing your association with Melbourne House, Dr. Bellingham?" she asked.

"I wish I could, Miss Thorne, but I . . ." He stopped, his face flushing as much with anger as embarrassment. "I am not a rich man, Miss Thorne. Maintaining a practice such as mine requires money, and connection. Physicians can be treated much like ornaments of fashion. We go in and out of style. If I am no longer Lady Melbourne's private doctor, my other clients may decide to consult other, newer men, and . . ." He bit his words off.

"I understand, Dr. Bellingham."

They regarded each other in silence for a long time. The corner of his mouth twitched, and twitched again.

"Yes," he murmured at last. "I expect you do. It is not easy, is it?"

"No, sir. It is not."

She let the silence settle again, giving the doctor time to make up his mind how far to extend this new sympathy between them.

"Well, perhaps . . . if it is not betraying a confidence . . ."

He stopped and started again. "I don't know how to speak about this, Miss Thorne. Not to you, nor to anyone. Mr. Goutier told me—showed me, really—a letter that was found among Mrs. Oslander's things. One that she should not have possessed."

Again, he waited for her exclamation of shock and surprise. Again, he seemed confused when it did not come. "Did the letter belong to Lady Melbourne?" Rosalind asked.

"It would seem so. I cannot . . . I don't know what she was thinking to keep it. The very idea of Mrs. Oslander acting improperly is repugnant. I cannot believe it. I will not." He spoke forcefully, as if ordering mind and heart to comply.

"It may be that I can help you, and Mrs. Oslander," Rosalind said quietly.

"How do you propose to do that, Miss Thorne?"

Rosalind chose her words with care. This man's distress was genuine. He had lost someone dear, and he was not free to grieve, or even to act, because he could not endanger his standing among his aristocratic patients.

"Dr. Bellingham, as I told you, I am here at Lady Melbourne's request, and at the urging of mutual friends to assist her during her illness. I am naturally concerned that Lady Melbourne is kept from any unnecessary excitement. She would be terribly distressed to find that even one of her letters had gone astray. Therefore, it is to everyone's benefit if this letter—and any more like it—are recovered, quickly and quietly. You see," she added, "like you, I have a great deal to lose if Lady Melbourne becomes disappointed in me, and says so to her friends."

Dr. Bellingham's doubt showed plainly on his face. Rosalind braced herself for arguments centered around her presumed delicacy and gentility. In the end, though, he just bowed his head.

"What do you propose, Miss Thorne?"

"That we work together to find the letters, and the truth

of how they disappeared," she said. "As indelicate as it may seem, there should be a . . . review of Mrs. Oslander's home. In case there might be other letters there. It should be done quickly."

Dr. Bellingham hesitated. He wanted to know the truth, but he must fear what that truth would be. "Yes, yes, of course. And when nothing is found it will . . . it will be a comfort."

He did love her, thought Rosalind. *He cannot say so, but he did.*

I wonder, did she love him?

"I cannot undertake such a mission today." Dr. Bellingham curled his hand into a loose fist, as if seeking to capture his frustration there. "After last night's entertainments, many of my . . . fashionable clients are demanding appointments for their heads and stomachs and throats and spleens and . . . well, I have already lingered here too long. If your message had come a half hour later, it would have missed me until eight o'clock tonight or even later."

"If you will trust me, Dr. Bellingham, it is something I can do. I have some small experience in such matters."

He stared at her again, and again she had the idea he was seeking some overlooked symptom to account for her extraordinary behavior.

What do you see, Dr. Bellingham? Do you believe me? Will you trust me?

"It will help Lady Melbourne, which is my charge, and Mrs. Oslander, which is yours," she reminded him.

At last, Dr. Bellingham pulled a small book and pencil from his pocket and began to write. "I am doing this only reluctantly, Miss Thorne, and I would not do it at all if Mrs. Oslander had any family." He tore out the leaf and handed it to her. "This is the house where she had rooms. I would give you a note for the landlady, but she would not know me. Except in cases of an emergency, I reached her through an agency."

"May I ask which one?"

"Mrs. MacKennan's, in Wallsingham Street." He hesitated, his eyes ticking open wide and pleading. "Miss Thorne . . . the runner, the man I spoke to, what he said about Mrs. Oslander being a thief . . . It is not true, Miss Thorne. It *cannot* be. I do not know what has happened, but you may rely on me absolutely should you have any need." He looked pleadingly at her. "Please, promise me you will tell me as soon as you find anything. Please."

"I will do my best, Dr. Bellingham, depending on what I discover. But I think we should not speak of this here. Even with the excuse of my throat, it will look strange if I call you again. If you meet me this evening at my house in Little Russell Street, we can speak again in private." *And we can speak freely. I am sure I will have new questions about Mrs. Oslander and your relationship with each other.*

The doctor nodded. "Yes, that makes sense. But it cannot be tonight. My patients, my schedule, I cannot . . . not even for this," he added in a bitter whisper. "Tomorrow. I can come tomorrow, at eight o'clock. Rather past polite visiting hours, I fear." He gave her a ghost of a smile. "But needs must as the devil drives."

"I do understand, Dr. Bellingham. Now, neither of us have much more time. Is there anything else you can tell me? Anything that might shed any light on Mrs. Oslander's actions?" *For instance, how you saw Lady Caroline give Mrs. Oslander a package to take to Henry Colburn?*

A soft knock came at the door. Dr. Bellingham whipped his head around as if he'd heard a thunderclap.

"I expect that is Mrs. Kendricks," said Rosalind. "She knows we are having a private conversation." She raised her voice. "Come in!"

But it was not Mrs. Kendricks. It was Claridge, tall and forbidding in her black dress and solemn demeanor. Rosalind bit her lip against a groan of disappointment.

Claridge made her entirely proper curtsey. "Lady Melbourne sends her compliments, Miss Thorne. She heard the doctor had been sent for and wants to make sure you are quite well."

Dr. Bellingham answered before Rosalind could. "You may assure Lady Melbourne that Miss Thorne is quite well except for a slight strain of her vocal chords." His face resumed an entirely professional demeanor without any of its ticks or hesitation. "However, I recommend that she remain quiet and rest to ensure against any worsening of her condition. We certainly do not wish to risk the recurrence of illness in the house so soon after all here have returned to health."

Claridge looked from the doctor to Rosalind and back again.

She does not believe him, Rosalind thought. *Why is that?*

But aside from that flicker of her gaze, Claridge remained impassive. "I will give Lady Melbourne that message," she said calmly. "Thank you, Doctor Bellingham, Miss Thorne."

Claridge turned away, but as she did, Rosalind caught the ghost of a satisfied smile on her face.

"Well, I must be on my rounds, Miss Thorne." Dr. Bellingham reclaimed his gloves and his valise. "Have that prescription made up, and please remember what I said about resting your voice." His smile and his bow were professionally indulgent, and he took himself from the room as smoothly as if this had been an ordinary visit.

Rosalind watched him go and hoped that her frustration did not show on her face. She made no move to stop him, though, because she knew he was wondering the same thing as she was.

Exactly how long had Claridge been standing outside the door?

And how much did she overhear?

CHAPTER 34

A Sojourn To Kentish Town

*I wish also to know if Scrope delivered the things
entrusted to him by me, as I have no news of that
illustrious personage.*

George Gordon, Lord Byron, private correspondence

As it transpired, Rosalind saw Mr. Harkness before he
saw her. She wasn't surprised. Mr. Harkness was on
horseback, side by side with a large black man who also
wore Bow Street's scarlet vest. This, she decided, must be Mr.
Goutier.

She, on the other hand, was in her plainest cloak and bonnet and carrying a stout valise, having walked the entire way
from Piccadilly to Kentish Town.

This was a lively, busy district. The dirt and cobble street
was clogged by carts and vans, and its sides were lined by
houses and yards of all description. Just this last quarter
mile, Rosalind had passed cook shops, butchers, a brewery,
and a cobbler. The smell was thick, even by London standards, and the usual sounds of a busy street were topped up
by the echoes of all the building going on by the canal.
Smoke and dust clouds rose from the nearby canal, and the
rush and rattle of dredging pumps underscored the sound of

hammering and the shouts of laborers and rush of the sawyers at their work.

There was another reason the Bow Street men failed to pick her out of the rest of the crowd. They, like many others, appeared engrossed in a particular form of entertainment taking place on the doorstep of a newish house on the corner where the mews met the high street.

A slender man—one far too well dressed to be a native of the street—stood on the stoop. A dark-skinned lady in a ruffled cap and worn gray dress faced him down from the doorway.

Rosalind turned her head as she passed, and turned it back quickly, grateful for her broad bonnet and its concealing sides

For the house was No. 12, and the man was Scrope Berdmore Davies.

Mr. Davies was gesticulating with his hands and his walking stick. That was surely his high-flyer across the way that a second crowd of boys, and not a few men, were gawping at. The high blood horses stirred and stamped uneasily.

Rosalind pushed past the scene, working her way through the other onlookers until she managed to fetch up beside Mr. Harkness's horse. He looked down, frowning, probably intending to tell her to take care, but she looked up.

He raised his brows. "You're late for the curtain."

"It was a very long walk."

He looked her up and down. "I can . . ."

"*Psst*, the pair of you," murmured Goutier. "I'm trying to watch the show."

". . . and you can just take yourself and your suggestions right out of here!" bawled the woman, who was almost certainly the landlady of No. 12. "This is a respectable house!"

Mr. Davies smiled and bowed, sweeping off his hat, probably as a grand gesture of apology. The landlady of No. 12 wasn't having any of it.

"I said clear off!" she shouted.

"Do you know who either of those is?" asked Mr. Harkness.

"Yes. The dandy is Mr. Scrope Davies."

"Is it now?" breathed Mr. Goutier. "He's punching above his weight."

Mr. Davies smiled again, showing all his teeth. "Of course you can't be expected to let just anyone into your rooms . . ." He reached into his pocket and brought out a couple of silver coins. "If, however, you would reconsider, ma'am, you'd find I am a most grateful . . ."

The landlady looked at the coins and then at Mr. Davies. Then she smacked his hand, hard. Laughter erupted from the onlookers. The coins went spinning into the street, setting off a general *Hurrah!* and a mad scramble. Mr. Davies stood there, startled. The landlady marched back into her house and slammed the door.

"Blast," muttered Mr. Harkness. "We'll never get in now. Not so soon after he's made an ass of himself."

"I can get in," said Rosalind.

Mr. Davies had lunged forward and began pounding frantically on the door.

"Ma'am! Ma'am!" he cried. "Please! Let me explain!"

The door flew open.

"Uh-oh," murmured Goutier.

The landlady stood in the threshold, a bucket in both hands. Davies reeled back, but not fast enough. In a single motion, she tossed the contents straight into Mr. Davies's face.

Rosalind slapped a hand over her mouth to muffle a most undignified squeak of surprise. The idlers showed no such restraint and guffawed openly.

The landlady slammed the door shut again.

Mr. Davies, to the hoots and applause of the onlookers, slumped back to his carriage.

Goutier looked at Harkness. Harkness looked to Rosalind.

"Are you sure you can get in?"

"Yes," said Rosalind. "I'll meet you at Little Russell Street at seven. We can talk then."

That should give us all plenty of time to pursue our separate courses, wherever they may lead.

Harkness nodded Then he and Mr. Goutier both nudged their heels against their horses sides to set them walking.

On the far side of the street, several of the idlers were making a great show of dusting down the step of Mr. Davies's high-flyer and offering helpful advice. Mr. Davies snarled and waved his stick at them, raising more laughter. As Rosalind watched, the dandy threw himself onto the seat and snatched the reins from the fellow who'd loosened them. He also snatched up his whip and looked as ready to use it on the crowd as on his matched bays.

But by then, Mr. Goutier had maneuvered his horse up right next to the team, within arm's reach of the bridles.

The dandy snarled a curse and turned, whip still in hand. But just in time he got a look at the white staff of office Mr. Harkness pulled from his coat pocket. The crowd saw it at the same time and scattered in all directions, leaving them alone with the dandy. Mr. Davies dropped his whip and pressed his face into his gloved hand.

Goutier took hold of the off-horse's bridle.

If words were exchanged, they were too soft for Rosalind to hear. Mr. Davies's shoulders shuddered once, then he looked up to heaven and gestured for Mr. Goutier to lead the way.

All the men touched up their horses. Rosalind turned back to No. 12.

It was time that she play her own part.

I only hope I haven't promised too much.

The woman who answered Rosalind's knocking was that same tidy dark-skinned lady who had so dramatically evicted

Mr. Davies from her doorstep moments ago. She glared at Rosalind as if perfectly ready to do it again.

"Good afternoon, ma'am. I'm looking for Mrs. Judith Oslander," said Rosalind. "I'm expected."

"Gor! If it ain't another one!" The woman folded her corded arms. "What's she done that all of a sudden she's got more callers than the queen!"

"I . . . I don't know. I've only just arrived. I've come all the way from Darbyshire." Rosalind gestured vaguely up the street. "She told me I could stay with her."

"Well, she didn't tell me anything about it," the landlady snapped. Then she took a second glance at Rosalind's face, and her bag, and her mud-spattered coat. This time, she softened, if only a little. "I'm sorry, my girl. Mrs. Oslander . . . she ain't been back here in days."

Rosalind let her chin quiver. "What should I do? I know no one else in town. Mrs. Oslander promised me. She wrote . . ." Rosalind fumbled with the catch on her bag.

The landlady shook her head. "Won't help you, dear. I told you. She's gone. Last I heard of her she was going to attend some patients over in Piccadilly. You want to ask at the agency. Mrs. MacKennan's, that'll be, over in Wallsingham Street. Might be they'd know more." She moved to close the door.

"Couldn't I just wait for her here?" pleaded Rosalind. "I've come so very far . . . and she promised she'd tell you. I don't understand what could have happened . . ."

The landlady set her mouth into a hard line, and for a moment Rosalind feared she was just going to shut the door.

"I've little enough for charity here, missy," she declared. "But I'll tell you this, you need to find yourself another friend. Mrs. Oslander ain't been back for days, she left no notice, and I've no rent from her this week. You best make up your mind she's not coming back."

Rosalind bowed her head and bit her lip. Then she said.

"She . . . I've nowhere to stay, Mrs. . . ." Then she lifted her head again, as if a thought had just struck her. "What if I paid what's owing?"

"Don't tell me you've got money?"

"A little. I saved."

The landlady sighed sharply and shook her head at Rosalind, the street, the world, and its ways. "Four shillings makes up what's owed and pays out the week," she said. "Have you got that much?"

"I've three . . ."

"All right, all right. I'll take two of that. But you'll have the rest for me Tuesday, or you'll find yourself on the street again, you understand? Hand it here." She gestured impatiently. Rosalind dropped the coins in her roughened palm, and she eyed them with all the skepticism of Mr. Faulks examining a new painting.

"All right. Top of the stairs. An' I'm Mrs. Courzant, should you need to shout for me, Miss . . . ?"

"Tanner. Rose Tanner."

"All right, Miss Tanner. It's not my day to do the linens, but I'll . . ."

"Oh, no, don't bother, Mrs. Courzant. Please," said Rosalind quickly. "You've already been so kind."

There was only one door at the top. It was not locked, and Rosalind let herself in.

Had Rosalind ever given over thought to how a diligent nurse would live, she might well have conjured a picture much like Judith Oslander's rooms. They were small, spare, and whitewashed. They were also scrupulously clean. The linen was spotless, as was the coverlet on the wooden bedstead. The colors of the rag rug by the hearth were bright and cheerful. There was a rocking chair in front of the polished brass fender and a bowl of flowers on the table. This was the only blot on the general neatness. The geraniums were sadly wilted, and red curling petals lay scattered across the scrubbed table.

The only other symptom of disorder was the sewing basket. It sat open on the table beside the flower. Reels of cotton, the ends of ribbons, spare buttons, papers of pins, and needles had all been rummaged into an untidy heap, as if the seamstress had just walked away for a moment and still meant to return to set all to rights.

The sight of that basket lent an extra sense of emptiness to the quiet, tidy rooms.

Rosalind set her bag down and undid her bonnet. She laid this beside the sewing basket. A square of new gray flannel lay folded on the table. Rosalind laid her hand on it. It was soft, good quality cloth, warm from the sunlight that filtered through the curtains on the little window.

A surge of emotion she could not name flooded Rosalind. She found she had to turn away quickly to face the empty flat.

Now, then, Mrs. Oslander. Rosalind squared her shoulders. *What have you left me?*

CHAPTER 35

In A Lot Of Wine, A Little Truth

*. . . it would be much better at once to explain
your mysteries. . . . What do you mean?—what is
there known? or can be known?*

George Gordon, Lord Byron, private correspondence

The One Tonne public house was low and dark, and Harkness didn't like the look of half the faces in there. Fortunately, Scrope Davies didn't object to sitting out in the yard where they could at least see what was coming at them.

"Anything," Davies growled as he flung himself down on the bench. "Just so long as you let me have a drink."

Goutier went to deal with the barman, and to everyone's surprise he came out with a bottle of red wine.

"*Vin ordinere.*" Goutier set it down on the plank table. "Compliments of the landlord."

Harkness cocked a brow. Goutier shrugged. "One Frenchman to another. The fellow's from Toulouse, and he swears it's genuine. Might even be telling the truth."

Davies snatched up the bottle. He pulled out a wicked-looking pocket knife to cut the wax seal and draw the cork. Bottle open, he poured himself a glass and drank it down like water.

He let out a harsh breath and poured another glass.

Harkness kicked his heels out and watched. Goutier took the bottle from Davies and poured out glasses for himself and Harkness. Neither Bow Street man drank.

The dandy took the bottle back and filled his own glass again, but this time he drank only half.

"Your man's right," he said to Harkness. "Genuine and quite ordinary, but . . . needs must." He shrugged. He also noted he'd left his knife on the table and tucked it carefully away in his coat pocket. "Now, sir. Am I arrested? May I know the charge?"

"You're not arrested, Mr. Davies," answered Harkness. "Not as matters stand."

"You know my name. I'm flattered." Davies raised his glass and then drained it.

Goutier raised his brows, and Harkness agreed. He had seen many a hardened drinker in his time, but this was genuinely impressive.

"Why were you so interested in speaking with the landlady back there at number twelve, Mr. Davies?" asked Goutier.

"Private business," muttered Davies.

Harkness's gesture indicated he understood this as a matter of fact. "Does that business involve Judith Oslander?"

Davies set his glass down. His hand was no longer as steady as it had been, but his eyes were clear enough as they shifted from Harkness to Goutier and back again.

"I think I don't care to speak of Judith Oslin . . . Oslander," he said with extreme dignity. "A man should not bandy a lady's name about in a tavern yard." He looked pleased, like a barrister who had made a particularly clever argument.

"What about the name of Lord Byron?" Harkness inquired. "A name you are said to be very familiar with. In fact, we've heard that you are acting as his agent on several matters of business while he's on the Continent."

Davies groaned and reached for the wine bottle yet again.

"God in Heaven! Could there be one more humiliation in this whole foul day?" He filled his glass and drank again.

Enough of this. Harkness pulled the bottle up close to him and out of Davies's reach.

The wine was doing its work, though, and driving the sense out of Mr. Davies.

"You know, I don't care for your tone, sir," the dandy declared. "You have no right, no business asking about Bryon! You could not ever understand him. He is beyond men such as you! Men without a glimmer of poetry in your souls!"

Goutier looked at Harkness.

"'This above all, to thine own self be true,'" remarked Harkness. "'And it must follow, as the night the day, thou canst not then be false to any man.'"

"*Tous les hommes sont semblables par les paroles, et ce n'est que les actions qui les découvrent différents,*" replied Goutier solemnly.

Mr. Davies gawped. Then, with the speed that comes to a man already in his cups, his contempt vanished and he laughed.

"Oh! I surrender! I am quite undone!" He pulled his lace handkerchief from his sleeve and waved it in the air. "Runners declaiming the Bard and—what was that, sir? Molière? Yes? Good lord! We are still in the age of wonders and I have badly underestimated the men of Bow Street. I apologize, truly." He mopped at his dirt-streaked face; paused for a moment's thought; and then undid his limp, stained cravat, balled it up, and pitched it right across the yard.

"All right," he said grimly to the discarded linen. "I do not deny it or hide it. I am acting in Byron's name, at least, he has wishes that . . . that he wishes I would wish to carry . . ." He stopped and took a deep breath. His cheeks were red with wine, embarrassment, and not a little anger.

"Byron wants to return to England," Davies said. "But there are some old . . . scandals that he thinks present a bar to him. That may or may not be so. What is true . . . what is . . . is there are some letters, indiscreet letters, that say too much about the matter. Byron wants them recovered, and preferably destroyed. I agreed to try." Davies paused, looking at his empty glass and then at the bottle. His brow furrowed, as if he could not understand how it had come to be so far away. But he did not reach for it. "I do not believe a man should live in exile for unproven crimes and . . . and . . . other things that are strictly personal. Strictly. And I do not believe England should be deprived of her greatest poet. So, I said I'd try, and try, try again," he added, smiling at his own feeble attempt at a joke.

Harkness did not smile. "And there is the matter of the money," he said.

Davies drew back as if he'd been struck. "Who told you that? That is a private matter between gentlemen!"

Mr. Davies, it seemed, had a wide range of items he considered private.

Goutier held his glass up to let the sunlight shine through it, shrugged at what he saw. After a quick swallow, he asked, "Then we may take it that his lordship does in fact owe you money?"

Davies shot to his feet so fast he swayed and had to grab the table's edge. "I demand to know who told you th-that!"

Harkness held himself still and waited. He had seen what money could do to a man. Lack of money could do more, and worse. It came to permeate a man, or a woman's, every thought, and would lurk behind every action. He had no doubt that what Mr. Davies told them was the truth: He wanted to help his friend return to England. But if Davies was in debt, or risk of debt, and Lord Byron owed him money, that also would spur him on, no matter what Davies might wish or want.

Scrope Davies dropped back onto the bench and let loose another long laugh.

"Ah! By all the gods! Is this what I've become! Standing on my pride while bargaining away my honor. God above! I should just shoot myself or join the Beau in exile." He shook his head. "But no, no such easy ends for me, I think. Very well. Yes, Lord Byron owes me money. He will not pay. He made that clear in his own inimitable way when I saw him on the Continent."

"And yet you still tried to get the letters from Lady Melbourne," said Goutier.

"Ha! You're wrong there, my fine runner! I did not try to get them from her!" Davies leaned forward and wagged a finger at Goutier. "I tried to find out if she still had them!" He paused. "It was that Miss Thorne, who thought she was so clever, told me she didn't." He paused again. "I shouldn't be surprised to find she was in on this. She had that look. Sneaking, stealing, might have them herself already . . ."

Harkness's hand shot out and gripped Davies's wrist.

"You will not speak of Miss Thorne again, sir," said Harkness calmly. "Not in a tavern yard or anywhere else."

"Oh-ho! Well, well, we must then consider Miss Thorne carefully, mustn't we. Delicate, fragile flower who knows too much and tells it to all . . ."

"Davies," said Goutier. "I'd be quiet now if I were you."

The pain in his wrist seemed to have finally made its way to his senses. Davies leaned forward and squinted until he understood the look in Harkness's eye. "I beg your pardon, sir," he said. "It is the wine."

"Yes," agreed Harkness, and let him go. "To return to the other question. What made you think Lady Melbourne might not have the letters?"

"Because Lady Melbourne is not the only person in this world to receive dangerous and indiscreet letters," Davies said loftily. "I received one of my own, sir, at my club. How it found me there, I don't know, but it did. This letter . . . this letter informed me that if I wanted the *Melbourne* letters, I should apply to Mrs. Oslander number twelve, Wolverton Mews, and bring . . . a sum of cash. You can imagine my surprise then when I heard from the little birds of Melbourne House that Mrs. Oslander not only had worked there but was dead." He took a breath and reached for the bottle again. Harkness let him have it. Davies drank deep again, and Goutier's face creased in a pained expression.

Harkness sniffed the wine and decided he was better off as he was.

"So," gasped Davies, "I went to number twelve to see if I could get into the rooms and retrieve the letters before someone else did, or before they were bundled up with the rest of her things to be sold to the secondhand shop. There." He slapped his hand down on the table and got to his feet, far more steadily than Harkness would have expected. "Does that satisfy you, my fine Robins Redbreast? I'm afraid I have unfinished business to attend to this afternoon." He paused, and a gleam came into his eyes as he picked up the bottle. "But! I think I shall begin with finishing this *vin ordinare*. Do you think I can persuade the fine gentleman from Toulouse to part with another bottle?" He sat back down and filled his glass to the brim.

"There is one question more," said Harkness.

"And what is that?" Scrope seemed to be having trouble getting the glass to his mouth.

"Which little bird told you Judith Oslander was dead?"

Davies drank deep, and Harkness wondered if he would answer at all. But at last he drew breath and he said, "Which one, sir? Why, the cuckoo, of course. The madwoman in the attic, Lady Caroline herself."

CHAPTER 36

A Thorough Examination Of The Circumstances

*What a suspicious person you are, on some points
you guess right, on others wrong . . .*

Elizabeth Lamb, Viscountess Melbourne,
private correspondence

Rosalind was determined to be methodical. The fact that Mr. Harkness found the initial letter in the lining of Mrs. Oslander's bonnet said that she was careful and she had practice in concealment. Even in a small set of rooms, that made for a great many possibilities.

She began at the front of the flat, moving slowly toward the back, which held the bedroom. She opened each drawer, set its contents aside, and searched the drawer itself before she unfolded or opened each item.

Mrs. Oslander, Rosalind discovered, had been a woman of plain tastes. All the linen was serviceable, clean, and neatly mended, but nothing more. Her three pairs of gloves were all stout—made for use rather than ornamentation. The wardrobe held two dresses, one for working days and the other a black crepe de chine for church or other formal occasions. Mrs. Oslander was not a lady for the theatre, or other public entertainments, and so had no evening gown. The diary Rosalind found was filled with notes on patients, appointments, and household accounts, about which she appeared especially meticulous. The letters in the little writing desk were likewise innocuous. There were bills, almost all of them paid. She found some slight correspondence with friends and pair of distant cousins, one in Suffolk and one in Wales.

They should be told. Rosalind put those letters into her valise.

What she did not see in all of this was any sign of luxury. There was no lace, no tapestry, no pretty china or other frippery to decorate the rooms. She opened the jewel box on the dresser and found nothing but combs and hairpins of the plainest sort.

Rosalind lifted out the inner tray of the box. Underneath, she finally saw the gleam of gold. There, she found a gold ring set with garnets It was not a costly thing. The band was slim, and the stones were muddy. But it did have the look of a wedding ring.

A keepsake from her previous life? Rosalind turned it over in her fingers and peered at it more closely. It had been engraved on the inside. Rosalind read:

P&J Aeternum

"Well," Rosalind breathed.

J was clearly Judith. But who was P? Her former husband? Rosalind's thoughts stopped, then reversed themselves.

What is Dr. Bellingham's Christian name?

She'd heard it. She knew she had. *What is it? What is it?* She squeezed her hand closed around the ring and squeezed her eyes shut as well, straining to remember.

This is Miss Thorne, whispered Lady Caroline indolently from the back of her mind. *Miss Thorne . . . this is Dr. Phillip Bellingham.*

Rosalind's eyes and fingers popped open at the same time. *He loves her.* Rosalind's earlier impression echoed in her mind. *But did she love him?*

She had once, or she would not have kept such a token. She had changed her mind, however, or she would have been wearing the ring when they found her. It would not be here in the bottom of her little box, beneath the plain combs and pins.

If, of course, it was Dr. Bellingham who had given her this ring. If her late husband's name had not been Peter, Paul, or Preston.

Rosalind moved to lay the ring back in the box, but at the last moment she hesitated and instead tucked it inside the valise along with the letters to the cousins. She did not like to do this. It felt uncomfortably close to theft. But she might need that ring to help convince Dr. Bellingham tomorrow night to tell her the truth about his relationship with Mrs. Oslander.

Rosalind snapped the valise closed and turned back to the flat. It was getting late and she was becoming worried. What if the letters were not here? What then?

Rosalind bit her lip. *Where else? What have I missed?*

There were only two windows in the rooms, one at the front and one in the bedroom. Their curtains were short and thin, unsuited to having letters sewn into the hems. She lifted the rag rug, which she could imagine Mrs. Oslander spending patient, quiet evenings plaiting. None of the floorboards was loose or new. She had no more success with the lining or bottom of the traveling case she found on the top of the wardrobe.

Rosalind was beginning to feel something of a fool. She dropped down on the bed with a sigh.

"Perhaps I have misjudged you," she said to the rooms and the invisible presence of Mrs. Oslander. "Perhaps you did have some friend whom you trusted, and the letters are with that person. Perhaps you already handed them over to the one who asked you for them. Perhaps that's why you went to Melbourne House that night. But then why keep back that one?"

She drummed her fingers restlessly on the pillow. And stilled them.

The pillows.

She snatched up the nearest—a fat, freshly stuffed feather cushion. She drew off the plain case and examined the seams in the ticking.

One had been torn out and neatly resewn. Rosalind squeezed it hard, as if she were strangling the goose that gave up those feathers.

There. She felt it. The slight, stiff crinkle of paper.

Rosalind closed her eyes and whispered a brief prayer of thanksgiving. When she opened them again, she picked up the pillowcase she'd discarded a moment before and she saw something else.

"Oh," she breathed.

On the spot by the headboard where the pillow had been laying was a neatly folded piece of dainty white linen. It had been delicately embroidered with pink and blue thread.

Oh dear.

Rosalind picked it up. But she didn't have hold of it right, and something heavy slid out and hit the floor at her feet. Rosalind reached down for it without thinking.

It was a packet of letters. *Of course it is letters. What else would it be?* But these were tied with a bow of pink ribbon.

Rosalind stared at the embroidered cloth. It was a Christening gown, and heavily creased from having been kept beneath the pillow. Rosalind's thoughts produced the sudden and searing picture of Mrs. Oslander in her plain flannel nightdress. She saw the nurse climbing into her bed and moving the pillow to touch this little gown, and perhaps press a kiss to it.

Oh.

Rosalind set aside the gown and looked at the letters. They were all directed to Mrs. Oslander. She leafed through them quickly, checking the franking and the dates. The last one had arrived just two weeks ago.

Rosalind bit her lip and pulled that letter out of the packet. She opened it up and she read, skimming quickly over the clumsy writing, conscious of a deep and ridiculous guilt at reading another person's letters without permission.

Rosalind dropped her hands into her lap.

Mrs. Oslander might or might not have been married. But she did have family.

"I'm sorry."

She had an aunt, all the way out in Bristol.

"I'm sorry."

And she had a daughter—living, growing, thriving—who missed her and was learning her letters and very much wanted to be able to write a letter of her own to Mummy soon.

"Oh, Judith," she breathed to the ghost in the room. "I am so, very sorry."

When Rosalind was able to make herself move, she folded the letter closed and tucked it back with the others in the bundle. She was satisfied now that she had learned all the flat could tell her. She just needed to find a way to make a graceful, or at least artful, exit. With the pillow and its contents.

Her first thought was to get the scissors from Mrs. Oslander's sewing basket and cut the pillow open at once. But even as she raised the blades, she paused. She would not be able to open the ticking without creating a spill of feathers, which would be noticed by the landlady in this tidy flat. She did not want to rouse Mrs. Courzant's suspicions yet. It was very possible Rosalind might need to come back here. She could have no reasonable explanation for willfully damaging a good piece of bedding.

Instead, Rosalind took a length of twine and a bit of brown paper from the cupboard. She bundled the pillow into an anonymous, if untidy, package and stuffed it into her valise along with the ring and the bundles of Mrs. Oslander's letters.

Then she stopped again. Because if Mrs. Courzant saw Rosalind taking her luggage out of the flat so soon, she'd want to know where Rosalind was going and why. As Mrs. Courzant was a sensibly suspicious woman who'd had other people knocking on her door and trying to get into these room, she might decide she needed to come up and make sure nothing was amiss. If she did that, she might notice a few things missing.

Rosalind rubbed her forehead and suppressed a most unladylike desire to curse.

Instead, she opened the window in the bedroom. There was a tiny dirt alley outside, empty except for a few pigeons and the lurking cat they hadn't noticed yet. She saw no one moving in the house to the far side or lingering at either end of the alley.

Rosalind dropped the valise down, startling and scattering the animals.

Then she reclaimed her coat and bonnet and went down the stairs. Mrs. Courzant was in her entrance hall with her bucket and scrub brush, scouring the whitewashed walls.

"Thank you so much for your help, Mrs. Courzant," she said. "I'm feeling much better. I'll go right round to the agency. Since I've a proper address, they can put me in their books as soon as I've interviewed with the head, and I've all my references with me." She touched her reticule.

The landlady nodded her approval. "That's right, my girl. No dawdling, no crying, just get on with it. Good luck to you."

"Thank you, ma'am." Rosalind took herself out the front door. Moving as casually as she could, she turned down the street and then turned into the alley.

The sides of her bonnet prevented her from seeing the dandified gentleman in the curricle who had his eyes fixed on her.

Rosalind shooed a pigeon away from her valise and then shooed the cat away from a pigeon as she strode into the next street.

She had passed a livery stable on her way to No. 12. She should be able to hire a hack there to take her, and all the letters, back to Little Russell Street. She could open the pillow there, with Mr. Harkness and Mr. Goutier to see and help her sort out what Mrs. Oslander had been doing.

She could tell them that whatever Judith Oslander's part in the theft and the blackmail, they at least now knew why she'd done it.

In the high street, Scrope Davies looked about himself. He did not see either of the damn runners watching. Good. It had been a simple matter to convince them he was drunker than he really was. He'd employed the tactic many a time at the races and the tables. That *vin ordinare* had been weak stuff compared to what he was used to. He could have downed three more bottles of it without ill effect. Indeed as it was, it had steadied his nerve and brain so he could finally plan. Still, he'd made a show of starting to sing and slip sideways as the men had left him in the tavern yard, evidently deciding they had better places to be.

As do I.

Davies touched up his horses and ordered them to walk on. Miss Thorne had clearly been more successful than he in her efforts to get past the dragon of a landlady.

And she'd found something—something she needed to take extra precautions to remove.

CHAPTER 37

A Quiet Meal In Good Company

*Hath he laid perjury upon his soul? No doubt he
will say so, as he always adds his sins to the other
obligations he has conferred upon me.*

George Gordon, Lord Byron, private correspondence

Mr. John Townsend was known as a man of surpassingly
regular habits. It was further known that it was at the
Prince of Wales's firm insistence that he gained his membership
at Watier's, a club that would otherwise never have admitted
anyone of his station or profession.

Most of Watier's other members tolerated Townsend, although
some to a greater degree than others. Many looked
on him as harmless and even amusing. Others saw him as a
potentially useful route for getting closer to the royal family.
Those who were less tolerant also tended to believe Mr.
Townsend perfectly oblivious to their quiet snubs and snipes.

This was not a mistake William Lamb made.

After his visit with Lady Jersey, Lamb went straight to
Watier's and stationed himself at a table in the famed blue
and gold dining room, with a dish of stuffed chops in a wine
sauce. As a result, he was there when Mr. Townsend walked
in at precisely two o'clock, according to his regular habit.

Many people considered nuncheon a habit for Frenchmen and ladies, who so easily grew faint. The Prince Regent was not of this opinion, however, and His Royal Highness was known to enjoy a hearty meal in the middle of the day. Therefore, it came as no surprise to anyone when Mr. Townsend had also adopted the custom.

When Mr. Townsend entered, Lamb—whose family also had some connection to the prince—stood and bowed. Townsend saw at once and made his stately way across the room to Lamb's table.

"Mr. William Lamb, is it not?"

"Mr. Townsend. Forgive me for not seeking a formal introduction. But I believe you know my parents?"

"Your father, Lord Melbourne, certainly. We've met several times at Newmarket."

The connection thus arrived at, Lamb inquired if Townsend would sit? Of course he would. Delighted. Would Townsend care to share a drink, or a chop? There it was going to be a long afternoon tonight, and Lamb had decided he'd better take precautions against the effects of having his supper delayed.

"Can't be seen nodding off while some damn fool in the opposition is droning on."

"Ha! Excellent, sir. And I'd be glad to join you. My thanks."

Extra plates and silver were brought. Lamb poured Townsend a glass of wine, and the men toasted the prince, the club, and the cook. Around them, other men seeking a quiet table or a good meal drifted into the room.

"How does your lady mother?" Townsend asked Lamb. "We were all much concerned to hear she had again fallen ill."

"She is rather better, thank you. D'ye know, Townsend, I was surprised not to see you at the Casselmaine ball the other night."

"I was requested to attend their Highnesses, the Dukes of York and Kent." Another man would have said it by way of apology. Townsend puffed out his chest and waited for some comment on his importance.

Lamb found he did not have the patience to oblige. He simply nodded in that way that caused so many people to consider him just a little thickheaded.

"Ah, so that would be why your man Harkness was there. He was acting in your place."

"Did you see him?" Townsend wiped his mouth and fingers delicately. "He didn't mention it, I'm afraid. I am trying to train the man in some of the proprieties, you know. There are days I do believe he wishes he was still out among the hedgerows stalking highwaymen." Townsend beamed fondly, as if speaking of a son rather than a colleague. "Despite that, Mr. Harkness has proved himself an exemplary officer, though, and sure to rise. He was with the highway patrol before he came to us, and is the youngest man ever to reach the rank of principal officer. If there's any matter at all that Bow Street can assist with, he's the first of our men I'd recommend for you."

Lamb let himself frown. "Well, I'm glad to hear you place such confidence in him, sir. But I fear that makes what I have to say all the more troubling."

Townsend set his glass down. "I do not understand you, sir."

Lamb folded his hands and considered the man in front of him. He also considered the clean tablecloth and his own finger ends. It was a tactic he liked to employ with his colleagues in Parliament. It made them restless. "My mother has been ill for some time," said Lamb. "She recently acceded to her doctor's wishes, and her family's, and asked a young gentlewoman to stay, one who could assist her with her correspondence and other such matters. The lady in question came highly recommended, by Lady Jersey, no less." Lamb paused to see what effect this had on Townsend, but for once Townsend seemed at a loss for words. "But I have heard, sir, that she has been taking private business—private business of my *mother's*—out of the house. In fact, I am told, she has been meeting with a man from Bow Street."

Townsend liked to appear an affable man, a genteel and mannered man who could appear in the highest circles and cause no irritation. Very few people had ever seen what Lamb saw now—the deep, thunderous flush of Townsend's anger creeping up from his thick neck to his furrowed brow.

"Is the lady's name Rosalind Thorne?" Townsend croaked.

"You know her then?" asked Lamb mildly.

"I know *of* her."

Lamb sighed and did not inquire as to the circumstances. "I recognize you've a job to do, Mr. Townsend, and I have always heartily supported the work of Bow Street, both in person and in committee before the house. But I am shocked that you'd allow such tactics as spying on the private doings of a man's home!" Lamb kept his voice regretful, conveying the impression of being conscious of his own shortcomings. "If there's something to do with some member of the household, of course it should be brought to my father's attention, or mine, but this . . . this, sir, is beyond the pale!"

Townsend controlled himself mightily.

"I must ask, sir, if you are certain of what you say."

Another man might have threatened insult. Lamb just looked sadder. "Do you doubt my word, sir?"

Townsend seemed to remember who he was talking to, or at least whose son he was talking to. "No, no, of course not. But it is sometimes the case that events are open to multiple interpretations . . ."

"I know what I have seen, and I know what I have heard." Lamb leaned forward and dropped his voice to a bewildered whisper. "Mr. Townsend, your man Harkness has planted a spy in my mother's house!"

CHAPTER 38

Following The Thread Of The Conversation

It is the common failing of an ambitious mind to over-rate itself . . .

Lady Caroline Lamb, Glenarvon

There were any number of constants existing between great households. One of them was the fact that there was always a tremendous amount of sewing to be done.

Therefore, it was only a matter of time before Mrs. Kendricks and Claridge should come to occupy the airy sewing room at the top of Melbourne House at the same time. Indeed, Mrs. Kendricks had stationed herself there as soon as Miss Thorne had left that morning, in the hopes that Claridge would arrive eventually.

The lady's maid did not seemed pleased to see her. She nodded civilly but stiffly and took a seat at the far end of the worktable. She brought out a pair of silk stockings flocked with green leaves and spread them on the table.

This won't be easy.

Mrs. Kendricks looked at the torn petticoat ruffle she was repairing. She considered the damaged seam, and possible ways to open the conversation.

But it was Mrs. Claridge who spoke first.

"I saw your Miss Thorne on the backstairs this morning." Mrs. Claridge opened her workbasket to get a stocking frame and pair of delicate scissors. "She must be feeling better."

"She is indeed," replied Mrs. Kendricks. "It was only a slight throat strain after all."

"Mmm. Well." Mrs. Claridge was silent for a moment while she slid the stockings over the frame and smoothed them into place. "I would think she'd have been helping with her ladyship's calls in that case, not slipping out like she'd something to hide." Mrs. Claridge examined the tear and snipped a single thread on the stockings, and then another. Her hands were as big and rawboned as the rest of her, but for all that, her motions were extremely delicate.

And she's too observant by half.

"Miss Thorne is about on her ladyship's business." Mrs. Kendricks tried for an impartially civil tone, and failed. "I don't ask questions as to how she does what's required of her."

"Her ladyship's business, is it?" Mrs. Claridge examined the stocking critically and snipped another thread. "Lady Melbourne said nothing to me about business today."

"No? Well. I'm sure I don't know why that should be."

Mrs. Claridge reached into her basket again, this time for a reel of delicate silk, which she held against the stocking to compare the colors.

"I must say, I'm surprised you're still here, Mrs. Kendricks, with your Miss Thorne out and about. Did she not need her maid?"

Mrs. Kendricks did not like these jabs, but she held her temper. Mrs. Claridge was obviously trying to start a quarrel by implying Miss Thorne was up to no good going out without her maid. But taking it up wouldn't do her, or Miss Thorne, any good.

"Normally, I would be with her, of course. But since we've had such a busy pair of days, she gave me leave to stay behind and see to my mending." Mrs. Kendricks paused to gather up a bit more of the ruffle onto her needle. "Miss Thorne's most anxious to present the neatest possible appearance. She's very sensible of her position as she's her ladyship's special guest, and aware she cannot appear at less than her best."

Claridge looked startled for a moment at this expression of humble gratitude, and then nodded in solemn agreement. "Well, it was thoughtful of her to give you the time to see to things. There's not many would do so much."

"Miss Thorne has always been an excellent employer," declared Mrs. Kendricks. Which was probably one of the last whole truths she'd tell in this conversation.

She supposed she should feel more prickings of conscience than she did. Like her, Claridge was very much at the mercy of the world. Everyone made shift and made do. When you had a place to keep, you sometimes did things, or allowed things to be done, that you wouldn't if you'd been able to choose freely.

Claridge had threaded her needle with the silk and begun stitching the tear closed, one slender thread at a time.

"You've a very fine hand there, Mrs. Claridge," Mrs. Kendricks said, which felt in some strange way like an apology. "I imagine keeping her ladyship's clothes in order is quite the challenge."

It was the right thing to say. Mrs. Claridge launched into a breathless rhapsody of the silks, satins, velvets, and laces that had passed under her hands. There was a whole litany of complaints—that were not truly complaints—of what endless trouble it was to care for all her ladyship's fine gowns.

"But that's all over now," Claridge said with a sigh.

"Over?" murmured Mrs. Kendricks. "From what I've seen, her ladyship is still honored by many friends. Her visiting hours seem to be filled to the brim."

"Yes, you'd think so, if you knew nothing of the old days."

A description of those old days followed—the dinners at Devonshire House in the company of the celebrated Duchess of Devonshire; the balls and parties at Clarence House at His Royal Highness's *personal* invitation; the travels to "foreign parts," where she was feasted and courted by royalty.

Mrs. Kendricks listened, glancing between her own work and Mrs. Claridge's face. She saw that the backs of her work-roughened hands were still smooth. The lines on her face were visible but shallow, and only a few streaks of gray sparkled in her dark hair.

Either you came to Lady Melbourne as a slip of a girl, or your real complaint is that you got here too late for all those glory days you're going on about. Mrs. Kendricks lifted the bit of seam she'd been working on and inspected the stitches. *I do start to suspect, Mrs. Claridge, that the most you've had to do with those fine gowns is turning and repacking them in their trunks so they don't crease.*

"Well, I must say," murmured Mrs. Kendricks when Mrs. Claridge finally drew breath. "It sounds like more excitement than I'd care for."

Again, this was the right thing to say. Mrs. Claridge lifted her nose, right up into the air. "I daresay it would not suit everyone. It takes a deal of skill to shepherd one's lady through such a life, but we always managed."

"I should think you'd find a chance to rest at home a pleasant change after so many years of hullabaloo."

"Rest," sniffed Claridge. "There's no rest to be had in this house."

"Well, caring for an invalid is always difficult, and I imagine her ladyship is one who's exacting in her illness."

"My lady is no trouble whatsoever," declared Claridge. "The trouble in this house lies elsewhere."

"I will confess Mrs. Claridge"—Mrs. Kendricks measured a length of cotton against her arm and snipped it off the reel—"that does not surprise me in the least."

"You mustn't take me for a gossip, Mrs. Kendricks."

Mrs. Kendricks ducked her head closer to her needle as she threaded it. "Goodness, no, Mrs. Claridge. I've been in many a house and seldom met someone who showed such honest devotion to her lady. I just meant, well, I've only been here a short while, but I've seen a thing or two." Mrs. Kendricks paused again. "Lady Caroline seems a very . . . changeable person."

"Changeable?" Claridge bit the word off like it was a piece of thread. "Oh, she's a deal worse than that," said Mrs. Claridge. "A very great deal. I hope, Mrs. Kendricks, your Miss Thorne hasn't been listening too much to that one."

"Only by way of trying to be of use to her ladyship," said Mrs. Kendricks. "She knows Lady Melbourne has been particularly troubled of late."

Mrs. Claridge was looking narrowly at her, trying to find the flaws she could pick at. Mrs. Kendricks smoothed out the petticoat on the table in front of her and ran her fingers across the seam, trying by feel to find if there were any additional tears or flaws she'd missed.

"Well," said the lady's maid loftily. "All I have to say is that some people should be glad that Claridge knows how to keep her own counsel, because she could say plenty if she wanted to."

"Perhaps we'd better leave it there," suggested Mrs. Kendricks. "I'll be the first to say I'm not one to gossip, but one never means to start telling tales, does one?" She peered at her work again. "Not that I'd repeat anything I was told in confidence, of course. Unless it was something that my employer absolutely needed to hear, you know what I mean, to avoid making some mistake, like trusting the wrong person."

Mrs. Kendricks watched Mrs. Claridge's face from the corner of her eye. *She's making up her mind. She's got something to say, and she's wondering whether she should, and if she*

*should, then how she should. Now, then, what's it to be? And
is it me you want to hear this . . . whatever it may be? Or is it
Miss Thorne?*

Claridge kept her eyes on her work, but she began to
speak, softly and clearly.

"Her ladyship was having one of her bad nights. We'd had
to call the doctor late for her, I remember. It was that bad.
There's times when she won't have anyone else touch her,
and there can be . . . a great deal to clean up afterward."
They shared a glance. They'd both attended sick rooms.
There was nothing more to be said about it.

"Was Mrs. Oslander not there to lend a hand?"

"Not that night. The spell had come on Lady Melbourne
that quick. She'd had to come up early from the dinner
downstairs. It was one of Lord Peniston's dinners." Mrs.
Claridge snorted. "All horse and political men. Some friends
of Mr. William's, hardly a one of them worth talking to, *I*
should think. But it's not my place, is it? My job is to care for
my lady."

"Just what I would have said, Mrs. Claridge." Mrs.
Kendricks paused. "This would be right after that Mr. Davies
came to pester her about some letters? I heard some talk
about that. I can't say I think much of that gentleman. Something about him that's not quite right."

"Oh, that's just the way it is with these dandified, poetical
gentleman. Always putting on a show." Claridge assumed an
indulgent and worldly air. Mrs. Kendricks grit her teeth just a
little. "They're pretty to look at, though, I must say," Claridge added wistfully.

Mrs. Kendricks made a skeptical sound deep in her throat.
"Well, I've seen a few of them in my day, and what I say is all
that so-called taste in clothes and horses, and I don't know
what else, leads them into trouble more often than not."

Mrs. Claridge shrugged and bent more closely over her
darning. "I dare say. Still, it does provide a bit of color now

and then, and who's the worse for that? But, yes, my lady had her spell after Mr. Davies came. At first I thought she might be using her illness as an excuse because she didn't feel like sitting with Lord Melbourne's guests, but it wasn't," she added with genuine sorrow. "It was that bad."

Mrs. Kendricks made a sympathetic murmur.

"Well, I'd finally gotten my lady to sleep. I was taking some things away to the laundry room and I happened to be passing the door to the yard and I saw it was standing wide open. Which it shouldn't be, of course. So I put my bundle down to go to close it. I remember thinking I should wake the butler, Mr. Wexford, and have him search the house. How was I to know there mightn't be a robber inside? I took a look out into the courtyard, just to see if one of the staff had slipped out quick like and gotten careless. . . ." She bit her lip. "But what I saw was Lady Caroline. Once you know her, you'll never mistake her, not even in the dark. She was running right across the yard. I ducked back and she barged through the door. She didn't even take the time to close it behind her, so she didn't see me there in the dark."

Mrs. Kendricks made sure her eyes opened wide in wonder at this. "What did you do? Did you go out to see what frightened her?"

"I meant to, but I wanted to make sure she was not going to make some disturbance. My lady had only just gotten to sleep. So I followed her."

"And you never saw what it was she ran from?"

"I'll tell you what I did see. Maybe you or your clever Miss Thorne can make some sense of it. I saw Lady Caroline run right into her writing room. She forgot to close that door as well, and I watched her snatch up a coat and gloves and toss them straight into the fire."

CHAPTER 39

Those Small Hidden Concerns

They fly so slowly, who fly from what they love.

Lady Caroline Lamb, Glenarvon

Rosalind stood outside the offices of the *London Chronicle* and watched George Littlefield and his friends leaving for the evening. There were a half dozen of them, all talking and laughing and pulling on their gloves. If George so much as glanced toward her, he did not recognize her.

Not that Rosalind could blame him for the failure. She hardly looked like herself. She was disheveled and still clutching her valise, and she was sure she was quite pale. She was physically tired, but more than that, the discovery of Mrs. Oslander's daughter had left her raw inside. She felt somehow that she should have known. That she should have done something. Stopped it somehow. Saved her somehow.

It was ridiculous, but there it was. She too had been abandoned young, and her heart went out to that unknown child, and no amount of reasoning would change that.

She wanted to do something for somebody. She wanted to put off the moment when she had to look at what she carried and have more disappointment, or fear, or sorrow. So, she was going to do the one thing she could think of. She was going to follow George Littlefield and find out where he went. She could do nothing to mend Mrs. Oslander's tiny family. She was probably going to break apart what tiny bit of stability Caroline Lamb and her son knew.

She could at the very least try to help George and Alice mend their fences.

And if you learn something you don't want to? Rosalind asked herself. *Then what?*

I don't know, she answered. *But it's better than one more secret festering in this world. It has to be.*

George and his friends stood about, shaking hands, slapping shoulders, and looking at the sky to judge the likelihood of rain. Then George tipped his low-crowned hat to them all and started up the street.

The exact opposite direction that he would take had he been heading home to the flat. Rosalind gave him a decent head start, picked up her bag and her hems, and followed.

She should not, of course, be doing this. However good her intentions, there was no excuse for surreptitiously trailing after a friend, a man who was very nearly her brother. She told herself she did it for Alice, and because George *was* very nearly her brother. If he was in difficulties, she needed to help. If he wasn't going to talk about those difficulties, she needed another way to find out what the problem was. This was the way that presented itself.

It was not, perhaps, the most satisfactory chain of reasoning, but it would have to do.

At first, Rosalind worried he might turn his head and see her. Soon, however, it became evident that George was entirely preoccupied. He was also in a hurry. Rosalind struggled to keep up the pace he set with his long legs while she was weighted down with her skirts, cloak, and bag.

At last, George turned into a curving alley. Rosalind stopped at the corner and pretended to inspect the contents of a jeweler's window. She snuck a glance around the other edge of her bonnet to see George stop halfway down the narrow street. This was a mercantile district. Not a haunt of the fashionable, like Bond Street, but simply one of hundreds of localities where things were bought, sold, and made. The shop at the end looked to be a dressmaker's. George headed straight toward it but stopped just outside the door.

Rosalind's brows puckered.

Then the dressmaker's door opened and a woman emerged, settling a straw bonnet onto her black hair. At this distance, Rosalind could make out very little about her except that she was neatly dressed in a pretty shade of pale blue.

And that George swept his hat off in a dramatic bow to her, and that she threaded her arm through his so they could walk away together.

Rosalind stared openly. She did remember to close her mouth. Eventually.

All at once, the young woman stopped, laughing and fussing with her bonnet ribbon. George reached up gently and undid the knot, retying it into a bow beneath her chin. From where she stood, Rosalind could not see the woman's face, but she could see George's. Rosalind had known George since he was a boy, and she had never seen such a smile from him. Rosalind felt her eyes open wide, and she forgot she was supposed to be hiding.

And then George looked up, right into her face.

"Rosalind?"

Of course the woman turned, and of course she saw that the man who was very clearly her beau was staring in shock and horror at a bedraggled woman carrying a traveling case.

Oh, George. Rosalind lifted her hem and walked quickly over to the couple. "Hello, George." She made her curtsey. "How do you do?" she said to the woman. "I'm Rosalind Thorne."

The woman returned her curtesy. She was a round woman

with an open and cheerful face and a pair of deep, intelligent, and dramatically dark eyes. "Hannah Gionetti," she said. "Very pleased to meet you, Miss Thorne."

"Very pleased to meet you, Miss Gionetti. You must excuse my appearance. I am at the end of a very long day."

"Oh, I understand what that is," said Miss Gionetti. "How is it you know George?"

"I was at school with his sister, Alice."

"Ah! I have not yet had a chance to meet Alice." She looked at George with mild reproof.

"George!" exclaimed Rosalind, looking him right in the eye. "How terribly negligent of you!"

"I've been meaning to arrange it, I just . . ." He shuffled his feet. Not only that, but George Littlefield—a man who wrote about murder, riot, and corruption, sometimes after witnessing the events firsthand—blushed like a schoolboy.

Miss Gionetti slipped a sideways glance toward Rosalind, and the pair of them shared a smile. *Men.*

"And are you a writing woman as well?" Miss Gionetti asked her.

"No, no. I'm a companion to a gentlewoman. I'm afraid I cannot stay talking, as much as I would like to, as she expects me back in time for her supper. But it was lovely to meet you, Miss Gionetti. I hope we can speak again soon. Perhaps if our free days coincide, you and I and Alice could visit the tearooms . . . ?"

This was finally too much for George. "I, erm . . . Rosalind, will you wait just a minute?" He grabbed Hannah's hand and hurried her up the street. Rosalind turned her back. She stared at the shop window in front of her.

I will not look back. I will not. It would be rude. We are in the street and George is clearly . . .

George was clearly finished with whatever he had to say to Hannah, because he marched up to Rosalind's side and seized her by the elbow. "Come along, Rosalind, I'll walk you back."

"Thank you, George—" Before she got any farther, George took off at such a pace she had to break into an undignified trot to keep up. "—But!" She shook his hand off. "I really have had a long day, and I think we'd be better off if we hired a hack, and Miss Gionetti is going to think there's something wrong between us if you insist on rushing me off like this."

George froze, his face gone white as the snow. He looked over his shoulder. Fortunately, Miss Gionetti was already gone.

Rosalind sighed, suddenly at the end of her patience. "There's a carriage house on the corner. Will you please go hire us a hack?"

George looked as if he'd rather jump headfirst into the Fleet Ditch, but he nodded, eventually. He also did as she instructed.

He did not, however, say a single word as they climbed into the badly sprung and listing carriage. Once he gave the driver directions, he sat back and stared out at the street. Clearly, it was going to be up to Rosalind to start this particular conversation.

"Miss Gionetti seems very nice."

George did not turn his head. "You won't tell Alice, will you, Rosalind?"

"Not if you tell her first."

George's reply was a belligerent silence. Had this not been one of her best friends in the world, and someone she knew to be a thoroughly sensible man, Rosalind might have described it as a pout.

"George, why won't you tell Alice you're walking out with Miss Gionetti?" asked Rosalind. "Is there something . . . wrong?"

"You mean is Hannah married, or Catholic, or something of the kind? No. Well, she is Catholic, because of her father, she's half-Italian . . ."

"Gionetti, yes. I had some idea."

But George wasn't listening. "But I don't expect Alice to

mind that, and I certainly don't . . . And, before you ask, Hannah does love me. She's said so. Which is nothing short of amazing, all things considered. You'd like her," he added suddenly. "She's sharp as a new pin and has a wonderful sense of humor."

"She sounds perfect for you."

"Yes. She is. Perfect." George turned to the window again. "For some man who can afford to marry."

"Ah," said Rosalind, because it was the only thing she could say.

"Yes. Ah." George exhaled. "Alice and I barely manage together. How am I to afford a wife on just my income? Yes, yes, she's a dressmaker and she brings in something, but what happens when the children come?" He stared at the passing houses, as if the arguments were pouring from the doorways rather than his own mind. "What happens if Alice . . . if Alice can't support herself?"

Now I understand. This was the root of both George's anger and his fear. He was afraid if he had a wife and children to care for, his sister might suffer.

"And you haven't said anything to Alice because you know she'd tell you to marry the woman you love."

"Of course she would, because, despite everything, she's still a romantic."

"And because she loves you and wants you to be happy," Rosalind corrected him gently.

George grimaced. "It's as well you don't work for the Major. You start far too many sentences with the word 'and.' "

"And what do you propose to do about it?" answered Rosalind.

George sighed, thoroughly and openly exasperated. "I'm going to have to break things off. What else can I do? It's not fair to Hannah to keep seeing her when I can't . . . I can't . . ." His fists tightened. "Hang it all, Rosalind, what else am I supposed to do? I can't abandon Alice!"

"Of course not, but you could trust her."

"You know I trust her!"

"Not enough to help you in this."

"That's not fair."

"It is true, however."

"Yes, all right, it is. But I won't let her martyr herself. I won't—"

"George." Rosalind cut him off sternly. "Exactly who are you arguing with? It isn't me, and it certainly isn't Alice."

George didn't answer for a long moment. When he did speak, Rosalind had to strain to hear him over all the sounds of the carriage and the street outside.

"I'm afraid, Rosalind," whispered George. "I've got so little to offer, so little to keep a family on. I . . . what if I can't do it?"

What if I'm like my father? Those unspoken words lay underneath everything that he did say. *What if I bring the ones I love into disgrace and disaster?*

Rosalind suddenly felt keenly aware of the valise at her feet.

"Speaking the truth will not do that, George," she said. "It's keeping secrets that brings down the disasters. If the three of us know anything, we know that."

George was silent for a while, but the mood between them felt different now. His belligerence had eased, and so had some of the fear. Finally, he nodded.

"All right, Rosalind. I'll talk to Alice. On one condition."

Rosalind frowned. "What possible condition could there be?"

"Alice told me about the engagement party. I promise I'll tell Alice about Hannah if you promise you will finally settle things with Devon one way or another. It's not fair to him to leave him dangling."

Rosalind felt her spine drawing itself up and her tone turning deeply, involuntarily icy. "I hardly think Devon Winterbourne, Duke of Casselmaine, is dangling."

George just returned a long, steady look, one that reminded her that this easygoing man had come from the same place as she, and had survived the same disasters she had. "Don't try to fool yourself, Rosalind," said George. "You won't like the results."

"I'm not fooling myself!" Rosalind cried.

"You are. In more ways than you know. But there." George slumped back and rubbed his face until that stern, steady expression was entirely wiped away. "Now I'm starting to quarrel with you, too, which puts the finishing touch on the work titled *George Littlefield Making a Complete Ass of Himself.* I'm sorry."

"It's already forgotten," she answered, but added nothing more, at least for a time, for her throat had tightened and her eyes were blinking far too rapidly.

"I can't do it, George," she whispered at last.

"Why not? You say I should be honest with Alice. What's . . ."

"Because I'd have to say good-bye to Charlotte," she croaked. "I'd never be able to see or write her again, and I've only just got her back. The Duchess of Casselmaine cannot acknowledge—cannot *have*—a sister who is a courtesan."

CHAPTER 40

A Matter Of Timing

*. . . Or am I one grown old in crime, and utterly
insensible to its consequence?*

Lady Caroline Lamb, Glenarvon

Harkness told Goutier to go home.

"I'm fine," said the patrol captain as his horse missed
its step on another cobble and Goutier winced, yet again. It
was clear the pain was bad. In fact, Goutier was beginning to
look as green around the gills as Mr. Davies had before he
started drinking.

"You're not fine," Harkness told him. "You need Sal to tie
those ribs up again."

"I can . . ."

"Do I have to make it an order, Mr. Goutier?"

"Probably," Goutier grumbled. "You'll come round as
soon as you've met Miss Thorne?"

"My word of honor."

With this, Goutier had finally relented. Harkness watched
him ride off, his elbow pressed tight against his wounded
side.

Little Russell Street was quiet when Harkness got there.
He'd made a detour to Bow Street and the stables to see the

horse taken care of, then walked the rest of the way. It was not that far. In fact, he'd sometimes strolled in this direction as he left the station for home. Just to make sure all was right in the street. Which was probably not the behavior of an upright man who lived entirely free of the regrets and pangs of unfulfilled affection, but he didn't seem willing to stop himself.

This was the time of day when folk were from home, mostly at their work. Adam took in the details of the street without really thinking—the idlers and porters on the corner, the houses closed and silent waiting for their inhabitants to come back from their work. Even the sound of children seemed distant.

Miss Thorne's house was as quiet as her street. Indeed, all its shutters were closed. But there was a light moving in the upstairs window.

She's gotten here ahead of me, he thought. He hoped that was a sign she'd met with success. Perhaps they could lay this business to rest before much longer.

Harkness put his hand on the gate, and paused. He felt his eyes narrow.

If Miss Thorne had gotten here ahead of him, of course she would not want to sit in a dark house. But why take all the trouble to make a light? Why not just open a window?

Especially the parlor window. For she was expecting him and Goutier. She would open the parlor to make it ready to receive them. The parlor window overlooked the street, and it was as firmly shuttered as all the others.

He looked at the upper story again and watched the light moving back and forth through the shutter slats.

A very unpleasant idea stole into Mr. Harkness's mind.

Jumping at shadows, Harkness, he told himself. *Who'd try burglary at such an hour?*

Someone who knew the house was closed up because the inhabitants were away visiting. Someone who knew a street like this was a quiet place in that space of time when afternoon faded to evening. At night, there'd be waking babies to rouse mothers who might look out a window, and barking dogs to alert their owners something was afoot, and men up late drinking or making or mending, and the fancy people in their carriages taking the side street to avoid the traffic in the high street as they headed to the Theatre Royal.

At this time of day, there were fewer people to see, and to wonder. The ordinary noises of London's ordinary business trickled over the fences and down the other streets. The sudden sound of a door slamming or something toppling over might be heard, but it would not be remarked on.

The light moved back and forth.

Harkness lifted his hand from the gate. *Maybe I'm being a fool. Maybe we'll laugh about it later. We'll see.*

Adam continued on, walking up the street until he came to an alley. Only then did he break into a run. He sprinted down the alley to the mews and back up toward Miss Thorne's house. A dog barked. Hoofbeats and wagon wheels clattered. All the cold, stale scents of London's back ways assailed him.

No one came to a window or a door to look.

He found the right gate. He pushed, and it yielded easily. Now Harkness was certain something was wrong. Mrs. Kendricks would never leave her house without latching the back gate.

Miss Thorne's back garden was a small rectangle of brick and packed dirt. Low walls divided it from the gardens belonging to the other houses in the row. What greenery there was stood in pots and the window box.

The back door had two steps leading up to it. That door also yielded when Harkness pushed. But this time, it was because the bolt had been shattered.

Harkness's first thought was to raise the alarm. There might be a day patrol near. But his shout would likewise give the alarm to whoever was upstairs, and maybe allow them a

chance to escape. Harkness flexed his fingers and felt that
same calm come across him that he knew from his nights in
the forest. The man had left himself an easy way out with this
broken lock and open door. He would leave the same way he
got in. Adam could wait.

As long as Miss Thorne doesn't come home.

He silently cursed Goutier's broken ribs. He could have set
the patrol captain on watch to prevent Miss Thorne from
surprising the burglar.

He thought to head up the stairs, catch the man in the act.
But no. The man might hear his step. He might be armed and
ready to fight.

Be sensible, Harkness. If Miss Thorne came, it would be
through the front door, openly and freely, with all the usual
sounds. The housebreaker knew his escape lay out the back.
He'd still run this way.

Harkness slipped into the scullery. Even with the door
open, this room remained deep in shadow. He waited, blinking hard to help his eyes adjust before he eased himself into a
crouch among the mops and pails. Harkness held himself still
and got ready to wait.

Footsteps passed back and forth overhead. The pace in-
creased. He heard a door slam. He imagined the would-be
thief freezing on the spot, his own heart hammering, wondering if he'd been heard. The steps began again, slower this
time, but speeding up quickly. He was taking the stairs now,
heading up to the attics.

Looking for the Melbourne letters? Probably.

Miss Thorne would be aghast to learn an intruder pawing
over her possessions, digging into what she worked so hard
to keep private. Adam, for once, found it harder to hold on
to his anger than to hold himself steady in the darkness. But
he'd be damned if he'd let it get the better of him. He would
not become a careless fool just because this was Rosalind
Thorne's house.

Upstairs, the noises continued—the scraping of heavy objects and furniture being moved, the restless footsteps hurrying back and forth. The burglar's patience was failing him. Desperation setting in. There would be breakage. Whatever pry bar or tool he'd used to shatter the back bolt would be used against trunks and drawers.

I'm sorry, Miss Thorne.

A voice shouted in the street. Another rose in song. They were accompanied by the noise of a light carriage and a team being driven too fast. It was getting late. Men were returning from work, women from their shops, the houses where they served. The houses were filling up with people who might notice a disturbance.

Upstairs, the noises ceased. The man had frozen in place again. He'd be close to panic now. He was out of time.

Does he know it?

Footsteps pounded down stairs.

Yes. One more moment, Miss Thorne. Just one more.

The sounds coming toward him were blundering and over-hasty. Adam shifted his weight and flexed his hands.

The scullery door flew open and a shadow bolted past. Harkness launched himself forward, wrapping his arms hard around solid shoulders.

"RAISE THE HUE AND CRY!" he bellowed. The old signal. The one everybody understood. Murder. Fire. *Thieves.* "HUE AND CRY!"

The thief rolled and kicked and struggled. They tumbled down the back steps and onto dirt and brick. Adam brought his knee in and his fist down.

Pain lanced through him, sharp enough and sudden enough that he saw stars. His grip fell away, and the thief twisted free. The next blow landed on Adam's chin and snapped his head back. He hit the hard dirt, vision blurred, ears ringing, mouth filled with the taste of hot iron and copper.

After that, he knew nothing at all.

CHAPTER 41

Mr. Townsend Decides

I have swum through Charybdis already . . .

George Gordon, Lord Byron, private correspondence

Rosalind arrived home to the unimaginable.

As the hack turned into Little Russell Street, she saw a crowd had gathered in front of her house. She saw men in red vests holding back her gathering neighbors and windows open so people might lean out and stare. At her house.

Rosalind did not entirely recall what happened after that. There was some confusion. She found herself out of breath and running up her front steps without remembering how or when she exited the hack.

She was told "wait" and "hold on, now" by a large number of (mostly male) voices.

Then she was inside her house, and inside her small parlor. Her writing desk had been broken open and papers scattered about the floor.

While I was in Judith Oslander's flat, searching so carefully for the letters, someone else was doing just the same. . . . The valise slipped from her fingers that had gone suddenly numb.

As Mr. Davies warned, men from Bow Street were everywhere. They were on the street keeping the crowds back and the traffic moving. They were in the yard, questioning the neighbors. They were in the kitchen. They were probably in the attics.

But there was one familiar man she did not see.

"Miss Thorne?" said a voice Rosalind felt she should recognize.

She turned and found herself face-to-face with Samuel Tauton. He was another of the Bow Street officers whose acquaintance she had made. He was an older, rounder man and was said to have one of the best memories for faces ever known.

"Mr. Tauton," she said. "I didn't . . . that is . . . I was expecting . . ."

"Mr. Harkness?" he asked. "I think you had better come with me."

The feeling of unreality she'd experienced when she first ran into her house returned as she followed Mr. Tauton up the stairs and into her bedroom.

Mr. Harkness was sitting up on her bed. It had been completely stripped, except for one sheet, and that sheet was stained with blood.

Blood.

A man in shirtsleeves was with Mr. Harkness, and those sleeves were rolled up past his elbows. He was digging in a black bag

Mr. Harkness's left hand was thickly bandaged in linen strips that had probably been torn from her sheets. He looked white as death, and a very odd combination of angry and profoundly embarrassed.

"My apologies," he whispered.

Rosalind just shook her head. This was the nightmare. Downstairs, that had been beyond imagining, but this—that he should be hurt and she should be unable to help—this she had feared, and that made it worse.

"I seem to have surprised a burglar in your house," Mr. Harkness went on.

"I see that, yes."

He closed his eyes. "I'm sorry," he said again.

"There is no need."

The man in shirtsleeves eyed Rosalind and Mr. Tauton. "Unless this woman has medical experience, Tauton, I want her out of here."

"As you say, Sir David."

Mr. Tauton steered Rosalind back into the hallway.

She swallowed. And swallowed again. "Is he . . . will he . . ."

"He'll be fine," said Tauton. "The wound's deep, I'll not lie. But he was found quick, and that's Sir David Royce with him."

"The *coroner?*"

"He's a physician trained in Berlin. Mr. Harkness is in very good hands. Let me take you down."

Rosalind wanted to protest, but she controlled herself ruthlessly. She could do nothing. She must not interfere. She must be calm. Clear-headed. She must.

She let Mr. Tauton take her arm and lead her downstairs. She had no strength or nerve left to insist she was perfectly capable, thank you.

"Clumsy bastard," muttered Tauton. "No idea how to find anything. Still, it looks to be a burglary, or at least a try at one" he was saying. "Did you keep any plate or jewels here, Miss Thorne?"

"There's the coffee service, but . . ." Rosalind's throat seized up. *The bank draft.*

Rosalind hurried to the desk. The drawers had all been opened, papers lay scattered everywhere. But there, in the center drawer, perfectly visible to all, lay Lady Melbourne's draft for five hundred pounds.

Rosalind lifted out the delicate paper. No mere thief breaking into an empty house would leave this behind. Whoever had come here had been looking for something quite specific.

Quite probably the Melbourne letters. Why else would anyone come here while she was away?

Rosalind became aware of the fact that Mr. Tauton was no longer looking at her. He'd stiffened to a species of attention. A moment later she saw why.

Mr. John Townsend, in his silk coat and broad-brimmed white hat, stood on the parlor threshold. He ignored his men and walked right up to her.

"Miss Thorne," he said.

"Mr. Townsend."

He bowed, and she curtsied. Because courtesy could not be neglected, even at such a time.

Townsend turned to the principal officer. "Mr. Tauton, I understand Harkness was injured in this business."

"Yes, sir. In the hand. Sir David's upstairs with him now. It looks good."

"I see," he said impassively. "Miss Thorne, how was it Mr. Harkness came to be here?"

Rosalind looked up at Mr. Townsend. She did not like this man. He did not like her. But he was the head of Bow Street, and she was . . . she was who she was.

Mr. Townsend mistook her hesitation. "Miss Thorne, you will come with me, please."

Mr. Townsend walked in front of her, out into her tiny back garden. He looked about himself, openly and entirely displeased with what he saw. Then he folded his hands behind his back and faced her.

"Miss Rosalind Thorne, I charge you, as an officer in the service of His Majesty the King, to tell me what has happened here."

He stood, tall and officious and utterly certain of himself, and waited.

He is waiting for me to lie, she realized, and then more. *He wants me to lie so he can catch me. So I become what he believes me to be.*

Rosalind took a deep breath. Her knees shook, and she stilled them.

Then Rosalind did as she was instructed.

She told Mr. Townsend about being taken to Lady Melbourne by Lady Jersey. She told him about the letters and Lady Melbourne's fear of blackmail. She told him about Sir David recruiting Mr. Harkness to find out the identity of the dead woman found in the Melbourne House courtyard, and how Mr. Harkness in turn asked her to assist him and to keep the matter entirely secret.

"So that together we might be able to spare Lady Melbourne and the whole family from unnecessary publicity and scandal. They have already been through so much."

Perhaps this last was a stretch, but when looked at in good light, it remained true.

She told him everything she knew for certain.

All the while, Rosalind watched Mr. Townsend watching her. His face remained a stone mask and his eyes did not flicker once. She remembered Mr. Harkness telling her this man had made his name pursuing radicals and other criminal rule breakers. Having seen him only as a flatterer, and courtier eager to pursue a place in society, she had not quite believed it.

She did now.

At the very last, Rosalind told Mr. Townsend about meeting Mr. Davies in the street and coming home and finding her door and desk open but the bank draft from Lady Melbourne still among her papers.

When Rosalind finally finished, she folded her hands. Now it was her turn to wait.

"I see." The mask of Mr. Townsend's expression did not shift at all. "Miss Thorne, you will oblige me by not leaving this house for the present."

Then he turned and went back inside.

It took Rosalind a long time to walk back into her parlor. Most of the Bow Street men had cleared out, but Mr. Tauton remained. She could not see Mr. Townsend.

"Here, sit down." Mr. Tauton pushed a chair, Rosalind's customary chair, toward her. "He's gone up to see Harkness. I don't know what you said to him, Miss Thorne." Tauton shook his head. "I haven't seen him like this since we unearthed that nest of Jacobites in Whitechapel."

"I told him the truth," replied Rosalind softly. "I hope that wasn't a mistake."

Mr. Tauton looked down at her. "I hope so as well."

After that, there was little to do but wait. A runner came to tell Mr. Tauton a cart had been brought to carry Mr. Harkness home, just as soon as ever he was ready.

"Loaded with plenty of clean straw. I saw to it personally."

"Good man," said Tauton, and he looked at the stairs.

Sounds of movement came from up above. Rosalind managed to find the strength to sit up just a little straighter. Mr. Townsend clomped slowly down the stairs.

"Now, men," he called over his shoulder. "Go careful. Wouldn't do to have Mr. Harkness damaged any more!"

Four men followed him down the stairs, with a lot of shifting and cursing. They'd made a sling of the bedsheet, and between were carrying Mr. Harkness in the middle of it.

"My insistence," said Mr. Townsend to Rosalind. "And Sir David's."

Rosalind got to her feet and went to the parlor door so she could see them carry him out.

Rosalind was only able to catch a glimpse of Mr. Harkness's face. He was far too pale but he still had that look of impatient embarrassment.

He turned his head and saw Rosalind there. Mr. Harkness

smiled, and she mustered a smile in return. His hand and arm were bound close to his chest in bandages that had probably been torn from another of her sheets. He managed to touch his brow with his good hand. Rosalind bobbed a curtesy and felt as if her whole frame must give way from the force of her relief.

More footsteps sounded, and Rosalind made herself turn to see Sir David coming slowly down her narrow stairs with his bag in one hand and his coat slung over his arm.

"Miss Thorne." The coroner stopped in front of Rosalind and bowed. "I'm sorry we haven't had a proper introduction."

"I'm sure under the circumstances we can forgo the formalities," said Rosalind. "I believe you say that Mr. Harkness will make a full recovery?"

"If he does as he's told, stays in bed and lets the thing heal, I am perfectly confident." Then he saw the worried expression on Rosalind's face and chuckled. "Don't worry, Miss Thorne. As it happens, I'm acquainted with Harkness's mother. She'll make sure he does as he should."

"Sir David has kindly offered to drive you back to Melbourne House," said Mr. Townsend.

Rosalind's head whipped around. *Surely I did not hear that correctly.*

For once though, Mr. Townsend was not looking at her. The door had been left open behind the men who were now carefully loading Mr. Harkness into the stout, straw-filled cart. He went to close it and peered at the latch, satisfying himself that the mechanism was still whole.

"I will tell you, Miss Thorne, that there has been some miscommunication at the house, and some confusion about what your role is there. You are not to worry. I will be addressing the matter myself."

"I . . ." Rosalind stopped, and began again. "May I ask the nature of the confusion?"

"As I told you, I will take care of the matter myself. In the meantime, I will take it as a personal favor if you continue on and make sure that this matter is cleared up exactly as Lady Melbourne asked." Mr. Townsend straightened and turned. His features were an impassive mask that would have done a butler at the Westminster Palace proud. "I might have lost one of my men today, Miss Thorne. In pursuit of his honest duties, as directed in obedience to a superior, and a lady of importance to the realm and the crown. I do not take this lightly."

"No, sir." Rosalind found she had to clear her throat. "Thank you, Mr. Townsend. Sir David. I am quite ready to leave as soon as you are ready."

Mr. Townsend promised he would see to securing her back door personally and post a man to keep watch. Rosalind thanked him solemnly and accepted his polite bow. Sir David drove his own gig and settled her in the back next to his bag and hers, for Rosalind was very careful to reclaim her valise before she left. She added the bank draft to the other contents.

Thankfully, Mr. Townsend did not choose to ask what she was carrying.

Sir David was an excellent hand with the reins. He drove smoothly through the traffic that was making its regular transition from daytime's vans and carts to nighttime's fashionable carriages.

The yard at Melbourne House was quiet when Sir David drew the gig up to the steps. He handed the reins to the boy, came around to open the door, and unfolded the step for Rosalind.

"I won't keep you talking, Miss Thorne," the coroner said as he handed her her valise. "I can see you're exhausted. But there are a few things Mr. Harkness wanted me to make sure you knew."

"I hope he was not too troublesome a patient," murmured Rosalind.

"Mr. Harkness is consistently troublesome. That is what makes him so very good at his duties." Sir David smiled. "He wanted to be particularly sure that I mentioned three items to you. In fact, he wouldn't let me begin work on his wound until I could repeat my lesson."

"That sounds very like him."

"Item one is that Mr. Davies wanted the Melbourne letters so he could convince Lord Byron to pay the money he was owed. Item two is that Davies knew the letters might be missing when he came to Melbourne House on the night . . ." Sir David paused. "I assume you know which night he meant?"

Rosalind nodded.

"Item three is that Davies had received a letter at his club that he said was from Mrs. Oslander. It contained an offer to sell him the Melbourne letters if he came to her house with the purchase price."

Rosalind bit her lip. "I see. That is, I think I will see when I have had a moment. You must excuse me, Sir David . . ."

"Yes, yes, of course." He held out his hand to help her down. "I thank you for all you have done, Miss Thorne, including handling Townsend as you did."

"I only told the truth."

Sir David smiled. "Knowing the right moment to tell the truth is a rare skill, Miss Thorne. I salute you for it." He bowed. "Take care of yourself, and be easy about Mr. Harkness. He will be well, just not as soon as he would like."

Rosalind thanked him and turned away. *I will believe this,* she told herself. *I will, because I must.*

The footman answered the door and took her things. No one else arrived to greet her. Rosalind steeled herself as she climbed past the first floor, but thankfully no door opened and no voice called. She was able to walk undisturbed to her suite and close the door behind herself.

"Miss Thorne!" cried Mrs. Kendricks, starting to her feet. She'd been sitting with her workbasket and one of Rosalind's slippers by the fire. "Great heavens, Miss! What's happened!"

In answer, Rosalind fell forward into her housekeeper's arms and began to cry.

CHAPTER 42

A Small Space Of Calm

*I would return from any distance at any time to
see you—and come to England for you—...
What a fool I was to marry!*

George Gordon, Lord Byron, private correspondence

Rosalind woke in her clean, soft bed in Melbourne House feeling oddly peaceful. There was a calm that came after a great storm of emotion, and she floated in it now. The slant of the sunbeams through the window told her it was past noon, which meant she was being unforgivably slothful, but she did not make any effort to rouse herself. She just lay on her back for a time and let her thoughts drift where they would.

Gradually, however, calm turned to restlessness, and to boredom. Even though part of her wanted to turn over, burrow under the coverlets, and never come out, she still pushed herself upright. Her cap had come off during the night; she replaced it and swung her legs over the edge of the bed.

At least somewhat upright, Rosalind rang the bell.

Mrs. Kendricks sailed into the room immediately and took in the situation at a glance.

"Back under the covers with you, Miss," she ordered. "I've your meal and a pot of tea on a tray, all ready for you."

"Thank you, Mrs. Kendricks. I will eat in the sitting room."

"You will not," replied her housekeeper sharply. "You will climb back into that bed, or you will get neither drop nor crumb."

Rosalind meekly swung her legs back into the bed and pulled the covers back into place.

True to her word, Mrs. Kendricks placed a loaded breakfast tray on Rosalind's lap and poured out a cup of extremely strong tea.

Rosalind ate and drank as if she were starved. Indeed, she couldn't precisely remember when her last meal had been. Surely not since before noon yesterday.

Yesterday.

Rosalind's throat tried to close around her last bite of toast and marmalade. She took a hasty swallow of tea to clear it.

"Are you all right, Miss?" Mrs. Kendricks stood at the foot of the bed in case anything was wanted, or in case Rosalind were to disobey instructions and try to get up before she'd finished her breakfast.

"Yes, yes," said Rosalind hastily. "Mrs. Kendricks, I had my valise with me when I came in last night. Where is it?"

"I put it in the wardrobe, Miss. I thought it shouldn't be left lying about, all things considered. Shall I fetch it?"

"No. It's better where it is for now." No one could casually glance inside of a valise inside of a wardrobe and discover . . .

What? What exactly was it she had?

Rosalind had proof positive in the form of a growing daughter that Mrs. Oslander had need of money. She had potential proof that Mrs. Oslander and Dr. Bellingham had been lovers. She had a set of concealed letters that might be the same letters so sought after by Lady Melbourne, and Scrope Davies, and Lord Byron, and possibly by one or more others that Rosalind did not yet have names for.

She also had the fact that Mr. Davies had known where

Mrs. Oslander lived and had received a letter threatening blackmail that bore her name and address.

She had the fact that some person in this whole dreadful mess was now so desperate, they had searched her house and attacked Mr. Harkness.

Rosalind closed her eyes against that memory.

"Miss?" said Mrs. Kendricks. "What is it?"

"Bad news, Mrs. Kendricks," Rosalind answered her. "I should have told you the moment I returned. I'm sorry . . ."

"You were in no shape to tell anyone anything, if I may say. Anything I might need to know, you can tell me now."

Rosalind thought to invite her to sit down, but she knew her housekeeper. Any such suggestion would be met with the declaration that she preferred to stand, thank you, miss. So, instead, Rosalind told her about returning from her search of Mrs. Oslander's rooms to Little Russell Street and what she had found there.

Mrs. Kendricks blinked. Mrs. Kendricks swayed on her feet.

"Will you excuse me please, miss?" she asked.

"Certainly."

Mrs. Kendricks left the room and closed the door behind herself.

Rosalind sat where she was. She clutched her cup in her hands. She would not get up. She would not go to try to offer comfort. She would not disturb this single moment of privacy Mrs. Kendricks requested. She would not interrupt the woman's anger, her grief, nor her right to maintain her dignity and station as she saw fit.

No matter how hard she had to bite her tongue. She would not do it.

The door opened, and Mrs. Kendricks returned, exactly as she had left, head erect and hands folded.

"I beg your pardon, miss," she said.

"There is no need at all, Mrs. Kendricks," replied Rosalind.

"All I can say is whoever did this better pray to the Almighty that he never come within my reach."

Rosalind felt herself smile. "Yes, I expect he'd better."

"With your permission, I'll go back as soon as can be arranged and see what needs to be done there."

"Ormande can take you in the chaise and stay to help."

"That would be most helpful, thank you. But before that . . ." She glanced toward the door.

"What is it, Mrs. Kendricks?"

Mrs. Kendricks's brow furrowed. "You should know, I did as you asked and spoke with Claridge. It was yesterday, early in the afternoon, while you were still gone."

"What did she say?"

"She had quite the story to tell, miss. All about the night Mr. Davies came begging for those letters and Mrs. Oslander was found dead. She says she saw Lady Caroline in the courtyard, quite late. She says she saw her run into her writing room and burn a coat and gloves."

Rosalind felt the blood drain from her cheeks. "Do you think she was telling the truth?"

"I don't know. But she very much wanted me to hear it, and to tell it to you."

"Did she say what she did afterward? After she saw Lady Caroline burn this coat?"

"No, miss. She did say the next morning the downstairs maid was cleaning the hearth and found some brass buttons, all burnt and melted. She says the maid showed the housekeeper anyway, and the housekeeper said there must have been some accident. Being as it was Lady Caroline's room, everyone was willing to let the matter lie."

Rosalind pressed her lips together in a thin line. "That's convenient."

"I thought much the same, miss. I did try to ask the housekeeper about it, but all she wanted to talk about was how lazy all the girls are and how many excuses they make up for not doing their work properly. As for Claridge herself . . ." Mrs. Kendricks considered. "I suspect she might not be entirely honest, but I don't know for certain that she's done anything beyond trying to make out as if she's done more and seen more than she has. We all do a little bragging and wishful thinking sometimes. May I ask . . . ?"

Rosalind took a fresh swallow of her cooling tea. "Lady Caroline told me a . . . a version of the story Claridge told you. In Lady Caroline's telling, she couldn't sleep and had gone out to the courtyard to look at the sky. She saw Mrs. Oslander's corpse, and she also saw a man—or a person in a man's overcoat—come out of the house to crouch over the corpse. She said she ran into the house after that."

Mrs. Kendricks frowned. "Mrs. Claridge said she didn't go outside to look so could not have seen anything of that."

"That is if she really didn't go outside to look. If she didn't go back to retrieve her laundry bundle, and see that the door was still open, and check to make sure nothing more was amiss in the yard."

Mrs. Kendricks was silent for a moment. "She'd have had to go back for the laundry at least. She couldn't leave that. She just might not have thought it worth mentioning."

"Possibly." Possibly all Claridge did say was true, but possibly only some of it, or none of it. Rosalind rubbed her forehead.

Someone, somewhere, was lying.

Dr. Bellingham said that Lady Caroline had paid Mrs. Oslander to take a packet of letters to Henry Colburn. Claridge said Lady Caroline had run away from Mrs. Oslander's corpse to burn a coat.

Mr. Harkness and Mr. Goutier said that Mrs. Oslander's corpse had not been dressed with a coat or gloves. How would Claridge have known to say Lady Caroline had burned a coat if she had not seen it?

Unless, of course, Claridge was lying about what she'd seen, and what she'd done.

Claridge would have had plenty of opportunities to speak with Judith Oslander and to watch what the nurse was doing. Come to that, Claridge would have had ample opportunity to address Mr. Scrope Berdmore Davies. She could even have done so under the guise of delivering a message from Lady Melbourne, were any disguise required.

There were, upon consideration, a great many things Claridge could have done.

Rosalind bowed her head over her teacup. There was a knock at the door, which Mrs. Kendricks went at once to answer. Rosalind felt a flash of genuine and irrational anger.

Am I not to be allowed one moment to think in this house?

Fortunately, she was able to calm herself by the time Mrs. Kendricks returned. "Speak of the devil and he shall appear," her housekeeper breathed. "Claridge is here. She sends her ladyship's compliments and asks if Miss Thorne will meet her in her bedchamber, if she is quite well after her excursions yesterday."

Mrs. Kendricks looked at Rosalind and straightened her shoulders. Rosalind did the same.

They could not ignore their hostess.

They did not have time to indulge her feelings any longer. They had work to do. They must get on.

Rosalind schooled her features into a properly calm and disinterested expression. Mrs. Kendricks nodded.

"Mrs. Kendricks, tell Claridge that Miss Thorne returns Lady Melbourne's compliments, and that I will be down just as soon as I am dressed."

CHAPTER 43

Loosening Secrets

*Her understanding had so adapted itself to her
passions, that it was in her power to give, in her
own eyes, a character of grandeur, to the vice and
malignity.*

Lady Caroline Lamb, Glenarvon

Lady Melbourne's private chambers were as airy and tasteful as her sitting room. The chamber was decorated in shades of pale green and pure white and hung with luxurious damask velvet. As it seemed was her habit, Lady Melbourne was seated in a chair by the hearth. A worktable had been set in front of her with several open letters on it so that she could read them without having to hold them. The sole concession to privacy and relaxation was the padded stool placed under her feet.

"Well, Miss Thorne!" Lady Melbourne cried as Claridge let Rosalind in. "You have been truant for an entire day. Tell me now, what have you learned? What progress have you made?" Lady Melbourne smiled her charming smile.

Rosalind felt herself staring. *I cannot give way*, she reminded herself. *I cannot be broken over this.*

Because if I am not calm, she will dismiss me out of hand, and then I will never understand what happened.

She also must not let her gaze flicker toward Claridge. She must treat the lady's maid as another anonymous piece of furniture, as one always treated servants while conversing with their employers.

But she needed Claridge to hear every word she spoke.

"Well, clearly, something has happened," said Lady Melbourne. "Otherwise you would not be making such drama over choosing how to start your story. Or is it that you are still not well? When I first sent for you, your maid assured me your throat strain had turned into a head cold." She smiled indulgently, signaling that she was perfectly aware this was a polite falsehood.

"No, I am quite well, thank you, ma'am." Rosalind answered as she took the chair that had been placed in front of Lady Melbourne. She folded her hands in her lap, very aware of feeling like a schoolgirl called before the headmistress. "But there have been some . . . troubling developments."

"After gadding about London for two days without pause, I should think there would be," Lady Melbourne said lightly. "Come, come, Miss Thorne, I find your drama beginning to pall. What is it you have to tell me?"

Rosalind forced herself to marshal her thoughts. She must step deliberately through this. She must say what she knew and what both these women needed to hear, but she must not do so in a way that would cause Lady Melbourne to cease to listen before she was done.

Despite her best efforts, Rosalind's gaze drifted toward Claridge, who stood in her usual place by the chimney, watching her lady, ready to anticipate any need.

"Mr. Davies is apparently in straits," said Rosalind finally. "And it is known that Lord Byron owes him money."

"Byron owes everybody money," replied Lady Melbourne. "I could have told you that much, had you asked."

"Yes, but that debt may be the reason Mr. Davies wants your letters."

Rosalind watched Lady Melbourne turn this over in her mind. "He means to hold them to extract payment from me. This is inherent in the notion of blackmail, Miss Thorne, and again, hardly a revelation."

"Except that he might not mean to ask you to pay. He might mean to ask Lord Byron."

The effect of this statement on Lady Melbourne was nothing short of remarkable. Her cheeks flushed red, and a moment later turned ashen gray. Claridge moved swiftly to the sideboard and poured three drops of some concoction from an apothecary's bottle into a waiting glass of water. This she held to her ladyship's lips, but Lady Melbourne jerked her chin away.

"Leave off, leave off!" she snapped. "I am quite well."

Claridge retired and set the medicine glass on the mantel. But she glared at Rosalind, her dark eyes as hard as marbles.

"Miss Thorne," said Lady Melbourne. "If all is as you have just said, those letters must be recovered from Mr. Davies at once. I authorize you—through whatever intermediary you see fit—to offer for them. *Any* amount . . ."

"Lady Melbourne, Mr. Davies does not have the letters."

"Then what on earth are you blathering on about! I am beginning to wonder if Lady Jersey's faith in you was just another of her absurd society notions!"

Rosalind reached into her sleeve, where she normally kept a clean handkerchief. She pulled out the copy of the letter Mr. Harkness sent her and laid it on Lady Melbourne's writing desk.

"What is this?" Lady Melbourne let go of the chair arm and with a crooked, trembling hand adjusted the paper's position. She read it through once, and then again.

When she spoke, her voice was nothing more than a hoarse whisper. "How did you come by this? Where is the original?"

So, she recognized the letter, and knew it well enough to

know this was only a copy. Rosalind took a deep breath to give them both a moment to gather themselves. "I received this from one of the Bow Street officers that I have dealt with in the past. He knew I had recently come to Melbourne House on a matter of private business."

"*And?*"

"And I am told that Judith Oslander was found with this letter on her person."

Claridge started. Openly, badly. Rosalind kept her gaze turned toward Lady Melbourne.

"Oslander?" Lady Melbourne frowned. "But . . . Dr. Bellingham's nurse? She has not been sent for for . . . a number of days now. Perhaps as much as a fortnight. What has she to do with this matter?" Lady Melbourne stopped. "You cannot tell me that Mrs. Oslander is the thief! I cannot believe it. She is utterly trustworthy!"

"Have you heard anything from Judith Oslander since the last time you employed her as a nurse?"

Claridge's eyes flickered from Rosalind to Lady Melbourne. Her folded hands knotted together.

"Nothing," said Lady Melbourne. "She left the house, and as far as I know had nothing more to do with any of us, and would have none as long as we remained in health."

"Did Mr. Davies visit at all while she was in residence here? I understand she was living in for a time to nurse Lady Caroline and Master Augustus."

Lady Melbourne's eyes darted back and forth as she tried to remember. Her mouth moved, sorting through her memories. But slowly, she slumped backward. Defeated. "I don't know," she admitted. "Claridge? What can you tell Miss Thorne about that?"

Claridge was clutching her hands together so tightly that her knuckles had turned snow white. "I can tell her nothing, my lady."

Claridge met Rosalind's gaze and did not flinch or blink.

Rosalind looked away first, but only to continue speaking to Lady Melbourne.

"This letter was indeed found on Judith Oslander's person. There can be no mistake."

"Where is she?" Lady Melbourne's words grated in her throat. "Where is that woman!"

"She is dead. She was poisoned."

Another person would have exclaimed in distress, shock, or sympathy. Lady Melbourne's chin trembled. Her fingers spasmed. "Where are the other letters?"

Rosalind shook her head. "I am still not certain."

"Why not! Why are her rooms not being searched? What have you been about all this time!"

"Lady Melbourne, Judith Oslander's corpse was found inside the gates of this house."

Claridge was flushed now. Rosalind could feel the heat of her anger and the outrage of her gaze. The maid wanted to shout. She wanted to hurl accusations and outrage.

But she was not permitted to so much as move.

"That's impossible!" announced Lady Melbourne.

"She was found the night of the dinner party, where Mr. Davies first came to ask you for the letters."

Lady Melbourne's face flushed bright red. "And I say it is impossible! I would know if such a thing . . . I would know! This is my house and I would know it!" Her swollen hand slammed down against her work desk. "I would know! *I would know*!"

Claridge took one step forward, but Lady Melbourne threw up her crooked, swollen hand to stop her in her tracks.

For a moment, Rosalind thought Claridge might cry aloud in her frustration.

"I agree, ma'am," said Rosalind quietly. "You should know all of this. It is difficult to keep anything from the mistress of the house."

The look Lady Melbourne turned on Rosalind was filled with such burning contempt, Rosalind felt her skin curdle.

"Are you calling me a liar, Miss Thorne?"

"I am telling you what I know, Lady Melbourne."

"And how do you know it? Who told you these things?" Lady Melbourne was rallying her self-confidence and her wit. In fact, she smiled. "If what you say is even remotely true, why wasn't this news in the papers? We should be under siege from the gutter press. They are always so eager to report every blood-stained anecdote they can get their filthy hands on."

"Because there are those who are keeping this in confidence least until more facts are known."

"Are *you* attempting to blackmail me now, Miss Thorne?"

Rosalind felt the warmth of her own anger rising. Every nerve in her was pulled taut by the strain of remaining calm. If Lady Melbourne challenged her composure with one more insult, she felt sure she would snap.

"Lady Melbourne, you asked me to trace your missing letters. Thus far, the only definitive trail leads to Judith Oslander. She took the letters. She also died of poison, in or near this house. My question now, Lady Melbourne, is if, given these facts, you wish me to continue my inquiries?"

This was important. This was vital. She needed Lady Melbourne's answer, and she needed Claridge to hear it. She needed to remove Claridge's ability to tell more lies, at least as much as possible. She could not leave Claridge any room to tell people, to tell Rosalind, that Lady Melbourne had changed her mind.

She needed Claridge to hear how close to the ultimate answer Rosalind had already come.

"And if I send you packing?" asked Lady Melbourne. She was attempting to make a joke, but the strain in her voice was palpable. "What will the famous Miss Thorne do then? Will it be Bow Street and the magistrates court for me?"

"If I am forced to leave now, you will still not know where the letters are. You must therefore ask yourself if hiding the truth would be worth that uncertainty."

"You present a cold dilemma, Miss Thorne, and you cannot begin to comprehend its nature."

"Then, Lady Melbourne, I ask that you tell me. Any information I have allows me to move more quickly. I know that the letters affect your family, I know they are a part of the larger question as to whether Lord Byron ever returns to England . . ."

"God forbid it should be so!"

Rosalind drew back in shock. Lady Melbourne saw this, and laughed—a bitter, heartbreaking sound.

"Oh, my dear, clever Miss Thorne, you haven't guessed? I kept the letters so that Lord Byron would *not* return to the country." Rosalind could not find her voice, and Lady Melbourne laughed again.

"Yes, you may well stare, Miss Thorne. I expect you have already heard what really caused him to flee in the first place. Well, now you can know the rest. When Lord Byron's worst and wildest moods are on him, he does not care what he does. He only wants what he wants and will dare the world to get it. If he comes back, if he comes into proximity of . . . of . . . certain persons, it will be all over for him, and for them. It is imperative that he remain abroad. The letters were the only means any of us had to make sure he would not try to return.

"His wife, Lady Byron, much against her own wishes, found them and gave them to me. You see, as her wedded husband, he might legally lay claim to any piece of her property. So she had to get them to someone who knew *exactly* what they represented. Even if that someone was otherwise regarded as an enemy." Lady Melbourne smiled sourly.

"That is why I kept them, as dangerous to me as they might

be. There." She lifted her chin. "I've given you enough to bury me in society's eyes ten times over. What will you do with it, Miss Thorne?"

"That depends, Lady Melbourne," Rosalind answered. "If you do not wish me to act any further on your behalf, I will take my leave. What I do after that is, of course, my private business. If, however, you wish me to continue to try to recover the letters as quickly as possible, then I will do so only on the clear understanding that this means I must also discover who killed Judith Oslander. Whoever that may be."

Claridge had returned to her place in the chimney corner. She had assumed the approved pose—erect, silent, not seeming to hear a thing. But this time it was not the servant's professional detachment. This was the look of someone who had been stunned.

Her hands hung loose and helpless at her sides.

Lady Melbourne saw none of this. Claridge was behind her, out of her line of vision. She just nodded her head once.

"Very well, Miss Thorne. It shall be as you say. Do as you see fit."

"I am sorry, Lady Melbourne." And Claridge. "I wish it could be different."

Lady Melbourne shook her head. Claridge did not move. "Please leave me. I find I am very tired. Claridge, go tell Cook I will have my supper on a tray this evening."

Claridge jerked to abrupt life. "Yes, my lady. Of course. After you, please, miss."

Rosalind walked out of the room into the corridor and was stunned when a hard hand caught her elbow and whirled her around. She stopped face-to-face with Claridge.

"If you speak that way to my lady again, I will see you done for." The maid's whisper was knife sharp.

"But you will not, Claridge," said Rosalind.

"You needn't think that you're the only one who knows

the ways of this world, Miss High-and-Mighty Thorne, or that such as you might be out of the reach of such a one as me."

"I would never make that mistake," Rosalind told her softly. "But I do know that you were the one who paid some carters to carry Mrs. Oslander's body to Bow Street."

CHAPTER 44

Goings On Belowstairs

*. . . These are your pupils . . . these sober minded
steady automatons. Well, I mean no harm to them
or you.*

Lady Caroline Lamb, Glenarvon

"Well, Mrs. Kendricks," said Rosalind. "It seems as if you were correct, as usual."

Claridge had followed Rosalind back to her rooms only reluctantly. Now she stood before the hearth straight-backed, hands folded in front of her, the very portrait of the proper lady's maid.

Or possibly of a prisoner at the bar.

Mrs. Kendricks looked her over and shook her head.

"I did say. It could be done by one person, if they knew how to keep a secret."

"And what do you intend to do to me?" Claridge asked. "Am I to be arrested, or simply sacked? Arrest might be better, as I believe they feed prisoners in the jails."

"I intend to ask you what happened," said Rosalind. "After that . . . I don't know."

Claridge very clearly didn't believe her.

"Was it that Mr. Davies?" asked Mrs. Kendricks. "He come

round begging for you to get him the letters? What story did he tell you? That he was trying to save Lady Melbourne from some trick of Lady Caroline's?"

"Mr. Davies?" said Rosalind. "You surprise me, Mrs. Kendricks."

"Oh, yes, miss. I'm afraid Claridge is not content with her lot. She thought she'd be a bit closer to the *ton* when she took this position. She reckoned on parties and glamour, not a sick old woman and soiled linen."

"How dare you!" snapped Claridge.

"If you don't like your place, you leave. You don't sneak and skulk and steal," said Mrs. Kendricks. "You break faith, you just make life harder for all the ones you leave behind."

If Claridge thought she might stare Mrs. Kendricks down, she was sorely mistaken. The two women faced each other for a long cold moment. But it was Claridge who—slowly, painfully—turned away first.

"I thought I was saving her."

"Who?" asked Rosalind quietly.

"My lady," said Claridge.

Rosalind looked to Mrs. Kendricks for confirmation.

"How could that be?" her housekeeper asked.

Claridge hung her head. "He told me . . ." She swallowed and laid her palm against her brow. "He told me she was in danger. He told me he was quite sure Lady Caroline had already taken the letters. And I told him . . ."

"You lied," said Mrs. Kendricks.

"I did not!" cried Claridge. "Not about that. I did see her arguing with the Oslander woman! I saw her press the letters into her hands. I heard the name of Henry Colburn. He has them and she gave them to him!"

"Then why didn't you tell Lady Melbourne when it happened?" asked Rosalind. "Or go get them yourself?"

"Because then she'd get away with it."

"I don't understand. Who?"

"The little witch! The so-called *Lady* Caroline. She's destroyed this entire house with her wildness and her foul bastard son. Oh, I know Mr. Lamb claims him, but such a man never sired such a . . . *thing*.

"If I went straight to Lady Melbourne, she'd just see it all tidied away. It's what she does. My lady knows that if she tries to make trouble, the witch will drag her name all up and down through the mud, open every old sore and rumor, though it drive her to an early grave!

"I had to wait. I had to find some way, any way, to get word outside these walls about what she'd done. I thought if I helped Mr. Davies she'd realize . . . *they'd* realize that they would have to get rid of her. Throw her out, send her away, something." Her voice broke. "And when the witch is gone, she will return to health, and everything will be exactly as it should."

She wants to believe that, thought Rosalind. *She's been holding tight to that, because otherwise what she has done will become too much for her to bear.*

"Did you let Mr. Davies back in the house? After the party?"

"Yes. We had arranged it. I had told him about what I'd seen between . . . Lady Caroline and Mrs. Oslander. He asked me to look in the desk for the letters, just to be sure, and tell him what I found.

"I met him in the library. I don't know what he meant to do. I was called away, because my lady had her spell."

"And when you found Mrs. Oslander in the courtyard afterward, you thought it was Mr. Davies who had killed her."

"It wasn't him!" she snapped. "I'll swear an oath to it! It was *her*. She knew that Mrs. Oslander was going to tell that she was the one who took the letters."

"But you don't know for sure," said Mrs. Kendricks. "You didn't see it."

"What if I did?"

"You didn't," Mrs. Kendricks replied firmly. "If you did, you would have said right away. You would have told your lady. You would have woken her from a dead sleep to tell her. But as it was, you weren't sure, so you made it so someone else could work it out."

"That's why you made sure Mrs. Oslander's body was taken to Bow Street," said Rosalind. "So that the matter would not be hushed up, and when the world came looking and asking questions, you thought you could help make certain suspicion would fall on Lady Caroline."

Claridge didn't answer.

Rosalind sighed. She thought to ask Mrs. Kendricks what should be done now, but no. She would not burden her housekeeper with that decision, or that secret. Not before they understood all the circumstances.

"Thank you, Claridge," said Rosalind. "You may go."

Claridge started. "Go?"

"Yes. I'm sure Lady Melbourne will have need of you soon."

Claridge's gaze slipped from her to Mrs. Kendricks, who returned her look of open confusion with one of cold certainty. Claridge swallowed.

"Yes, miss." She bowed a proper curtsey—back straight, eyes lowered. "Thank you, miss."

Mrs. Kendricks closed the door behind her. "I'm not sure that was wise, miss."

"Maybe not," said Rosalind. "But I am not feeling qualified to sit in judgment just yet." She got to her feet. "At least not until I know what I found at Mrs. Oslander's flat. We need the scissors, and a clean bedsheet to catch the feathers."

While Mrs. Kendricks fetched what was needed, Rosalind opened the wardrobe and pulled out the package she had made of the pillow.

What if I have been wrong all this time? She took the scissors Mrs. Kendricks handed her and cut the string and opened the paper. *What if these are not Lady Melbourne's letters? What if there is nothing at all in there but some straw and old packing to fill out a few thin feathers?*

Or some other set of letters? From the lover who gave her her daughter, perhaps? Or somebody else?

Mrs. Kendricks spread the sheet on the bed, and Rosalind laid the pillow down.

What if . . . what if Claridge was right and the letters are with Henry Colburn and it was Lady Caroline who took them and killed Mrs. Oslander because she found it out?

What if William Lamb killed her to keep his wife safe?

In one swift movement, she slit the pillow straight down the middle. Feathers flew everywhere. Rosalind ignored them all and pulled the three bundles of letters out of the middle of the rapidly deflating case.

Three bundles of letters, all tied in red ribbons. All of them addressed to Lady Melbourne.

Relief made Rosalind's knees shake.

She'd done it. She'd found the letters.

You could leave now, whispered a treacherous voice in her mind. *You have done what you promised. You could hand these straight back to Lady Melbourne and leave at once. Let someone else finish this.*

Rosalind closed her eyes tightly against the tears.

No.

Rosalind set the letters down. She walked out of the bedroom into the sitting room and stood there, doing nothing but trying to get her breathing under control.

"Miss?" said Mrs. Kendricks behind her. "What are we going to do? Should we tell Lady Melbourne?"

Rosalind drifted to the window and looked out over the beautiful formal garden. The other times she had looked across this view, it had been still and empty. She'd wondered if anyone ever visited this lovely private bit of parkland. Now she saw that someone did.

Lady Caroline was down there, playing with her son. The two of them chased each other around the fountain. Mostly, Augustus chased his mother, and Rosalind could see her dancing and turning, keeping herself just out of reach. Just as he seemed to be losing breath and patience—aha!—he caught her, wrapping his arms around her waist. She grabbed hold of his hands and spun them both around. The boy laughed, a loud donkey's bray. He pulled himself away from her and stumbled across the gravel path, spinning himself onto the lawn. Lady Caroline laughed and clapped and ran to join him. Both of them twirled beside each other, arms out, spinning side by side.

I do not want it to be her, or William Lamb. I want it to be Mr. Davies, or Dr. Bellingham or Lord Byron come back in some disguise, sitting in a darkened room, weaving a spider's web of a plot.

I want Claridge to be a better liar than I ever could imagine and strong enough to give Mr. Harkness a fight and make him believe her to be a man.

She did not believe Lady Caroline to be an innocent. She did not believe her to mad.

But Rosalind knew what it was to not fit in the world. She knew what it was to be lonely and to wish for love and understanding. She knew what it was to be confused about one's place and to wish for something different, even when one kept being told one had everything.

And if Lady Caroline was taken away, what would become of the boy—that ungainly, awkward boy with his flawed understanding and spirits?

If William Lamb was taken away, what would happen to both wife and son?

She knew that her heart ached for the other child, the one who did not yet know she had been orphaned. She knew that she wanted to save this child for the sake of that one.

What if it is her? Or him? What will I do?

There is only one way to find out.

"Mrs. Kendricks, tell Ormande to get the carriage ready," she said. I will go to Mr. Colburn at once. If he confirms Claridge's story . . ." Rosalind did not finish. "I only hope he will be at his office today." She paused. She thought about Claridge, somewhere on the back stairs and the quiet rooms. "And, Mrs. Kendricks, I have an errand for you. I think it might be a good idea to get these letters out of this house."

CHAPTER 45

The Offices Of Henry Colburn, Publisher

*I have been lately in a terrible state of plague &
vexation . . . Accounts must have reached you in
the Country of a most extraordinary publication
having appeared in the World.*

Elizabeth Lamb, Viscountess Melbourne,
private correspondence

"Miss Thorne! Please do come in and make yourself
entirely at home."

It seemed to Rosalind that when it came to a matter of life,
death, and blackmail, the answers should properly lurk in
darkness in a fog-choked lane or dank cellar. They required
what Alice would call "appropriate and expected atmos-
phere." They should not be neatly stored in a wooden cabinet in a private office in the heart of the city, where a warm
fire burned in the grate and the rain drummed softly against
the windowpanes. Neither should they be held by such a man
as Henry Colburn.

Mr. Henry Colburn was a bustling little man with a paunch
that strained his brown brocade waistcoat and the tiniest feet
Rosalind had ever seen. His hairline had receded early from
his broad, speckled brow, and his eyes were large and liquid.

He smiled readily and was filled with a host's earnest energy as he inquired whether her chair by the fireplace was quite comfortable, informed her that the tea was ready, and asked if she took lemon and would she agree to try a slice of the seed cake that Mrs. Colburn had baked this morning?

Rosalind accepted cake, tea, and lemon. Mr. Colburn seated himself in the other chair opposite the low tea table.

"Thank you for agreeing to see me on such short notice, Mr. Colburn. I understand you must be terribly busy."

"I am never too busy for a friend of Miss Littlefield's." Mr. Colburn waved his stubby hand.

This was not entirely true. It was three o'clock. Rosalind had initially presented herself in Mr. Colburn's reception room at noon. The harried clerk had been prepared to dismiss her out of hand. Indeed, he took her name into his employer only after she'd mentioned Alice Littlefield. When he'd returned, he'd been terribly apologetic. Mr. Colburn's schedule could not be cleared before three. Would she like to wait? Or would she be so good as to return?

Rosalind declared she would return and had spent the intervening time most profitably at Clements' Circulating Library purusing the many and varied publications that Mr. Colburn had made available to the reading public.

The work had restored some measure of calm. It had at the least given her some productive distraction for her thoughts.

"I did not realize Alice had spoken to you about me."

"She did, several days ago. 'Mr. Colburn,' she said, 'a particular friend of mine may be calling at your offices. I do hope you will be able to see her,' and naturally, I am glad to oblige."

This did not sound entirely like Alice, but Rosalind did not see any advantage to be gained in pointing this out.

It was somewhat amazing to Rosalind that she could adopt such a collected manner. So much was happening right now in so many other places. Mrs. Kendricks had returned to Little

Russell Street to survey the damage of their home and to lock the Melbourne letters in the silver cupboard with the plate. The would-be thief had already searched the house, and now there was a Bow Street man at the door.

They will be safe there, she told herself for the thousandth time. *No one will take them. No one will think to look. No one will come to harm Mrs. Kendricks.*

The greater worry was Claridge and Lady Melbourne, back in Melbourne House, sitting in their rooms and Lady Caroline in hers, all with their own secrets and all knowing that something must give way soon.

None of them were women accustomed to waiting on others for their answers, or their instructions. They might be saying anything to one another. They might, together or separately, be deciding that something must be done to protect themselves, to protect the house or the family.

And there would be nothing Rosalind could do about it. She would not even know it had happened.

She must be here. She must find the last strands of the tangle she had undertaken, for so many reasons. Not the least of which was that tonight she had promised to meet with Dr. Bellingham. She must know what to tell him, and what to ask him, to put together the final pieces so she could be done with this.

Mr. Colburn, seeming to realize that all was not entirely right with his guest, picked up the platter of potted meat sandwiches.

"Will you try one of these, Miss Thorne? They are from Bailey's and my sister swears by them. And you must try one of these vanilla cakes as well." He put one on her plate without waiting for her agreement. Seemingly satisfied that she now had enough nourishment to carry on a proper conversation, he poured himself his own cup of tea and added a lump of sugar from the bowl. "Now, then. How may I be of assistance?"

Rosalind drank some tea (which was very good), sampled a vanilla cake (which was even better), and considered. She had never met a publisher in his business offices before this, and had not been entirely certain what she would find. Especially not from a man who had published *Glenarvon*, which set the fashionable world howling, and then followed it up with another book titled *France*, which had the critic at the *Quarterly Review* accusing its (female) author of everything from Jacobinism to libel to blatant impiety.

She had never met with anyone when so much seemed to hang on the results.

I must put that aside. I must concentrate on this moment, now.

She made herself look closely at Mr. Colburn. He was clearly a man used to putting ladies at their ease, which meant he was an expert at drawing room artifice. Rosalind was conscious of wishing she had Mr. Harkness with her, or Mr. Goutier. The presence of a Bow Street officer would shift the balance of conversation, and influence. But the first was nursing his wounded ribs, and the second . . . she could not even think of troubling him so soon after he had been so seriously wounded in her house.

She was alone in this.

Rosalind set her plate and cup on the little spindle-legged table at her elbow.

"Mr. Colburn, I am here about a rather delicate matter. There is . . . some suspicion that Lady Caroline Lamb has acquired a set of letters from some female correspondents of Lord Byron's."

"Lady Caroline Lamb is a female correspondent of Lord Byron's," said Mr. Colburn with a twinkle in his eye.

"Indeed, but these letters are not hers to keep, or to give away. I have been further informed that she might have given these letters to you, with the intent that you should publish them."

Mr. Colburn took another drink of tea, added another lump of sugar to the cup, stirred, and drank again.

"May I ask what your interest is in this matter? According to Miss Littlefield, you have many friends among our finest families. Might some of these letters have your name in them?"

Rosalind found she had to control a rush of temper. And a blush.

"Not my name, no," she answered evenly.

Mr. Colburn nodded again. "I see. At least, I think I may see. Well." He drank his tea, added yet another sugar lump, and stirred. Again satisfied, he drank a long swallow and set it aside.

"Miss Thorne, I'm not certain if you will believe this, but if Lady Caroline did present me with such a set of letters, I would not print them."

"I confess, that surprises me, Mr. Colburn."

"You mean why would a man who has profited so much from Byron's name turn down such an opportunity?" He smiled, completely at ease.

"Yes," Rosalind answered honestly. As she had perused the stack of Colburn-published periodicals at the library, she had reached one inescapable conclusion. Mr. Colburn was extremely fond of Lord Byron. Hardly a month in the past four years had gone by that some Colburn periodical did not feature an article, commentary, or serial about the poet. There were biographical pieces, gossip pieces, and essays. There were even pieces of fiction attributed to Byron, possibly not always accurately.

But if Mr. Colburn was at all shocked or worried about the turn of this conversation, he hid it with a degree of expertise Rosalind had never seen before. His eyes twinkled as he calmly freshened his tea and added yet more sugar. "I see you are a practical woman, Miss Thorne, and I think you and I may speak openly of practical matters. You will understand, I am not a gentleman, I'm a businessman. I work for profit. Byron's name brings in great profits. But!" He held up one blunt finger. "A businessman has to understand who he does business with, and for me, that includes genteel ladies. They write for me, and share what they choose to share—be it adventures of travel, or heartbreak, or the sharpest society gossip. I cast the books in a form that will entice the public and have them printed up. If their material is good and my advertising works as it ought, we all make a nice sum. But my ladies must trust me. Some of them come when they are in difficult circumstances. They write because they need the money to make up for some failure or indiscretion on the part of their menfolk." Rosalind waited for him to bring up Alice again, but he did not. "If I were a gentleman, I'd say it was my duty to protect their reputations. But I am a businessman, and it is my business to protect their ability to keep working for me. That includes making as sure as I can that what I print does not actually harm them, or me.

"If I publish any of Byron's letters that come to me from Lady Caroline, I will be harming her. If I am careless with her, I'll never get another lady worth her salt, or my time, to enter my door. So I won't do it." Mr. Colburn folded his hands across his considerable stomach and waited for Rosalind's reply. "My name can be bandied about the drawing rooms for a great many causal offenses, but it will not be for the willful destruction of a vulnerable woman."

Rosalind took her time. Mr. Colburn's speech had been a lengthy one, and she needed a moment to think it over, to watch the man in front of her and decide whether she believed it.

Outside, the rain had ceased to fall. The office was quiet except for the crackle of the fire in the grate and the ticking of the clock on the wall.

Rosalind made up her mind.

"Mr. Colburn, you have spoken frankly with me. I will be

frank with you as well. Lady Caroline is accused of stealing some private correspondence from her mother-in-law. These missing letters have become entangled in the death of a woman named Judith Oslander. It has been suggested that Lady Caroline gave the letters to Mrs. Oslander, with instructions that she should bring them to you."

Mr. Colburn sat as he was for a moment. Then he pursed his lips and let out a long, low whistle.

"There are days when I believe I've heard everything, and then the sun comes up again and I find I'm wrong."

He dug his fingers into his waistcoat pocket and brought out a ring of delicate keys. These he took over to one of the room's many cabinets. He opened a drawer and brought out a portfolio bound with black tape. He undid the knot and passed it over to Rosalind.

"A woman calling herself Mrs. Oslander did come here," he said. "And she did have papers from Lady Caroline with her."

Rosalind's heart plummeted. She took the portfolio in both hands.

"It's not letters," said Mr. Colburn. "It's a manuscript for a new novel. It's not good, and it's far from finished, and I've put off writing her back with my opinion. I was concerned that Lady Caroline might be going through one of her periods of disordered spirits and I did not want to make things worse." He nodded toward the portfolio. "You can look if you like. I'll trust in your discretion."

Rosalind opened the portfolio's cover. Inside waited a small stack of ink-spattered papers with so many lines crossed out and written over as to be nearly illegible. She turned over several pages but could only make out a word here and there.

She remembered Lady Caroline scribbling frantically at her desk, and how the ink dripped and spattered. This certainly could be the work of her hand. But it made no sense that Judith Oslander would have it. Lady Caroline did not trust Mrs.

Oslander. Why would she give an important charge into the hands of someone she thought was a spy?

Unless.

Rosalind remembered the state of Lady Caroline's study, the piles of papers and books. The way she unceremoniously dropped yet more papers, unbound and unsorted into a drawer before she locked it.

Maybe she did not give them up knowingly.

Rosalind remembered how very easy it was to open Lady Melbourne's desk. She also remembered Lady Caroline's outraged description of Mrs. Oslander searching through her things.

It would have been a matter of a moment for Mrs. Oslander to lift some papers from the bottom of one of Lady Caroline's great heaps and spirit them away.

"Mr. Colburn, were there any letters with these pages?" Rosalind asked. "A note from Lady Caroline, perhaps?"

Mr. Colburn frowned. "No, nothing. Mrs. Oslander communicated Lady Caroline's message directly."

"You read a great deal of writing. Is there any possibility that this might be . . . an earlier work? Not something new, but something written a while ago? Perhaps even several years?"

Mr. Colburn frowned. "May I see them?"

She handed the portfolio back toward him. He pulled out the papers, tossing the cover aside. He leafed through them, pausing only here and there. His lips moved soundlessly as he read, and his fingers, stained with ink and crisscrossed with tiny scars, flicked the pages with surprising speed.

He put the stack down and stared at it, and then at Rosalind.

"It's possible," he said. "I had not noticed the signs before, but now I would say it's very possible. What made you think so, Miss Thorne?"

"I think that Mrs. Oslander might have used the excuse of Lady Caroline's manuscript to gain entrance to your offices."

Mr. Colburn said nothing, but he did take another drink of tea. "It is possible, and obviously, it worked." He chuckled ruefully. "Well, in that case, I'm going to ask that you return these to Lady Caroline, with my apologies." He knotted the ribbon again and handed Rosalind the portfolio.

Rosalind took it with thanks and held it on her lap. "Did Mrs. Oslander say or do anything else while she was here?"

Mr. Colburn added another lump of sugar to his cup. This time, Rosalind could tell he was using the time to try to make up his mind. "Yes, she did," he said finally. "Mrs. Oslander wanted to talk about the possibility of writing for my house. She suggested that her position as a nurse provided her a unique look into the lives of the grand and the great."

"You did not find this strange?"

"It's my business to buy such stories. Why would I be surprised when someone comes trying to sell them?"

"Do you remember what answer you gave her?"

"Not specifically. Quite probably I told her I would be happy to read whatever she might bring me. She thanked me, and left, and never returned."

"Did you mention her name to anyone?"

"Why would I? To be honest, she was not that interesting to me. If she'd actually *had* a manuscript, it would have been different. But she had nothing beyond what I've showed you. Also, she told me she was acting in confidence for Lady Caroline, and I do not care to break faith with the author of a profitable book. She still might give me another such work. I won't let my wagging tongue cheat my wallet."

He was being blunt. She could not accuse him of trying to shock her, but he was quite deliberately removing all his own varnish so she might see who he was. Rosalind did see, and she believed him.

"I have one more question, Mr. Colburn. Have you ever been visited by a Mr. Scrope Berdmore Davies?"

Mr. Colburn sipped his shockingly sweet tea, his eyes distant as he consulted what Rosalind was sure must be a capacious memory. "I have heard . . . ah! Yes, he's a friend of Lord Byron's, is he not? I think I have heard his name, possibly from Mr. Hobhouse . . . but no, he has never come to see me. I wish that he would, though. If you meet the gentleman, Miss Thorne, you might tell him I'd pay for an article about . . ."

"Thank you, Mr. Colburn." She got to her feet. "I will not take any more of your time."

Mr. Colburn also stood. For the first time since she came into the office, he appeared openly hesitant. "Miss Thorne? You say Mrs. Oslander is dead? Is . . . is Lady Caroline accused?"

The image of Claridge's murderous face rose in Rosalind's mind.

"Not yet. But it may be she will come to be . . . suspected."

Mr. Colburn folded his hands behind his back and looked out his window. Rosalind watched as he tapped one hand against the other. "I understand professional men are frequently hired in such matters. If there's a question of fees, or character, or any such thing, you may apply to me at any time."

"Thank you, Mr. Colburn. I do have one other request."

"Certainly."

This time Rosalind hesitated. This was not a request she would normally make, but the circumstances and the people involved were exceptional in a vast number of ways. "I cannot tell how much longer it will take to clear these matters up. Not long, I hope. But in the meantime, please do not tell Lady Caroline what happened between you and Mrs. Oslander. There is yet more to discover, and I would like to be able to present all the facts to her at once, to spare her the suspense." *And to keep her from running to Lady Melbourne with accusations, or doing anything else on impulse.*

Now Mr. Colburn looked confused. "But Lady Caroline knows," he said. "I didn't write her about her manuscript, but I did write to tell her to be careful how much she entrusted to Mrs. Oslander."

CHAPTER 46

A Bad Spell

*. . . it is this; it is feeling too keenly, it is suspecting
evil perhaps never intended that makes me so
harsh, so violent, so odious, forgive me . . .*

Lady Caroline Lamb, private correspondence

Rosalind had seldom felt so alone as she did returning to
Melbourne House that evening. She had spent the entire
ride back trying to find some way past the worst of the possible truths.

Coward, her conscience whispered. *You cannot refuse to
see what is.*

Rosalind knew this was right, but that did not make it any
easier.

*I just need a moment to be still and think. I need to decide
what to do, and what to say, and how.* She clutched the portfolio with Lady Caroline's pages in it to her chest and started
climbing the stairs.

"Psst!"

*I may have missed something. I'm sure I must have missed
something.*

"Psst!"

Mrs. Oslander knew how to steal and how to hide what

she'd taken. But why would someone like that make such open and clumsy approaches, first to Mr. Colburn and then to Mr. Davies?

There was an easy answer to that. But it did not answer the question of how . . .

"Miss Thorne! *Psst!*"

Rosalind was several steps past the first landing. Preoccupied as she was, she failed to see the door to Lady Caroline's writing room open, or that Lady Caroline herself stood on the threshold, beckoning frantically.

Rosalind resisted the urge to raise her eyes to Heaven for patience. Instead, she schooled her features into a polite mask, turned, and went to see what Lady Caroline wanted.

Lady Caroline waved her inside the writing room and shut the door behind them. She pressed her finger to her lips and darted past Rosalind to close the door to the connecting room.

"We must be a little quiet," Lady Caroline whispered as she sat herself on the sofa. She patted the spot next to her, signaling that Rosalind should sit as well. "Augustus is asleep. He was very tired after his play this afternoon, and I told him he could sleep in here. For a treat. Now, you must tell me all, Miss Thorne! I have been looking for you forever, but you have been always gone! I was beginning to think Lady Melbourne had thrown you out into the street and would not tell me! What did you learn? What have you found out about Mrs. Oslander? Do you know who took the letters yet? Is that them? Are they recovered?" she cried, waving her hands at the portfolio. "Was it Mr. Davies, creeping back in after the party? Are we to be murdered in our beds? Is Lady Melbourne to be finally revealed for all she is?" She squeezed Rosalind's hand in her delicate fingers. "You *must* tell me!"

Rosalind took a deep breath, trying to resist the current of Lady Caroline's rapid and enthusiastic speech. "I will certainly tell you everything I can, Lady Caroline, but I ask you to excuse me for the moment. I am tired and I was hoping to rest and change before . . ."

Lady Caroline, however, was not in a mood to be patient. "But Lady Melbourne means to claim you, and you will certainly not refuse her, and then I will not know anything for hours! You *must* tell me! I have been in a state of the most dreadful suspense!" She smiled and pressed Rosalind's hand again.

Rosalind sighed. She needed time to order her thoughts. *It seems I am not to have that time.* "Lady Caroline, I did learn something about Mrs. Oslander today, but I think you will not be pleased by it."

Lady Caroline drew back. Her eyes searched Rosalind's face restlessly, and all trace of excitement faded. She did make a visible attempt to rally some calm by shaking back her red curls and folding her hands in her lap.

"I am ready. You may tell me."

Rosalind glanced toward the connecting room. The door remained closed. She thought she heard the rumble of a snore from the other side.

"I went to see Mr. Colburn today. Mrs. Oslander had taken him some manuscript pages that she said came from you."

Color slowly crept up Lady Caroline's neck and into her cheeks. "She did *what*?"

"You told me that you had seen her rummaging through your papers. I believe she may have removed some of them and used them as an excuse to gain an appointment with Mr. Colburn." She held out the portfolio. "He asked me to return them to you, with his apologies."

Slowly, with trembling hands, Lady Caroline reached for the portfolio. After several false starts, she was finally able to undo the ribbon, open the cover, and read the contents. "She took these?" Lady Caroline whispered. "She gave these to him and he kept them!" She flipped through the pages, slowly, and then faster, and faster. "He told me nothing! He should have told me! Why did he not write to me *immediately*!"

"He says that he did."

"He did not! I received no such letter! I . . . I trusted him! Is he a traitor, too? Is he another liar! I should never!" She let the papers slither off her lap to the floor and dug her hands into her red curls. "This is my punishment, my punishment for daring to speak the truth!" She shook her head violently. "No! Not mine! It is her doing! Hers! She got to him, paid him off!" Lady Caroline's voice rose to a shriek.

Rosalind started forward to try to urge Lady Caroline to calm herself, but before she could catch hold of her, Lady Caroline's cheeks went from scarlet to gray and she doubled over in pain.

Fear shot through Rosalind. She wrapped her arms around Lady Caroline's shoulders, hoping to straighten her, or at least comfort her.

"Lady Caroline, please, calm yourself . . ."

"I cannot! I cannot! Oh! Oh!" Lady Caroline pressed her fists against her chest. "My heart! My heart! I cannot stop! I cannot!"

Rosalind scrambled for the bell. Before she could reach it, the connecting door opened and Augustus Lamb tottered out, rubbing his eye with the back of one hand.

"Mother?" He yawned. "Mother?"

Oh no. "Master Augustus, please . . ." Rosalind tried to force at least a little calm into her voice and made to shoo the boy toward the door. Behind her, Lady Caroline groaned and wrapped her arms tightly around herself.

Augustus stared at his mother and did not move. "She's having a spell," he announced. "My father is home. Father knows what to do."

"I'm sure . . ." began Rosalind, but she had no chance to get any further.

"Father knows what to do," repeated the boy, and he teetered out the door.

Rosalind did not try to stop him. She rang the bell and then ran back to the sofa to wrap her arms around Lady Caroline. The other woman was flushed as with fever, but her hands were ice cold.

"We must get you to bed." She thrust her arms under Lady Caroline's and heaved her to her feet. But as soon as they were both standing, Lady Caroline's knees buckled, and she nearly dragged Rosalind down with her.

"I cannot!" Lady Caroline gasped. "I cannot! It is my fault! My fault! I did this!"

Rosalind was the larger of the two of them, but even so, attempting to support Lady Caroline's limp, weeping form into the connecting room took all her strength. Rosalind wished desperately for Mrs. Kendricks, but Mrs. Kendricks was as far away as the moon.

"Caro!"

Rosalind looked up as William Lamb dove into the room. He swept his wife out of Rosalind's unresisting arms.

"William, no!" cried Lady Caroline. "William, you cannot be here! William, it's over! It's over! I've killed you! I've killed her and killed us all!"

Mr. Lamb ignored this and laid Lady Caroline down on the daybed. "Her medicine is in the bottom drawer of that vanity," he said to Rosalind. "She needs a half glass of water and the bottle labeled Windford's Preparation. Quickly, woman!"

Rosalind ran to the small marquetry vanity table. A pitcher stood on the matching washstand, along with a glass. Augustus stood by the door, watching solemnly as his father covered his mother over with quilts and pushed a bolster under her feet to raise them.

Rosalind pulled open the vanity drawer to a great rattling of glass.

The drawer was filled with bottles. She counted at least a

dozen, and each and every one of them for laudanum. Rosalind stared for a startled moment and then reached blindly for one bottle nearest the front. To her relief, it was the Windford's Preparation. She turned to hand it and the glass to Mr. Lamb.

Lamb uncorked the bottle and held it up to the light with the water glass, murmuring under his breath. He poured three careful measures into the water and swirled it.

"Here now, Caro," he said, kneeling down beside her and slipping an arm under her shoulders. "Here is your medicine. For your heart. You must drink."

"No! I won't! I should suffer! It's my fault! Mine!"

Firmly, Lamb brought his hand up to the back of her neck and pressed the glass to her mouth; in one swift motion he raised her and tipped the glass. Lady Caroline gagged and swallowed, and gagged and swallowed again. Lamb held the glass in his hand and kept pouring the medicine until she had swallowed it all. Through all her struggles, he held her tight, his face utterly impassive.

"That's it, that's it," he murmured when he took the glass away at last. "There. Done." He lowered her back onto the bed.

Lady Caroline looked up bleakly at her husband and at Rosalind. "You see what I am become?" she asked. Her skin was gray and her lips tinged with blue, but the panic had at last subsided.

It was then the maid finally arrived. "See to her ladyship," Lamb ordered. He took Rosalind's arm in one hand and Augustus's in the other and steered them both out of the room.

In the writing room, he released them. "She'll sleep now," he said. "And she will be better when she wakes."

"Father knows what to do." Augustus beamed with satisfaction.

Lamb ruffled his son's hair. "So do you, Augustus. Good lad. Come now, let us take you back to the nursery so Mother can have her rest." He laid a hand on his son's shoulder and glanced toward Rosalind. "Would you be so good as to meet me in the library, Miss Thorne? I would like to talk with you about what's happened here."

She nodded agreement and watched Mr. Lamb lead his son away.

Rosalind opened the connecting door again. The maid was busy adjusting pillows, elevating Lady Caroline's feet, and closing the drapes. She said nothing as Rosalind opened the vanity drawer again. Rosalind stared at the laudanum bottles crammed in their drawer. She noted how many of them were empty and how many were full.

She glanced about the pretty little room for any other decanter or bottle and did not find it.

Only then did she do as she was told and take herself down to the library.

CHAPTER 47

The Price Of Loyalty

*You love ... and he who made you alone can tell
to what these maddening fires may drive a heart
like yours.*

Lady Caroline Lamb, Glenarvon

The library of Melbourne House was a large chamber with curving walls. The domed ceiling had been decorated with a mural that depicted the muses draping themselves over assorted philosophers. The shelves were lined with all manner of volumes, probably collected across generations. It was likely that serious men in black coats had been hired for the purpose of curating and collecting them all.

Rosalind wondered idly how many of them had actually been read.

The room was arranged for the comfort of the occupants as well as to impress their visitors. There was a window seat, and several soft deep chairs. An array of crystal decanters stood in a neat line on a sideboard in case the master of the house or any of his guests should want a drink.

There was no fire in the hearth, and her folded hands quickly grew cold. The single lamp cast a steady circle of gold light, but the rest of the room was sunk in twilight.

The rain had started again.

Rosalind sat down in one of the wingback chairs, as was proper. The silence of the room fell heavily across her shoulders. There was not even a clock ticking to distract her. Rosalind found herself staring up at the portrait over the mantel. It depicted three lovely young women, holding hands as they circled a steaming cauldron. The central figure was very clearly a young Lady Melbourne. Rosalind looked into her merry painted eyes, searching for something. But she could not have said what.

At last, the door opened and Mr. Lamb strode into the room. His collar was opened, and his rumpled cravat hung loose about his neck. He went immediately to the table with the glasses and decanters.

"Well, the house is settled, at least for now. I've sent for the doctor, but hopefully the worst is past. I'll have to tell Mother, of course, which I am not looking forward to." He shook his head and surveyed the array of decanters in front of him before selecting one. "Will you take sherry, Miss Thorne? You look like you could use it."

"Thank you."

Mr. Lamb handed her the glass, and she sipped. He opened a second decanter, and the strong scent of French brandy filled the still, cool air. He poured himself a tumbler full and drank deeply.

Rosalind turned the stem of her sherry glass between her fingers. "Mr. Lamb, this may seem a strange question, but may I ask where Lord Melbourne is? I have not seen him at all since I've been here."

Mr. Lamb chuckled once, and the sound was utterly without mirth. "My father, I expect, is either in the country or at Tatterstalls. Possibly at Newmarket. He doesn't tell me where he goes. He doesn't tell Mother, either, unless he needs her to give orders to Cook for dinner. He prefers to leave what goes on inside the house in my mother's hands." He paused. "And mine."

"I see." Rosalind took another drink of sherry, welcoming the warmth it brought her.

Mr. Lamb was watching her. "Miss Thorne, I think you have seen a great deal, and now that great deal includes our house and our family at its worst. Well, almost its worst," he murmured to the liquid in his glass. "And I expect that you, like everyone else, wonders why I don't divorce Caro. Why I don't send the boy away to some country place where he will be decently cared for but entirely out of sight. I can then marry a new, thoroughly respectable woman and start a new, thoroughly respectable family suited to a man with political ambitions."

Weariness pressed hard against Rosalind's mind, threatening her ability to remember her manners. There was no help in the sherry glass. She set it aside. "Forgive me for being blunt, sir. But I am aware that is none of my business."

Mr. Lamb smiled thinly. "In this case I rather think it is, because it speaks to my state of mind and the breadth of my actions, both of which are important to forming your opinion of the nature of this household. Spare me your surprise, Miss Thorne," he added. "You are one of my mother's agents. She has had others for other purposes. You will be reporting to her shortly, and you may tell her what I say now. Well and good. I wish that you might. She might listen to you." He drank off the last of his brandy and poured himself another. "So, to return to the original question. Why don't I divorce Caroline? I don't because I"—he pointed at his chest—"am the one responsible for her predicament."

"I don't understand."

She thought he would sit then, but he did not. He carried his brandy to the window and looked out across the courtyard, watching the rain pour down. Then he turned and stalked back to the fireplace. He stared at the clean grate where the coal and the paper twists waited for a light to be applied.

"We fell in love very young, she and I," he said. "I was dazzled by her. I still am, when she is well. You have no idea the strength of her mind and her heart. But it runs wild, you see. Given time, given understanding, it might have been calmed, or at least been channeled. But . . . I didn't have time, and I didn't have understanding, and I certainly didn't see . . ." He stopped and drank the rest of his brandy.

"I didn't see that my mother took such dislike to her. That she decided she would split us apart, and when I would not simply fall away, Mother decided she needed a wedge. Lord Byron presented himself as an opportunity. Damn the man, and damn the woman." He stared up at the portrait of Lady Melbourne and her friends, witches around the caldron.

For a moment, Rosalind thought he would throw his glass at it. She thought about how Claridge had called Lady Caroline a witch as well.

"Mother and Byron ended up using each other for their own ends—ego, malice, greed, desperation—pick which one you will. Poor Caroline got caught in the middle of them, and then poor Anne Isabella—Lady Byron as we must call her, and even, oh God help her, poor Augusta. None of them had a chance."

And yet in the end they did unite, at least for a time. They smuggled the vital letters away and formed a kind of alliance to keep themselves safe and Byron at bay.

She looked at the smiling witches with their sharp and clever eyes again. She thought about all the ways in which a woman could and would make shift and make do, and how enemies could become allies when they all needed each other.

All the things that the gentlemen for all their power and prestige would never see, no matter how hard they tried.

"Then why . . ." began Rosalind, but Mr. Lamb didn't let her get any further.

"Then why not release Caroline? To where? To what? She is already an object of utter scorn. Her family is as useless as my own." He sighed. "I have failed to love her as she needs. All I can do now is protect her, and I will do that to the best of my abilities as long as she and I, and our son, live in this world."

Now he met her gaze directly, and his own was confused and filled with cold disappointment, but not weakness. There was nothing weak about William Lamb.

"I do understand," Rosalind told him.

He nodded. "Yes, I believe that you do. Be merciful toward us, Miss Thorne. I know that you are trying to help my mother, but must her desires once again be gratified at my wife's expense?"

Rosalind rubbed her hands together uncertainly and then stilled them. *I must not lose my composure.*

"I do not wish to do so," she said. "I came here in order to help."

He smiled at this demure answer. "Then let us work together. The sooner those letters are found, the sooner calm is restored and you can be shut of us and all our troubles." He sat down in the chair opposite her. "I understand you visited Henry Colburn today," he said. "What sent you there? What did Colburn have to tell you?"

That a letter may have gone astray. That Judith Oslander has information to pass off, perhaps about your family. Perhaps about others.

"There was the possibility that Lady Caroline herself stole the letters and sent them to Mr. Colburn for safekeeping, or publication."

Mr. Lamb rubbed his chin. "Yes, I can see that might have happened. And what came of it?"

This conversation, among other things. You telling me that your father is seldom here, which means that the staff will certainly bring you the mail first when it arrives in the house. It is tradition. It is protocol. You might even read those letters before you distribute them to the rest of the family. Who is to prevent you? Who would think you would do anything wrong, or that might draw a rebuke from your mother?

"Mr. Colburn indicated that he had not been in communication with Lady Caroline for many months."

Mr. Lamb was silent. He looked at his shoe tops and his finger ends. Rosalind could see him turning her words over in her mind. Abruptly, she remembered Devon on the terrace, smiling gently at her.

Being active in Parliament, you see, has taught me the finer points of debate . . .

Mr. Lamb had noticed her careful phrasing, and he did not like it at all.

She remembered Lady Caroline's story of the figure in the dark coat bending over Judith Oslander's body.

She considered that if any part of that story was a lie, it might be that Lady Caroline did not recognize that man. That she might have found the coat and gloves in the family's private rooms, or in this library. Claridge might really have seen Lady Caroline try to burn the garments, but not to protect herself.

She did not want to put any of these things together. She wanted to remember the child. Weak and ill as he was, he had parents who refused to abandon him. She wanted to look at Mr. Lamb now and see only the man of principle who refused to abandon his wife and hide his son.

"Let me ask another question," said Mr. Lamb. "Do you know where the letters are?"

Rosalind met his gaze. "Not for certain, no. I believe they were taken by Judith Oslander. I believe that she meant to use them for blackmail."

"Blackmail? A serious charge, Miss Thorne. But you have had her rooms searched, have you not? And you did not find them?"

Rosalind felt Mr. Lamb's mild, careful gaze pressing against her. *Just like his mother's.* "Not yet."

A flicker of anger passed behind Mr. Lamb's eyes, but it was quickly gone, replaced by a mild disappointment.

"Tell me, Miss Thorne, do you know a man named Fullerton?"

"Mr. Fullerton!" Rosalind gasped as if she'd been shoved hard from behind.

"Yes. He knows you. In fact, he spoke with me the other day, specifically to warn me against you."

"I . . . I don't know what to say to that, sir. Mr. Fullerton is no friend of mine. I have interfered with some of his plans in the past."

"I thought that might be the case, but you can understand why I'd be concerned to hear your name in the mouth of a known blackmailer, especially when the question of blackmail has arisen again." He looked at his finger ends again. His nails were very clean and neatly polished. "You cannot seem to get away from the practice. Lady Jersey had a great deal to say about it when I spoke with her."

Rosalind said nothing.

"I know, of course, that you are a friend to your ladies and make yourself useful in many ways great and small. I believe Mother said you not only were helping locate her letters but had been helping her write them."

Rosalind said nothing.

"Again, this is all by way of being helpful." He glanced up at her, his face solemn, serious, and entirely free of guile. "We should know what is being said about us, don't you agree?"

"It is generally best."

"Yes. Now. I'm exhausted, Miss Thorne. I've got to check in on Mother and let her know what the uproar was about. I suspect you will not want to bother changing for dinner. A meal on a tray in your room's the thing, don't you agree?"

"Yes, certainly."

"Then I'll bid you good evening now."

He waited. Rosalind rose to her feet. She made her curtsey. He made his bow. Rosalind turned and walked toward the door. The distance seemed very great. Mr. Lamb watched her the entire way.

Perhaps he would stay here awhile after he was satisfied she had done as she was told. Perhaps he would take another drink of his fine French brandy.

Mrs. Oslander had been poisoned with a mix of brandy and laudanum. Both of which William Lamb had to hand. He was also quite clearly familiar with usage and doses.

William Lamb said that he would protect his wife and his son. William Lamb was underestimated, quiet, competent, and possessed of steadier nerves and greater conviction than many around him. He was the son of a mother who would dare the entire world to do what she must for her family.

And Rosalind had seen for herself that he knew how to force a woman to drink more than she wished.

She closed her eyes. *I do not want it to be true.*

But perhaps it wasn't. Because there had been someone else in the library that night. Waiting in the shadows, waiting for word about the letters.

Mr. Davies.

CHAPTER 48

All The Tangled Threads

*... She—was not the person marked out by provi-
dence to be their avenger.*

George Gordon, Lord Byron, private correspondence

Rosalind returned to her rooms to find the lamps had been
lit. So had the fire. Mrs. Kendricks had probably instructed one of the upstairs maids to make sure everything
was done properly this evening. She may even had used a bit
of the housekeeping money to make sure it happened.

It was nearly dark outside, and the rain had started again.
The curtains had been closed against drafts, so she could not
see it, but she could hear it sheeting against the window.

The rooms were entirely empty. Rosalind was alone except
for the sound of the fire and the ticking of the mantel clock.

Rosalind stood as close to the fire as she dared. She was
cold. Her hands were trembling. But she could not tell whether
it was fear or anger.

*Neither will serve. I must think. I have the answer. I must.
I have seen so much ... I must have seen the truth somewhere in the middle of all this mess.*

*I must, because I cannot stay here another day. I have
reached the end of my nerve.*

Mrs. Oslander is the key. I must think of Mrs. Oslander.
Mrs. Oslander could remove letters quietly from a great house. She could hide them so she could not be found. She was a good thief.

But she was an incompetent blackmailer. Rosalind felt her chin lift. She'd sent a letter straight to Mr. Davies that used her own name. That was too direct. She'd bluffed her way into Mr. Colburn's office and hinted about gossip about the grand and the great. That was not direct enough. Certainly neither attempt was the work of someone familiar with the subtle and hazardous arts of blackmail.

Rosalind, by necessity, knew something about those arts. She had seen how Mr. Fullerton worked his schemes. He was subtle, insinuating with his threats, gentle and civil with his demands. And so very reasonable.

In fact, he was a little like Mr. Lamb had been just now in the library, as that gentleman had showed Rosalind how easy it would be to accuse her of extortion.

Dear God.

Judith Oslander was an experienced thief. She stole because she needed the extra money to support her daughter. But when it came to the actual process of blackmail, she was just a beginner. All that Rosalind had learned showed a woman stumbling, even blundering about, and she had nothing to show for it except disaster.

That meant she'd had a partner. She must have. Not just for this one house, this one packet of letters, but for others. She might have been stealing for and with that other partner for years.

For an eternity.

Which was an old word, with Latin roots, which she had learned at the dame school.

Eternity. Latin. Noun. *Aeternum*

Rosalind pressed her hand over her mouth. *Dear God in Heaven. What a blind fool I have been.*

Judith Oslander's death had nothing to do with Bryon and his crimes, or Lady Caroline and her madness, or Lady Melbourne and her past. The answer was with Judith Oslander herself. With what she was doing and what she wanted and how much she needed the money.

The great and the grand had not made a victim of Judith Oslander. She had overturned their lives of the grand and the great and sent them all scurrying.

She did not die because she had offended the powerful. Mr. Harkness had said it at the very beginning of this business. *She might have been trying to go around her employer.*

Only it wasn't her employer. It was her lover. Perhaps he had customarily paid her for everything she brought him, like a receiver of stolen goods at a secondhand shop. Perhaps when she told him what she could get out of Melbourne House, she'd said she wanted more money this time. Maybe she pleaded. Or demanded, and he had refused her.

They quarreled. They parted, and suddenly Judith Oslander was alone and did not know what to do. She still needed the money. She took the letters. She thought she could sell them, but it turned out to be harder than she realized. She was barging about, calling attention to the fact that she had the letters. She was going to get herself caught.

And if she was caught, she might tell someone about her partner, and their scheme, hoping her honesty would lessen her punishment.

Or maybe she would even tell them that the whole idea had been his from the beginning. Make herself look like the poor wronged creature, the victim of a seducer. It was a story a jury of men just might be ready to believe.

He could not risk it. Not even for the woman he once loved.

Because, of course, Mrs. Oslander's partner had been Dr. Bellingham.

Dr. Bellingham had been in Melbourne House that night.

He had been sent for because Lady Melbourne had had a spell. He could have seen Mrs. Oslander arrive. He could have spoken urgently and lovingly with her and convinced her to wait for him somewhere. It was a big house. There were many quiet rooms.

He might even have suggested the library. At a supper party, the guests would be in the dining room, the billiards room, the sitting rooms and parlors. The library would have been dark and cold and quiet.

He was a doctor. If he didn't happen to have any laudanum in his bag, he would know where it was kept in the house. He could have dosed the good French brandy. He could have soothed her, told her what she wanted to hear while they drank together.

When she was stupefied, he could have poured the poison down her throat.

But she didn't die. Not right away. Either she was strong or he'd been in too much of a hurry to make sure. Or both.

The library's big bow window looked out over the courtyard. Mrs. Oslander would not have even needed to go out into the corridor to make her escape. She'd staggered out into the yard, forgetting her coat but remembering her bonnet and its precious hidden letter.

Lady Caroline had seen her.

Claridge had seen her.

Perhaps Dr. Bellingham stood in the shadows and watched them all. Perhaps he'd let himself believe that it had all gone even better than he could have hoped. When he saw Claridge send for the cart and not rouse anyone else to help, he must surely have believed that she meant to simply make this problem go away. Which is what a loyal servant to a dying woman would do.

How could he imagine she would want to raise suspicion rather than suppress it? What a shock it must have been to find out what Claridge had really done.

The little carriage clock on the mantel started to chime, which made Rosalind turn and look, and remember something else.

The blood and strength drained from her heart in a single instant, and she had to grasp the mantel to keep from falling over. As soon as she could move again, she lunged for the bell and rang until she thought she must break the cord or her hand.

According to the chimes, it was seven o'clock. She was supposed to meet Dr. Bellingham at Little Russell Street at eight. They were to talk. She was to tell him what she'd found out and where she meant to find out the truth about his relationship with Judith Oslander.

Little Russell Street, where Mrs. Kendricks was at work setting the house to rights. Alone.

Except, of course, for the Melbourne letters.

CHAPTER 49

For There Is No Honor Among Thieves

*They say 'the best Men are moulded out of
faults'—I am sure it ought to be impressed upon
the minds of all unmarried Ladies—the Married
ones know it.*

Elizabeth Lamb, Viscountess Melbourne,
private correspondence

According to the mantel clock, the time between Rosalind shouting orders to the maid to have the carriage brought round and the maid's return to say that Ormande was ready and waiting lasted twenty minutes.

In Rosalind's mind, it was a year. More. It was ten years. Twenty.

When the maid came, Rosalind already had hat and coat on. She flew down the stairs and out the door. She skidded badly on the rain-slick stairs but stumbled forward, to be caught by Ormande.

"Careful, miss!" he cried.

Rosalind pulled herself free and scrambled into the chaise. "Little Russell Street!" she cried. "Hurry!"

Ormande did not question or hesitate.

"Get those gates open!" he shouted. The carriage rocked as he threw himself onto the box. "Shift it, Acre. Go!"

The whip cracked hard and the carriage lurched forward. Rosalind clung to the seat.

It will be all right. Even if he gets there first, he will not hurt her. He has no reason. He has already searched the house. He knows the letters are not there.

But they were there now.

He will not know that. He cannot know that.

It had been Bellingham who broke into her house. He wore a dark coat. As a doctor, he would have a knife or a pair of scissors with him always and could have brought them when he ransacked her rooms, just in case they were needed.

And, of course, he knew where she lived because she herself had told him. Because she believed he loved Mrs. Oslander. Because she was too slow to understand that if Mrs. Oslander had an employer, the obvious candidate for the position was the doctor she had worked with for so many years.

The doctor who told Rosalind he could not meet with her last night. He had something else he needed to do.

But she hadn't seen it. She hadn't thought it. She'd been distracted by her belief and her fear that some resident of Melbourne House must be the driving force behind this disaster. How could a maid and a nurse and a doctor—ordinary, anonymous souls—overturn such titled, illustrious, notorious people? People who had sailed through every storm and every scandal no matter how dire?

What are they saying back in the house? Who saw me running away, and what must they think? I should have kept my calm. I should have pretended nothing was wrong.

It's too late. It doesn't matter. What matters is that I get to Mrs. Kendricks before Dr. Bellingham does.

The carriage rocked dangerously. A horse whickered. A man cursed and bystanders shouted. The chaise hesitated and lurched forward again.

It will be all right. Even if he is there first. There will be a runner on guard. He will not hurt her while there is a runner

*just outside the door. Mr. Townsend promised there would
be, because the back door is broken.*

Because Dr. Bellingham smashed it open. Because Dr. Bellingham was convinced that Rosalind had the letters.

*The runner will be there. He might even be in the kitchen.
Mrs. Kendricks will surely have invited him in for a cup of
coffee.*

The carriage bounced. Rosalind bit her tongue and tasted
blood.

*I will get out at the corner. I will send Ormande on to Bow
Street to raise the alarm. If there is a runner outside, if she
did not invite him in to get out of the rain, I will call him in
right away . . .*

The carriage rocked to the side, then slowed.

Rosalind sat up straighter, her heart hammering. Someone
outside was shouting. Ormande was shouting back, but she
couldn't hear what he was saying.

"There's no time to argue, man!" shouted a person outside.

Rosalind's hand flew to the curtain, but before she could
draw it back, the door flew open. A man clambered into the
carriage and dropped onto the seat across from Rosalind.

"My apologies, Miss Thorne."

It was Dr. Bellingham.

CHAPTER 50

Casual Conversation

*My God, you shall pay for this! I'll wring your
obstinate little heart!*

George Gordon, Lord Byron, to Caroline Lamb,
in conversation

Shock turned Rosalind's mind to a perfect blank. The doctor knocked on the carriage roof with one gloved fist. "Turn around, Ormande! Melbourne House, quick as you can! Lady Caroline is taken ill!"

"Miss Thorne?" called down Ormande.

Dr. Bellingham lowered his gaze to her. Did he see how pale she had gone, or how tightly she clutched the edge of the seat?

Rosalind forced herself to call out. "Yes! Melbourne House, Ormande!"

This is good. This is fortune taking a hand, just once.

"Just as you say, then!" Ormande touched up the horses. The carriage tilted just a little as he took them around a corner and into the next street, a far easier operation than trying to turn the carriage in the middle of a crowded street.

This will keep him away from Mrs. Kendricks and the letters. We are going to where there are people. To where I can have a message sent to Bow Street.

Dr. Bellingham removed his hat. Water sluiced off the brim and splashed onto the carriage floor, and Rosalind's hems.

"I suppose I should not be so surprised," she murmured. "I did hear Mr. Lamb say the doctor had been sent for. But how is it you come to be in the street?"

"My horse threw a shoe." He shook more rain from his shoulders and collar. "I was making my way on foot when I saw Ormande." He waved toward the front of the carriage. "I suppose you must have been on your way to keep our appointment."

"Yes." Rosalind made her fingers loosen their grip on the edge of the seat. *It will be all right. I need only sit and be calm.*

". . . and what can you tell me?" Dr. Bellingham was saying.

Rosalind jumped.

"I'm sorry?"

The corners of his mouth ticked up into a smile. "I asked what you can tell me. About what you have learned." He spread his hands. "As we have been thrown together, we may as well talk now, or I fear it will be at least another day before we can talk at all."

We may as well talk now. She imagined his mouth smiling in its odd, hesitant way as he stood in the darkened library at Melbourne House. She could imagine him telling Mrs. Oslander to sit.

"So, what is it we know, about . . . the letters and Mrs. Oslander? What have you learned?"

He would have gotten her a drink. He would have asked her to talk to him before she went to Lady Melbourne, or Mr. Lamb, and asked them for money for the letters.

"Miss Thorne?" Dr. Bellingham's eyes shone in the light from the carriage lantern. She'd thought his face was damp with rain, but he was perspiring. In daylight, his face would be quite red. In the shifting darkness, it looked to be a strange and unnatural shade of gray.

What can I tell him? What lie will he believe?

"Miss Thorne, what is it? What's happened?"

"I'm sorry," she said, and her voice sounded far too harsh in her own ears. "It's been a difficult day. But . . . I believe I know who the blackmailer is."

His brows ticked together. She suddenly remembered thinking how it was as if he was struggling to find the appropriate expression. She had thought that, for a doctor, he had difficulty with manners and conversation.

"But who is it, Miss Thorne? Who do you think did this thing?"

She had not thought his difficulties arose from an attempt to pretend he didn't know his mistress was dead.

Tell the smallest lie. Tell him the mistake I almost made.

"Mr. Scrope Davies."

Dr. Bellingham fell back. His expression collapsed. For a moment she was seeing the real man, and he was as tired as she was, as frightened and considerably more desperate.

He had so many reasons to be. But for now, he was also entirely relieved.

I will just sit and be calm. I will say as little as possible. I can do this.

Dr. Bellingham pulled out his handkerchief and rubbed his sweating face. "I should . . . it should have been obvious, I suppose. Do you know why he should do such a thing?"

"He was short of funds and Lord Byron owed him money," she said.

"I see. I see." He wiped his face again. "That is disappointing. Then I may assume you have found the letters?"

Now it was Rosalind's turn to pause. *Don't be surprised. Don't be surprised. It is a natural enough question.* But it was too late. Dr. Bellingham saw her hesitation.

"I'm sorry. I suppose that was an impertinent question." He laughed just a little. "What strange circumstances we are in. Actually, I suppose you must have them with you?"

"No," she said. "I didn't bring them. They are safe."

"Where?"

Rosalind mustered an offended frown. "Does that matter, Dr. Bellingham?"

His brows ticked upward. Searching for the correct position, the plausible expression.

"No, no, I suppose not. Not to me, certainly. I imagine you have returned them to Lady Melbourne already."

"As soon as I got them," said Rosalind. "After all, it was what I was brought to the house to do."

"Of course, yes. Of course, that is what you would do."

He moved, too sudden for her to scream or even to get out of the way. In the space of a heartbeat he was looming over her, his knee on her skirts, trapping her legs under the fabric so she could not kick out. His hand gripped her wrist. His palm pressed brutally against her mouth. She could not scream, could not open her teeth to bite.

"I could choke you, Miss Thorne, choke you dead right now, you'd be surprised," he whispered. "I could tell Ormande you'd had a fit and fainted. I'm a physician. Her ladyship's physician. He would believe me. So you will not scream. You will do nothing foolish. You will continue to talk to me calmly and sensibly. Do you understand?"

She nodded. There was nothing else to do.

He lifted his hand away but did not release her skirts or her wrist. His breath was hot and sour. He smelled of onions and lavender and his harsh, sick sweat.

"Where are the letters?"

"You still mean to sell them." *I will not give way.*

"They are still valuable and I need the money. Where are they?"

"My arm hurts," she said. *I will not give way. You cannot make me.*

"I'm sure it does." He leaned closer. His eyes were wide and bright. A fresh trickle of sweat ran down from his temple to his chin. "There is no reason for this, Miss Thorne. We are natural allies, you and I. Two people who must make our own way among our *betters*." He turned the word into a sneer.

"My arm hurts," she repeated. The words came out as a whisper. She sounded weak, tired.

Like she was ready to give in.

Dr. Bellingham snorted and let go of her wrist. Rosalind brought it close across her body.

The carriage hit a loose cobblestone and rocked.

"You know what they are, Miss Thorne. Petty and selfish, hoarding their money and their power and making sure the rest of us bow and scrape and smile, or we're out in the cold. How many lives has Lady Melbourne ruined with her scheming? Let the world see what she really is, and the world will be the better for it!"

"And those others who will be harmed? Lady Caroline, her husband and son? And Mr. Scrope Davies, who is guilty only of bad judgment?"

He laughed. "Hardly a pack of innocents!"

"What of Judith's child?"

His face fell again. This time the surprise was real. "*What?*"

You didn't know. "She had a child. A daughter who lives in the country with an aunt. Judith sent them money and kept all their letters hidden so no one would know." She paused and looked him in the eye. "Is she your child, Dr. Bellingham?"

Don't do this.

"You think I would kill the mother of my child!"

The rain drummed on the carriage roof. Outside, the other conveyances passed on their way home or to the theatre. To dinner. To a ball.

Be meek. Give in. Let him think he is convincing you. Hide your feeling. You know how to do that.

And yet, now that her life depended on it, Rosalind found she could not.

"You killed Judith Oslander because you were afraid if she was caught she would name you a blackmailer," said Rosalind. "Even if no case was ever brought to court, even if nothing were ever proved, just the accusation would destroy your reputation. No person of wealth or consequence would ever take you on again. How am I to know if the fact of a child would stop you from trying to save yourself?"

The carriage was slowing. The doctor felt it, too. His head jerked up. He still held her skirts trapped. She could not kick out, could not throw herself out of reach. She had no room to swing, to punch.

The carriage lurched to a halt. Shouts, calls, and curses rumbled through the windows and over all, the coachman's shout.

"Here, Acre!" shouted Ormande "Get yourself out there and see what the matter is!"

"What's the delay?" shouted Dr. Bellingham. She saw his throat bared. Could she choke him? Not fast enough.

The carriage rocked. *I know what's happening.*

"Can't say yet, sir. The traffic's stopped dead." He paused. "It's an overturned brewer's van, sir! They're trying to clear the road, but there's no telling how long it'll be."

The carriage rocked again. *One chance. I have one chance.*

"Well, back us around! There's not a moment to be lost!"

"Would willingly sir, but there's no room." He paused. She heard footsteps on the cobbles. Ormande had climbed off the box. He was coming around.

Rosalind screamed. She screamed with all the force in body and soul. Straight into the doctor's face.

He reeled backward. His weight shifted, and her skirts loosened. Rosalind screamed. The door opened and Ormande was shouting and Rosalind threw herself backward and she screamed.

She screamed like it was the end of the world. She screamed like it was the last thing she would ever do.

"Murder! Murder!"

She felt hands grab for her and miss. She hit the cobbles, splashed into water and mud and worse and did not care.

"Ormande! Hold him!'

"She's in hysterics!" cried Dr. Bellingham. "Hold *her*!"

Rosalind grabbed hold of someone's arm. She levered herself to her feet. She was smeared with mud and filth. She looked like a madwoman.

She looked like a witch.

She lifted her hand and pointed at him. Dr. Bellingham shrank back.

"Raise the watch!" she cried. "There's been murder done!"

"She's gone mad!" shrieked Bellingham. "Mad! Ormande, help me restrain her!"

Ormande looked at her, dripping and foul. He looked at the doctor.

He made up his mind.

"Grab him!" he called. "Murder! Murder! Raise the hue and cry!"

Bellingham turned. He plunged into the mass of carriages and horses and men.

He never had a chance.

EPILOGUE

Your confidential letter is safe—and all the others.

George Gordon, Lord Byron, private correspondence

George Littlefield achieved a tremendous success, and a raise in salary, by being the first one to report on the scandalous blackmail scheme being run by respected London physician Philip Bellingham, who had died from being kicked by a startled horse as he fled through the streets in a futile attempt to escape the Bow Street runners who had so cleverly and relentlessly tracked him down under the eagle-eyed guidance of Mr. Jonathan Townsend.

The other papers picked up the story, repeated it, enlarged on it, and in some cases reprinted it wholesale. Not one of them mentioned Melbourne House, or Lord Byron, or Lady Caroline Lamb.

Rosalind Thorne held a small and entirely unreported supper gathering in her restored and repaired dining room in Little Russell Street. There, Miss Alice Littlefield met Miss Hannah Gionetti, and all parties got on famously.

Mrs. Judith Oslander was buried quietly in a simple Christian service, with a headstone commending her to the world and her creator as a devoted mother. The ceremony was attended by a Mrs. Kendricks, a Mrs. MacKennan, and several nurses who had worked with the deceased and liked her, despite the fact that she was so frequently quiet and prickly.

From her bed, as she was recovering from the chill she took by being out in the rain, Rosalind wrote a letter to Mrs. Fidelia Ross. In it, she explained that Mrs. Oslander had died in an accident but that she had left an annuity for Mrs. Ross and her daughter.

The details of which I have enclosed, she wrote, *along with the name and address of Mr. Hughes, the banker who has charge of the fund.*

After this, there was only one thing left to do. Well, perhaps two.

Perhaps three.

Rosalind walked into Lady Melbourne's sitting room. Nothing had changed from the first day. Except she did not know the woman who stood in the chimney corner.

Rosalind made her curtsey and received her ladyship's answering nod. She opened her bulging reticule and took out two packets of letters. She laid these on the table at Lady Melbourne's elbow.

Lady Melbourne lifted one hand and nudged at them with her fingertips.

"I did not think you would bring them back."

"They are not mine to keep," she replied. "May I ask where Claridge is?"

"She has gone home," Lady Melbourne answered. "We agreed it would be best."

"I think perhaps that was wise."

Lady Melbourne cocked her head toward Rosalind. "You believe me a foul, sinful woman. You hold me in contempt. I see it in you."

"I do not choose to spend my strength in that way, Lady Melbourne." She made her curtsey. "I bid you good day."

She did not wait to see if that good day was accepted. She turned and she left, and she let Lady Melbourne watch the way in which she did not look back. It was not quite the cut direct. But almost.

Rosalind also did not wait for a footman or maid or other servant. She had not let anyone take her things, as she had never planned to stay. She just started down the stairs toward the front door. She had already said her thanks and farewells to Ormande and . . .

"*Psst!*"

Rosalind looked up. She had passed the landing again. This time, Lady Caroline leaned over the marble railing and grinned.

"Well, Miss Thorney Rose. Do we say farewell here?"

Rosalind felt herself smile. "I believe we do. I am glad to have known you, Lady Caroline."

Her blue eyes twinkled. Today was clearly one of her good days, and Rosalind was glad to see it.

Lady Caroline turned her head one way and then the other, as if trying to judge what angle suited her best. "May I write to you?"

"I should be glad to receive your letters."

"Oh, you say that now! But I shall take you at your word."

And Rosalind curtsied on the landing, and Lady Caroline straightened up and returned a gentleman's bow.

Smiling, Rosalind left the house and walked out into the sunshine.

Now, there was only one thing left to do.

The Harkness home was an old house in an old, cramped, busy lane. The door was opened by a stout woman with a worn apron and an air that was at once cheerful and no-nonsense.

"Well, bless me!" she cried as soon as she saw Rosalind. "You must be Miss Thorne!"

"I, yes . . ."

The woman did not wait to hear anymore. "I'm Adam's mother. You come right in, miss." She swept ahead of Rosalind down the flagstone entry hall. "Adam! You've a visitor!"

Mrs. Harkness took Rosalind straight through the kitchen and into a plain black parlor. Mr. Harkness sat in the worn chair by the open window. The sound of chickens and geese tumbled through with the sounds of the lane and the laughter of children and scolds of their mothers.

Mr. Harkness struggled to his feet. He was also blushing. Blushing, as if sitting in a comfortable chair with a quilt on his lap was a shameful act.

"None of that, Adam Harkness," said Mrs. Harkness. "You sit right back down. Miss Thorne doesn't need to see you make your manners while you're recuperating. Sit down, Miss Thorne. Let me get you some tea. You look all in. Adam's told me what's been happening. I should be confined to my bed for a week if I was you!"

Rosalind thought this most unlikely, but she just smiled and took the slat-backed chair she was offered. "Thank you, ma'am."

"And you mustn't spare any worry for my son. As you can see, he's doing fine and will be back on his feet in no time."

"I would not doubt it for an instant."

"Now, let me get you that tea. We've a lovely new tin, a gift from Mr. Goutier and his wife, and then you two will have to excuse me. I've dinner to prepare. The army will arrive any minute now."

"She means my brothers and sisters," said Mr. Harkness. "We are very like an army. Unruly, ill-kempt, and always hungry."

"You are all neat and clean as can be, thank you very much, Adam Harkness," said Mrs. Harkness loftily. "And if you're not, it is not my fault."

"No, ma'am," said Adam humbly.

Mrs. Harkness bustled back to her kitchen. A silence fell between her and Mr. Harkness.

It was strange, reflected Rosalind, for all the time Mr. Harkness had been in her parlor, this was the first time she had been in his. It was plain. Everything in it was hard used but clean and comfortable. It felt right for him.

And somehow, she could think of nothing to say.

"I'm very sorry about your hand," she said finally.

Adam shrugged. "My own fault, and Dr. Bellingham's. You have nothing to be sorry for."

Rosalind tried again. "I would have come before, but . . . that is . . ."

"You needed to finish matters," Mr. Harkness finished for her. "Mr. Goutier told me the whole of it. And what he could not, Mr. Townsend did."

"Oh. Mr. Townsend was here?"

Adam nodded solemnly. "A visit of state, practically. To let me know that he is waiting to welcome me back as soon as Sir David gives me leave." He raised his bandaged hand. "Which I hope is soon."

He truly did look well. His hand was swaddled in clean bandages, and his face was slightly flushed, but his eyes were perfectly clear.

He is well. He will be well. I'm the one who cannot settle or decide.

Mrs. Harkness returned then with a mug of tea, and an indulgent smile, and swept out again, her mind already on her dinner.

Rosalind sipped the very strong tea and found, perhaps oddly, it was just what she wanted.

"Miss Thorne," Mr. Harkness said gently. "I can't help but feel there's something you want to say to me."

"Yes," she agreed, and took another drink of tea. "I wanted . . . Mr. Harkness, I'm going to be away for a while."

The familiar, patient stillness settled on him, and he just said, "Oh?"

"Yes. I'm . . ." Rosalind stopped, again. *This is ridiculous. Why can't I just say this?* "I'm going to the country to stay with Mrs. Showell and the Dowager Duchess of Casselmaine. I'll be helping with Louisa Winterbourne's wedding."

"Ah," said Adam.

"I . . ." Rosalind swallowed some more tea. Why was this so difficult? She should just say it and be done. She could even leave it there. Mr. Harkness would tell her she owed him no explanation. This was in some ways true. Despite that, she wanted him to have one.

"Mr. Harkness, when I was seventeen, just before my father ran away, Devon Winterbourne, as he was then, had asked me to marry him. We were very much in love." He said nothing, only waited and watched her. She felt a stab of annoyance that she could see nothing but patience in his blue eyes. *What do you think of me?*

"Then my world fell apart, and so did his. His brother died. He—Hugh—was drunk and fell from his horse into a snowdrift. When they found him, it was too late. Suddenly, Devon was Duke of Casselmaine and I . . . was a gentlewoman of reduced circumstances with a sick mother and no prospects whatsoever."

"And he left you?"

"No!" said Rosalind. "Never that. If anything, I left him. I was so ashamed of what had happened, of what was happening. It was my godmother who showed me how I might survive and keep some shred of dignity. But every day, she reminded me how my reputation and gentility was all I had left and I must preserve them at all costs. I must be humble, useful, poised, and perfect. I must always face the world with calm and perfect etiquette and courtesy. Otherwise, I would be cut off, and then . . . well, there was no then. There was nothing outside the drawing room world."

The words came out of her tumbled and halting by turns. She had never spoken like this to anyone. Not even Alice. With Alice, she had never had to, because Alice knew it all.

"I believed it with every fiber of my heart. And so, I became who I am and . . . and then Devon, Lord Casselmaine, we met again. And he said . . . he said he wanted to honor his previous promise, if I wanted that as well."

"And what have you told him?"

Rosalind turned the mug in her hands, grateful for the warmth against her palms. "There are complications. With my family, which you know, and he does not yet. That is my fault. And there are other . . . complications. With my life, as it is, and with who I have become."

She lifted her eyes, finally able to meet his quiet, patient gaze. *What are you thinking?* she wondered again, because she could not tell. He was holding himself back, waiting to hear all she had to tell. But he remembered. He must remember the other time, when they were alone, face-to-face, not in sunshine but in shadow.

"But I want to be sure," Rosalind said. "Of my own feelings, first. I do . . . some part of me . . . is . . ."

"It's all right," said Mr. Harkness.

Rosalind nodded gratefully. "But there is more. If I refuse Devon's offer, I will be refusing a great deal with it. For the past eight years my one goal—my only goal—has been to keep my place. But my wish has always been to return home—to be fully a part of the world where I grew up. If I turn from him, I turn from that wish, then . . . where do I go? Who do I become? I will remain betwixt and between forever, and I do not know if I have the strength for that."

"You would not be alone," Adam reminded her. "You would still have your friends. The Littlefields to start with, and Mr. Faulks."

And me. She heard the words clearly, although he did not speak them. He did not need to.

"I know," she said, in answer to those unspoken words. "But I cannot stay true to myself and turn away from someone who has been a friend, who still feels for . . . not just the girl I was but the woman I am. I want . . . I want to understand all of this before I choose."

Mr. Harkness bowed his head. Rosalind found she could not breathe. She feared him pulling back, separating himself.

She had said too much and said the wrong things. She had already cut herself off.

But when he looked at her again, he was still himself, still here with her.

"There is only one thing I would ask," Adam said. "No matter what you decide, you will come tell me. It will not be left to a letter of any kind." His mouth curled into its small familiar smile. "I find that I'm rather tired of letters right now."

"I promise," replied Rosalind. "Thank you, Mr. Harkness."

He bowed where he sat. "And thank you, Miss Thorne."

There was everything to be said after that, and at the same time nothing at all. And when Rosalind took her leave, turning up the crowded lane, she realized that she had no idea what would happen next, but she did not mind. Her heart was whole and her life was sound.

Rosalind Thorne would take the world exactly as it came.

ACKNOWLEDGMENTS

No book actually gets written by one person on their own. I'd very much like to thank all the help and support of my many friends; of Rosalind's readers and fans, who keep letting me know how much they enjoy her problems, and solutions; all the members of the Untitled Writers Group, who never fail to ask the hard questions; my fabulous editor and equally fabulous agent; and, as always, my husband and my son, who are last on this list but first in my life.